12/19

BAD FAITH

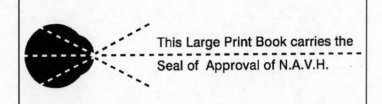

This Large Print Book carries the
Seal of Approval of N.A.V.H.

BAD FAITH

ROBERT K. TANENBAUM

THORNDIKE PRESS
A part of Gale, Cengage Learning

GALE
CENGAGE Learning·

Detroit • New York • San Francisco • New Haven, Conn • Waterville, Maine • London

GALE
CENGAGE Learning®

LIBRARY OF CONGRESS CATALOGING-IN-PUBLICATION DATA

Tanenbaum, Robert.
    Bad faith / by Robert K. Tanenbaum.
        pages ; cm. — (Thorndike Press large print thriller)
        ISBN 978-1-4104-5030-2 (hardcover) — ISBN 1-4104-5030-9 (hardcover)
    1. Karp, Butch (Fictitious character)—Fiction. 2. Ciampi, Marlene
(Fictitious character)—Fiction. 3. Trials (Murder)—New York (State)—New
York. 4. Large type books. I. Title.
    PS3570.A52B33 2012b
    813'.54—dc23   2012018213

Published in 2012 by arrangement with Gallery Books, a division of Simon & Schuster, Inc.

Printed in the United States of America
1 2 3 4 5 6 7 16 15 14 13 12

To those blessings in my life:
Patti, Rachael, Roger, Billy,
and my brother, Bill;
and
To the loving Memory of
Reina Tanenbaum
My sister, truly an angel

ACKNOWLEDGMENTS

To my legendary mentors, District Attorney Frank S. Hogan and Henry Robbins, both of whom were larger in life than in their well-deserved and hard-earned legends, everlasting gratitude and respect; to my special friends and brilliant tutors at the Manhattan DAO, Bob Lehner, Mel Glass, and John Keenan, three of the best who ever served and whose passion for justice was unequaled and uncompromising, my heartfelt appreciation, respect, and gratitude; to Professor Robert Cole and Professor Jesse Choper, who at Boalt Hall challenged, stimulated, and focused the passions of my mind to problem-solve and to do justice; to Steve Jackson, an extraordinarily talented and gifted scrivener whose genius flows throughout the manuscript and whose contribution to it cannot be overstated, a dear friend for whom I have the utmost respect; to Louise Burke, my publisher, whose enthusiastic support, savvy, and encyclopedic smarts qualify her as my first pick in a game of three on three in the Avenue P park in Brooklyn; to Wendy Walker, my talented, highly skilled, and insightful editor, many thanks for all that you do; to Mitchell Ivers and Natasha Simons, the inimitable twosome whose adult supervision, oversight, and rapid responses are invaluable and profoundly appreciated; to my agents, Mike Hamilburg and Bob Diforio, who in exemplary fashion have always represented my best interests; to Coach Paul Ryan, who personified "American Exceptionalism" and mentored me in its finest virtues; to my esteemed special friend and confidant Richard A. Sprague, who has always challenged, debated, and inspired me in the pursuit of fulfilling the reality of "American Exceptionalism," and to Rene Herrerias, who believed in me early on and in so doing changed my life, truly a divine intervention.

PROLOGUE

The handsome young New York Fire Department paramedic jumped from the back of the ambulance with his gear bag and looked up at the old four-story walk-up on the Upper West Side. Once a haven for junkies, including the infamous Needle Park, much of the neighborhood had been gentrified and cleaned up. However, the West 88th Street building, located between Amsterdam and Columbus Avenues, had fallen into disrepair. The steps leading up to the building's entrance, like the sidewalks along the narrow, tree-lined street, were cracked and uneven; a rusted fire escape climbed the faded red bricks of the façade; what paint remained around the windows was peeling away.

There was certainly nothing charming about the bitter November evening air, nor the three large white men standing in front of the stoop who moved to block the paramedic. "False alarm," said the man on the left, the words coming out from his bearded lips in puffs of condensation that hung briefly in the chill breeze before dissipating.

"Sorry, but we got a 911 call about a child in medical distress, and I have to check it out," the paramedic replied. He tried to step past, but the man in the middle — the tallest of the three and ruggedly handsome, with long wavy gray hair swept back from his tan face — placed a hand on the young man's shoulder and stopped him.

"Sorry, brother, but as Brother Frank just told you, your services are not needed here," the man said, fixing the paramedic with his intense blue eyes. He was smiling wide, his big white teeth flashing in the dusk, but there was nothing friendly about his demeanor.

The paramedic scowled and brushed the larger man's hand off of his shoulder. "I'm not your, brother, mac, so keep your mitts to yourself."

"What's the problem, Raskov?"

The paramedic, Justin Raskov, turned at the sound of his partner's voice. "Yo, Bails, these jokers won't let me in the building," he replied to the other paramedic coming up behind him.

"Well, it ain't up to them," Donald "Bails"

Bailey Sr. growled as he moved ahead of his partner to glare at the three big men confronting them. "We got an emergency call for this address and we legally have to check it out. And you, my friend," he added, thrusting his jaw at his opponent's face, "are breaking the law, and I'm maybe two seconds from siccing New York's finest on your ass."

In his experience, Raskov was used to seeing even the most recalcitrant people move out of the way when stared down by his pugnacious partner, a muscular middle-aged black man who'd been a staff sergeant in the army and still carried himself like one. But the three other men closed ranks, two behind the third, who was obviously the leader and now raised his hand palm-outward and thundered, " '*YOU SHALL NOT PASS THROUGH, LEST I COME OUT WITH THE SWORD AGAINST YOU!*' "

At the unexpected outburst, Raskov took a step back but Bailey stood his ground and rolled his eyes. "Frickin' great," he sighed. "We got us a Bible thumper. Numbers 20:18, right? Yeah, I know the Good Book, too, and I'll take that as a threat." He looked back at the ambulance, whose driver had his head out of the window and was listening to the exchange. "Hey, Dougy, call the

11

cops and tell them we got three morons preventing us from responding to a 911 medical emergency, and one of them just said he was going to attack us with a sword."

When he finished, Bailey looked back at the three men and tilted his head with a slight smile on his face. "Tell you what, asshole. If there's somebody in that building who needs our help and doesn't get it on time because of your cute little antics, it'll be on your head."

Disconcertingly, the big man smiled back. "The true believers of this household are under the protection of the Lord."

"Yeah, we'll see how that works when the cops show up," Raskov said.

As if on cue, a patrol car swung around the corner and pulled over to the curb behind the ambulance. Two officers got out and hurried up to the knot of men. "What seems to be the problem here?" the older officer asked.

"Hey, Sergeant Sadler, how ya doin'?" Raskov said to the cop. "We got a 911 call that a child has a medical emergency in apartment 3C. But these jokers won't let us check it out."

Sadler nodded at the paramedics. "Evening, Justin, Don," he said before frowning and turning to the three men on

12

the stoop. "One of you want to explain?" he asked.

The man who'd shouted the biblical verse stepped forward. "I am the Reverend C. G. Westlund and God's emissary at the End of Days Reformation Church of Jesus Christ Resurrected. I speak for the family in apartment 3C. The call was in error and any intervention by these gentlemen would be against the family's religious beliefs."

"Well . . . reverend . . . is it true there's a sick kid in there?" the sergeant asked, his voice indicating that his patience was not going to last long.

"The child's infirmities of the body are being healed by the power of prayer," Westlund answered. "God's will and compassion are the only medicine the child needs."

"Then with all due respect . . . get your ass out of the way, and let the paramedics do their job," Sadler barked. "That or you, me, and your pals here are all going to take a little ride down to the precinct house, where I'll toss your butts in the pokey for obstructing these fine officers of the NYFD in the performance of their lawful duties."

Westlund turned his head slightly to his right, and the man he'd identified earlier as "Brother Frank" suddenly rushed forward with a growl as though to attack the sergeant. But Trent Sadler, a grizzled old veteran who'd been dealing with street thugs and violent criminals for more than twenty-five years, was ready. He stepped neatly to the side and in one swift motion pulled a Taser stun device from the holster on his belt and applied it to the neck of the would-be assailant.

Brother Frank yelped and fell to the sidewalk in a twitching heap. Keeping his eyes on the other two, Taser at the ready, the sergeant spoke to his partner. "O'Leary, handcuff this quivering mass of idiot and hand him over to the backup when they get here," he said just as another patrol car wheeled around the corner with its lights flashing. "Speak of the devil. Now, reverend, I didn't like the little nod to your 'brother' here, so I wouldn't mind lighting you up, too. Having said that, you need to answer this question: Do you want to find out what a Manhattan sidewalk tastes like, or will you get the hell out of my way?"

The smile disappeared from Westlund's face and he glared at the police sergeant. But he then moved aside, followed by his man. *"'The god of this age has blinded the minds of unbelievers, so that they cannot see the light of the gospel of the glory of Christ, who is the image of God,'* " the preacher warned them.

"What?" Sergeant Sadler replied.

"It's Second Corinthians 4:4," Bailey said. "The guy is a walking Bible quote. Loony tunes if you ask me."

"Yeah, well, I like a good sermon on Sunday," Sadler replied. "But not when it's wasting our time and there's a kid who needs help. Follow me; I'll make sure no one gets in the way. O'Leary, bring up the rear as soon as you hand Brother Frank over to the backup . . . and tell them to keep the good reverend out of the building, otherwise he and his other goon are free to go."

With that the sergeant entered the building with the two paramedics hustling along behind him. Reaching apartment 3C, he pounded on the door. "Police, open up!"

An older woman with frizzled hair, poorly dyed to a sort of burnt orange, answered the door. "Are you believers?" she asked.

"Yeah, sure," Sadler replied. "We believe there's a sick child on the premises, and these two men need to see him."

The woman's eyes widened and she tried to close the door. "No doctors! Blasphemers!" she shrieked. "You can't come in!"

"Like hell we can't," the police sergeant replied, and pushed the door open with his shoulder, entering the apartment with the two paramedics as the woman continued to protest.

The apartment was enveloped in shadow; the shades were drawn over the windows, and no electric lights were turned on. The only illumination was from dozens of candles that had been lit and placed around the small living room and tiny kitchen. But even in the half-light, the police officer and paramedics could see that the only adornment on the walls were portraits of Jesus and of the Reverend Westlund.

Several people were sitting on a couch and on a few chairs pulled into a circle in the living room. They'd appeared to be praying when the men entered but had stopped and now only stared up at the intruders.

"We're looking for a sick child," Sadler announced. No one answered. "Who called 911?" Again there was no answer. Instead, the group returned to their prayers, their voices droning on.

"Come on," the sergeant said to Razkov and Bailey. He led the way down a hallway to a back bedroom in which more than a dozen adults and several children were crowded around a bed praying. A young boy lay on the bed, nude except for a pair of underwear, his skin nearly white except for

16

the dark circles below his closed eyes. His thin chest rose and fell slightly and he groaned once.

The paramedics pushed through the crowd and checked the boy's vital signs. "He's comatose," Raskov said, looking up at the police sergeant. "His pulse is weak and breathing shallow, we need to transport him to the hospital now!"

"You can't," one of the women in the prayer circle said. "My name is Nonie Ellis and I'm Micah's mother. My son will be cured through God's will; Western medicine is the false hope of Satan. We will heal him with prayer!"

"He hasn't got a prayer if we don't move him now," Bailey replied.

"I want you to leave," Ellis demanded. "You have no right to force us to accept your ways."

"And I'm ordering you to stand back," Sadler told her. "In fact, if anyone in this room delays us one more second, I'll have the whole lot of you hauled down to the Tombs — and if you want to meet devil worshippers, that would be the place to spend the night."

A worried-looking man walked over and stood behind Ellis. "Nonie, honey, I think we have to let them take him," he said as he

17

tried to put his arms around her. She shrugged him off but made no more attempts to stop the men and instead ran from the room.

Bailey picked the boy up in his arms. "No time for a stretcher," the paramedic said, "this kid's dying."

The sergeant looked at the man who'd tried to console the boy's mother. "And you are?"

"David Ellis," the young man replied. "I'm Micah's father. Please help him if you can."

This time the paramedics led the way out of the apartment and down the stairs to the ambulance. Waiting on the sidewalk, having been joined by the people who'd been in the living room, the Reverend Westlund yelled when he saw Bailey emerge with the child. "There they are! The new centurions! No different than the Roman soldiers who helped the Jews murder Christ!"

"Blasphemers!" someone shouted.

"Satan worshippers!" yelled another.

"Stop them!" cried a third.

The crowd of Westlund followers started to surge toward the ambulance even as Bailey laid the boy on a gurney to be loaded into the back. But before they could reach the paramedics, Sadler and the other three officers on the scene had placed themselves in the way.

"Hold it right there!" the sergeant yelled, his booming voice rising above all the others. *"Back off, or we will arrest each and every one of you!"*

The crowd hesitated. But then from the rear Westlund cried out, "Don't be afraid, my brothers and sisters! *'Blessed are they which are persecuted for righteousness' sake; for theirs is the kingdom of heaven!'* This is a direct affront to the will of God!"

Again the crowd, which had been augmented with those who'd been praying in the boy's bedroom, started to move forward. The sergeant pressed the button to the radio transmitter on his shoulder. "Dispatch, we have a situation and are in urgent need of backup," he said even as he pulled the Taser from its holster again. He and his men prepared to defend the paramedics.

"Stop this!" a voice suddenly shouted. It belonged to David Ellis, who inserted himself between the crowd and the police. "Micah is my son, and I don't want anyone else hurt," he said to the angry mob. "Please, we appreciate your prayers and your concern. But just go home now. Please."

The crowd stopped and seemed unsure of what to do. A few of them yelled but no one moved to interfere with the police and medics.

Sadler turned to Ellis. "Thanks, son, that could have got ugly," he said. "Now, do you and your wife want to ride in the ambulance with your son?"

The young man turned to find his wife and saw her standing next to Westlund, who had his arm around her shoulders as she sobbed. "Honey, do you want to go with Micah?" he asked.

His wife stopped crying long enough to glare at him. "I will not sin! Micah was in the hands of the Lord and now you're taking him away."

Westlund pointed his finger at David Ellis. "Whoever removes the boy from his fellow believers is responsible for his passing from the world and will face the wrath of God."

The father's shoulders sagged and he looked back at Sadler. "I'd like to go, thank you," he said.

The sergeant directed him to the back of the ambulance. "Then let's hurry, son, your boy needs more than prayers right now."

David Ellis climbed in and sat next to his son, his hand caressing the boy's ashen face. "Please, God, take care of Micah," he whispered, and began to cry.

1

Four Months Later

The two men tried to look as calm and nonthreatening as possible as they waited in line for the ferry that carried tourists to Ellis Island and then onto Liberty Island, where the Statue of Liberty stood bathed in the morning sunlight. They had arrived at Battery Park early that Monday to make sure that they would be on the first boat to the islands.

Both men were Muslim, one an American-born twenty-one-year-old of Pakistani descent. The other was a twenty-five-year-old native of Afghanistan who'd come to the United States two years earlier on a student visa. According to plan, the Afghani attended classes at New York University, but acting like a student was only a ruse. His attendance had been spotty at best, and when a month ago he'd begun preparing with other members of the team for the Ellis

Island event, he stopped attending school altogether.

As the student and his partner stood in line, they chatted idly about the late-March weather, relatives, and schoolwork while occasionally — to reinforce the image of themselves as innocent sightseers — smiling at their fellow passengers and chuckling at the antics of children, all of whom would be dead by noon. *God willing,* Aman Ghilzai thought as he bent over to pick up a stuffed animal dropped by a toddler who was being held in the arms of his mother.

"Thank you so much," the doomed woman said to him.

"You are very welcome, a beautiful child," he replied.

A native of Afghanistan, Ghilzai had been recruited by the Taliban as a teenager living in the tribal areas of Pakistan and then, when he complained that their focus on Afghanistan was too narrow, by al-Qaeda. Several other members of the team were also from abroad, places like Yemen and Somalia. They, too, had entered the land of the Great Satan at various times over the past several years to await orders that would carry them to martyrdom. The remaining members were Americans brought into the fold by the Chechen mujahideen Ajmaani, a beautiful and mysterious blond woman who'd become a legend even in al-Qaeda due to her savage attacks on the infidels.

Ghilzai sighed. He hoped at least one of the virgins who would be attending to him when he reached paradise would look like Ajmaani. A year or so prior to meeting her there'd been rumors that she'd been killed or captured by the Americans, but then she'd reappeared a month ago carrying coded instructions from a trusted al-Qaeda courier telling Ghilzai and the others to co-operate with her. He'd been impressed with her plan and her cold-blooded viciousness; she had no regard for the lives of Americans, whether they were adults or children.

It did not occur to him that she also had no regard for the lives of his team, or that of any Muslim tourist who might happen to be killed as well. He wouldn't have cared either way. His only complaint was with her reliance on the American-born jihadists she assigned to the team, such as his fellow sightseer, Hasim Akhund. Although these men were enthusiastic about taking part in the attack, they liked to boast to each other — like men who had to talk in order to keep their courage up — and pose for photo-graphs with their weapons. They all seemed to have some nebulous complaints about their treatment in the United States, such as not being able to get good jobs, which they blamed on racism and anti-Muslim prejudices; or that they didn't have girlfriends; or that they were just what Americans called "losers" with nothing else to do.

They said all the right things and prayed fervently in the days leading up to that morning, but Ghilzai thought their reasons for volunteering for jihad were insignificant or petty, rather than to strike a blow for Allah and repressed Muslims all over the world. He didn't trust them; he worried that their boasting would get beyond the group, and he worried they wouldn't come through when it mattered. But he was not in charge, and he could only hope that the other foreign-born jihadists, who like him had fought the infidels overseas, would be enough if something went wrong.

So far, everything seemed to be going right. Ghilzai had seen Ajmaani that morning as he'd crossed State Street to Battery Park. As prearranged, she'd been haggling with one of the Somali sidewalk vendors who sold knockoff purses to tourists. When she spotted him, she held up two purses, the sign that he was to proceed with the plan. As he and Akhund walked toward Castle Clinton National Monument to buy tickets and get in line for the ferries, he placed a quick call from his cell phone. *"Allahu akbar,"* he said quietly, and then hung up.

Purchasing the tickets, the pair proceeded to the dock, where they discovered that they weren't the first arrivals. A young couple was first in line, acting like newlyweds with shameful public displays of affection, kissing and hugging as though no one else was near. The man was lean and carried himself like an athlete, while the young woman was tan, pretty — though her nose was a bit prominent by Western standards, Ghilzai knew — and green-eyed. Other than giving friendly nods when Ghilzai and Akhund walked up to stand behind them, the couple paid them little attention. When they weren't kissing, they laughed and joked without a care in the world, and it pleased Ghilzai, who had never had a woman's love, to know that their day would end tragically.

Ghilzai pretended not to notice when Ajmaani got in the line just in front of a middle-aged couple. He quickly studied the pair, looking for signs of danger. The man was a fit, square-jawed type with close-cropped gray hair — the sort Ghilzai disdainfully thought of as a wealthy business-man who spent too much time at the gym

25

and barber; his woman was tall, buxom, brunette, brown-eyed, and, the terrorist conceded, a match for Ajmaani in beauty. Although they were more discreet than the young couple standing next to him, they were obviously in love from the way they looked at each other and their hands occasionally met. But they didn't seem particularly interested in Ajmaani, who caught his eye and gave him a slight nod.

At last, the guard at the entrance announced that the ferry would begin loading. Entering a large white tent, passengers were told to remove belts, shoes, coins, and anything else metallic, as well as all cameras and electronic devices, and place them in a basket to be viewed by security personnel. Then passengers had to pass through metal detectors, all part of the fallout from the 9/11 attacks on the World Trade Center.

Ghilzai and Akhund did as requested, knowing they had nothing to worry about — everything they needed was already on board the ferry, placed there by a member of their team who'd gained employment years before with the company that ran the ferries.

As the pair walked aboard the boat, they were greeted by an Asian-looking man who, according to a tag on his lapel, was named Tran and was a volunteer guide. "Do you have any questions about where to go for the best views?" he asked pleasantly.

"No," Akhund answered curtly.

Ghilzai noted with alarm that his partner was sweating profusely and looking around nervously. "No thank you," he added politely, and then pointed toward the stairs leading to an observation deck. "Let's go up there."

After he'd separated Akhund from the volunteer and anyone else who might overhear, Ghilzai whispered through clenched teeth. "Relax. You are beginning to act suspiciously. The plan is going according to schedule; this will be a great day for Allah and all of us. Do not bring attention to us."

Akhund swallowed hard and nodded. "I'm okay," he said. "Just some nerves and excitement."

"Do not let either interfere with your duty to Allah and your comrades," Ghilzai warned him.

Up on the observation deck in the open air, Akhund seemed to settle down and Ghilzai actually enjoyed the ride out to Ellis Island, his third trip in four weeks. However, what pleased him wasn't quite the same as what engaged the tourists around him, who pointed and laughed and took numerous photos of the Manhattan skyline, the Statue of Liberty, and themselves. What lifted his heart was looking at the empty space where he knew the WTC Twin Towers had once stood. It also pleased him to know that while the morning's events wouldn't cause as many deaths as that attack, they would be spectacular in their own right. After all, terrorism wasn't so much about how many deaths resulted — though large numbers were good for publicity; it was the way in which the infidels died, suddenly and in a place they considered safe.

Arriving at Ellis Island, Ghilzai was surprised to see another ferry tied up at an adjoining dock. A number of men and women in ferry-company uniforms bustled about on board the other boat but no tourists were in sight. "I thought we were the first ferry this morning," he said to the volunteer, Tran, as they were departing to view the American Family Immigration History Center.

"Engine trouble last night," Tran explained. "They had to send another ferry to pick up the passengers. They should have it up and running again soon."

As though on cue, the other ferry's engines

suddenly roared to life. "See," Tran said with a smile. "Those guys are good."

Leaving the boat, Ghilzai and Akhund wandered through the buildings where, from the early to mid-twentieth century, more than twenty-five million immigrants were processed and granted legal entrance to the United States. The two looked at the photographs of immigrants on the walls and read the inscriptions, feigning great interest in the hopes and dreams of the people looking back at them from long ago. But as soon as they dared without arousing suspicion, they got back in line to reboard the ferry for the trip to Liberty Island and the Statue of Liberty.

Waiting in line, Ghilzai noted that the young couple he'd been behind in line were nowhere to be seen. He knew from his previous trips that it was not unusual; there was no requirement to ride the same boat and sometimes tourists tended to linger on Ellis Island and take a later ferry to Liberty Island. *Their lucky day,* he thought regretfully, *a gift of their lives to them from Allah.*

Nor did he see Ajmaani. But he also knew that was according to plan, as she was going to wait until they'd commandeered the boat, just in case there was trouble and they needed backup from an unexpected source.

As the engines roared and the crew prepared to cast off, the terrorist took a deep breath and tapped his partner on the back. "It is time," he said as he pulled his cell phone from his pocket and called the number he'd reached earlier that morning. "We're moving," he said, and hung up again.

Walking over to the railing, Ghilzai glanced around and, seeing that no one was paying attention to him, dropped the phone overboard as he'd been instructed by Ajmaani. "There is no need to call again if you carry out the rest of your mission," she'd said the night before at their last meeting. "If you're caught before you can accomplish your task, I don't want the American agents to have the other phone number to locate your comrades."

Being out of contact with the rest of the team troubled Ghilzai. He understood security measures and no one was ever quite sure about the capabilities of American counterterrorism agencies, but this seemed extreme. Still, Ajmaani had a reputation for dealing forcefully and fatally with anyone who questioned her instructions, and he wasn't going to risk it.

With the cell phone swirling down into the depths of New York Harbor, Ghilzai and Akhund sauntered in the direction of the pilothouse as the ferry's engines revved and the boat lurched. The plan was to now take control of the vessel, which would then be met in the waters just off Liberty Island by the rest of the team in a speedboat. The others would board, killing anyone who resisted, and then prepare to turn back any attempt to retake the boat while they negotiated with the authorities. Of course, the negotiations were just a way to stall for time and make sure the American media had been alerted so that when the ferry — with the Statue of Liberty in the background — was blown up with all on board, the moment would be caught for posterity and the glory of Allah.

It had been more than ten years since the images of the collapsing WTC buildings had been etched into the minds and psyches of Americans and the West. How many times had those images been shown? Thousands? Tens of thousands? Every time there was a story about terrorism, there was a mention of al-Qaeda. Every anniversary and every event related to 9/11 received attention. He was convinced that the images of an exploding tourist ferry with that green monstrosity of a statue behind it would get similar billing and reach audiences around the world for another ten years. *At least ten,* he thought

31

to himself with a smile.

"The American media ought to pay us for giving them such great videos for their newscasts," one of the other jihadists had joked at their last meeting.

If they knew about this, they probably would have, Ghilzai thought. *Nothing is sacred to the media in this country, not even images of slaughter. They are our best propaganda tool, and it doesn't cost us anything more than our lives.*

Ghilzai and Akhund reached the pilot-house deck without being challenged. They stopped beneath a net that held a dozen orange life preservers and reached up to remove three, which had been marked with a black X. Instead of lightweight vests meant to save people in water, these were heavy — the first two, which they quickly put on, were filled with C4 explosives and ball bearings, all connected to a detonator. All they had to do was yank the cord hanging from the front of the vest and death and mayhem would result. Inside the third vest were two Glock nine-millimeter handguns — not a lot of firepower, but enough to overcome an unarmed crew.

With the vests on and the guns in their hands, they ran for the pilothouse, where they encountered a thick-shouldered, bronze-colored man wearing a ferry employee shirt. "Hey, you're not supposed to be here," the man complained.

Ghilzai pointed his gun at the employee's head. "Open the door," he said, nodding at the pilothouse entrance.

The man held up his hands and cried out in terror. "Okay, okay, please don't shoot." He fumbled with a set of keys attached to a chain on his belt. He found the key he was looking for and unlocked the door, then stepped to the side and cowered.

Ghilzai pushed past the employee and jumped into the room. *"Allahu akbar!"* he exclaimed, holding up his gun. "Nobody move or everyone dies!"

Akhund followed him, shouting in a high-pitched voice, "Death to America!"

2

Gilbert Murrow held up the piece of paper. "I found this taped to your building's entrance. It's addressed to you and says, *'The fear of the Lord adds length to life, but the years of the wicked are cut short.'*"

The little pear-shaped man in the vest and bow tie put the paper down and folded his pudgy hands on his round belly. He was sitting on the couch in the Crosby Street loft Roger "Butch" Karp shared with his wife, Marlene Ciampi, and their children, looking across the living room at the kitchen, where his hosts stood next to each other, leaning back against the granite-topped island. "If that's not a threat," he said, scrunching his nose to move his round, wire-rimmed glasses back into place, "I don't know what is."

"It's Proverbs 10:27," answered Marlene, an attractive and petite, sexually appealing woman. She glanced up at her six-foot-five husband with a smile and shrugged. "Catholic school upbringing."

Karp chuckled. "Glad Sacred Heart High School was good for something, as it appears the nuns' other influences may have waned over the years," he said, giving his wife a wink.

"You complaining?" Marlene asked, raising an eyebrow.

"Absolutely not! Merely stating the obvious," Karp replied, and they both laughed. They'd been married since they were young ADAs in the office of legendary DA Francis Garrahy, and while Marlene's face had its share of care and smile lines, and vanguards of gray had crept into the tight curls of her dark hair, he still considered her the most beautiful woman in the world, as well as his best friend.

"Very funny, you two," Murrow said with a sigh. "But I'm serious, and now they apparently know where you live. Here's another one that came to the office: *'Whatever they plot against the Lord He will bring to an end; trouble will not come a second time.'* That's Nahum 1:9, by the way."

"Really? I'm impressed," Marlene said. "I didn't know that you were a biblical scholar, Gilbert."

"I'm not," Murrow retorted. "I Googled

it." He shook his head. "Look, I know you two think you're immortal, but these people are nuts, and one of them just might go off. That snake-oil salesman, the so-called Reverend C. G. Westlund, has his demented disciples convinced that you're the anti-Christ, Butch."

Karp stopped smiling as he looked at the worried face of his friend and colleague, who'd shown up unexpectedly to walk with his boss to the Criminal Courts Building at 100 Centre Street for the Monday morning bureau chiefs meeting. As the district attorney of New York County, which encompassed the island of Manhattan, Karp had become the lightning rod for Westlund and his followers after the District Attorney's Office charged David and Nonie Ellis with reckless manslaughter in the death that past November of their ten-year-old son, Micah. It hadn't alleviated the situation when the DAO also charged Westlund and one of his henchmen with a misdemeanor for "obstructing a paramedic from the performance of his duty" outside the Ellises' apartment building, which had resulted in a sentence of sixty days in the Tombs and a fine of a thousand dollars for the preacher and his follower.

As anticipated, the indictment against the

Ellises ignited a firestorm of controversy between the proponents of "faith healing" and those, such as Karp himself, who believed that parents had a legal duty to provide "an accepted standard of care" for sick children. Lined up against Karp and the DAO were the religious zealots, who labeled the charges "a direct affront to the will of God," and also so-called Constitutionalists, who railed about the government infringing on parents' rights under the First Amendment's freedom-of-religion protections. However, the debate wasn't confined to the DAO versus the far end of the political-religious cult spectrum; it had also become a hot topic for newspaper editorials, as well as television and radio talk shows.

Although Karp didn't pay much attention to the ever-fluctuating pulse of public opinion, Murrow, his adminstrative assistant, kept him updated on the general tenor of call-in radio shows, as well as letters to the editors of newspapers. The gentler remarks were that the district attorney was a heartless wretch who needed to be run out of office; some simply suggested that God should remove him for his transgressions.

Even those who agreed that Micah's

parents should have sought medical attention for their son were often convinced that the DAO was overreaching in accusing the Ellises of reckless manslaughter. Many of them argued that the "poor parents had suffered enough" and that attempting to convict them and send them to prison was cruel and unnecessary.

After one such briefing in his office by Murrow, Karp had shaken his head. "These people have forgotten that this isn't about religion or the Constitution, it's about a ten-year-old boy who suffered and died because his parents didn't take him to a doctor," he'd said. "It's about a dead child and parental responsibilities, not a theoretical debate."

Given the controversy, Karp would have preferred to try the Ellises himself. It was the sort of case that to him went to the heart of the justice system. He also understood that his taking the lead in trying cases set an example for the attorneys who worked for him; it demonstrated that he believed, as had his mentor, Francis Garrahy, that the New York DAO should pursue cases based on the rule of law — not popular opinion or political expediency — and that they were to keep foremost in their minds that before presenting a case to the grand jury they must have factual evidence of the guilt of the accused and legally admissible evidence to convict beyond a reasonable doubt.

However, he'd had another trial to prepare for and prosecute, which precluded his day-to-day direct involvement in the Ellis case, but he still kept vigilant oversight. He'd approved assigning Kenny Katz — one of his protégés in the Homicide Bureau, who'd sat second chair with him on several high-profile cases — as lead counsel, with an old colleague, Ray Guma, sitting in as the supervisorial seasoned mentor.

With jury selection for the trial starting in a little more than a week, Karp had been satisfied with Katz's preparations under Guma's watchful eye. The young man had avoided getting caught up in the hype surrounding a high-profile case and approached it professionally, as he would any other homicide case — with thorough preparation. And at the meeting this morning, he would be presenting his case to the bureau chiefs and various other assistant district attorneys to be dissected.

Katz had avoided any appearances in the media, directing all inquiries to Murrow, who'd mostly relied on the old "we won't be trying this case in the press" noncomment. But Murrow had grown increasingly alarmed at the vitriol of those who thought that the Ellises should not have been charged and that Karp was the devil incarnate. When Murrow called that morning to say he was dropping by "to talk," Karp knew it was because his friend was worried about his safety.

"It's a lot of rhetoric, Gilbert," Karp said. "If I responded to every threat, we'd never get anything done. Clay is on it and is taking the usual precautions, which as you know with him means Secret Service–type surveillance."

Murrow sighed. Although trained as a lawyer and originally hired as an assistant district attorney, his duties now were to run the daily administrative operations of the office, including keeping Karp's schedule and acting as his mouthpiece with the media. His "other" job was as Karp's political adviser, which, while not a thankless task — as the boss frequently expressed his appreciation — was a difficult one to juggle since Karp hated that part of his job. But Murrow did his best to dance between his employer's distaste for politics and the exigencies of his having to run for office every four years.

When the decision was made to charge the Ellises, Murrow shook his head, knowing what was to come. But he knew better than to argue judicial philosophy with his apolitical, merit-driven boss, so after glumly pointing out what to expect and from which corners, he accepted the fact that the case would go forward. Then he'd done his best to defend the DAO when the press came calling for comment, or when unfavorable and unfair editorials and "talking head" opinions came out, which again was no easy task as Karp could not have cared less what the media thought.

Nor was Karp going to give in now on the idea of beefing up security. It wasn't that he was oblivious to the threats or trying to be a hero, but Karp wasn't going to let his personal safety affect how he ran the office and his life. Nor did he think it would save him if he did. As he'd explained to Clay Fulton, the NYPD detective sergeant who was in charge of the detectives assigned as investigators to the DAO as well as Karp's security, and to Murrow just a few days earlier, "If someone really wants to get at me, they're going to do it. We take reasonable measures to prevent any incidents, but we all know from experience that a determined assassin will find a way to strike."

Karp was not as matter-of-fact about the security for his twin boys, his daughter, and

41

Marlene. However, even there he had limited control because of the rather unique makeup of his nuclear family.

Marlene, a former ADA herself who'd started the office's sex crimes unit, was tough as nails. She had turned in her prosecutor's badge to start a firm that provided VIP security services. Ultimately, the firm became highly successful and was purchased by a publicly held operation for millions. Lately, experiencing an apparent midlife crisis, she'd started taking on special cases in which her talent as a private investigator, as well as her law degree, were needed. Over the years, including "volunteer" work protecting abused women from brutal spouses and boyfriends, she'd shown a surprising proclivity for meeting violence with violence and coming out the winner. So when he'd mentioned the idea of increasing police protection for her and their children, she'd scoffed.

"I'm quite capable of taking care of myself," she noted pointedly — she'd barely managed to shoehorn some of her dealings with abusers and other miscreants into the strict confines of the law. "I've made plenty of enemies in this world without worrying about a few more nutcases. And even if they are dangerous, I'm probably more aware of my surroundings and potential threats than my dear, but somewhat naïve, husband, and he won't allow any extra security for himself. And to be honest, I certainly don't want to rely on some cop watching my back; it might give me a false sense of security, trusting someone I don't know. So I'll watch my own, thank you very much."

Karp had no more luck with his daughter, Lucy. But considering that she and her fiancé, Ned Blanchett, worked for a secretive "off-the-books" antiterrorism agency that exposed them to grave danger on a regular basis, there was no reason to think that an NYPD officer or two was going to make much of a difference.

In fact, Lucy and Ned, who made their home in Taos, New Mexico, were in town on assignment for the agency, which was run by an old family friend and former FBI agent, Espey Jaxon. They'd had dinner with the family and spent the night in Lucy's childhood bedroom. Karp had heard them stirring before dawn and got up, catching them heading out the door with to-go cups of coffee.

"Off to a boring ol' meeting," Lucy said unconvincingly. "We should be home by dinner, but if not, don't wait and don't worry."

When the door closed, he'd walked into the kitchen to check out the television monitor mounted in a corner that was connected to a security camera above the outside door. He shook his head when a black sedan with tinted windows pulled up to the curb and the two young people got in and then sped off into the dark. *Boring ol' meeting, my ass,* he thought. He'd already been filled in on the events transpiring that morning by Jaxon, but he knew that his daughter and future son-in-law were precluded from discussing it and he honored their silence.

That left the twin boys — Zak and Giancarlo — to worry about. The problem with them was that they were in high school and, as with any teenagers, they liked their freedom and sense of independence. They were active, involved in sports, the music scene in the Lower East Side, and whatever else two teens who considered Manhattan their playground might be up to at any given time. When he'd suggested that a plain-clothes police officer be assigned to tag along "discreetly and at a distance" until after the Ellis trial, they'd complained mightily, saying, "a cop would cramp our style." They threatened to "ditch the tail" as soon as possible.

"I'm not worried about a bunch of crazies; I'll club them with this," said Zak, the larger and more rambunctious of the two. He sounded disturbingly like his mother as he raised his right hand, which was in a cast due to his having broken it punching a larger, older upperclassmate who was bullying his brother and another player on their high school baseball team.

So for the time being, Karp had let it be. The truth was that while the biblical verses about God's wrath were thinly disguised threats, they were no more alarming — indeed, quite a bit less alarming — than others the Karp-Ciampi clan had dealt with in the past. Because of his job the family was a magnet for trouble. They had been fending off a variety of sociopaths, terrorists, and other assorted killers and thugs since he and Marlene had met at the DAO and started dating. Marlene had even lost an eye opening a letter bomb intended for him before they were married and had kids. Lucy's version of all these events was that the family had a spiritual calling to battle the "forces of evil."

"We better get going," Murrow said, standing up.

Karp looked at his watch — it was almost eight o'clock — and nodded. "Sure, let's roll," he said, pulling on an off-the-rack blue suit jacket.

3

Lucy Karp noted the look of surprise on the terrorists' faces after they burst into the pilothouse and the crew hardly reacted except to cast hard glances at them before going about their business. Only the captain said anything, which was, "Go to hell." He muttered the sentiment with his back turned to them.

The crew members were not the only other people in the pilothouse. Besides Lucy, there were the two young men who'd been standing in line — agents for USNIDSA, the United States National Inter-Departmental Security Administration, which her agency had teamed with for this operation. They both had their guns trained on the intruders, identified at the morning's briefing as Aman Ghilzai and Hasim Akhund.

"Drop your weapons!" the lead agent demanded as he sighted down the barrel of his gun at Ghilzai's forehead.

"Girnaa aap ka bandooq!" Lucy said, repeating the command in Urdu.

Swift as a cobra the terrorist pointed his gun at Lucy and pulled the trigger. His face registered surprise again when there was an empty click but no loud report and no bullet left the barrel.

Ghilzai dropped the gun and reached for the cord hanging from the faux life preserver to detonate the C4 explosives packed inside and spew ball bearings and fire throughout the pilothouse. He braced himself for the expected flash that would carry him off to his reward, but his path to martyrdom took a detour when his weapon failed him again.

"Maghloob ho jana," Lucy yelled. "Surrender!"

Ghilzai sneered at her. "I speak good English, *randi.*"

"Well then next time you call me a whore, I'm going to slap that ugly mustache off your ignorant face," Lucy replied.

The agent next to her smiled. "Sorry about that, asshole," he said scathingly to Ghilzai. "The bomb's a fake and the guns are loaded with dummies. You and your pal are my prisoners."

Ghilzai wasn't just some poorly prepared, brainwashed recruit from New Jersey. As they'd been told at the briefing that morning after she and Ned left her parents' loft, he had been trained at a top-notch al-Qaeda camp in Pakistan. "Remember, he is able and dedicated, and he will be determined to carry out his mission," Jaxon had said. "When he realizes the mission has been compromised, he will adjust and try to kill as many Americans as he can. Precautions have been taken, but that doesn't rule out some surprise. Be careful."

Suddenly, the second terrorist screamed something incoherent, dropped his gun, and started to run from the room. But he only reached the doorway before he was knocked back onto the deck of the pilothouse, where he lay clutching his midsection and gasping for air. A bronze-skinned man wearing a ferry company uniform stepped in behind the downed man, followed by a tourism volunteer named Tran, according to his name tag.

Lucy tried to smile when she saw her fellow agents John Jojola and Tran Vinh Do enter the room, but it was a weak attempt. She'd known that the guns the terrorists were going to "find" in the life preservers wouldn't be loaded. Still, it had been unnerving to have one pointed at her head and to hear the sound of the hammer striking the shell. She felt nauseous and dizzy, so she concentrated on the bantering between Jojola and Tran.

"Jojola! I thought we agreed that I would get first shot at these guys if they made a run for it," Tran complained. *Tham lam lon!*"

"He just called you a greedy pig," Lucy said, relieved to have something to take her mind off the incident. A super-polyglot, she had a savant's ear and tongue for languages, more than five dozen of them by last count. She'd learned Vietnamese, which Tran had used to insult Jojola, by age twelve.

"I understood him, Lucy," Jojola replied dryly. "My Vietnamese may be rusty but I heard enough versions of that back in '68 to last me a lifetime, so I knew what the *ngu ngoc khi* was saying."

"What the hell?" said the lead NIDSA agent, pointing his gun at Ghilzai while his partner handcuffed Akhund, who was still trying to catch his breath from a blow to the solar plexus.

"He," Lucy said, pointing to Jojola, "just called him" — she pointed at Tran — "a 'stupid monkey.' It's a pretty typical insult in Vietnam."

The lead agent's jaw dropped and then he scowled. "I could give a rat's ass what they're calling each other."

50

"This is what we get working with amateurs and old men," added the second agent, placing flex cuffs on the downed terrorist's wrists.

Jojola and Tran stopped their squabbling to look hard at the agent who'd insulted them.

"Amateurs and old men?" Jojola said, seething. "Look, you baby-faced James Bond wannabe. I was kicking the asses of tougher men than these two before you were born."

"You mean we were kicking your ass," Tran retorted before sneering at the agent and adding, "But yeah, *trè em imbecile* —"

"Sort of French-Vietnamese for 'imbecile child' . . . ," Lucy interpreted helpfully.

"— all I see are cheap suits, bad haircuts, and snot-nosed children playing at being men," Tran continued.

"All right, boys," Lucy interrupted. "I think we still have work to do, and we need to move on."

She smiled and shook her head. She'd met Jojola, a member of the Taos Indian tribe, when he was the tribe's chief of police and had teamed with her and her mother to catch a serial child-killer in New Mexico. A decorated army veteran who'd served during the Vietnam War, he was a spiritual man

51

who had not been surprised that the crossing of their paths, and the seemingly coincidental events that had twisted their fates together, led to his joining Espey Jaxon's small counterterrorism agency.

At least it was no stranger than the participation in the agency of Tran Vinh Do, a longtime family friend, mostly because of his dedication to Lucy's mother, Marlene. Tran was a former Vietcong leader during the war in Vietnam and was now currently a gangster in New York City. Although she didn't need convincing that there was more than coincidence to all of their lives crossing, it didn't surprise her to learn that Jojola and Tran had been sworn enemies during the Vietnam conflict, even though they'd since buried all but the verbal hatchets and were the best of friends.

The federal agents glared at Jojola and Tran for a moment but then the lead agent shrugged. As he turned Ghilzai around, he looked at Akhund and said, "Good work, Hasim. We'll put in a good word with the judge."

Akhund furrowed his brow, trying to understand what the agent was saying, but Ghilzai got it right away and lunged at his partner. "Traitor!" he spat as the agent restrained him. "I knew you could not be trusted! As Allah is my witness, you will die for this and your soul be cast into the pits of *jahannam!*"

Hasim Akhund's eyes grew wide with fear. "I did nothing," he said. "They are trying to make me look like a traitor!"

"Okay, you two, break up the love fest," the lead agent said. "Captain, would you make the announcement? Meantime, you two assholes stand there against the window. You might enjoy what you're going to see."

The ferry captain picked up the microphone to the public address system and spoke. "Ladies and gentlemen, please remain in your seats. Our sister ferry tied up next to us is ready to get back in service and so we're going to let her go ahead. We hope you enjoyed your visit to the American Family Immigration History Center and we'll be under way for Liberty Island shortly."

With that, the captain turned off the microphone and nodded to the agents and Lucy. "Good luck," he said.

"Thanks," Lucy replied as she and her two cohorts quickly moved toward the door. She'd remained aboard the ferry when it docked so that she could listen in with eavesdropping equipment on any calls placed by Ghilzai's cell phone. She knew the code words he was going to use if the attack was going forward, but if he had changed his mind and contacted his counterparts speaking in Urdu or Arabic, her talents might have been needed. They knew a lot of what was planned, especially regarding the attempt to hijack the ferry, but they did not know how to locate the other part of the terrorist team — only that they were going to attack by boat. Now she had to get to the other ferry.

Lucy ducked out of the pilothouse and hurried past curious, but not alarmed, tourists. She quickly made her way to the other ferry, stepping aboard as the crew cast off and the boat pulled away from the pier.

4

It was a lovely spring morning in Gotham when Karp and Murrow emerged onto Crosby Street and turned the corner onto Grand Street for the half mile or so walk to the Criminal Courts Building on Centre Street. The trees were beginning to bud and although the sun had yet to peer over the tops of the skyscrapers, their fellow pedestrians smiled and chatted beneath clear blue skies as they wove their way through the throng on the busy sidewalks.

Reaching the front of the massive Criminal Courts Building, Karp pointed to a newsstand. "I'll be up in a minute," he said. "I'm going to go pick up the *Times* and say hello to Warren."

As Karp approached, "Dirty" Warren Bennett, who owned the newsstand, looked up through thick, smudged glasses and grinned. "Hey, Butch . . . asshole bitch . . . how are you this morning?" the thin little man with the long, pointed nose asked.

Karp smiled back. Bennett hadn't earned his nickname because of the state of his clothes or personal hygiene, though both were in need of a good washing. The moniker was due to his Tourette's syndrome, which, in addition to causing muscle spasms and facial tics, made him involuntarily swear like a longshoreman.

"Hey, I got one . . . oh boy shit whoop crap . . . for you," Bennett said.

Karp's smile disappeared and was replaced by his game face. He and the news vendor had been playing movie trivia for years, with Bennett trying to stump Karp, which he'd yet to do. "Well, pilgrim, draw if you've got the *cojones*," he replied with his best, though poor, John Wayne imitation.

Bennett sneered. "Oh yeah? Okay then, Mr. Wayne. In 1944 Lux Radio Theater featured . . . whoop whoop oh boy . . . a radio adaptation of this movie with Betty Grable, Carmen Miranda, and John Payne," he said. "Name the movie and be exact."

Karp scoffed. "Appropriate choice for this morning," he replied. "*Springtime in the Rockies*. That exact enough for you?" He waited for Bennett's face to show the first sign of triumph before he shattered his friend's hope of finally scoring a point. "But it's a trick question, Mr. Bennett," he said, watching his opponent's hopeful expression immediately fade. "John Payne played the part of Dan Christy in the film, but Dick Powell replaced him for the radio version."

"Damn it, Karp, you bastard," exclaimed Bennett, whose responses weren't always tied to Tourette's. But he shook his head and smiled. "Man, you're . . . oh boy shit piss . . . good."

Karp wiggled his eyebrows. "Don't mess with the Duke of Trivia, pilgrim."

Both men laughed as Karp picked up a newspaper and paid the vendor. But as he turned toward the Criminal Courts Building, a shout interrupted his good mood.

"There here he is! There's Karp!" The shout elicited jeers and epithets.

Looking in the direction of the voices, Karp saw a dozen or so protesters, some carrying picket signs, walking swiftly toward him on the sidewalk. Emerging from the middle of the pack to lead them was the Reverend C. G. Westlund, who didn't yell but smirked as he approached.

"I'm getting a little . . . tits oh boy . . . tired of these jokers," Bennett snarled, leaving his newsstand to confront the mob.

"It's just words, Warren," Karp said, placing a hand on his friend's shoulder and pulling him back. He then stepped toward his detractors. "Let's hear what they have to say."

Westlund marched up until he was only a couple of feet from Karp and blocking his way into the courts building. "Repent, Brother Karp, and drop the charges against the Ellises, who were faithful to the will of God!" he thundered.

"I believe we'll leave that for a jury to decide," Karp replied evenly. "Now, if that's all you've got to say, I have more important things to do."

But Westlund stepped closer as his followers drew in, their faces angry and some a bit wild-eyed. "More important than answering our questions about God's place in the home of simple Christian Americans? Have you forgotten that this is a nation founded upon Christian ideals of faith in God, or do those of the Jewish faith not recognize the efficacy of prayer? Or the rights of Americans to ask God for deliverance from earthly ills and deny the ungodly arrogance of Western medicine that seeks to supplant God as the arbiter of life and death? Granted, most doctors are Jewish, as are most lawyers."

"'Yield unto Caesar that which is his sayeth the Lord,' get it, Westlund?" Karp replied.

"Break the law here and you're going to be held responsible. And more accurately our American heritage is founded upon Judeo-Christian values, which you don't adhere to."

As the crowd pressed in, Karp had to admit it was the sort of situation in which one crazed person, agitated by Westlund's words, might decide to act. He was ready to defend himself, but the need was suddenly averted when a large black sedan pulled up to the curb a few feet from where Karp was standing toe-to-toe with the preacher and his followers.

A thick, broad-shouldered black man emerged from the vehicle. "Morning, Butch," Clay Fulton said, walking up to stand next to his employer and longtime friend. He then looked at Westlund and his followers. "What seems to be the problem here?"

Just from the big detective's body language, Karp could tell that Fulton was spoiling for a fight. He couldn't blame him; he was half tempted to rock Westlund himself for his anti-Semitic remarks. But he wasn't going to play that game. "Good morning, Clay," he replied. "The good reverend and his flock were just enjoying their First Amendment right of free speech and now will be getting out of my way so I can go to work. Isn't that right, reverend?"

Westlund's eyes narrowed. " *'The wicked flee when no one pursues, but the righteous are bold as a lion'!*" he shouted as his supporters cheered.

"If you're going to quote Proverbs 28 . . . whoop oh boy . . . quote all of it!" Bennett shouted back. " *'Those who forsake the law praise the wicked, but those who keep the law'* . . . oh boy bite my ass . . . *'strive against them. Evil men do not understand justice but those who seek the Lord'* . . . crap bastard . . . *'understand it completely.'* "

Karp looked back at his friend with surprise. "Why thank you, Warren," he said. "Write that down for me sometime."

"My pleasure," Bennett replied, his face twitching as he sniffed and then wrinkled his nose as if he'd caught a foul scent. "I know a false prophet . . . asswipe . . . when I smell one."

Westlund glared at Bennett and then Karp before stepping aside. "Just trying to save your soul, brother," he said to Karp, then turned to Bennett. "God has afflicted your mouth for the foulness of your soul. Repent and you might yet be saved!"

"Why you piece of . . ." As he spoke, Bennett tried to get at the much larger man but Karp held him back.

"He's not worth it, Warren," Karp said.

"Don't worry, little man," Westlund snarled, "God has ordained that we'll meet again."

Moving so quickly that the preacher flinched and took a step back, Karp got in Westlund's face. "Let's be very clear about something, Mr. Westlund," he growled in a voice so low that only those closest to them could hear. "You and I are the ones who will be meeting again, but it's going to be in court and you'll be sitting at the defense table."

Westlund recovered quickly, though he moved away from Karp. "You see, my brothers and sisters, when faced with God's truth, the evil resort to threats!" he told his followers, who shouted and cursed.

Karp ignored them and looked at Bennett. "You okay, Warren?"

Bennett's angry eyes still followed Westlund as the preacher led his followers away, but he nodded. "Yeah, to hell . . . crap oh boy ohhhh boy . . . with that asshole," he said. "But thanks for . . . whoop whoop . . . sticking up for me."

"Seems to me we were sticking up for each other," Karp replied, and clapped the smaller man on his shoulder. "If he bothers you, just let me know."

Bennett smiled, blinking up at Karp, his light blue eyes magnified behind his glasses. "Thanks, Karp. But I can handle that guy . . . or I have friends who will."

Leaving Bennett at his newsstand, Karp entered the Criminal Courts Building on the Hogan Place side. Fulton then headed for the building's security office and left him to ride the elevator up to his office on the eighth floor alone. As the car rose, he felt his face burning with anger. Some of it was for Warren Bennett, a good, hardworking man and one of several local street people who kept watch over the environs and people around the courthouse, especially Karp and his family. Although unsure of how exactly their system worked, Karp was aware that they reported to David Grale, the "mad monk" who believed God had appointed him to rid the city of evil men he believed were possessed by demons. The irony was that the killer had made it part of his mission to safeguard Marlene and the kids, especially Lucy, whom he'd met when they were both working in a Catholic soup kitchen.

Exiting the elevator and walking into the conference area of his office, he noticed that his receptionist, Darla Milquetost, was setting up and preparing for the bureau chiefs meeting. He wished her a good morning and entered the inner sanctum of his personal private office space, still thinking about the confrontation with Westlund and his band of lunatics. He regretted being drawn into a war of words with the bellicose preacher, but it had been hard to stomach the man's anti-Semitic remarks.

Those and more bigoted comments had begun shortly after the Ellises were indicted. Early on, Westlund's attacks were subtle. He couched Karp's ethnicity as a "possible explanation" for why the DAO was "persecuting" the Ellises, as well as himself and his followers.

"Nothing against the Jewish people, but I suppose we should expect," the minister had explained to a radio talk-show host, "that someone of the district attorney's faith would fail to recognize true Christians' right to place their faith in God and not the false god of modern medicine."

Other times, Westlund's prejudices were thinly disguised as backhanded compliments. "Jews, such as our district attorney, are known as a 'practical' race of people who tend to believe more in science and man's infallibility than Christians, who put

God first. That's why Jews are so successful at business and secular professions, while Christians place more stock in spirituality."

But after being jailed for obstructing the paramedics, Westlund had ramped up the vitriol. Upon his release from the Tombs, the firebrand preacher told a waiting television crew, "Karp comes from a long line of predecessors who enjoy persecuting Christians; that's why he's out to crucify me and my brothers and sisters in the End of Days Reformation Church of Jesus Christ Resurrected."

When his comments were challenged by an editorial writer the next day, Westlund backtracked. He complained that his remarks had been "taken out of context" when aired on the evening news. By "predecessors," he said, he'd meant other district attorneys and law officers, not Jews. And his reference to crucifying, he added, was just a metaphor to illustrate how the Ellises were being "unfairly and harshly" treated for their spiritual beliefs.

As the trial date neared, Westlund was savvy enough to let his followers make the most inflammatory comments, up to and including that the DAO was prosecuting the Ellises solely because Karp was an evil Jew who hated Christians. Occasionally when one of his followers stepped over the line enough for the media to raise their collective eyebrows, Westlund would issue a press release through his church saying that he did not "condone hate speech." He attributed the venal comments to "a few overwrought church members who are reacting to the district attorney's attack on the fundamental American right to practice religion without the interference of the government. It may have been an inappropriate way to express their feelings, but I think what you're seeing is their frustration as yet another one of their God-given rights is taken from them."

As Karp's reflection continued, he was reminded that Westlund and his ilk weren't the only ones using God's name in vain to further their hateful personal agendas. But his thoughts were interrupted when his receptionist announced the arrival of Murrow, who stuck his head in the door. "Ready, boss?" he asked, referring to the bureau chiefs meeting.

"Yeah, let's go," Karp replied, wondering how this day that had begun so full of beauty would end.

5

Espey Jaxon looked up from the deck of the ferry, saw the news helicopter circling in the distance, and then noticed Nadya Malovo out of the corner of his eye. She'd come out from the interior of the boat with Agent Mike Rolles, her National Inter-Departmental Security Administration handler, and walked over to stand beside him. She looked across the water at the motorboat filled with armed men that stood motionless in the water.

"I thought the idea was to keep her out of sight," Jaxon said to Agent Rolles with a frown.

Before the agent could answer, U.S. Marshal Jen Capers emerged from the ferry and strode up to where the three stood. "It was," she answered angrily. She pointed her finger at the agent and said, "This violates the agreement."

"Relax," Rolles said with a smirk. He

reminded Jaxon of a college fraternity type playing at secret agent. "What's she going to do, swim for it? She's cuffed, and she's with me. She just wanted to watch, and after all, she's the reason Ali Baba and the Forty Terrorists on that boat over there are screwed. Or would you have rather watched this ferry and a few hundred tourists get incinerated on the news tonight?"

"She couldn't care less about innocent people dying," Capers spat, fixing Malovo with a hard stare. "She's looking out for herself. Now she goes inside, or I'll haul her sociopathic rear end back to that nice little cell we have for her at FloMax penitentiary. She's still a prisoner of the U.S. Marshals Service."

"Afraid national security trumps your little escort service," the agent said scathingly.

"Yeah?" Capers replied, pulling out her cell phone and holding it up to him. "You want to explain to your boss and mine what your playing Pinocchio to her Geppetto has to do with national security? Maybe she's yanking your strings, or something else, a bit too much and you need to be cut loose. Now, what's it going to be? You want to make the call or should I?"

Rolles's smirk dissolved into an angry glare and his face flushed. But then he turned to Malovo and nodded toward the door. "Go inside," he snapped.

"Yes, of course," Malovo replied in heavily accented English. She looked up at the news helicopter hovering in the distance and smiled at Capers. "I'll leave you with your boyfriend and watch the festivities with someone who appreciates my . . . contributions. Such fire in a woman . . . a shame you only like men."

Capers ignored the comment and signaled to a young marshal standing close to the ferry door. "Hank, escort the prisoner back inside," she said, "and this time if she moves from where I told her to stay, cuff her to the rail."

Hank Masterson, a former Navy SEAL and prior to that a college linebacker, nodded. "Yes, ma'am. And if Double-oh-seven has a problem with it, should I cuff him, too?"

Rolles bristled. "You want to go, big boy, let me know," he shot back, but turned away when Masterson just laughed at him.

When the others were inside, Capers looked at Jaxon. "Sorry about that," she said. "I had to call in to headquarters and couldn't get any reception inside the ferry. Hank was supposed to stay with her but Rolles convinced him to wait for me. Good man, Hank, but he's still learning."

"Not a problem," Jaxon replied as he smiled and then turned back to study the idling motorboat through his binoculars. "And it was worth listening to you cut that jackass down to size with the Pinocchio comment — 'yanking your strings, or something else,' that's classic. Still, I have to admit, I'm glad she tipped us off on this one."

Capers didn't respond to his last comment and he knew why. A year ago, Malovo had posed as the legal assistant of a lawyer who was helping defend a terrorist, the imam Jabbar, in a trial Karp was prosecuting. She poisoned a former leader of the Sons of Man as he was about to testify about his secret society's role in aiding the defendant in an attack on the New York Stock Exchange. Malovo had then escaped from the courtroom and made her way to Il Buon Pane bakery, where she intended to murder the owner, Moishe Sobelman, just to torment her nemesis Butch Karp, who had befriended the old man. But Moishe's wife, Goldie, had somehow made her hesitate, and then Capers arrived at the shop and got the drop on her.

It had taken every ounce of her professionalism for Capers not to pull the trigger and arrest her instead. Just a few months earlier, Malovo had led an attack that killed Capers's partner. It rankled Capers that she now had to play babysitter for Malovo, who'd worked out some sort of deal with the NIDSA higher-ups in which she supplied information on radical Islamic sleeper cells.

"The powers that be decided we don't need to know all of what she's getting in exchange," Capers told Jaxon one evening when they were discussing the arrangement over dinner. "We just know she'll be going into WITSEC; but what else she gets, your guess is as good as mine, and for some reason it's a big secret."

Jaxon now grimaced remembering the conversation and Capers's distress that instead of languishing in a tiny isolation cell with a shoebox-sized window for light twenty-three hours a day — or receiving the death penalty — her enemy would be placed in WITSEC, the federal witness protection program. There Malovo would, at the very least, be given a new identity, a place to live, and money to live on, and, most galling of all, the U.S. Marshals Service would be responsible for her safety.

"I'm sorry, *querida*," he said now, using his pet name for her as no one was close enough to hear. "It's just wrong. No matter what she gives us now, it doesn't absolve her of the evil she's done."

Capers patted him lightly on the shoulder. "Don't sweat it, pumpkin," she replied. "My partner would have gladly given his life to save innocent people, even if it required our making a deal with the devil."

"A she-devil," Jaxon said, turning from the rail to face her.

"Yeah, and I'm worried about what she's really got planned in that twisted mind," Capers replied. "I have a hard time envisioning her settling down in some small obscure town in the Midwest and joining the local Junior League, all under the watchful eye of my office. That's a leap too far if you get my drift."

"I do," Jaxon said. "But I feel safer knowing that you're itching to put a bullet in her if she so much as blinks in the wrong direction."

Capers nodded. "I wouldn't mind."

Jaxon smiled. "I rather enjoyed playing the old married couple in line this morning," he said.

Capers returned the smile. "Yeah, something I could get used to," she said, and then sighed. "Of course, a girl would have to be asked first."

When she saw his expression change, she laughed again and said with a light drawl she'd picked up in her hometown of Austin, Texas, "Why bless your heart, Agent Espey Jaxon, you're as red as a chili pepper. I do believe you're feeling a tad backed into a corner?"

"No, I . . . um . . . well," Jaxon stammered. "I just wasn't expecting —"

Capers laughed again. "Don't worry. You're off the hook . . . for now. I'll let you go back to capturing terrorists while I check on my prisoner and hope she tries to escape."

"We still on for dinner at Butch and Marlene's place tomorrow night?"

"Wouldn't miss it for all the oil in Texas," Capers replied.

As she disappeared back inside the ferry, Jaxon glanced over at where Ned Blanchett lay prone on the deck, looking through the scope of his sniper rifle at the terrorists on the other boat. A few feet beyond him, Lucy Karp and several NIDSA agents hovered around communication equipment set up for negotiating with the terrorists on the boat.

Lucy looked up as he approached and shook her head. Jaxon looked at his watch: 8:50. The terrorists had until nine to surrender or face attack.

He had insisted that his agency be in charge of this operation while the NIDSA agents took a backseat. Jaxon's argument was that Malovo was vital to his agency's attempts to root out the remaining members of the Sons of Man and should stay his prisoner. Under normal circumstances, a bigger national security group like NIDSA would have laughed and taken over. But the powerful man who had formed Jaxon's agency in secrecy and asked him to run it carried a lot of weight in the nation's capital, and his team leader got what he wanted in this case.

After complaining vigorously, the chief agent for NIDSA gave in but insisted that his man be the liaison between Malovo and Jaxon's agency. He had no choice but to agree; the assassin would only talk to the agent. Other agents with several agencies had tried to interrogate her after her arrest, but it wasn't until the current macho man came along that she agreed to make a deal. Exactly what it was wasn't clear, but it started with her not spending the rest of her life in FloMax, the maximum-security federal penitentiary in Florence, Colorado, that housed the worst of the worst, including the Blind Sheik and the Unabomber.

So Jaxon had to rely on the agent to pass on any information that was pertinent to the Sons of Man. Occasionally, Jaxon was allowed to question Malovo in the presence of the NIDSA agent about information she had provided. But most of what he learned was relayed in briefings.

Currently, she wasn't divulging much about the Sons of Man. She'd diverted the focus to a series of terrorist plots aimed at the New York metropolitan area that she said her sources had told her were in the works. The sources believed that she was her alter ego, Ajmaani, a Chechen Muslim terrorist, and she'd used that to infiltrate the sleeper cells to find out their plans.

It was how they'd learned about the impending attack on the ferry. She said she'd been told that two men would board the ferry and wait until the boat was leaving Ellis Island before signaling to their comrades waiting in another boat and then commandeering the lightly guarded vessel using weapons they believed had been stashed aboard by an accomplice. Once the boat was in their control, they would order it stopped in the waters just off Liberty Island. They would then blow it up with everyone on it, including themselves and every man, woman, and child.

"For propaganda purposes," Malovo had explained.

Thanks to Malovo's information, they'd been able to identify Ghilzai and Akhund; knew where the accomplice (who'd since been arrested) had hidden the weapons, which had been exchanged for harmless fakes; and were waiting for Ghilzai to pass the word to proceed to the others when the ferry started to leave the dock.

Originally, they had considered remaining on the regular ferry and continuing with the journey, inviting attack even with the tourists aboard, so that the waiting terrorists would not note anything amiss. But there was too much of a risk that the attackers might get through the first line of defense and hurt or kill an innocent adult or child. So they'd come up with the idea of switching ferries, bringing the second ferry with the armed agents over in the middle of the night.

Malovo knew that the main terrorist group would be approaching the ferry from the water, but she said she wasn't sure of the boat they would be using as they planned to steal one in the night. And that was a source of concern. On any given day in the spring, New York Harbor was jumping with watercraft, from oceangoing freighters and Hudson River barges to cabin cruisers, yachts, and small sailboats. The feds would have to let some of them approach close enough to be sure they were the enemy or risk tipping the terrorists off and allowing them to escape to plan some other attack.

It was the reason Malovo had been brought along for the ride. She would make her appearance from the pilothouse and then go back inside once the attackers had revealed themselves. And indeed that's what happened.

When they reached the waters off Liberty Island in front of the statue, Malovo walked out of the pilothouse and the captain shut his engines down as if he was following the instructions of Ghilzai. That's when a large cabin cruiser that had been in with the other boat traffic suddenly veered toward them.

Jaxon had waited for the terrorists' boat to separate from the vessels around them and move to within a few hundred yards, then gave the word. Suddenly, a half-dozen New York Police Department speedboats and a U.S. Coast Guard gunboat with a fifty-caliber machine gun mounted on the bow materialized seemingly out of nowhere. The gunboat swerved into the path of the cabin cruiser; the terrorists tried to escape, but they were cut off by the NYPD craft surrounding them. At the same time, two dozen federal agents from Jaxon's office and NIDSA transformed from supposed tourists milling about on deck to armed men ready to repel boarders. They were then joined by an NYPD helicopter with a sharpshooter perched in the open side door.

Surrounded, the terrorists had fired a few shots before cutting their engines and stopping in the water. After a half hour, they'd agreed to talk, and a small rubber dinghy had been launched from the gunboat with a cell phone. Apparently, the group was split on how to proceed; some of them wanted to surrender, but others — apparently foreigners, as they spoke to Lucy in Arabic and Urdu — refused. They'd been told they had until nine, which was now only a few minutes away.

"Something's happening!" Blanchett shouted.

6

The din of two dozen men and women carrying on a variety of conversations stopped the moment Karp walked into the conference room and took his seat at the head of the long table for the weekly Monday morning bureau chiefs meeting. On either side of him, the New York DAO's chiefs and assistant chiefs, and a smattering of assistant district attorneys, waited expectantly, some sitting at the table, others occupying whatever seat they could find around the room.

The room itself reflected Karp's own minimalist attitude, its walls unadorned, the table and chairs about as basic and worn as the building itself. There wasn't time to worry about the décor. In fact, Karp had never even noted the putrid green color that coated the walls of the corridors, courtrooms, and offices at 100 Centre Street until Marlene had commented on them a few years earlier.

All that mattered in that room was the fair and effectual process of dealing with the administration of justice for the victims and perpetrators of an average of four hundred murders, twelve hundred rapes, seventeen thousand felony assaults, eighteen thousand burglaries, nineteen thousand robberies, and thirty-eight thousand grand larcenies — not to mention tens of thousands of "lesser" crimes — inflicted every year upon the citizens of New York County.

The meetings had been a fixture of Garrahy's administration, and while they'd gone by the wayside during the decline of the office after his death, they had been reinstated when Karp was elected to office years later. Outwardly the purpose of the meetings was for assistant district attorneys to present their pre-indictment cases to the other prosecutors in the room, who would then do their best to dissect and question the authenticity and credibility of the evidence, as well as discuss the expected response and counterattack of the defense. And woe to the ADA who came into that meeting unprepared to answer the questions.

On a larger scale, the meetings were to ensure that the office's two guiding principles for prosecuting the accused were being followed. Also something Karp had picked up from his mentor Garrahy, the principles required that they be 1,000 percent convinced of the accused's factual guilt and have the legally admissible evidence to prove it. It was not enough to believe that the defendant was "probably" guilty, nor was it acceptable to go to trial without the evidence to prove the case — no matter how convinced the ADA was of a person's guilt.

As Karp looked around the table, he noticed Kenny Katz off to his left. The slim, muscular young man with dark curly hair had a troubled look on his face and didn't appear to be tuned in to what was happening in front of him. With the Ellis trial set to start the next week, he knew that his protégé was probably feeling the pressure of being in the driver's seat of his first high-profile case. He decided it was time they had a private talk.

"Tommy Mack," Karp said, addressing his Homicide Bureau chief, "take over. I just remembered I had something I wanted to discuss with Mr. Katz. . . . Kenny, could I see you in my office?"

Once inside Karp's office, Katz took a seat on the edge of a leather chair beside the front of Karp's desk. It didn't take long for the ADA to validate Karp's assessment of what was bugging him. "You know, you hear a lot about how this is a religious-freedom First Amendment case," Katz said to his boss, who settled behind his desk. "And then even in the office there's quite a bit of disagreement about whether reckless manslaughter was the appropriate charge."

Karp studied the young man for a moment, seeing himself as he'd once looked when he sat in that chair, in front of that desk, confessing his own doubts to the legendary DA Francis Garrahy. It reminded him that one of the most important aspects of his job was training the next generation.

"Look, Kenny, first of all let's deal with the First Amendment bullshit," Karp said at last. "Nowhere in the Constitution, including the Bill of Rights, does anyone get immunized against committing murder or child abuse. As Justice Robert Jackson said, the Constitution is not a suicide pact, and it is certainly not a 'get out of jail free' card. And as far as our case is concerned, no one is infringing on the defendants' rights to practice their religion when it comes to their personal decisions. As adults, if they want to put their trust in prayer and eschew modern medicine, even at the risk of their own lives, that is their right. However, there is nothing in law that says that one person's individual constitutional protection is absolute or trumps the rights of someone else. Or, for that matter, protects someone who commits a crime. For instance, how about the recent example of the leader of that polygamist sect in Arizona? He was charged with sexually assaulting underage girls who he claimed were his wives and said that such a practice fell under religious protections in the Constitution. Do laws against sexual assault, particularly against minors, not apply because someone claims that it's part of his religion?"

"No, of course not," Katz said.

"Good, then let's move on and look at the facts of this case and whether it was charged appropriately," Karp said. "The way I see it, this is a case of child abuse, plain and simple. And what's more, such a severe case of child abuse that a ten-year-old boy died as a result. Regardless of the parents' religious or philosophical beliefs, when they take on the responsibility of bringing a child into this world, they have a duty to provide for that child, including seeking commonly accepted medical help when that child is sick. Talk about rights; that child had the right to count on his parents to protect him and keep him safe, as well as make decisions on his behalf that he was too young to make for himself."

Karp stood up and looked out the window at the view of the park in Chinatown. "I know you're well versed in all of this, but I think it helps sometimes to review it, get it clear in your head. I know it does for me. So let's go over the categories of murder we have in New York."

He turned back to Katz and held up a finger. "Beginning at the top, there's 'intentional murder' — that is to say that the defendant intended to cause the death of the deceased and then in fact caused the death of the deceased. I think we can all agree that the defendants in this case did not intend to cause the death of their son. They knew their son was very sick, but we'll assume that they truly believed that prayer would cure him."

"But then doesn't that get us back to the question of constitutional protections to practice their religion as they saw fit?" Katz asked, warming up to the discussion.

"If that's the case, then what about Islamic extremists who claim that their actions are sanctioned by God and, in fact, that jihad is their religious duty? Did that give them the constitutional right to murder more than three thousand innocent people on September 11, 2001?"

When Katz didn't answer, Karp moved on. "The second theory, if you will, of murder in New York is what we call felony murder — a death that occurs during the course of and in furtherance of committing or attempting to commit an underlying felony, such as robbery, rape, or kidnapping. For instance, the wheelman in a robbery; he doesn't intend for anyone to get killed when he pulls up in front of a liquor store so that his armed accomplice can rob the store. But inside the store, the gun goes off, the store owner drops dead — the wheelman is just as guilty of felony murder as the gunman. In this case, however, there's no evidence that the Ellises were committing some other felony and in the course of committing that felony, or to cover it up, their son died. So felony murder isn't appropriate either."

Karp sat on the edge of his desk. "So that brings us to the theories of 'reckless' and 'negligent' homicide, and even here you have to add the concept of 'depraved indifference' murder. A simple explanation of reckless homicide is that the defendant was aware of the risk that grave physical injury or death might occur due to his actions, but he consciously disregarded the danger and someone died as a result. Depraved indifference has to do with the defendant's state of mind. For instance, throwing a gasoline bomb into an apartment building at night knowing people are asleep inside is not merely disregarding the danger; it is viciously, wickedly indifferent to the likelihood that your actions will harm or kill other people — depraved. You may not have intended to kill any particular person, or even cared if someone died, so it is not intentional murder, but it is certainly reckless to the degree of depraved indifference."

"Then didn't the Ellises show depraved indifference to their son's suffering and potential for death?" Katz asked.

Karp shook his head. "They did not purposely do something to place their son in danger, not caring if he lived or died. In fact, I think there is ample evidence, which the defense is sure to introduce at trial, that they were shocked and devastated by his death. So we come at last to whether to charge them with negligent homicide or the more severe reckless manslaughter; for that I'll use an analogy I've used many times when explaining the difference for grand juries."

A man who thought best on his feet, Karp rose again and began to pace. "In this scenario, a man takes a child to the rooftop of a New York high-rise to check on his homing pigeons. When they get there, the man notices a gun lying on the ground. He doesn't bother to see if it's loaded, nor does he put it in a safe place, but just goes on about his business. But the child goes over, picks up the gun, it discharges, and the child is killed. That's negligent homicide. The man failed to exercise reasonable judgment to protect the child. He violated the reasonable man's standard of care."

Katz nodded and took over the anecdote. "In the second scenario, the man sees the gun, picks it up and discovers it is loaded, but places it back down where he found it. The child picks up the gun and is killed — that's reckless manslaughter. He was aware of the risk but consciously disregarded it."

"Right," Karp agreed. "So were the Ellises aware of the risk that their child would die?"

"Well, they certainly knew that he was very sick and in a lot of pain," Katz said. "He'd suffered seizures and was probably blind before he went into a coma."

"I think you just answered the question," Karp said. "They were aware of the risk that their son was so sick that without medical attention he would die, but they consciously disregarded that fact to stick with their religious belief system, which, again, does not protect them from the criminal act of recklessly disregarding their son's worsening medical condition."

Karp looked at Katz and smiled. "So we cool?"

"Yeah, we're cool," Katz said.

Suddenly there was a knock on the door; Fulton entered and without speaking turned on a television mounted in the bookcase. The screen was immediately filled with an image, obviously taken from the air, of a ferry sitting still in the waters off Liberty Island. A bold headline across the bottom of the screen announced, "Breaking News: Terrorists Attack Liberty Island Ferry."

As the videographer went to a wide shot, Karp could see that about one hundred yards from the ferry what appeared to be a cabin cruiser also sat still in the waters. Between the two were a number of smaller boats, several of them with the word "police" clearly visible on them.

"We're taking you now to the Nine News Sky Copter and reporter Tessa Laine for the latest on this breaking event," the news anchor said. "What can you tell us, Tessa?"

"Well, so far only that police have apparently intercepted an attempted terrorist attack on a Liberty Island ferry," Laine reported. "It appears that the police are attempting to negotiate with the terrorists, who are in that boat you see surrounded by police boats."

"Can you see what is happening on board the ferry?" the anchor asked.

On cue, the cameraman zoomed in on the ferry. "Only that there appear to be armed men on the ferry," Laine answered, "but as the police seem to be concentrating on the other boat, perhaps the armed men on the ferry are on our side. We're going to try to get a better picture of the people on the deck of the ferry."

"Jesus, is that who I think it is?" Fulton asked.

Although the images were small and jumped around quite a bit from the movement of the news helicopter, the screen suddenly showed Karp's daughter, Lucy; her fiancé, Ned, who was peering at the terrorist boat through the scope of a rifle; Espey Jaxon; and U.S. Marshal Jen Capers. However, Karp knew that his friend's exclamation wasn't because he'd seen them. It was because of the blond woman who was standing with them, looking at the news helicopter.

"It is," Karp growled. "It's Nadya Malovo. She's back in town."

7

Jaxon rushed to the railing next to where Blanchett lay looking through the scope of his rifle. "What have you got?" he asked, lifting the binoculars he had hanging around his neck.

"Not sure but there's a lot of movement and they appear to be arguing, or at least making a lot of aggressive-looking hand gestures," Blanchett replied.

"They're fighting," Lucy confirmed. "One of them just called and said they wanted to give up, but then the phone went dead —"

At that moment, a shot rang out across the water. "That wasn't at any of us," Blanchett said. "I think there's a mutiny —"

Suddenly, a man jumped from near the terrorist boat's cabin onto the bow carrying a long tubular device.

"Rocket grenade!" Blanchett yelled.

"Take him out, Ned!" Jaxon shouted back. The words were hardly out of his mouth before Blanchett's M40A3 sniper rifle boomed. The man on the bow of the cabin cruiser reacted as though attached to an invisible wire that jerked him backward and off the boat.

The 7.62-millimeter bullet reached him not a moment too soon as while falling, he pulled the trigger on his weapon, launching a rocket-propelled grenade. However, having a hole blown in his chest destroyed his aim and the grenade soared almost straight up before plummeting down harmlessly into the water.

Everything was quiet for a moment, and then all hell broke loose. The cabin cruiser's engines roared to life and the boat surged forward toward the ferry. Those on board began firing at all the police vessels, the gunboat, the police helicopter, and the ferry.

A burst of automatic fire stitched its way across the water and up the side of the ferry, passing only a few feet from where Jaxon stood. At the same time, a rocket was fired from the cruiser, striking one of the police vessels, which erupted in a ball of fire.

The response was furious. The Coast Guard gunboat opened up with its fifty-caliber, tearing chunks out of the cruiser as it roared across the water toward the ferry. The police officers on the smaller boats also joined in the shooting gallery while trying to run interference for the ferry.

Someone aboard the terrorist boat aimed at the news helicopter and opened fire. Struck, the helicopter began to bellow thick dark smoke and spun out of control into the water.

On board the ferry, the NIDSA agents fired away with their handguns while Blanchett's big gun boomed again and again.

Jaxon glanced over at where Lucy had been standing when the shooting started and was horrified to see her lying on the deck, bleeding from an apparent shoulder wound. She was trying to help a NIDSA agent who lay motionless on the ground next to her, a pool of blood growing beneath him. Blanchett looked over at the same time and stopped shooting.

"I've got her, Ned," Jaxon yelled, and ran to Lucy even as more automatic rifle fire raked the ferry, clanging off steel and whistling overhead.

"I'm okay," Lucy yelled. "Just nicked." She looked back at the agent she'd been trying to help. "But I think he's gone."

Blanchett's expression turned from concern to anger as he nodded and began to shoot again, the big gun's bullets punching hole after hole into the cruiser's cabin and taking out gunmen whenever they appeared.

The battle ended as quickly as it began. Thousands of rounds had been exchanged, and the cabin cruiser was again dead in the water, only now there was black smoke pouring from it and a small fire was visible in the rear. The men on board had stopped shooting, though none could be seen.

Ascertaining that Lucy was not in any immediate danger from her wound, Jaxon moved to the railing and studied the terrorist vessel through his binoculars. He was still watching when a man on the cruiser dove into the water and another man ran to the rail and shot the diver. Blanchett immediately dispatched the shooter.

The Coast Guard vessel swept in closer. "Throw down your weapons and raise your hands," a voice demanded over the gunboat's loudspeakers.

Jaxon saw several men start to comply. He and everyone else around him began to relax as the police vessels cautiously moved toward the terrorists. Resistance appeared to be over.

Lucy, who'd picked herself up and was listening in again, yelled, "They want to surrender! I think —"

Suddenly, the terrorist boat erupted in a

massive fireball that also consumed the police vessel closest to it. The heat and concussion could be felt on the ferry, still fifty yards away. Then all that remained was debris, some of which was still falling out of the sky, and small oil fires on the surface of the water. There were no signs of any survivors.

Jaxon heard the ferry door behind him open and turned to see Capers leading Malovo out, joined by Rolles and her partner, Masterson. "They do that or us?" Capers asked.

"Them," Jaxon replied. "We weren't shooting when it happened." He slapped his hand on the railing. "Damn it, I would have liked to take those guys in and see if we could get them to talk. This was pretty sophisticated, media-savvy planning, and I'd like to know who was behind it."

Malovo, who'd been looking with satisfaction at the debris on the water, shrugged. "Good riddance, no?" she said. "Besides, maybe the other two will be able to tell you something." Capers turned to Malovo, who was looking at the fires burning on the water with a satisfied grin. The assassin laughed. "There's just something about death that turns me on," she purred. "Is it the same for you?" she asked, turning to meet Capers's gaze.

Eyes blazing, Capers swung Malovo around and cuffed her wrists behind her. "Yeah, well, you're going to have to take care of that all by yourself in a cell tonight."

Malovo laughed again. "It would not be the first time, my beautiful friend, but perhaps someday we can let the men yell while we help each other with such things?"

"Not on your life," Capers shot back. "There wouldn't be enough hot water in the world to get the stench off."

The smile disappeared from Malovo's face for a moment, but then her eyes glittered and she grinned. "Perhaps someday we will take a shower together and find out, no?"

As they disappeared into the interior of the ferry, Jaxon looked over at Lucy, who was frowning and looking at the water where the terrorist boat had been. "What is it, Lucy?" he asked as he walked over.

"I'm not sure," she replied. "I'll talk to you about it later."

Late that afternoon, Jaxon arrived in a dark sedan at a private entrance on the Hogan Place side of the Criminal Courts Building in downtown Manhattan. Clay Fulton was waiting for him there and escorted him to the elevator. They took it to the eighth floor and the anteroom that led directly into the inner office of the New York district attorney.

"I take it you've seen the news," Jaxon said when he opened the door and saw Karp waiting for him.

"Yeah, caught it this morning and a few dozen replays since," Karp replied. "Just got back from Beth Israel Hospital. Lucy's lucky the bullet didn't hit any organs or major blood vessels." He paused for a few moments. "So everything went down like you told me it was going to."

"Yeah, pretty much," Jaxon responded. "I was hoping we could take more prisoners."

"What's the body count?" Karp asked.

"Not sure on their side, maybe a dozen," Jaxon responded. "We lost five police officers, two more badly burned, and one federal agent — the guy who'd been next to Lucy. Also, the pilot of the news helicopter is in serious condition, though the reporter seems to have gotten away with nothing worse than a dunking."

"Could have been worse," Karp noted.

"Much worse," Jaxon agreed. "If we weren't able to intercept these guys, it would have been a catastrophe. Hundreds dead. A big public-relations coup for al-Qaeda."

"So we owe Malovo our thanks?" Karp asked, shaking his head.

"I wouldn't go that far," Jaxon replied. "She's looking out for number one, herself."

"I'd rather be prosecuting her for murder and putting her on death row," Karp said.

"I won't argue with you there."

"You know she can't be trusted."

Jaxon sighed and nodded. "Funny, but you're not the first one to say that to me today."

8

"Honey?" David Ellis called out as he entered the tiny apartment on West 88th Street. There was no answer, nor sound of any kind aside from street noise outside. The shades in the living room were drawn, the windows closed, adding to the gloom and stillness.

She's probably napping, he thought as he stood for a moment in the entranceway before closing the door behind him. Nonie, his wife, napped a lot and had ever since Micah died. And when she wasn't asleep, she walked around as if in a daze and spoke in a monotone devoid of any emotion. The only time her voice was animated at all was when she talked about the Reverend C. G. Westlund, or if David said something that irked her, particularly if it could be construed as critical of the reverend.

In fact, Westlund was the reason David had feigned an illness at his job as a computer programmer so that he could come home and talk to his wife about her obsession with the man and their trial, which would start with jury selection in two days. He would have waited to talk until that evening after work, but when he got home she would usually already be in bed, or would soon rush out of the apartment to attend a church meeting or some other business with Westlund and wouldn't come home until late, after he'd gone to bed. Awake, he'd listen to her slip quietly into the apartment and then would hear the door leading to their son's old room, where she slept, click shut.

It had been a long time since they'd slept in the same bed, a fact he'd even once brought up with Westlund after Micah's death, when he still thought of the reverend as a friend and spiritual guide. When he complained that his wife refused to have sex with him, Westlund had counseled him to be patient. Women whose children "are taken into the arms of God" often lose their sex drive as they grieve, the reverend advised. "Give her time," he said.

However, time had only seen his marriage go from bad to worse, and he now considered the reverend a big part of the problem. When he complained to Nonie that she should be turning to him, her husband, when she needed consoling, she bitterly retorted, "The reverend is the only person who understands me." She wouldn't come right out and say it, but she implied that Micah would not have died if David's faith had been stronger. And he knew where that was coming from.

More and more frequently she referred to Westlund by his first name, Charles, and his effect on her mood was increasingly evident. Alone in their marriage bed at night, David sometimes wondered if there was something more going on between his wife and Westlund than spiritual guidance. But his mind recoiled at the thought of such a betrayal.

He'd met Nonie at Tennessee Christian College when he was a senior computer science major and she was a junior studying early childhood development. She'd been the prettiest girl he'd ever met, with a nice smile and a laugh he could hear in his mind even when she was gone. He'd fallen in love, and to his surprise and delight, when he finally worked up the nerve to tell her after they'd been dating for four months, she confessed that she loved him, too.

They'd been married shortly after that and though they'd both been virgins, he believed that they enjoyed their sex life. *But not anymore,* voices whispered to him from the dark corners of the master bedroom on sleepless nights. *Perhaps she is enjoying it with someone else.* He tried to shut the voices off, but they only grew louder each time she spoke Westlund's name with the tenderness she'd once used when saying his.

They'd met the Reverend C. G. Westlund shortly after Micah's first series of treatments for brain tumors had ended at the Elvis Presley Memorial Children's Hospital in their hometown of Memphis. The holy man's timing could not have been better.

Several months earlier, the Ellises' beautiful blond-haired, green-eyed, then-eight-year-old son had started complaining about headaches that as time passed were often accompanied by nausea and vomiting. They'd taken him to a pediatrician, who diagnosed migraines and suggested bed rest "in a quiet dark room" whenever he felt a headache coming on. The diagnosis changed when Micah began to say that sometimes when his head hurt, he had a difficult time seeing.

They began to doubt the doctor when their formerly athletic little boy seemed to lose coordination in his muscles, stumbling for no apparent reason and regressing in some of his fine motor skills, such as writing. Then one night, standing with his parents in the kitchen of their small home in East Memphis, Micah grabbed his head as he cried out and then collapsed to the floor. His body went rigid, arching and racked by muscle spasms as though he was being electrocuted; his eyes bugged out from his head and froth appeared around his mouth as he made strange guttural sounds.

After an evening in the ER of Memphis General Hospital, Micah had been transferred to the state-of-the-art Elvis Presley Memorial Children's Hospital, where an MRI of his brain revealed a type of brain tumor the pediatric oncologist who spoke to them afterward called an astrocytoma. The doctor had gently explained that there were two types of astrocytomas: nonmalignant, noncancerous tumors, and malignant tumors, which were cancerous. Although both types could affect the brain's functions, such as coordination, the cancerous tumors would spread and eventually result in death. And Micah's were cancerous.

The doctor had explained the possible treatment options. The preferred method was to remove the tumors surgically, he

101

said. However, due to the location of Micah's tumors, deep inside the cerebellum, and the way they had integrated with normal brain cells, he felt the surgery was too risky "except as a last resort." He believed that the best course of action was chemotherapy, in which Micah would be given drugs that specifically targeted fast-growing cells, such as cancer cells, and destroyed them. The drawback was that they could expect "significant" side effects because the drugs also attacked fast-growing "normal" cells such as hair, stomach, intestine, and blood cells. The results could include nausea, vomiting, hair loss, fatigue, anemia, and muscle/nerve pain, about which the doctor told them, "You as an adult would probably describe it as the absolute worst flu ever, so bad you might wish you were dead. And of course, it can be even worse for a frightened child."

And that wasn't all the bad news. The chemotherapy would be followed up with radiation treatment, "probably once a day, five days a week, for as long as seven weeks." Again, there were side effects, many of them the same as for the chemotherapy, as well as a potential for what the doctor euphemistically called an "intellectual decrease" and damage to Micah's pituitary gland, "which could affect his growth."

Worse, the doctor couldn't guarantee that one chemotherapy/radiation treatment would be enough. "Sometimes the first treatment doesn't quite get it done, or even the second. We have to go after this thing until it is completely gone, or it will just come back."

It all sounded so frightening, the proverbial "cure is worse than the disease" scenario. However, the doctor had cautioned them that without treatment, Micah would die . . . and soon. "With treatment, we have an eighty percent survival rate of at least five years," the doctor noted, which didn't sound great, but it was better than death.

So they'd signed the consent forms to have Micah treated. As predicted, the chemotherapy drugs and first round of radiation made Micah's life, and theirs, a living hell.

As they'd watched their boy suffer, the Ellises prayed, begging for mercy and compassion. Although their attendance at church had fallen off considerably since their college days at a Christian school, they were both people of faith. He'd been raised a Southern Baptist, and Nonie had been brought up in the Pentecostal church, which included faith healing — healing by prayer and "laying on of the hands" — among its main tenets. So when the tall, handsome preacher — back then he'd been called John LaFontaine — with the striking blue eyes; deep, smooth voice; and long brown hair showed up on their doorstep after a particularly rough day for Micah, she was already ready to believe.

"Good afternoon and God bless you, ma'am, sir," Westlund had said, smiling as he peered into their home through the screen door. "I am Doctor of Divinity John LaFontaine of the Holy Covenant Church of Jesus Christ Reformed and I am in your neighborhood today to bring you the Word of the Lord and healing for body, mind, and soul. How are you today, brother and sister?"

"Uh, fine, but we're not interested . . . ," David said, but before he could ask the man to leave, the preacher stepped up to the screen and sniffed. He made a face and stepped back as if he'd smelled something foul. "I am sorry to disturb you," he said, shaking his head sadly and looking at them with such empathy even David felt drawn to the man. "There is a terrible sickness in this house, and I am intruding." He paused and bowed his head, then spoke without looking up as he held out his hand toward the door. "A child is suffering . . . an injury to his head . . . no . . . a disease . . . a disease of Satan's design."

Suddenly he looked up, first at Nonie and then at David. "There may still be time," he said. "May I see the boy?"

Wondering how the man was so certain about his diagnosis and that their child was a boy, David hesitated. After a pause, he was about to ask him to leave when Nonie touched his arm. "Please, David, let him see Micah," she said. "What can it hurt?"

So in spite of his misgivings, David unlatched the screen door and invited the man into their home. Without another word, Westlund marched back to Micah's room, where their son lay on his bed, pale, thin, and exhausted. With his bald head and dark circles beneath his pain-filled eyes, he looked like a child on the verge of death. Clutching the bowl he used when nauseous, Micah stared up at the stranger with fear.

Nonie started to reassure her son. "It's okay, Micah, Mr. —"

"Doctor," the man said quickly, correcting her, which made Micah cry out unexpectedly.

"His recent experiences with doctors have not been good ones," David explained.

Westlund nodded and then turned to the

boy with a smile. "It's okay, Micah, I don't think much of those doctors either. I am not here to hurt you. I am a doctor of the soul and my cures are painless. I bring you tidings of God's mercy and compassion."

Micah smiled slightly at the man's words and the sound of his voice. He visibly relaxed.

"Would you mind if I placed my hand on your head, son?" the preacher asked.

Micah nodded. "That would be okay."

Westlund leaned over and put one of his large hands on the top of their son's head and closed his eyes. Although they could not make out the words he began mumbling, he appeared to be praying. Then he shuddered and looked up at the Ellises' worried faces.

"Satan's cancer has taken root inside his head," he said.

"Yes, that's right," Nonie replied as if the preacher was viewing some sort of supernatural MRI to confirm the doctors' diagnosis.

Westlund nodded and closed his eyes again. Then he frowned. "You've been trying to heal the boy with poisons," he said in a slightly accusatory tone. He straightened up and removed his hand from Micah's head. "I'm sorry, but I can't help."

"Why? What's wrong?" they asked in unison.

Westlund started to speak but then bit his lip as he looked from Nonie to David to Nonie again. "I'm sorry, but you've placed your faith in the false miracles promised by purveyors of Western medicine," he said as though it pained him to have to say it. "Only God chooses who lives and who dies; these attempts to thwart His will are a direct affront to Him."

"But we believe in God," Nonie said. "We pray every day and every night for Him to help Micah."

Westlund looked down at Micah and shook his head. "The boy's spirit is strong but the faith in this house is weak. You cannot ask God to heal and then hedge your bets with medicines that are brewed through Satan, who ever seeks to place himself on a level with the God who created him and us."

The preacher cocked his head to one side as if there was something he didn't understand about the Ellises. "I take it you do not regularly go to church?"

Nonie bit her lip. "We miss more often than we go," she said, glancing at David. "We've just been so busy with Micah and David's out of work —"

Westlund held up his hand. "I hear your words, but they are just excuses," he said. "You have time for hospitals and doctors, but you do not have a couple of hours to spend with God even once a week." He reached down and touched Micah gently on the head. "My heart breaks for this innocent child, but as I said, there is nothing I can do. You have chosen where to place your faith and now you must abide by that choice. I can only hope that God, in His infinite mercy and compassion, will forgive your transgressions, recognizing that you made them for all the right reasons and have been led astray by the false gods of medicine, and that God will help this innocent child."

"What should we have done then?" David said, suddenly angry that this stranger had entered his house, touched his son with the promise of healing, and then decided he couldn't help because their faith wasn't strong enough.

Westlund ignored the anger. "Prayed," he said. "Placed all of your faith in Almighty God, and prayed for the healing that can only come through the sacrifice of His son, Jesus Christ, who healed the sick and brought Lazarus back to life."

"Please, please help us," Nonie suddenly

pleaded, grabbing the preacher's hand.

Westlund withdrew his hand from her grip. "There's nothing —" he said as he began to turn toward the door. Then he stopped and looked at David. "You're struggling with finances, brother," he said. "You say you've recently lost your job?"

It was true. "What about it?" David replied sullenly.

"There's no shame in being hit hard by a capricious world," Westlund said. He looked from the parents to their son and back to the parents. "Forgive me if I came off as criticizing you regarding your son. It's hard to have faith when it appears that the world, and God, has turned against you."

Westlund reached into his shirt pocket and pulled out a business card. "Give my assistant, Brother Frank Bernsen, a call," he said. "We are a small ministry, and not a wealthy one, but we do have an emergency fund to help good people such as yourselves."

"We'll be all right, but thank you," David replied, somewhat sheepishly after his angry reaction.

Westlund nodded. "I understand. You're a proud man and not one to take handouts. That's why this would be a loan, not a gift, though in accordance with the Bible's prohibition of usury, we can't accept interest. Take only what you need, and pay it back."

The preacher studied their faces and then smiled benevolently. "Look, we've just met, and in less than happy circumstances, so if it's too soon to extend the hand of friendship in Jesus' name, I understand. But do call if we can help."

David accepted the business card and held out his hand, which Westlund shook. "Thanks again," he said. "That is kind of you to offer and to have stopped by."

"Would you say a prayer tonight for Micah?" Nonie asked.

Westlund turned to David's wife and placed both of his hands on her shoulders. "I'll do better than that," he said. "I'll get down on my knees with you right here and now. It is never too late to place your faith in God as the true healer."

And so the Ellises found themselves kneeling next to their son's bed as Westlund placed a hand on Micah's head and gripped Nonie's with his other. "O Lord, our God, we come before Thy face, bowing before Thy majesty in recognition of our unworthiness and giving thanks for all Thy good gifts, which Thou dost again and again give us for body and soul . . ."

"Nonie?" David called out again as he walked back to their son's former bedroom and opened the door. The room was dark but he could make out the familiar silhouettes of teddy bears and toy airplanes. But his wife wasn't in the bed. He wondered where she could be, if for no other reason than they needed to prepare themselves for the start of the trial.

The shock of Micah's death had been compounded a few weeks later when police detectives arrived at the apartment, informing them that they'd been indicted on the charge of reckless manslaughter and were under arrest. At the time, he'd been outraged. Wasn't it enough that his beloved son had died?

Westlund had, of course, been outspoken in their defense, and he'd soon been joined by an unlikely consortium of supporters, including Ivy academic lawyers who'd offered their services to fight what they said was an unconstitutional attack on their religious beliefs. Indeed, they'd received letters of support, even money, from people all over the country, ranging from antigovernment types to religious zealots.

However, as time passed, David had started to wonder if the charge against him and his wife was perhaps legitimate. He'd never thought of himself as a bad father. He loved Micah with every ounce of his being. But the more he listened to Westlund and the others turn the case into a theoretical discussion, the more he began to question if he and Nonie were indeed guilty. But Nonie would hear none of it. She believed every word out of Westlund's mouth and bitterly denounced the New York District Attorney's Office as "a den of Satan worshippers."

Already suspecting that she held him in part responsible for their son's death due to his lack of faith, he'd never told her that he was the one who called 911 when Micah lay dying. He'd gone out for a walk and found himself in a grocery store, where he purchased one of those cheap prepaid cell phones and called. But it had been too late.

He left the room and made his way back down the hallway to the kitchen, where he noticed a pile of open mail on the table. Or rather he noticed a single envelope that was separate from the others. It was from an insurance company and addressed to David and Nonie Ellis. "Important document enclosed" was stamped on the outside.

David frowned. He didn't remember doing any business with that particular insurance company. Probably an advertisement, he thought, but he still opened the envelope and pulled out the letter inside.

It was, after all, an important document. It explained that "pending the outcome of the legal actions" the Ellises were facing, the company was withholding the death benefits for Micah as a rider on a life insurance policy taken out in the name of his parents, David and Nonie Ellis, and assigned to the Reverend C. G. Westlund.

A sob escaped David's mouth as he crumpled the letter in his hand and stormed out of the apartment.

9

Bruce Knight sat in his one-man law office staring at the telephone, willing it to ring. The silence remained unbroken except for the creaking and knocking of the ancient radiator that had kicked on as evening fell on the city. *Thank God it's March,* he thought. *At least the heating bill will be going down.*

There weren't any sounds from the minuscule reception area outside of his office, either, not even a secretary typing at a keyboard or talking to friends about her boring job. He'd had to let his assistant go a month before due to the reason behind the silence — a dearth of paying clients. A young woman with short black hair, tattoos, and a nose ring, she still came in on Fridays to help him out with filing, declining his efforts to pay her, even with post-dated checks.

"You're a good man, Bruce Knight," she'd

said the previous week when she left. "One of these days, you'll be back on your feet and can make it all up to me."

It's only Monday afternoon; things will pick up, he told himself for the hundredth time that month as he glanced over at the stack of envelopes perched precariously on the edge of his desk. Most of them remained unopened; he knew what they would be — demands for payments from collection agencies, threatening notes from his landlord regarding missing rent checks, utility bills several months in arrears. He just didn't need the aggravation, and it wasn't like he could do anything about it. So they sat unread and unanswered.

Knight combed his fingers through his prematurely thinning hair and thought ruefully back to the days when he'd been a young Turk fresh out of law school and already climbing his way up the ladder of one of New York's best boutique law firms. As with his current practice, he'd specialized in criminal law and fit right in with the firm's take-no-prisoners reputation. But unlike his current practice, his clients then had been wealthy men and women, mostly accused of white-collar crimes or those crimes of passion the rich sometimes indulged in — sexually assaulting domestic servants, or shooting one's spouse and his mistress as they romped about on the Mulberry silk sheets.

By New York standards, the firm had been small, only seventy-five attorneys as opposed to a Wall Street–Madison Avenue white-shoe firm — which would have hundreds, along with satellite locations in Chicago, Los Angeles, London, and Paris — but charged gold-shoe prices. They often took clients referred by the white-shoe firms that either weren't as capable at fighting it out in the trenches with the New York District Attorney's Office or didn't want to scuff the polish on those shoes by getting involved in ugly cases.

With the aid of his clients' deep pockets for hiring "expert witnesses" who would say anything for a price, Knight's success rate had outshone that of even some of the firm's more experienced attorneys, earning him the notice of the partners. The more acquittals he won, or cases he got dropped, or cases he pled down to a slap on the wrist, the more important cases he was assigned to and the higher his salary and bonuses climbed. With the sort of praise he was earning in firm meetings, he even dreamed of becoming the youngest partner in the firm's ninety-year history.

Unfortunately, he did not handle success well. He discovered a penchant for beautiful women, expensive cars, and forty-year-old Glenfiddich single-malt Scotch whiskey, which at $2,500 a bottle was one of the world's best and priciest. But even a great single-malt sometimes needed, at least in his mind, a snort or two (or three) of cocaine to balance the high.

He didn't worry about where all that might be leading; he was young and had the world by the balls. However, those late nights, beautiful women, drugs, and Scotch started taking a toll. He found that it was getting increasingly tough to get up in the morning and into work without a couple more lines of coke to go with a pot of coffee. Before long, he was sneaking snorts at his desk and even in the men's stalls of courthouse restrooms during breaks.

When he was almost caught snorting a line off his office desk by one of the partners, he started to worry a little. But he reasoned that he was under a lot of stress and *needed* cocaine to handle it for the time being; he'd tone it all down after he made partner. At least that's what he told himself on mornings when no amount of eyedrops got the red out and blood appeared on the tissue when he blew his nose.

The pressure to perform just kept getting more intense, which meant more cocaine and more booze. Then he started making mistakes: arriving late for court and angering the judges; forgetting to file paperwork on time; rushing in late to meetings — once missing a meeting entirely as he slept one of his binges off. He called in and said he had the flu, but it had not saved him from being told to report to the office of one of the senior partners when he arrived at work late, the next morning.

"What's going on with you?" the partner, a middle-aged Harvard grad with movie-star looks, asked bluntly after Knight sat down in the chair in front of the man's massive desk.

"What do you mean?" he replied, feeling a wave of nausea rise in his throat that was partly from fear and partly from the excesses of the previous night.

"I think you know what I mean," the partner said sternly. "Bruce, when you started here, we all were impressed with your work as an attorney and with you as a person. You had a great chance of making partner at an early age —"

Knight did not like how the man was speaking in the past tense about his dream. *Had a great chance.*

"— but the quality of your work has fallen off considerably," the partner continued, "and to be honest, your reliability is in question, too. We take this very seriously; this firm has a ninety-year reputation for excellence. We are nothing without our clients, and if we fail them, they'll go elsewhere."

The partner leaned across the desk and locked eyes with Knight. "Do you have a drinking problem? Because if you do, we'll get you help."

Knight shook his head. "No . . . some social drinking after work, but nothing outrageous," he said, having never wanted a drink more in his life than at that moment.

"What about drugs?"

"Drugs?"

"Yes, illicit drugs . . . speed, pot, coke, heroin. Are you doing drugs?"

Again Knight denied the accusation. "No . . . not since a little experimentation in college," he replied, hoping that the man didn't notice the sweat he could feel popping out on his forehead.

The partner remained quiet for a moment and then nodded. "Okay, I hope not. But whatever it is that has been affecting you and your work, it needs to stop now. I'm letting you know that you are officially on probation. We'll be watching to see how you respond to this little chat."

Knight left the office and almost collapsed in the hallway with fear. He vowed to quit the boozing. *And no more coke.* And he meant it. He wasn't a bad guy; he called his parents back home in Columbus, Ohio, every week, gave to charities and even the occasional bum on the street. He'd just been enjoying life a little too much, and he could adjust . . . *tone it down.*

When he got back to his office that day, he reached into his desk drawer and withdrew the small bindle of coke. He got up and went to the bathroom, intending to flush the drug down the toilet. But as he stood there looking at the snowy white powder, he decided that it would be a waste of money. He'd have one last blowout that weekend and be done with it. To celebrate his upcoming sobriety, he dipped a fingernail in the powder, brought it to his nose, and sniffed.

The only problem was that once it was gone that weekend, he wanted more. At first he resisted the drug's call. He even started working out at the firm's gym, ate healthy, and went to bed early — without the beautiful women. But then there was that night he went out with an old law school buddy and twin brunettes, each wearing the same

120

low-cut dress. "His" twin kept telling him how turned on she got after snorting cocaine and, well . . . the rest was history.

Knight tried to hide that "toning it down" wasn't working by spending a lot of time at the courthouse and the firm's law library. But he was sinking and he knew it. He considered going to the partners and accepting their offer of "help" with his addictions, but he also knew that would be the kiss of death for his dream of becoming a partner. They might pat him on the back and pay for rehab, even keep him on as one of the firm's low-level attorneys, but they would never trust an addict — even a recovering addict — with important cases or the firm's reputation again. So he just tried his best to hide his problem, knowing that sooner or later it would have to end.

It came sooner. After one particularly wild night, he slept through his alarm clock on the morning of an important pretrial hearing. There wasn't time to shower or shave, and he put on the first suit he found lying on the floor, albeit a Brooks Brothers. He arrived in the courtroom ten minutes late to find an irate judge and a panicked, angry client.

It was then that it struck him that his lifestyle wasn't just affecting him; it was playing Russian roulette with the lives of his clients. He'd sworn an oath to zealously protect the rights and freedom of the people who trusted him, and he was failing miserably.

There was still enough left of the boy from the Midwest who'd been raised to believe in old-fashioned values like honesty, integrity, and earning his paycheck. He got through the hearing, but when he returned to the office, he walked into the senior partner's office and resigned.

After that there was only one thing left to do; he spent what little savings he had on a hedonistic cocaine-fueled month-long binge that he half hoped would kill him. It didn't. Then when the expensive cars and furniture were sold and the money was gone, he was evicted from his apartment and found himself living on the streets. He was too ashamed to go home to his parents or beg friends — most of whom no longer wanted to know him anyway — for a place to stay or a hand back up out of the gutter.

Instead, he learned where the homeless shelters were located, and when they were full, the heating grates and nooks and crannies of buildings where he could shiver the night away. He did odd jobs when he could, raided Dumpsters for food and things to sell or trade, and sold his blood. He couldn't afford cocaine or Glenfiddich anymore, but by panhandling he could usually afford a bottle of the cheapest whiskey or rotgut wine and tried to drink himself to death.

A year later, he looked fifty-five, not thirty-five; his nose was perpetually red and his blue eyes had the haze of the perpetually drunk. He'd sunk about as low as he could get one night four years earlier when he climbed down from a subway platform, planning to end it all. . . .

Knight's recollection of the dismal past was broken by the sound of someone entering the reception area. He jumped up from his desk to see who it was, worried that it might be a bill collector. Since he couldn't risk losing a client, he opened the door of his office and stopped. His jaw dropped; he could not quite believe what he was seeing.

Standing in the doorway to the hall was the partner from his former firm. The look on the man's face was one of scorn, but he brightened when he saw Knight. "Good afternoon, Bruce," he said pleasantly.

"Uh, h-hello," Knight stammered, and then just stood, mouth agape, wondering if he was dreaming.

The man tilted his head to the side and smiled. He pointed to the office behind his former employee. "Mind if we sit down and have a little talk? I may have some work for you . . . and if you don't mind my saying so, it looks like you could use it."

Knight finally shut his mouth and nodded. He couldn't believe it. Work? From his old firm? "By all means," he said, stepping aside to indicate that the man should enter. "I apologize, my receptionist needed to leave work early today so I am manning the fort by myself."

"Of course, I understand," the man replied as they entered the office.

"Would you care for a cup of coffee?" Knight asked, wondering if he had any coffee to make.

"No, thank you. It's too late in the day for me. I'd be up all night."

Knight laughed a bit too long and loud as he sat down at his desk and pointed to the worn chair across from him. "Please, have a seat."

The man looked down at the chair, which had seen better days many years earlier. He declined to sit. "I won't take much of your . . . valuable time," he said, "but I've come to offer you a job for a client that I think you'll find both lucrative and interesting."

Lucrative. Knight's heart skipped a beat

and then started pounding like a drum. "I'm all ears," he said, wondering if the smile on his face looked as desperate as it felt. "May I ask the client's name?"

His former boss smiled back. "Of course. Her name is Nadya Malovo."

10

Westlund groaned impatiently when his cell phone on the nightstand next to the bed started playing an old Rolling Stones song. He usually wouldn't have answered a call in the middle of having sex with a member of his congregation, but "Sympathy for the Devil" was the ringtone for his chief of security, Frank Bernsen, a little inside joke between the two of them. Bernsen knew better than to interrupt his boss when he was "entertaining" unless it was important.

"Pardon me, angel, but the Lord's work calls," he said, sitting up in bed and swinging his long hairy legs over the side. He grabbed the cell phone as he stood and walked toward the bathroom so that his guest wouldn't hear the conversation. "Yes, brother, the Lord's peace upon you," he said loud enough for her to hear before closing the door.

"What's up, bro?" he growled.

"We have a visitor," said Bernsen, who was known as Frankie the Cat in another life, when he and Westlund both rode with a motorcycle gang. "Ellis. He says he wants to see you."

"About what?"

"He won't say, except that it's between you and him. . . . But he's pretty hot."

Westlund frowned. This didn't sound good the day before the Ellis trial. "Did you tell him that I'm . . . uh . . . busy?"

"Yeah, but he says he'll wait in the chapel," Bernsen said. "You want me to toss his ass out on the street?"

Westlund smiled at the thought. "Sounds good, bro," he replied with a chuckle. "But I better hear what the man has to say. It may be nothing, or at least nothing I can't talk him out of; if I still don't like what I hear, we'll figure out what to do about it then. Give me ten minutes and then send him up."

"You don't want me to come with him?"

"Nah, I can kick that punk's ass blindfolded. Just frisk him; I don't want any surprises."

Westlund hung up and thought for a moment before returning to the bedroom. "I apologize, my love, but the blessing of our union will have to wait for a few minutes," he said to the woman curled up on a set of red satin sheets.

"Do you want me to leave?" she said, disappointment verging on despondency welling in her eyes.

"No, not at all, sister," Westlund replied, leaning over to stroke her face with his hand. "In fact, would you do me a favor and stay in here as quiet as Lazarus before the resurrection, and just listen at the door to what is being said?"

"Listen? Why?"

Westlund kissed her gently on the lips. "You'll understand soon enough," he said as he stood. "But I believe that Satan may have entered my visitor's heart with the purpose of posing a threat to my ministry here in this evil city."

The woman's eyes narrowed. "Why would anyone do that?" she demanded. Then tears sprang to her eyes and she buried her face in her hands. "I couldn't stand it if something took you away from me."

Westlund placed a finger on her lips. *This one is always on the verge of a psychotic breakdown.* "Shhhhh," he whispered. "Just listen . . . would you do that for me? Would you do that for this love that God has given us?"

The woman nodded. "Of course," she

128

whispered back. "I love you. God sent you to me in my hour of need . . . I would do anything."

"As I would for you," Westlund replied. "Now I have to get dressed. . . . And, sister, my love . . . bless you, you are an angel."

As Westlund pulled on a track suit, he thought about the day he introduced himself to the Ellises in Memphis, Tennessee, two years earlier, when he was going by the name of John LaFontaine. *Doctor John LaFontaine of the Holy Covenant Church of Jesus Christ Reformed,* he reminded himself with a chuckle.

Westlund was no believer, but he played the part well. That day after he'd knelt with the Ellises at their son's bed to pray — just a simple Pentecostal prayer he'd picked up from the Internet — he patted the boy on the shoulder and stood. "I'll keep you in my prayers tonight, too, son," he said kindly.

The parents had risen with him and stood looking down on their son with hopeful expressions. "How do you feel, Micah?" Nonie Ellis asked.

The boy shrugged but smiled slightly. "A little better I think. Is Jesus going to help me not be sick?"

Westlund seized the moment to grab the

boy's hand. "If you believe, Micah. Jesus provides miracles!"

The preacher could feel the hope, and his opportunity, enter the room like a ray of sunshine through clouds. Even the father, who Westlund could tell was going to be a tougher sell than the mother, smiled and patted the boy's leg. Meanwhile, Nonie shook his hand effusively and asked him if he could stop by again and pray with the family.

Westlund had scrunched up his face and shaken his head, noting that his was a "traveling ministry" and that he had "a lot of ground to cover in this evil city." He then paused to allow the mother's face to register her disappointment, before adding, "But I'll do what I can to find some time."

He'd then waited a few days before showing back up at the Ellis house. Long enough for the woman to start despairing, but not so long that her husband's reticence took over again.

There was another reason for the delay. He'd done his homework and talked to the right people, and he knew that the more time that passed immediately after the brutal chemotherapy treatments stopped, the better the boy would feel as his body healed itself. And, if he timed it right, the child's recovery and general feeling of well-being would coincide nicely with prayer sessions and the laying on of hands.

As for the disease itself, the astrocytoma tumors, his "research" indicated that the chemotherapy would probably cause the tumors to shrink, at least at first, which would — along with the cessation of the treatments — alleviate the symptoms caused by the disease. He was aware that normal protocol would be for Micah to return to the hospital to be tested and, if circumstances warranted, to begin a new series of chemo sessions. So he also had to time his appearance on the worried parents' doorstep, to "spread the Word of God" and pray over their sick child, so that he got to them before they returned to the hospital for the tests and resumption of treatment.

The Ellises weren't the first victims of this particular con, and he'd perfected it along the way. Of course, it didn't always work out. Sometimes he got the door slammed in his face. Or the parents would politely reject his offer to pray over the child. But if he chose his marks right and did his homework, more often than not he would find himself on his knees praying with desperate parents, and from there he was well on his way to worming into their confidence and their lives.

The next step was to convince them that their child could only be saved by renouncing Western medicine and placing "one hundred and ten percent" of their faith in praying for God's mercy and compassion. Part of his "research" was identifying which parents had religious leanings, and then he relied on biblical scriptures related to Jesus' healing the sick by laying his hands on them and invoking the Holy Spirit. There were several Christian denominations that practiced "faith healing," especially Pentecostals, which he'd learned relied on an intermediary, such as a preacher, to serve as the conduit for the Holy Spirit.

When he returned to the little house in East Memphis, he brought with him "Sister Sarah," a sometime girlfriend and shill who helped him with the con. "She knows what you're going through, as well as the temptations and lies those who preach the gospel of Western medicine use to lure you into their web," he told the Ellises. "But, as I'm sure she'll tell you, she turned to faith and her child was saved."

Nonie had immediately asked Sarah to tell her story, but as he instructed her, Sarah insisted that they first pray with Micah.

When the prayer ended, the boy was again queried as to whether he felt better, and looking up at his mother's hopeful face, he said yes.

Westlund then suggested that Sister Sarah share her story over a cup of tea. As though reliving a nightmare, the other woman wept and shuddered as she recounted how her young son, "Kevin," had been diagnosed with a rare form of leukemia. The doctors at the Children's Hospital had warned her that without chemotherapy her son would die, but added that the treatments they felt were necessary were "experimental" and could even kill him outright.

"As you already know, the things they put my poor little boy through were horrible," Sarah whimpered. "My child was being tortured and poisoned, but I thought it was the only way to save him . . . that's what those . . . *doctors* told me." She hung her head and wiped at her cheeks with a tissue handed to her by David Ellis. "But I didn't know what else to do. My husband had left me when Kevin was diagnosed and I had no one to turn to . . ."

Sarah stopped and smiled sweetly at Westlund. "Our great friend, our blessed brother John LaFontaine, spoke at our little church, and with the truth he gets from

God, he turned me away from liars and to Christ. It wasn't easy . . . he had to battle first for my soul so that I could believe enough . . . I had been a terrible sinner —"

"Yes, you were, sister," Westlund said, and chuckled.

"— and my sins were visited upon my innocent child," Sarah said to Westlund, "but you saved me."

Westlund had held up his hand. "Not I, sister, it was your faith in the Lord Jesus Christ, who caused the Holy Spirit He'd once used to heal the sick and raise the dead to move through my hands so that I could cleanse your son of the disease Satan had planted in his blood."

Sarah had reached into her purse and pulled out a photograph of a young boy with blue eyes and blond hair. "This is my son now," she said, "three years after the doctors said he would die. Oh, they claim his recovery is a 'spontaneous remission' without a known cause, but I know who cured him . . . the Lord and this good man here." She'd paused to show the Ellises the photograph.

"He's a beautiful boy," Nonie Ellis said. "Like my Micah, only older . . ." She suddenly burst into tears.

Ready for the moment, Sister Sarah

jumped to her side before even David Ellis could get there to console her. "It's okay, Nonie," the con woman cooed. "Help is here. All you need to do is trust in the Lord . . . and Doctor LaFontaine."

Nonie had been persuaded ever since. But David had been a tougher sell, though he'd gone along with his wife's wishes and, as his son improved, warmed somewhat to Westlund. However, the woman had confided that her husband sometimes argued with her about getting Micah checked at the hospital. So one day when Sarah, who often came on his visits, was occupying Nonie with Micah, Westlund asked David if he could talk to him alone.

"Brother, I know you have reservations about me and my work," he said after they sat down in the living room. "And I wanted to say that I understand your reluctance to embrace what I'm telling you. Not many people know this, but I was a ferocious sinner until one day I met a man of God hitchhiking by the side of the road and I was overcome with the Holy Spirit through what he had to say. It was the Truth, and I knew it when I heard it. And, in that moment, I went from a hell-raising, motorcycle-riding, womanizing spawn of Satan to preaching the Word of God. That roadside preacher

135

told me that I had been given a gift, the gift of healing body and spirit. And, brother, I have tried my best to share that with you and your family."

Not quite sure what to make of the conversation so far, David looked confused but then nodded. "I understand that and I really do appreciate all the time you've spent with us," he said. "And Nonie, well, she thinks the world of you, and I know Micah does, too."

"Thank you, brother. But what about you?"

The question caught the young man off guard. He stammered a bit before answering. "Well, I think you're great as a person and you obviously care about other people. It's just that . . . well, just that I'm not convinced that prayer is the only thing we should be doing for Micah right now. I think that God works in different ways, including medicine."

Westlund held the young man's gaze for a moment, then dropped his head and nodded. "I hear ya, brother, I really do," he said. "And to be quite honest, I was afraid we'd reach this point. You see, for me to heal through the Holy Spirit, it's not enough for the afflicted to believe, or for some of the people who love them to believe, or even for those people to believe but not with every bit of faith they have. I know there are many gray areas in this wicked old world, but I believe that faith is an all-or-nothing proposition. What sense does it make for a man to say, 'I have faith in God to heal my son, but I don't want to take any chances so I will place some of my faith in hospitals and doctors and the poisons they want to pump into my child'?"

Westlund paused and appeared to wipe away tears that had apparently formed in his eyes. "I'm sorry," he said. "I know I get worked up about this, but it's because I truly have come to care about you, Nonie, and Micah . . . he is such a beautiful child."

Suddenly, Westlund stood. "However, I respect your beliefs, and after all, he is your son. Yet I cannot in good conscience continue my work here when I know that your faith is torn between God and man's arrogance. I'll just say good-bye to Micah and Nonie, and then I will leave you to your fate — though I will, of course, continue to pray for all of you."

As expected, David Ellis had looked at him in alarm. "Really, I don't mind your being here," he said. "I believe in God and Jesus. I just think that —"

Westlund held his hand up. "No need to

explain, brother, I understand," he said. "I respect your position, but I'm afraid I need to be going."

At that moment, Sarah entered the room with Nonie, who saw the two men facing each other and asked, "What's wrong?"

Westlund smiled and shrugged. "There is nothing wrong, dear little sister, just a difference of opinion. But it is time for me to leave your family in peace and go where I am of more use."

"What? No!" Nonie cried in alarm, looking from her husband to Westlund and back to David. "What did you say?" she demanded.

Westlund pretended to play the part of the peacemaker. "It's all right. God gives us free will to make decisions and David is exercising his, but it means I must leave."

David began to protest. "But I never said —"

"I explained to your husband," Westlund interrupted, "that for Micah to be saved through the Holy Spirit, those who love him the most must give themselves over entirely to faith in God and no other."

"But I do believe," Nonie cried out, bursting into tears. "And Micah believes. Please don't leave us!" She turned to David, her eyes flashing with desperation and anger as she snarled, "How could you? Haven't you seen what he's done for Micah?"

"Honey, I didn't ask him to go," David pleaded. "I just think that maybe we should follow up with the doctors for Micah . . ."

Nonie glared and her voice hardened. "What? So they can poison our son with the devil's lies again? You want to put him through that torture? Next they'll want to use surgery that they already told us might kill him!"

"I just want what's best for our son and —"

"I don't care!" Nonie shrieked. "I don't care what you want . . . our son is going to die and it's because of you! I hate you!"

David Ellis looked like someone had hit him over the head with a two-by-four. Now tears welled in his eyes until at last he nodded and looked at the ground. "You're right," he said to Westlund. "It's all or nothing. I believe in God or I believe in the doctors." He looked at his wife, who nodded and began to smile. "I'll believe in God with you, Nonie."

As the woman beamed at her husband, Westlund placed his hands on David's shoulders. "Hallelujah, brother!" he exclaimed. "I've been waiting to hear those words for so long. I believe, Sister Sarah, that we have witnessed another miracle in the making of a new warrior for Christ. Let us get down on our knees and thank the Lord!"

"Hallelujah!" Sister Sarah shouted.

Hallelujah indeed, Westlund thought as he waited now for David Ellis to arrive at his apartment door.

11

Waiting in an interview room at the Varick Federal Detention Center Facility in downtown New York City, Nadya Malovo opened the buttons on her jail jumpsuit to reveal a hint of cleavage. One of the jail matrons was sure to make her button it up again later, but for this meeting she hoped to make good use of her physical assets. She glanced over at the one-way mirror, nodding at the man she knew was watching from the other side.

Settling back into her chair, Malovo gave her short blond hair a final shake and smiled slightly, satisfied. Everything was going according to plan. *But these are only the first steps, and there are many more,* she reminded herself.

She knew that even with her meticulous planning, she was walking a razor's edge; all it would take was one slipup and it would all be over. However, it did not trouble her that her plan was a desperate one; it was simply a fact that she used to keep herself focused. She'd been walking an edge since her early twenties, and if anything she needed that adrenaline rush to feel alive.

Nadya Malovo, a.k.a. Ajmaani, had been an orphan scraping for a living on the cold hard streets of Moscow, where her nascent criminality and her unreal physical abilities as a sometime cat burglar got her noticed by the authorities. But instead of prison they sent her to a "special school for girls" to be trained as a spy and assassin.

Roughly twenty-five years later, she now killed without remorse, and while she would do anything to avoid being killed, she didn't fear it. *Fear of death will get you killed.* She could still hear the harsh voice of her old KGB mentor. He'd been a great teacher, though she thought of him without affection. After all, he'd been a merciless overseer of her training who had her brutally raped by some of her male "colleagues" so that no enemy would ever be able to use that degradation to break her down. When it was over, she showered, tended to her wounds, dressed herself, and reported for duty as if nothing had happened.

There was one lesson he'd never been able to get her to accept. *A professional has no*

time or desire for revenge; it is business.
Revenge burned in Malovo like the coals of last night's fire, waiting to be fanned into a sudden flame, and she never passed up the opportunity for it if it fit her plans. Many years later, long after the dissolution of the Soviet Union, when she was working as a freelance assassin and agent provocateur, she found her former mentor in a remote cottage in the Urals, where he'd retired. She castrated him and left him to die slowly in the snow while she sipped a glass of wine and watched from the front porch of his home.

Her current plan was intertwined with the threads of revenge as well. Threads that involved her nemesis, the six-foot-five New York City DA Roger "Butch" Karp and his loathsome family. Just thinking about the man made the coals in her dark soul glow brighter.

The eventual success of her plan depended on her being out of Florence ADX, the maximum-security prison in Colorado, which normally only housed the worst, most violent and dangerous male prisoners but had made a special allowance for Malovo. There was no escaping from "the Alcatraz of the Rockies," as the prison was known, so she had to scheme to get out as an undercover informant for the U.S. government.

So her part of the "deal" with the Americans was that she would infiltrate so-called sleeper cells of Muslim extremists as her alter ego the Chechen terrorist Ajmaani; learn their plans; and pass the information on to the agencies. She'd been able to convince her captors that according to her sources, al-Qaeda was planning a series of strikes in New York City, culminating with one massive attack on a date and location that were as yet unknown; they only knew it would be within the year and hit Manhattan.

Of course it was all a lie to get out of the prison and back to New York City. Except for the massive attack . . . *That is real,* she thought.

In reality, it was Ajmaani who contacted the sleeper cells — which she'd known of prior to her arrest — and with forged documents purported to come from higher-ups in al-Qaeda, or some other extremist organization, planned attacks and set them in motion. Then she turned around and betrayed the terrorists to win the confidence of the Americans, starting with the attack on the Liberty Island ferry.

The attack on the ferry and its aftermath could not have gone better. She'd located Ghilzai and other foreign-born members of that cell, sprinkled in some American jihadis to ruin the cohesion of the group and sow distrust, and then told them that the time had come to "strike a blow for Allah and attack the Great Satan."

As she had ever since assuming the role of Ajmaani, first for the Russian government trying to destroy the Muslim separatist movement in Chechnya and later for the highest bidder, she found the mujahideen to be extremely gullible, and the one involved in the ferry attack was no exception. It wasn't that they were all stupid or uneducated or even poor, though some were all three. But whether it was their religious upbringing or dissatisfaction with their lives, or a psychological predisposition to accepting the orders of authority figures as gospel, it didn't take much to convince them that sacrificing their lives to kill others would earn them a place in paradise.

"Of course their leaders never volunteer to kill themselves for Allah," she'd laughed cynically when talking to the NIDSA agent Mike Rolles as they drove back from the harbor following the attack. "They have enough fools to use as cannon fodder for God."

And cannon fodder is what they've become, she mused as she waited for her new attorney to arrive. *No survivors. No witnesses.*

It was all part of the plan to not only escape her captors but live well and on her own terms after that, with each piece of the plot that would win her freedom snapping into the others like a jigsaw puzzle. One piece had been to establish herself as the fearless Ajmaani and take part in the attack. But in addition to wanting to be present in case something went wrong and she needed to intervene, she had to be able to send a message to certain people that she was in charge of events.

Another piece had been to select the most fanatical foreign-born terrorists to be on board the attacking vessel, who were told to avoid capture no matter what the cost to their lives. "If you are stopped from completing your main mission, blow yourselves up; it will still make a dramatic statement in the media, especially Al Jazeera television. You will be heroes and martyrs for Allah," she'd told the boat leader the night before the attack.

Even then she'd taken no chances. Her appearance on the ferry when the talks with the attackers had stalemated was to send a signal to one of her men stationed in a hotel room on the southern end of the island with a view of what was happening. When it was apparent that at least some of the attackers on board the boat survived the barrage of fire from the police, he'd use a remote-control detonator to set off the bomb that had been planted belowdecks unbeknownst to the attackers.

She tried to consider everything, even making Ghilzai believe that Akhund was the traitor. Ghilzai would never talk, and Akhund would never survive jail. She would also make sure of that.

In return for helping thwart the terrorists, Malovo had worked out a deal in which she would be placed in the federal witness protection program and given a quiet new life in some out-of-the-way community. *I'd rather rot in prison than suffocate in suburbia.* She had no intention of doing either.

However, she needed to convince the authorities that it was what she wanted, though she knew that the agent Espey Jaxon and U.S. Marshal Capers, who had refused to relinquish total control of Malovo to NIDSA, would be suspicious. She would have to deal with them and made a mental note to file away their obvious personal feelings for each other, information that could be useful later on.

After her arrest, Malovo refused to say much of anything to U.S. interrogators other than the occasional tantalizing tidbit about people she knew, including traitors within the U.S. and Russian governments and the supersecretive Sons of Man. It was enough for the feds to send in a stream of agents, men and women, hoping she'd open up to one of them. But not until NIDSA agent Michael Rolles entered the interview room did she begin to "spill her guts." Of course there was a reason for that.

When he was sure they were alone, he quietly said, *"Myr shegin dy ve, bee eh."* It meant "What must be, will be" in Manx, the language of the Isle of Man. It was also the mother language of the Sons of Man, who had grown from a group of pirates and smugglers in the eighteenth century into a clandestine syndicate of powerful and wealthy descendants bent on U.S. and world domination. It was the signal she'd been waiting for; help had arrived . . . for a price.

Gradually, so as not to arouse the suspicions of anyone watching, she warmed up to Rolles, and in their first two-hour interview "revealed" a smidgeon of information that had led to a bomb-making operation in the Bronx. Her captors, including Espey Jaxon and U.S. Marshal Capers, appeared to have final say in where she went and when. But she was NIDSA's prize due to her relationship with Rolles, as she made it look like he had touched some vulnerable part of her psyche to the point that several months into his appearance, she flirted shamelessly and suggestively with Rolles. The irony was that Rolles wouldn't have been susceptible to her feminine wiles even if that had been part of her plan.

Testing the waters, Malovo — who had spent a lifetime studying the weaknesses of her enemies, most of whom were men — did "test the waters" with Rolles, just in case seduction would come in handy later. But he just smirked and said, "Don't bother. I don't like women, if you know what I mean."

Just like the SOM hierarchy to send a homosexual as their emissary and close that door for her. But there were many ways to a man's heart. Sex was one. Power and money were others. Rolles wanted both, and she was his ticket to a seat at the SOM board table.

She told him her plan, or what she wanted him to know of it, and what she had to offer. Something SOM wanted very much, and they were almost blind in their desire to get it.

■ ■ ■ ■

There was a knock on the door and a young, balding, and paunchy man in a cheap suit entered. She'd been expecting him, knew who he was and even what he looked like; he was the key to her plan.

"Who are you? Where is my lawyer?" Malovo hissed.

"I'm Bruce Knight, your attorney," the young man responded. "I was retained as an independent counsel by the law firm that was hired to represent you, which is, by the way, my former firm. I'm in . . . I'm in my own practice now."

Malovo narrowed her eyes. "I see," she said. "The evil terrorist is too hot to handle for those fat old men. Pressure from Washington? So they find some flunky to provide some window dressing and forget about her."

Knight's face flushed. "I will say that the firm retained by your . . . *benefactors* does want to fly, as I was told, under the radar with you regarding the state and New York County charges against you. I mean, true or not, allegations of blowing up school buses, murdering children and police officers, attacking the New York Stock Exchange, and killing a prosecution witness in a Manhattan courtroom make you a public relations nightmare," he said tightly. "But I'm no flunky. I've won my share of tough cases, and I don't back down from anyone, including the government. However, if you're not happy with my representation, you are free to find someone else. I'll inform the firm."

Malovo gave him an appraising look, as if she might have misjudged him. *That took some balls, as it would mean giving back the fifty-thousand-dollar retainer, and if my sources are right he's already spent a good part of it.* "At least you have some fire in you. That's good."

Suddenly her head dropped and her shoulders sagged. A small sigh escaped her lips.

"Are you okay?" Knight asked.

Malovo shook her head without looking up. "How can I be?" she moaned. "All of my life, I have been used by evil men toward their own ends. KGB. Russian mob. Terrorists and power brokers. I have been raped and abused, made to fear for my life." She sighed. "I was just a child; first they told me it was for my country, then for my life and vicious men like Andrew Kane."

"Andrew Kane?" Knight asked. "The guy who was running for mayor . . . then he got mixed up in some criminal plot, didn't he?"

151

"Yes, that's him," Malovo said. She sighed again. "I will not lie to you. I participated in many of these deeds, though the government has greatly exaggerated my role, but I have been searching my soul and I want to make up for these things if I can."

"And go into the witness protection program," Knight said. "I was told of your deal with the feds."

"Yes, of course," she replied with a shrug. "Who wants to live their life in prison?"

"I understand."

Malovo leaned across the table, the shadow between her breasts drawing Knight's eye as she patted him on the hand. "Thank you, Bruce. I am very glad you understand." She leaned back in her seat. *Enough of a show for now.* "Yes, I think I'll keep you."

An hour later, Knight finished droning on and on about the charges Karp had personally indicted her for in New York County, including multiple counts of murder, for which Karp had already filed the paperwork necessary to pursue the death penalty. As with a life in suburbia, she had no intention of ever facing those charges. She had an entirely different purpose for Bruce Knight, who finished his presentation and left.

The door to the room on the other side of the one-way glass opened and Michael Rolles entered. "I still don't understand what this guy has to do with your mission," he said.

"As I've told you, you will learn that when you need to," she responded with a glare. "You have been told to cooperate with anything I need. . . . And I am not about to give away the ace up my bra; then you will have no need of my services, and I'm sure that would put me in a very dangerous position."

"Up your sleeve."

"What?"

"The expression is 'up your sleeve' 'the ace up your sleeve,' " Rolles said, correcting her.

Malovo smiled. "And how would you know where I keep my ace?" she said. "You don't like women, remember?"

Rolles's eyes narrowed in anger. "Just remember who you work for," he warned her.

"How could I ever forget?" Malovo replied. She smiled, thinking about her old mentor dying in the snow. "I never forget."

12

"He'll see you now," brother Frank announced as he entered the chapel where David Ellis sat looking at the plain gold cross behind the lectern, wondering what Jesus would say about the Reverend Westlund and his End of Days Reformation Church of Jesus Christ Resurrected. David stood and started to walk past the bodyguard but was stopped by the other man's hand on his shoulder.

"I'll need to pat you down," Frank Bernsen said. He was smiling but his eyes were anything but friendly.

"Why?" David asked sarcastically. "Surely no one would want to shoot the Reverend Westlund, or whatever his name is today."

Bernsen cocked his head and the smile disappeared. "There have been some threats. Nutcases who resent Brother John speaking out for you and your wife. Don't take it personally; everybody gets the same treatment."

"I do take it personally," David retorted, but he held his arms out to his sides and allowed himself to be frisked.

"Go ahead," Bernsen said when he'd finished. "You know the way."

Unfortunately, he's right, David thought as he walked to the elevator that would take him up to Westlund's third-floor loft. He and Nonie had been in the building many times since moving to New York City; now he regretted it.

Several months after meeting Westlund, David had been offered a good job with his former company. He'd been thrilled, except that it meant relocating to Manhattan. It wasn't that he minded the move so much — in fact, he would have been happy to leave Memphis and the reverend behind — but he knew that Nonie was going to balk at going.

And he was right. She adamantly refused and said she would stay behind "until Micah is completely cured." But he knew it wasn't just about Micah, who seemed to be improving by the week. She'd thrown herself into her renewed faith and her work for the church — visiting the sick with Westlund or sometimes with other mothers, like Sarah, who had seriously ill children who'd been "cured by God"; attending prayer meetings; and even soliciting "donations" on the street. She was so completely in thrall to Westlund that the first nagging doubts about her marital faithfulness entered his mind. He'd seen the way Westlund looked at his wife, tracing her body with his eyes, though he seemed to have an innate sense of when to pretend that he was merely thinking when he felt David watching him. He wondered if Nonie looked at the preacher in the same way when David wasn't around.

Yet he loved his wife and knew that if push came to shove, he'd stay in Memphis. But then he'd received support from where he least expected it. After hearing of the job offer, Westlund had told Nonie that it was her duty as a Christian wife to support her husband and go with him to New York. She reluctantly agreed, though her mood turned sour and she was often tearful, until the evening a week later when she came home from a prayer meeting and happily announced that the preacher had decided to relocate to New York City, too.

As she explained it, Westlund had "prayed on it" and decided that he could reach more sinners in the big city than he could in

Memphis. "And he's become so attached to us that he doesn't want to lose contact," she said, beaming.

"Praise the Lord," he replied less than enthusiastically, but she didn't notice.

Shortly before they were due to leave, Westlund sat them down in their living room to "ask a favor." He said he'd been receiving death threats — he wasn't sure of the source but suspected either members of "apostate" churches "or maybe the medical community," which he said saw him "as a threat to their ill-gotten gains." So, he said, he was leaving not just Memphis, but his name and the name of his church behind.

"I fear that if they can find me, they will carry out their evil agendas," he lamented. "It came to me in a dream that I shall now be known as the Reverend C. G. Westlund of the End of Days Reformation Church of Jesus Christ Resurrected. I trust that you, my dearest friends, will understand my reasons and guard them."

The Ellises had moved and Westlund followed a couple of weeks later, staying with the young family in the tiny apartment on West 88th Street until he could find accommodations, which turned out to be the loft on Avenue A and 6th Street in the East Village. The building was owned by a widow named Kathryn Boole, whom Nonie had befriended one day in Union Square Park. Boole was feeding the pigeons and kept wiping at her eyes until Nonie realized the woman was crying. A gentle soul, Nonie walked over to a nearby coffeeshop and bought two cups — one for herself and one for Boole.

Grateful for the act of kindness, Boole told Nonie that she'd recently lost her husband of twenty years to an illness and that she saw little point in going on herself. Nonie shared her story and the "miracle" of Micah's recovery, which had continued unabated when they moved to New York.

Nonie introduced Boole to Westlund, who shook his head and lamented that they had not met when her husband was still alive "so that he might have been healed through the power of prayer." Boole quickly fell under his spell and was soon convinced that the physicians who attended her husband had all but killed him. Before too long, she was even more obsessed with Westlund than even Nonie and seemed to go beyond just reliance on his spiritual guidance. He noticed that she cleaned up, started wearing makeup, and dyed her hair a sort of burnt orange.

As it turned out, Boole's husband had

been a moderately wealthy businessman who dabbled in Manhattan real estate, including the building on Avenue A, an old warehouse that had been converted into a furniture store on the bottom level; the next floor was office space, and the top floor was reserved for a large, three-bedroom loft. While Boole was obviously taken with the preacher, it still came as a surprise when Westlund announced at the beginning of a prayer meeting that the church would be relocating to the Avenue A building. "Our dear Sister Kathryn has been moved by the Lord to offer the building to house our ministry as well as our bodies," he proclaimed with tears rolling down his ruddy cheeks.

As Westlund went on to effusively praise Boole, David glanced over at the woman. She was blushing wildly at each word of praise. But there was something else. A hunger in her eyes for the preacher. The woman never missed a prayer meeting or a chance to "work the streets" with Westlund.

When Micah became sick again, she'd been the loudest and most invested of those praying. And after his death, she was always at the forefront of the protests against the district attorney. David didn't like the woman, and yet he felt responsible for her falling into Westlund's hands because of his wife. It was Nonie who had filled a grieving widow's broken heart with the "miracle" of Micah's recovery. But they had both vouched for the preacher's character; at the time, even David had been won over by his son's apparent health and wife's happiness.

We opened the door and let the serpent into Kathryn's soul, he thought as he rode the elevator up.

David arrived on the third floor and knocked on the door of the loft. There was an electronic buzz and metallic clicking followed by Westlund's deep voice from within. "Come in, and may the Lord bless you."

Entering the loft, David was again struck by the opulence of the décor. He was no furnishings expert but he knew expensive when he saw it. He had often wondered if the place was already furnished when Westlund moved in or whether the preacher was living high on the hog off of Boole and donations. *And life insurance policies taken out on dying children,* he reminded himself angrily.

A policy clearly signed by your wife, *who allowed Westlund to forge your signature,* said a mean little voice, interrupting his thoughts.

Yes, signed by my wife and Westlund . . . how do I live with that?

Westlund was rising from a leather chair, a wolfish smile plastered on his face and his arms outstretched as if to embrace David. "Welcome, brother," the preacher said warmly. "This is an unexpected surprise."

David stopped with enough distance between them to avoid being hugged. "Where's my wife?" he demanded.

Westlund's smile remained on his face but now it more closely resembled a smirk. "She's not here, brother," he said calmly. "Did you expect to find her? I don't believe we had an appointment. Have you checked for her at home?"

"She's not home," David spat. He looked behind Westlund toward the bedroom door, which he saw was partly ajar, and tried to move toward it.

Westlund stepped into his path. "I'm sorry, Brother David, but I can't allow this intrusion into my privacy."

David attempted to go around the bigger man but was grabbed by the arm. "Nonie!" he yelled. "Nonie, come out!" He tore his arm out of Westlund's grasp.

"What's this about?" Westlund demanded.

"What is it about?" David said, stepping back, his lip curling into a sneer. "It's about

161

you using people's pain and suffering to worm your way into their lives. It's about destroying people's faith. And it's about this, you son of a bitch." He pulled the crumpled letter from the insurance company from his jacket pocket and waved it in Westlund's face.

Westlund looked at the letter, his face growing dark. He was well aware that without medical attention, the children he prayed over would probably die, but that was part of the plan.

When talking to parents of seriously ill children like the Ellises, he always emphasized that only God decided who lived, who died, and when — "Not physicians, who play at God; not even humble servants of the Lord such as myself," he told them. "However, we believe that if we place our complete and undivided faith in God, we can pray for Him to spare the lives of our loved ones."

To cover his bases, he cautioned the parents that no amount of praying would save their children. "God teaches through suffering as well," he warned them, "and if He calls your sweet angel home, in spite of our best efforts, we must accept His will. But you may still be comforted to know that your expression of faith will assure your child a place at Jesus' table, where you'll see him again someday."

Then, if and when the moment was right, he would mention that in the "unfathomable" event of their child's death, some earthly good could come from their suffering. He hated to ask, he'd say, but if he was going to reach his full potential as a "warrior for the faith" it would take money, and one way to support his work would be for the family to take out a life insurance policy naming the church and himself as the beneficiaries.

It was a carefully constructed grift. He knew that the parents would have to submit to a medical examination, as well as a review of their medical records, but as predominantly young, healthy couples, most would pass easily. However, he was also aware that insurance companies rarely checked on the children attached to their parents' policies as "riders." He did emphasize that when the insurance underwriters contacted them regarding their child's prior medical history they should deny any problems.

"It's not a lie, it's a question of faith," he would explain. "We believe that the cause and cure of any illness is a matter between God and the patient. As true believers we do not accept the word of physicians; to do so would be to place the faith we owe to the Lord in the hands of men who play at being God. Therefore we reject their test results and diagnoses as little more than witchcraft. The truth is that God decides which of their patients live or die."

When some parents questioned whether insurance companies might find their children's medical records at the Children's Hospital, where they were treated, Westlund assured them that God would take care of the problem as long as they believed.

As an experienced con man, he knew that no grift was perfect; there was always a chance for a mistake. But he thought that as much as possible he had all the angles covered. Even if the parents didn't have the money to pay the premiums, he paid for them "from donations." He'd suggest different insurance companies to avoid suspicion and kept the benefits low — typically $250,000 — so that the companies would be inclined to write it off rather than investigate and attempt to get the money back, even if they did suspect larceny.

Of course, it meant Westlund turning a blind eye to a child experiencing a slow, usually painful death with nothing more to alleviate their suffering — because "the church" did not believe in painkillers — than a room full of fellow believers, some of them hired for the part, praying like nobody's business.

It's not like I gave them cancer, Westlund thought with a shrug on the rare occasion he reflected on what he was doing. *If these rubes believe that God can save their brats, then they can blame God for letting them die. The kids are good as dead anyway, I'm just taking advantage of the inevitable. In fact, I provide a service by offering a few months of hope that little Johnny will live to be a high school graduate, and when he doesn't, that they'll all meet "on the other side." Hell, they should pay me for that alone.*

A couple of times, the kid did survive due to either a great response to the first chemo treatment, or what the doctors labeled "spontaneous remission." Such events were always a disappointment in that there would be no insurance payoff, but he learned to use even that to his advantage. He'd take credit for the "miracle" and the grateful parents, who would be convinced that his intercession with God was responsible for their child's survival, would happily donate significant amounts to his ministry. And it was good advertising, with the happy parents unwittingly helping him con other parents with their home visits and testimonials.

Westlund had to be careful not to press too hard. He didn't need any suddenly suspicious parents going to the cops or telling the doctors at the hospital about him. As with the Ellises, one parent or the other was often more skeptical about his motives; sometimes both scowled when he got around to donations to the ministry and the life insurance policy. If they balked, he immediately backed off and waited for them to come back to him, often having decided to go along with the plan because they felt guilty about not supporting him. But as his ability to pick the right marks increased over time, he had less to worry about.

The South in general had been a lucrative place to do business with the prevalence of Pentecostal and other churches that believed in faith healing. But all good things must come to an end, and an experienced con man like Westlund knew that the longer he worked an area, the greater the chance that he'd slip up and get caught. And it had finally happened in Memphis.

Nonie Ellis wasn't the first mother of a critically ill child he'd talked into taking out a life insurance policy without her husband's knowledge and with Westlund forging the signature. In the other case, the woman's husband had balked and she'd come to him with tears in her eyes and desperation in her voice. One of the side benefits of his profession was that the women were often young and some, like this woman and Nonie, quite pretty. They were also vulnerable to a holy man full of assurances that all would be okay, which their husbands could not compete with. He'd give them a shoulder to cry on, and often as not he'd get them into bed, explaining that it was all part of God's compassion for them in their hour of need.

In the previous case, the woman had fallen in love, as they often did when he turned on the charm, but he was surprised when she announced that she'd decided to leave her husband to become her minister's wife. Doctor of Divinity John LaFontaine had scrambled to "admit" that he was in the process of divorcing his wife — "a harlot" who had cheated on him repeatedly — and until the paperwork was final, they'd have to remain "secret lovers in Christ."

The woman had been satisfied to wait, but now her husband had refused to take out an insurance policy and sign over the benefits to Westlund. She was worried that Westlund would leave her and stop praying over her terminally ill daughter because of her husband's "selfishness." Westlund told her that she didn't have to worry — that he loved her and her child and wouldn't leave either of them. But his visits to the home became noticeably less frequent and his lovemaking rushed and lacking his old passion. Then one day, she'd come to him with "an idea to help Jesus" — she'd take out the insurance policy and Brother Frank could play her husband when the insurance medical examiner came by the house.

At first, he "resisted" her plan, saying he didn't want her to go against her husband's wishes. Then, after an afternoon of lovemaking, he relented "because the money goes for the greater good, God's work, and that isn't a sin."

His frequent prayer visits to the house had resumed, as did his ardor in bed. Then the woman's daughter died, normally a time when he expected the woman would turn to him for comfort. But rather than leaning on him, after signing over the insurance check she instead became overwhelmed with guilt and told her husband about the affair and the insurance scam.

A large redneck, the husband then made two mistakes. He should have gone to the police, but instead he dropped by Westlund's house one evening to demand the money back for his silence. "And it'll keep me from putting a load of buckshot in your ass for taking advantage of my wife, you sorry piece of crap," he added.

The second mistake the man made was not looking out for trouble the next night when he went to take out the trash. He was a big man, a tough man, but he was no match for three other large men wearing ski masks and wielding crowbars. The first blow to the back of his head had knocked him down and out; the several dozen more that followed eventually killed him after he spent a week in a coma, during which he never regained consciousness. That's when Westlund had paid the widow a visit to offer his condolences, and a piece of advice. "You're still alive, and I wouldn't want anything bad to happen to you," he said without a hint of his former affection for her.

Westlund thought that was the end of it until a Memphis homicide detective, Willie "Wink" Winkler, came calling. The detective said he'd been assigned to the husband's murder case and in the course of his investigation he had checked the wife's phone log. "And it looks like she calls you a lot."

"Of course she does, I am the family's spiritual adviser," Westlund answered. "This has been a difficult time for them with their daughter's illness and tragic demise . . . and now this murder. Terrible . . . just terrible."

Westlund had felt reasonably secure that the detective would never be able to make a case against him. There'd been no witnesses to the attack, and the crowbars had gone into the Mississippi River. The wife was scared to death and apparently hadn't said anything to the detective about the insurance payment. But he knew from his first stint in prison — for a simple Ponzi scheme that had cost him five years — that detectives sometimes lie in the weeds and wait for their targets to relax.

So when David Ellis got a job in New York City, Westlund had told Nonie she needed to go with him, and then announced that it was time to move his ministry north to "battle evil in that modern-day Sodom." Brother David was lukewarm about his plan, but Nonie, whom he'd set his lustful eyes on, had been ecstatic.

The move had paid off even better than he expected. His sometime partner in Memphis, Sister Sarah, told him that the detective had come by the widow's home but the frightened woman had stuck with the story that there had been no romantic liaisons with Reverend LaFontaine and that she believed he'd moved on to California. Sarah, whom he'd asked to keep an eye on his victim, had dropped by for "a visit" right after the detective left her home to let her know that she was being watched.

Meanwhile, Nonie introduced him to the widow Kathryn Boole, and he'd charmed her into turning over the Avenue A building to him. He'd also been duly grateful when she told him that she'd amended her will to leave the building to him, along with the balance of her estate, when she died.

Although he'd so far been unable to duplicate the system he had in Memphis for identifying the families of critically ill children, he'd been pleased when his plans for the Ellis kid, Micah, had apparently come to fruition. As he'd known was likely, the symptoms of the tumors returned and then grew steadily worse.

When it became apparent that Micah was fading fast, David Ellis's "faith" had begun to waver, and he spoke to his wife about taking the child to the hospital. Of course, Nonie, who leaned increasingly on Westlund as her son's condition grew worse, told the reverend about David's plans. He turned that around to blaming the husband's qualms for the lack of faith that was dooming their child. Fortunately for him, the child died before David could change his wife's mind.

However, Westlund hadn't counted on the New York District Attorney's Office bringing charges against the Ellises. In Memphis, whether it was due to the religious politics of the region or something else, the district attorney had never pursued a faith-healing case. But Karp was a different breed and determined to pursue the parents for their recklessness.

Westlund could not have cared less about what happened to the Ellises. But Nonie had told him about the letter from the insurance company. It was simple: if the Ellises were found guilty of the reckless-manslaughter charge, the insurance claim wouldn't be paid. It was worth a quarter of a million dollars to get the case dropped, and if that didn't work, to make sure the Ellises were acquitted. He didn't like putting himself in the limelight, just in case someone in Memphis saw him on television, but his ego and desire for money had led him to bring the protests against the DA's office, as well as contact the lawyers who'd taken on the case on First Amendment freedom-of-religion grounds.

Now here was David Ellis angrily waving the insurance letter in his face. "I meant to thank you for that," he said, acting as if they'd all known about the policy. "It was a generous gesture, brother."

"You trying to tell me you didn't sign my name on the policy?" David Ellis demanded.

"I swear on the Bible," Westlund said. *Not even a lie,* he thought. *Brother Frank signed it.*

"I don't believe you!"

"Brother, I understand that you're on edge with the trial starting tomorrow, but it's going to be all right and —"

"There's not going to be any trial," David interrupted. "At least not for me. Nonie can make up her own mind. But I'm going to plead guilty in the morning." He held up the paper again. "And I'll be giving this to the district attorney."

Westlund looked aggrieved. "If it's the money you want, you can have it. I thought it was a gift for Christ."

David shook his head as tears came to his eyes. "Money? You can't give me what I want," he replied. "I want my son back. We were fools to believe in you and your lies. I was a fool to let you into my home. . . . And just so you know, I was the one who called 911 that day . . . but I was too late, so I lost my son, and now my wife. But I'm going to do what I can now to atone, may God forgive me."

David Ellis turned and left, but Westlund followed him out of the apartment to the elevator. "You're sure we can't reach some understanding, brother?"

"Don't call me 'brother,' and the answer is no," David said. He paused and, with his voice breaking, added, "And if you see my wife, send her home."

When the elevator door closed, Westlund called Bernsen. "Hey, bro, we got a situation," he said. "Get someone to follow Ellis. We may have to find us some more crowbars, if you get my drift."

Returning to the loft, Westlund paused for a moment inside the foyer and then went to the kitchen, where he opened a drawer and looked at the two handguns there — one an automatic, the other a revolver. He took out the latter. *Any idiot can use a revolver.* He then went into the bedroom, where the woman was waiting, the hand with the gun in it hanging loosely at his side.

"I can't believe that David would . . ." Her voice trailed off. "What are you doing with that gun?"

Westlund's shoulder sagged. "I would have never expected David to react that way either, but the devil has taken his heart and soul," he said, shaking his head sadly. "Now I'm afraid the authorities will misinterpret. You know the district attorney, Karp, has it in for me and won't rest until I am in prison."

The big man began to cry quietly. "I will not go to prison to be set upon by the agents of Satan," he said, looking down at the gun. "You need to go now, my love, and we will meet on the other side someday."

"You can't! I won't let that happen!" the woman declared, rushing into his arms.

Westlund kissed her fervently, dropping the gun on the floor, then picking her up and carrying her to the bed, where he set her down. "How much do you love me?" he asked as he pulled off his sweat suit.

"More than life, my darling, more than life!"

13

Bruce Knight stepped out of the D train at the 125th Street station in Harlem and immediately regretted it. It was well after midnight and the only other people in sight were three young black men whose exposed arms and necks were covered with dark tattoos. They immediately stopped smoking whatever it was they had been passing among themselves and watched him intently. He went over to a bench and sat down with his back to them, hoping he didn't look as much like a target as he felt.

Conscious that his suit alone, never mind the color of his skin, in that neighborhood at that late hour invited criminal avarice, he was also sorry that he'd brought the sophisticated new cell phone with all the bells and whistles that his former and now-current employer had delivered to him with a note that read "A gift so that we can communicate effectively. All apps and the

monthly data plan paid for one year. Enjoy."
He wondered how he'd explain what he'd
been doing in Harlem in the early A.M.
when robbed of his wallet and new toy.
They'll think I was looking for drugs, he
thought, *which I guess is better than their
knowing what I'm really doing.*

He heard footsteps behind him. *Oh well,
here we go.* The thought was immediately
overwhelmed by a stench so powerful he
nearly gagged. He expected to hear a demand for his wallet and started to rise but
stopped at the sound of the voice behind
him.

"Evening, Mr. Knight . . . crap tits whoop
whoop . . . sorry we're a little late."

Knight relaxed and looked behind him as
he stood up. There were no gangbangers
around, just "Dirty" Warren Bennett and an
enormous, bearlike man from whom the
smell emanated. "Hi, Warren, good to see
you," he said. "And your friend . . ."

"This is Booger," Dirty Warren replied.
"Sometimes known . . . oh boy . . . as the
Walking Booger."

Knight looked back at Booger and noted
he was aptly named, as the man had a
sausage-sized finger shoved knuckle-deep
up a nostril. Booger appeared to be wearing
several layers of filthy clothing that covered

177

all but his hands, neck, and face, all of which were in turn covered with coarse dark hair, further enhancing his ursine appearance.

The giant apparently did not believe in bathing. However, he was friendly enough, extending the unoccupied hand, which Knight chose not to examine as he shook it.

"Please a meet choo," Booger mumbled. He may have even smiled, though it was difficult to tell through his furry face.

"Likewise," Knight replied. "What happened to the 'bangers who were just here?"

"They . . . oh boy tits cocks whoop . . . took off," Dirty Warren replied, then pointed at his companion. "They're afraid of him. Booger's just a big teddy bear unless . . . whoop . . . you get him riled, then he's *Ursus horribilis* . . . a grizzly."

"Grrrrrrr," Booger growled for effect, then laughed. "Booger Bear hong-ree. Go."

"You're always 'hong-ree,' Boog," Dirty Warren replied. "But you're . . . asshole whoop whoop scumbag whore . . . right. David's waiting." He looked at Knight. "You remember the way?"

Knight looked down the subway tunnel to where the rail disappeared. Most people would have cringed at the idea of walking into the darkness, but while he would have

178

rather been home in bed, he felt nostalgic at the same time. "Not really, but I know we go that way," he replied, pointing down the tunnel.

Dirty Warren patted him on the back as he walked past and hopped down from the platform onto the tracks. "Good start. Remember to stay away from the third rail."

Knight walked to the yellow warning line at the edge of the platform and hesitated, recalling the first time he'd climbed down from another platform looking for a place to sleep.

Some four years earlier, on a bitterly cold February night, he'd been homeless and living on the streets. There were no more spaces available at the Bowery Mission, so he stumbled down into the nearby subway station to stay warm. Craving a drink but without enough money to buy a half pint of even the cheapest bourbon, he contemplated giving up, just stepping off the platform in front of the next train or touching the electrically charged third rail.

However, although he frequently contemplated suicide, the will to live kept glowing in him, though he did little to fan the flames. So he hopped down from the platform and headed along the track looking for some dry spot and a little warmth. As each train passed, he wondered if any of the occupants looking out caught a glimpse of his haggard face and booze-hazed eyes and, thinking they'd seen a bogeyman, screamed.

A little ways down the track, he found a nook in the tunnel wall leading to a doorway marked MAINTENANCE ONLY, above which hung a dim lightbulb that cast a faint orange glow, giving the space a Halloweenish look. He tried the door but it was locked. Still, the alcove was reasonably dry and the color of the light at least offered the illusion of warmth, so he curled up in a corner, the backpack that held all his earthly possessions his pillow.

He fell asleep between the passing of each train, which in his exhaustion merely stirred him to semiwakefulness, after which he'd slumber again. So it had taken him quite a while to realize that he was being shaken by someone and then, once he was awake, to believe he wasn't still dreaming.

Thinking that he was being robbed or assaulted by some other subway dweller, he pulled the small steak knife he'd found in a Dumpster and slashed at the dark figure bending over him. But it was like fighting a shadow, as his assailant easily evaded his frenzied swinging. He was soon exhausted and stood numbly, realizing he was at the mercy of the stranger, who he now realized was a tall bearded man in a hooded robe.

During their "fight" he caught glimpses of the man's pale, gaunt face, which was framed by long, dark hair and dominated by two black eyes that flickered with an inner fire. Now, as he stared into those eyes, Knight knew he was looking into the face of a killer who, if not totally insane, was walking insanity's razor edge. Yelling in terror, he made one last lunge at the stranger, only to have the knife knocked from his hand. Then, as fast as a cat after a rat, the man moved around him and kicked behind his knees, driving him painfully into the ground; his attacker then yanked his head back, and with one hand digging into his eye sockets, he took the other and placed a sharp blade at his throat.

"For the love of Christ don't kill me!" Knight cried out. He had no idea why he'd chosen those words, which he hadn't heard or used since leaving his Midwest home and Presbyterian upbringing. But they seemed right at that moment.

The man suddenly released the grip he had on Knight's hair and the knife disappeared. "Stand up! Let me look into your eyes," the stranger demanded.

Trembling, Knight did as he was told. The man then leaned forward and stared deep into his eyes. He had no idea what the stranger was looking for, but a moment later, the hard stare softened into a kindly look that matched the smile that came to the man's face. "I do not see evil in you," the man said, "or I would have had to release you from that body. But you are safe now, brother. I will not harm you."

The stranger offered his hand. "I'm David Grale. What's your name?"

"Bruce Knight," he replied, still wondering when he would wake from this new nightmare. But whether he was dreaming or not, he recognized that whatever insanity battled for control in the man's brain, he spoke the truth. He was safe . . . at least for the moment. "I was trying to stay warm."

"And not doing such a good job of it, brother," Grale said. "You look hungry. Follow me and we'll see if we can take care of both."

Grale then turned and entered the maintenance door, followed by Knight, who wondered how he'd opened it and from which side. Stepping through the door and watching the other man march off down a dimly lit hallway, he hesitated. *Maybe he's taking me someplace to kill me,* he thought, then shrugged before hurrying to catch up to his long-legged benefactor. *If he wanted to kill me, I'd already be dead.*

Grale led him down the maintenance tunnel for a bit and then went through another door, which took them to a ladder that led down into a sewer pipe, judging by the ankle-deep water, smell, and cat-sized rats that hissed and scurried away. In places where there was no light, Grale turned on a flashlight, though Knight got the impression it was more for his sake than his guide's.

Knight had quickly lost his bearings and had no sense of what direction they were heading. In general it seemed to be ever farther down, though they sometimes had to go up a ladder in order to go down three more levels. They passed through a variety of doors and openings, including some that were not man-made but clefts in the rock leading to paths that linked with their man-made counterparts.

They'd been walking for perhaps a half hour when they reached a dimly lit intersection of several tunnels. Grale stopped, motioning for Knight to do the same as he called out, "I'm looking for the entrance to the kingdom of heaven."

"And how do you gain entrance?" a voice

183

shouted back from the dark outside the circle of light.

"The love of Christ," Grale replied before turning to grin at Knight. "It seems you knew our password."

"I have no idea why I said that," Knight said. "Dumb luck and fear, I guess."

Grale shook his head and placed a hand on Knight's shoulder. "Not luck, brother, no such thing. It was divine intervention," he said as he resumed walking toward the other voice. "Good evening, brothers."

Two men materialized out of the dark — one carried a bow with an arrow nocked, the other an older-model rifle, and both had long knives on their belts. Dirty and ragged, they appeared to Knight to be ordinary street people, except for the fact that their eyes were clear and steady, and on second glance looked more like photographs he'd seen of Czech resistance fighters from World War II.

"Evening, father," said the older of the two, tipping his cap to Grale. "A visitor?"

"God be with you, my son. Yes, Brothers Harvey and Chuck, meet Brother Bruce. I vouch for him," Grale replied, making a vague sign of the cross before turning away from the pair and continuing their journey into the bowels of the city.

" 'Father'? 'My son'? Are you a priest?" Knight asked.

"No. I was a Catholic layperson on the outside before I inherited my kingdom," Grale replied. "But the Mole People seem to have accepted me as their spiritual leader while adopting my mission to fight against the coming darkness. We have quite a few Catholics and Lutherans, and with no one else to serve their needs, I am their de facto priest. Others of different faiths, and even the stray agnostic, have picked up the honorific."

"The Mole People? I think I read an article in the *New York Times* a while back about the Mole People — something like thirty thousand homeless people living beneath the city in subway tunnels and sewers," Knight said as they walked.

"I'm aware of the article," Grale said, his voice hardening. "It was replete with errors, misinformation, and lies. For one thing, the article cast a large umbrella over many people and called them all the Mole People — murderers, rapists, the depraved, and criminally insane lumped in with those whose only crime is poverty. Oh, they may be tormented by addictions to alcohol and drugs, maybe even struggling with mental illness, but by and large they are good people down on their luck. However, they were all painted with the same broad brush by the article, which further isolated them from society — they're now avoided on the streets by 'normal' people rather than extended the hand of Christian charity."

As he listened to Grale, Knight realized that his guide was more a philosopher than the usual street person. When they were able to walk side by side, he stole glances at the other man's face as he spoke.

Grale was gaunt to the point of skeletal, with deep-set eyes, hollow cheeks, and a sharp aquiline nose above his thick mustache and beard, but he had clearly once been a handsome man and there was still a nobility to his visage. He was also younger than Knight first thought, fooled by the creases that radiated from the man's eyes and mouth and crossed his forehead. Knight guessed him to be in his midthirties.

"I found it alarming that the article missed that most of the real Mole People aren't society's castoffs and misfits, nor are they coming from the ranks of the traditionally poor, though that class has grown, too," Grale said. "Whatever our makeup ten years ago, currently our ranks swell with the recently impoverished, the great disappearing middle class, who find themselves suddenly homeless, penniless, and now among the 'have-nots.' These are the new immigrants to my kingdom beneath the streets, and this country had better wake up or there will be no middle class, only class warfare."

"That's the third reference to your 'kingdom,' " Knight noted. "So you are a guardian, a de facto priest, and a king?"

Grale did not answer immediately but trudged on. They rounded a corner, and although he couldn't see beyond the reach of his guide's flashlight, Knight could feel that he had stepped into a large open space. The flashlight wasn't the only illumination as all around him there were odd diffused lights; some even climbed partway up the dark space across from where he stood.

"This, Mr. Knight, is my kingdom, the kingdom of the Mole People," Grale said, and called out loudly to the dark, *"The peace of Christ be upon you!"*

"And upon you!" dozens of voices called out from around the space.

"We have a new visitor tonight," Grale announced. "Brother James, would you please turn up the house lights for a minute so that Brother Bruce can get a good look at our home."

"Now, father? It's after hours," a voice

whined off to their right.

"It's just for a moment, Jim," Grale replied, sounding perturbed. "Newcomers are disoriented enough without being able to get a sense of their surroundings. And, besides, he knew the password."

Knight was soon aware that the light was growing, and with that came the realization he was standing at the entrance to a cavern the same approximate size as Madison Square Garden. The glowing lights turned out to be electric bulbs behind cloth hung in front of living quarters built or carved into the walls. Curious, the Mole People peered out from their hovels — men, women, and even some children.

"Welcome to my kingdom," Grale said with a grand sweep of his hand. "Come, follow me to my throne."

Knight followed Grale over to a long, raised cement platform, looking around as they walked. Although much of the cavern appeared to be natural, or at least carved crudely from the bedrock of Manhattan Island, the rest was obviously constructed by engineers.

"A long time ago this was a subway station," Grale explained. "They were trying to expand when engineers discovered a dangerous fault in the rock, and the station was abandoned and another built quite close to here. Although there are a number of other places beneath the city where my people reside, this is the inner sanctum, accessible only to those who know the password."

"You have electricity," Knight said, stating the obvious.

"Courtesy of the New York transit system," Grale said with a laugh. "The Mole People come from many walks of life, including electricians capable of tying into the juice that runs the subway. It's all magic to me, but apparently they even know how to shut the whole system down with a flick of a switch, though of course we use only enough power to light and provide a little heat for our humble homes."

Grale led him up onto a raised platform on which sat a large leather overstuffed chair that might have once dominated a Fifth Avenue penthouse living room but had seen better years. Several smaller chairs formed a semicircle to either side of the "throne." He was invited to have a seat on one of the lesser chairs while Grale plopped down on the leather chair.

Reaching above him to turn on a standing lamp, Grale called out, "Brother James, would you please dim the lights again so our family may sleep?" Brother James didn't answer but the house lights dimmed and then went out, leaving only the lights in the living quarters around the walls and Grale's lamp.

When they'd settled in their seats, Grale leaned forward, the shadows of his face deepening beneath the light of his lamp. "So, Brother Bruce," he'd said, "do you want to tell me how you came to be shivering on the doorstep of the Mole People?"

Knight was still thinking about that night as he and his two escorts approached a vaguely familiar intersection of tunnels. He had not recognized much of the route they'd taken, though he knew from experience that the Mole People rarely took the same way back to their homes. As Grale had explained to him that first night, they had many enemies. "Some are criminals and violent men who seek revenge on some of us or think we'd be 'easy' targets," he'd said. "But some are officers of the law, even federal agents, looking for some of us."

Grale had laughed. "It might alarm you to know that if I was caught, I'd be arrested and tried for multiple counts of murder," he said. "But I can assure you I've never killed anyone who didn't deserve it."

There was one other group whose presence made the Mole People take the security of their home seriously. "We call them the Others," Grale explained. "They live beneath the streets, too. Vicious, deranged killers who have formed their own communities ruled by whoever is the most violent and evil. They are demons who have taken over the bodies of human beings. As called upon by God, we hunt them, but they in turn hunt us, especially if we wander the dark paths alone and unarmed. You must always be on guard against them."

Having started to relax around Grale, Knight was taken aback by the comments about demons. *He really is quite deranged himself,* he'd thought at the time, *though I have to admit there is something else about him that makes me feel safe.*

Now, passing through one sewer tunnel with Dirty Warren and Booger, Knight noticed large, elaborate, and quite well-done paintings on a wall. "I don't remember this," he said.

"It's the . . . whoop oh boy ass . . . latest thing in the underground art scene," Dirty Warren explained. "They're the crème de la crème of graffiti artists, who sneak down and paint on sewer walls and subway tunnels. Some are actually pretty famous in the art world; I've even seen some photos of

their art in the magazines I sell at my newsstand. Unfortunately . . . piss tits . . . we
sometimes have to chase them off — con-
tributing of course to urban myths about
bogeymen who live beneath the streets.
They're harmless, and I think a lot of their
stuff is pretty good and . . . whoop whoop
ohhhhboy oh boy . . . livens up the place,
but we don't want anybody accidentally
stumbling on the kingdom and giving us
away to the police or our enemies."

As they approached the familiar-looking
intersection, Dirty Warren called out, "I'm
looking for the . . . piss damn whoop . . .
entrance to the kingdom of heaven."

"And how do you gain entrance?" a voice
shouted back.

"The love of . . . whoop . . . Christ."

Knight looked amused. "You haven't
changed the password in four years?"

Dirty Warren shrugged. "David doesn't
see the . . . oh boy crap . . . need. Let's keep
moving, David's a bit more . . . uh whoop
whoop . . . temperamental than maybe the
last time you saw him."

"Temperamental?" Knight said.

"Yeah, and it's getting . . . oh boy . . .
worse," Dirty Warren replied.

Knight caught the scowl on his guide's
face and the worried tone in his voice. *So*

the madness continues, he thought, again harkening back to his introduction to the Mole People.

After telling his story to Grale that first night, he'd been given a hot meal and a cot to sleep on. The next morning, he stood before his benefactor again.

"I trust you slept well, brother," Grale had said, stroking his long beard as he sat on his leather throne. "At least it had to be better than a concrete floor in a subway tunnel."

"Much," Knight replied. "I'm very grateful."

Grale nodded. "As I said to you last night, I believe there is more at work here than mere chance or dumb luck. What that may be we shall learn in God's own time. Meanwhile, I'd like to make you an offer. You are welcome to join us. You'll be given a place to stay and share in our meals. You'll be expected to join one of our work parties — everybody who is able does — but nothing too onerous."

"That's very kind of you," Knight replied, thinking that at least for the winter, having someplace warm with food was an attractive option, even if it was underground.

"Good," Grale said, smiling, then he frowned. "However, we do have rules here, starting with no alcohol or drugs, which, along with any criminal activities or acts that place my people or our home in danger, will be cause to have you expelled. And in the case of traitors, the punishment is much worse. Do you understand?"

Gathering what Grale had just implied, Knight could only nod. He wondered if he could do without the alcohol — craving a drink even then — though he saw a glimmer of hope that enforced abstinence might free him from its influence. He had no intention of doing any other sort of criminal activity, or of being a traitor, so he knew he was safe in that regard and tried not to think what the punishment might entail.

Grale looked long and hard at him before nodding. "One more thing: you are welcome to leave us at any time. However, for the first few months — before you've proved yourself and know your way around — you will always be led outside by escorts who will confuse the way back to the kingdom. If you choose to leave us, you can't come back without an escort. And finally, a word of caution: if you try to leave on your own, or return on your own, we will deal with you harshly. However, we will probably not need to; if the Others find you wandering the labyrinth, there will be no helping you."

Grale's lecture had sent chills up his spine, but having nowhere else to turn, he'd opted to remain with the Mole People. And he soon learned to like most of the kingdom's inhabitants and their king.

As Grale noted during one of their many conversations, the Mole People society was based on early Christian communities where everyone worked for the common good, sharing the successes and hardships of their lives together. Those who could not work — including women with small children, the infirm, and those too ill — were taken care of by the community. Those who could work were divided into various parties. Some begged on the streets, others scoured Dumpsters and alleys throughout the city for food and anything that might be useful or sold at a secondhand store. Some even worked menial jobs, bringing their wages back to put in the community pot.

Grale oversaw all of it. Although he delegated some authority and day-to-day functions to trusted lieutenants, he was every bit the warrior-king who ruled on disagreements; presided over social events, including officiating at marriages; ruled on matters of the community's laws; and meted out punishments. While he could be imperious and harsh, he was also gentle and loving, spending long hours walking among his people offering words of encouragement and tending to the sick. Most called him "Father," though he took no offense when some simply referred to him as David. Nor was there a requirement that his people believe in any particular religious credo, so in addition to Christians, there was a sprinkling of residents of other faiths, as well as agnostics and atheists.

There was another side to Grale, however. His people referred to his "dark moods," when he would sit on his throne for hours, even days, hardly moving, or even talking, except to himself or to lash out over small or imagined issues. Often during these periods, he would roam his subterranean world, or the streets above at night, killing — murdering, Knight reminded himself — men and even women he believed were evil and inhabited by demons.

The vigilante killings rankled Knight as a man and as a defense attorney. He had a hard time stomaching Grale's self-appointed position as judge, jury, and lord high executioner, but he said nothing, knowing it would do no good. Although Grale seemed to enjoy his conversations with Knight and they'd spent hours discussing philosophy, the law, and world events, he didn't come to him for advice on how to rule his dark world.

Indeed, the only man who seemed to have the king's ear was Brother James, a small, gnomish man who had apparently once been an electrical engineer and was responsible for many of the "civilized" attributes of the kingdom. He had once had a family and a good job, but something — no one knew quite what — had caused him to lose both, and he'd found his way to the Mole People, among whom his technical abilities, despite his bitter personality, had made him welcome.

When Grale was in one of his moods, James would often be seen standing behind the throne, bent over and talking in a low voice, a smirk on his face. Whatever it was he said, it often seemed to push Grale farther into the dark recesses of his mind, and only a "hunting trip" would bring him out of it.

The little man had few friends and he didn't bother to hide his dislike for Knight, whom he seemed to see as a competitor for Grale's favor. The women in the community were known to avoid him and his leering face and searching eyes. But Grale seemed not to notice and did nothing when others complained about him, other than to point out that they owed their light and heat to James.

Despite his distaste for Grale's vigilante efforts, Knight generally liked the man and felt a great debt to him. In all he spent six months with the Mole People, six months that sobered him up to the point where he no longer wanted a drink. He'd been assigned to the "Dumpster diving" crews, something that before meeting Grale would have appalled him. Yet it gave him a sense of purpose to bring something of value back to the odd community that had taken him in. He felt at home.

So he had been dismayed when one night, Grale summoned him to his throne and announced, "My brother, it is time for you to leave us."

"Why? Have I done something wrong?" Knight asked.

Smiling, Grale shook his head. "No, my brother, but it is time. Some of these people will never leave; they are incapable of dealing with the outside world. But others, like our friend Warren Bennett, who runs the newsstand in front of the courts building and lives in a small apartment, and you — now that you've rid your body of the poisons you poured into it and have discovered what it means to be part of a community — have a life on the outside they need to follow. And, in truth, I have another reason."

Grale explained that he wanted Knight to resume his law practice. "From time to time, my people need the services of an attorney, and it would be very helpful if I could count on you."

Although the idea frightened him, Knight also felt something awaken in him. He knew that Grale was right. His life was on the outside, and if he could repay his friend by resuming his career, he would do it.

Grale had even given him enough money to rent his small office on the Lower East Side, as well as a tiny apartment. Knight was humbled by the gesture, knowing how hard the Mole People worked to come up with that kind of money, and from the day he hung his shingle again, he'd refused to take any more funds from them.

It hadn't been easy. A one-man law office didn't bring in much to spare, and there'd been days when he'd vaguely contemplated going out for a drink, especially when his former receptionist, Danielle, had suggested it one night. But he recalled that night four years earlier when he'd thought about jumping in front of a subway train and the thought of alcohol made him nauseous.

■ ■ ■ ■

As he and his two escorts now approached Grale's lair, he was experiencing trepidation in light of what he was planning to do. This was more than getting one of the Mole People out of jail or representing them for some petty crime like vagrancy or trespassing.

When his former employer told him his new client's name was Nadya Malovo, it only vaguely rang a bell, and not in the context of Grale. When he read her file and the affadavits placed there by the New York DAO, he assumed he'd heard her name in news accounts of her alleged criminal activities. None of which would have caused him to contact Dirty Warren at his newsstand in front of the Criminal Courts Building.

No, Knight's visit to Dirty Warren was inspired by Malovo herself, when she mentioned having worked for Andrew Kane, the former mayoral candidate who'd somehow been embroiled in criminal plots and terrorism. Once the darling of his party and the media, both of which had seen him as presidential material, Kane was apparently more of a Lex Luthor, a criminal mastermind, than a John F. Kennedy.

When Knight lived among the Mole People, it was well-known that Grale considered Kane to be a mortal enemy and a demon of the first degree. He had devoted himself to tracking the man, waiting for an opportunity to strike. And although Knight had not seen Grale in several years, the Mole People grapevine — mostly in the form of Dirty Warren — had informed him that his friend had indeed captured Kane and kept him a prisoner, though to what end, no one seemed to know.

Knight didn't know if it would be important to Grale that his client, a vicious terrorist who was now working with the feds in the hope of being placed in the witness protection program, had talked to him about working for Kane. But he thought it was worth telling Dirty Warren and was only a little surprised when the news vendor called on him at his office and said that Grale wanted to talk to him in person.

On his way to meet his guides, Knight had wrestled with what he was doing. One issue was the fifty-thousand-dollar retainer check he'd been handed to take on Malovo's case. He'd immediately paid his bills and rehired Danielle, even paying her for the times when she'd volunteered. The money was a godsend and he wished he could keep it. But he figured he was now going to have to give it back, maybe even repay what he'd spent except for the few hours he'd worked on the case, and then tell his employer that he needed to retain another lawyer.

But more than that troubled him. By talking to Grale about his work for Malovo and the conversations he had with her, he was betraying the attorney-client privilege and his oath as a defense attorney. It didn't matter that she was without a doubt a cold-blooded killer; she had the absolute right to legal representation.

He argued with himself that there was no reason to discuss her with Grale. She merely mentioned that she regretted working for Kane. Maybe she was trying to turn over a new leaf and was just an attractive woman who had been used by men all of her life for their own evil ends. The same ethics that had caused him to give up his practice in the first place now nagged at him.

Still, he felt compelled to let Grale know that he was working for her. He owed it to the man who had given him his life back. He would find a way to assuage his conscience later.

As he had once before, Knight felt, rather than saw, the moment he stepped into the inner sanctum of the Mole People. "Welcome . . . fuck you oh boy . . . home," Dirty Warren said, patting him on the back. "We're to take you straightaway to David. . . . One word of caution: he is edgy these days and his moods are darker and last longer. He's also got a bad cough but won't go see a doctor; maybe you can talk him into it."

Approaching Grale's platform, Knight could see his friend slumped in his chair, but someone else was missing. "Where's Brother James?" he whispered.

"Gone," Dirty Warren spat. "He was caught stealing from the treasury, and there's always been . . . whoop whoop . . . his leering at the women. David kicked him out and told him never to return on penalty of death."

"Good riddance," Knight said. "I never did like that guy."

"No one did," Dirty Warren said. "Bastard."

Drawing closer to Grale, Knight could see that the years had not been kind. His long hair was streaked with gray and the lines in his ashen face were deeper. The sleeves of his robe had been pulled up, revealing how thin he was, the muscles standing out against the pallid skin like ropes. He coughed into his hand, a deep, wet bark, as they walked up.

"You should get that cough checked out," Knight said.

Grale turned his head slowly to look at him. "God is my physician."

"Which medical school?" Knight shot back. He heard Dirty Warren suck in his breath in shock.

But Grale laughed. "I see you haven't lost your sense of humor, brother. That is good. We could do with a little more laughter around here, couldn't we, Warren?"

"Hell . . . whoop whoop . . . yeah," the news vendor replied. "I'll leave you two alone until . . . oh boy my ass . . . you need me to take Bruce home."

"Thank you, Warren, we won't be long," Grale replied, and then turned to Knight. "I hear you have a new client?"

Knight nodded. "Yes, Nadya Malovo. She is —"

Grale held up a hand. "I know all about that evil woman. It is fortunate that you were picked to be her attorney."

"Dumb luck, I guess," Knight replied.

Grale's eyes blazed angrily for a moment, but then he nodded. "As I told you once, it wasn't dumb luck but divine intervention. I had heard that she was in town again."

"She's working for the feds to root out

204

some terrorist sleeper cells," Knight said, surprised at how easy it was to betray his client.

"So she says," Grale said scathingly. "I believe there is more to it than that. But come, tell us everything she said and did."

Knight recounted what he'd seen in her files, as well as what she told him in their interview. When he got to her request for him to meet with her cousin, Grale laughed.

"Boris Kazanov is no cousin of Nadya Malovo," he said. "He's a brutal killer, including of women and children, who he particularly likes to torture first. A dangerous demon I have been trying to find for years. Have you arranged this meeting?"

"Yes, two nights from now," Knight replied. "On the boardwalk at Coney Island. Should I not go?"

"Oh, no," Grale said. "You should definitely go. But I will be there, too."

Knight swallowed hard. He didn't like the sound of Grale's voice. He almost forgot to tell him what Malovo had said about working with Kane, but then remembered.

At the mention of Kane, Grale reached down and picked up the end of a dog leash, which he yanked hard. There was a yelp and a man — at least he seemed to be a man, though he crawled on all fours and simpered

205

like a whipped cur — appeared from the other side of Grale's throne. His clothes were in tatters, his long blond hair matted and filthy; the leash was attached to a collar around his neck. But the true horror was that when he looked up, his face was a mass of scar tissue through which two blue eyes burned with madness and hatred.

"Meet Andrew Kane," Grale said. "I'm afraid that a face transplant he once received to avoid detection by the authorities has fallen into disrepair without the antirejection drugs it requires."

Grale gave the leash another yank, eliciting a doglike snarl and then insane gibbering from Kane. "You hear that, Andy? Apparently your old friend Nadya has not forgotten you."

14

Karp heard the door to the private elevator
slide open in the anteroom adjoining his office and a woman's laugh. The elevator led
to a secure private entrance on the Hogan
Place side of the Criminal Courts Building
and was used only by judges, the district attorney, and special visitors. Such was the
case this morning.

There was a knock on the door. "Come
in," he said as he stood up behind the
enormous mahogany desk that had once
belonged to Frank Garrahy.

The woman laughed again, and he smiled.
It's good these two found each other, he
thought as the door opened. His mind must
have been easy to read as the woman, who
entered first, saw his expression and
blushed; for that matter, so did the man
who followed her in.

"Hello, Butch," Espey Jaxon said. "We
were discussing our mutual friend Nadya

Malovo."

"Uh-huh, I could tell. Nadya makes me laugh, too," Karp replied with a wink. "Marshal Jen Capers, always a delight to see you."

"You too, Mr. Karp," Capers replied, blushing deeper.

It had been a week since the terrorist attack on the ferry and several days since Jaxon and Capers had dropped by the loft for dinner with Karp, Marlene, Lucy, and Ned, while the twins were off visiting friends overnight. By unspoken agreement, they'd kept it primarily a social occasion and avoided talking much about the attack or Malovo's involvement, though Karp had been briefed on the situation beforehand.

This morning's appearance was to bring him up to date as part of the agreement that kept Malovo in federal custody and out of his reach for prosecution on the New York charges. It galled him that a vicious killer was escaping justice, and was even being offered a new life, in exchange for her exposing other vicious killers. He was only partly appeased that hundreds, even thousands, of innocent lives might be saved by the arrangement.

He didn't trust that Malovo was just looking for a new start in life. This feeling was echoed by his visitors after they filled him in on the latest. "She has infiltrated several more cells," Jaxon said. "Some are only in the talking stages, others at the beginning. I think the public would be shocked, if not completely terrorized, to know how much homegrown terrorism exists just in the five boroughs."

"So what are your plans to take these guys down?" Karp asked.

"If they get beyond the planning stage, we'll act," Jaxon replied. "But we're hoping that by watching and letting them think they're safe, we'll get a better understanding of how organized — or not — they are, and maybe who's directing them."

"Anything sound imminent?" Karp asked.

Jaxon shook his head. "We're checking out a supposed mosque in the Bronx that Malovo says is in the early stages of setting up as a bomb-making factory. Other than that there's just some nebulous rumors of 'something big' going down, apparently this fall and planned for Manhattan, but our girl hasn't been able to pinpoint anything more."

"You think she's leading you on?"

Jaxon shrugged. "Yes. Jennifer — Marshal Capers and I both think she's up to more than trying to spend her days in a nice house with a white picket fence. We're keeping tabs on her as best we can. If she messes up, the deal is off."

"And so is our deal," Karp said. "If we get our hands on her, you feds are not getting her back."

"Wouldn't bother me any," Capers said. "Oh, almost forgot, she's got herself a new lawyer who's supposed to be handling her state cases. His name is Bruce Knight."

Karp furrowed his brow and drummed his fingers on his desk for a moment. "Bruce Knight? Name's familiar . . . yeah, I remember him. Good young attorney, used to work for one of the hotshot boutique firms; gave my guys fits in court, but haven't heard of him in quite a while."

"Well, I'm guessing you will soon," Capers said. "Not sure how he fits into her plans though."

"I think this is a case of giving her enough rope to hang herself," Jaxon added. "And in the meantime, she can keep giving up other bad guys. Right, marshal?"

Capers nodded but then frowned. "Call this intuition, or maybe it's just something I'm picking up from little things she says, but whatever devious plan she's working on, I think it would involve you. She doesn't come right out and say it, but she hates you with a passion."

"There's a long line of haters out there, lots I don't even know," Karp replied. "But I'm sure you'll keep an eye on her for me."

"Like a hawk," Capers replied.

Jaxon stood and was joined by Capers. "We need to be rolling," Jaxon said. "And I know you're busy. You have that double-homicide trial coming up . . . the Columbia University Slasher case."

"That's correct, my friend," Karp said. "We also have the Ellis trial's jury selection starting today. I'll be glad when that one's over."

"No doubt," Jaxon replied. "Funny how, Christian or Muslim, these supposed spiritual leaders never seem to pay for getting others to do their dirty work."

The couple had only just closed the door behind them when the intercom on Karp's telephone buzzed, followed by the sugary-sweet voice of his receptionist, Darla Milquetost. "Misters Guma and Katz to see you," she purred.

Karp rolled his eyes. *It must be spring,* he thought. *Love is in the air, and not just Jaxon and Capers.* Milquetost, a widow closer to sixty than fifty, and his longtime colleague and friend Ray Guma, a notorious office

211

lothario in his younger days, were also an item, and his appearance in the reception area always brought out the honey in Darla. He pressed the button on his intercom. "Send them in, please."

The door opened a moment later and Guma, followed by Kenny Katz, entered. They were both nearly breathless with whatever news they were bringing, which was surprising to see in Guma, who, while passionate in the courtroom, was an old hand and not given to excitement over a momentarily titillating tale du jour. He was also a cancer survivor, an ordeal that had turned his curly black hair white almost overnight, emaciated his once-muscular physique, and cut deep lines into his face. Some days it looked like it was all he could do to get out of bed, much less make it to work.

"Shouldn't you two be headed to court?" Karp asked. "Or am I wrong to think that jury selection in the Ellis case begins in" — he looked at his watch — "twenty minutes?"

"You'll never believe what just happened," Katz said in reply.

Karp arched an eyebrow. Although thirty years younger than Guma, Katz was no wet-behind-the-ears excitable puppy either. He'd served with the army overseas in Iraq and Afghanistan, where he engaged in combat, was wounded, and received the Purple Heart. He had also been awarded several medals for heroism. To say he was calm under fire was an understatement, which was part of why Karp thought his protégé might someday be the one sitting behind the mahogany desk. "Try me," he said.

"Belinda King just called," Katz replied. "Apparently, David Ellis has hired her to represent him. King says he wants to give us a statement on the record and then plead guilty."

"I know Belinda; fiery redhead and a tough, hard-nosed attorney. Rolling over can't be her idea," Karp said. He furrowed his brow. "Did she say what he's willing to plead to? Are they asking for a lesser plea?"

"That's the strange part," Guma answered. "I could tell she wasn't pleased, but she says he's going to plead as charged to reckless manslaughter."

"What about his wife?" Karp asked. "Where's she in all of this?"

The two ADAs shrugged simultaneously. "Apparently King was just hired, and she said she didn't know much about what brought this on or what he wants to say in his Q & A statement to us," Katz said. "Or what Nonie Ellis is doing; she's only representing David."

"What about jury selection?"

"I spoke to the judge, and he's agreed to delay until after lunch while we see what this is really all about," Guma replied.

"Good. So when's this supposed to go down?" Karp asked.

"Now," Guma replied. "We were just dropping by to let you in on it, and now we're going to meet them curbside to escort them up to my office."

Karp rose out of his chair. "I was just about to get a hot dog and a knish for an early lunch from my favorite street-side vendor," he said. "I'll go down with you."

Exiting the Criminal Courts Building a few minutes later, Karp and his colleagues were spotted by Westlund and the group of protesters who'd arrived for the first day of the Ellis trial and taken a position across Centre Street, as well as the television crews on the scene.

"Repent, Karp!" Westlund, who was standing on a milk crate, shouted into a megaphone. "Stop your minions from carrying out this unholy travesty and attack on religious freedom. Or face the wrath of the Lord!"

"So now we're minions?" Guma said with

214

a chuckle.

Across the street, Westlund thundered, "Fear God and give Him glory, because the hour of His judgment has come! Worship Him who made the heavens, the earth, the sea, and the springs of water!"

Karp walked up to the hot dog stand and greeted the vendor, who asked, "The usual, Mr. DA?"

"Yeah, with mustard in the middle of the knish, and mustard and kraut on the dog; you got it," Karp replied.

"Boy, that guy Westlund gives me the creeps," Katz said. "He's going to push some nut's button someday and somebody's going to get hurt. . . . Hey, isn't that Edward Treacher setting up shop next to Westlund?"

Karp turned to see what he was talking about. "That's him," he said. "Now, this should be interesting."

Treacher was another of the local street denizens who hung out around the court-house and the park across the street. He was a former college English professor who, legend had it, took too much LSD back in the 1960s. Treacher wound up as an itiner-ant sidewalk preacher known for shouting biblical quotations, which he combined with panhandling. Tall, thin, and dressed in patched and threadbare clothing, he even resembled an ancient desert prophet with his long, frizzy gray hair and wildly rolling eyes, though Karp knew that much of his sometimes incoherent ramblings was an act and he was perfectly capable of holding an intelligent conversation when he wanted.

As Westlund ranted and stirred up his followers, who shouted at Karp, Guma, and Katz, Treacher calmly placed a small milk crate just outside the circle of protesters and climbed aboard with his own megaphone. He then waited for Westlund to speak.

" 'Cursed is the one who trusts in man,' " Westlund shouted, " 'who depends on flesh for his strength and whose heart turns away from the Lord!' "

Treacher picked up his own megaphone, turned up the volume, and shouted back. "That would be in Revelation. Not bad . . . for a false prophet. And you know what Zechariah had to say about false prophets: 'If a man still prophesies, his parents, father and mother, shall say to him, "You shall not live, because you have spoken a lie in the name of the Lord." When he prophesies, his parents, father and mother, shall thrust him through.' "

Westlund and his followers turned to Treacher with frowns on their faces. Some booed and shouted for him to go elsewhere. He simply smiled at them and shook a large soda cup with the word "tips" written in black marker on the side.

Turning to the television cameras and crews that had flocked to the area, Westlund held up a hand. *" 'And these signs will accompany those who believe: In my name they will drive out demons; they will speak in new tongues; they will pick up snakes with their hands; and when they drink deadly poison, it will not hurt them at all; they will place their hands on sick people, and they will get well!' "*

Westlund's followers were working themselves into a frenzy. One woman suddenly screamed something incomprehensible and fell to the sidewalk, where she writhed.

Treacher looked amused, as did a gathering crowd of tourists and other pedestrians. "I need to get me one of those," he shouted into his megaphone. "How much do you pay her? I do like the use of Mark 16:17–18; I've found it very handy for lunch money."

The crowd laughed. Treacher bowed and shook his cup at them, blessing those who contributed.

Scowling, Westlund turned to yell across the street at Karp.

" 'For our struggle is not against flesh and

blood, but against the rulers, against the authorities, against the powers of this dark world, and against the spiritual forces of evil in the heavenly realms.' "

Treacher looked over at Karp and waved. "Hello, Mr. Karp. That was Ephesians 6 . . . always good when you need something for railing against the Man. I think a good comeback would be Matthew 5:11: *'Blessed are you when people insult you, persecute you and falsely say all kinds of evil against you because of me.'* I used that the last time I had to go to court for trespassing."

Karp waved back. "I do believe that Westlund has more than met his match," he said in a low voice to Guma and Katz, who both laughed.

"Oops, looks like our appointment has arrived," Katz said, pointing to a yellow cab that had pulled up to the curb.

Accompanied by a redheaded woman dressed in a business suit, David Ellis emerged from the cab. Across the street, Westlund spotted him and pointed as he yelled into the megaphone. " *'The fool says in his heart, "There is no God." They are corrupt, their deeds are vile.'* "

Katz and Guma started walking toward Ellis. Suddenly, the crowd around Westlund surged into the street, bringing traffic to a

218

screeching halt. Several police officers assigned to the courts building as well as traffic cops rushed out to try to herd them back.

One protester, however, avoided the cars and the officers and continued walking toward where Ellis stood, a confused look on his face, with his attorney. Karp noticed the protester, too, a middle-aged woman with her hair poorly dyed to a burnt orange; in fact, he recognized her from earlier protests. There was something about her face that drew his attention; her lips were drawn up into a snarl, and her eyes blazed with anger and madness. When he noticed that she kept her right hand in her large purse, the alarm bells went off in his head, and he started to move toward Ellis and his colleagues.

"Ray, Kenny!" he yelled as he started to run.

Katz turned toward him with a confused smile as he saw his boss point past him toward the street. He looked around and sensed the danger as well. But it was too late.

As the woman came around the back end of a taxi, she pulled a revolver from her purse. *"Judas!"* she screamed as she lifted the gun and fired twice into David Ellis's chest.

Ellis fell back into the arms of his attorney and they both crumpled to the ground. The woman then swung around and pointed the gun at Guma, but even as she pulled the trigger, Katz leaped and knocked Guma aside, taking the bullet himself.

Panting, her eyes rolling wildly, she aimed again at Guma, who had been knocked to his knees. Karp yelled, *"No!"*

It was enough to distract the woman, who instead pointed the gun at Karp. He raised his hands. "You don't have to do this," he said.

"Evil, you are evil!" the woman cried out.

"Who are you?" Karp replied. "What's your name?"

The question seemed to confuse the woman. "Kathryn . . . Kathryn Boole," she said after a moment, though she kept the gun aimed at Karp's chest.

"Kathryn, please, hand me the gun," Karp said, holding out his hand. "There's been enough bloodshed for one day."

Boole looked at the weapon in her hand as if she wondered how it got there. She started to lower the gun but then Westlund shouted from across the street. *" 'Blessed are they which are persecuted for righteousness' sake; for theirs is the kingdom of heaven!' "*

The woman looked back at the preacher and nodded. The gun came up and she began to pull the trigger even as Karp lunged for her.

There was a gunshot, but Karp didn't feel anything as he knocked the woman to the ground. He expected her to struggle, but she didn't move, so he raised himself.

Something warm, wet, and sticky was on his face; he wiped at it and his hand came away covered in blood. But he quickly realized it wasn't his. Kathryn Boole, however, lay gasping from a bullet wound in her chest and as he watched, she took one last breath and died.

"Who fired that shot?" he demanded as he picked himself up.

"Me," said a man's voice from near the taxi.

Karp looked over and saw one of Westlund's bodyguards place a handgun on the hood of the taxi and raise his hands as two police officers ran up and cuffed him. "It was you or her," the bodyguard said. "I'm licensed to carry in the city."

Turning away from the man, Karp quickly ran over to where Katz was sitting up on the pavement, held by Guma. He was bleeding from the shoulder but nodded toward the taxi. "I'll be okay," he said. "Check on Ellis."

Karp walked quickly over to where Belinda King was trying to apply pressure to the wounds in Ellis's chest. A woman he realized was Nonie Ellis rushed past him and knelt at her husband's side.

"David!" she cried.

David Ellis frowned. "Why?"

Nonie looked confused. "Why what?"

"Why are you Westlund's lover?"

"What? Oh no, David, I was never . . . ," Nonie cried.

"But I thought . . . ," he whispered.

"No, sweetheart, he's just a minister. Is that why you didn't come home last night?"

David nodded. "I walked around until it was time to come to court. I was going to plead guilty. I *am* guilty for Micah's death."

Nonie's face turned pale. Tears fell from her cheeks. "No. I'm the one who placed my trust in the wrong man. I'm sorry, David, I love you. Please don't leave me . . ."

But for the second time that morning, it was too late. David Ellis was dead.

15

Heedless of the rats that scurried to get out of his way, David Grale swept through the sewer tunnel cursing the art world. He'd been on his way to Coney Island when he received word that the guardians at one of the entrances had intercepted two graffiti artists. Normally, he would have let his men handle the trespassers — usually by frightening the wits out of them — but this was the closest to the kingdom that they'd penetrated and he wanted to question them himself.

He wished that the current fad would quickly run its course. Word of the underground artwork had spread — helped by an article with color photographs in *The New Yorker* magazine — and his world was suddenly popular with artists, their fans, and the media. One of New York's eccentric high-society mavens had even thrown a black-tie party, complete with catering and champagne, at the "opening" of a show by one of the hot young spray-painters beneath Grand Central Terminal. What had once been a haven for society's castoffs and rodents, and a playground for teenagers, was being invaded, keeping the guardians busier than they'd ever been.

And they're getting closer. Grale seethed as he rushed along in the near dark. The fact that two had made it through the warren of tunnels to one of the main entrances was alarming.

Arriving at a dimly lit intersection of the tunnels, he found his two men guarding the prisoners, who were seated on the ground with their hands tied behind their backs. They looked up in fear as he stalked up to them.

"What have we got here, Harvey?" he growled, speaking to the older of the two guardians.

"Artists," Harvey said scathingly before a coughing spell interrupted him. When it stopped, he added, "Meet Adrian and Chad."

"What are you doing here?" Grale snarled at the flinching prisoners.

"Just looking for a place to paint, bro," said the one identified as Adrian, nodding at the spray-paint cans and lantern lying on the tunnel floor. "It's a free country, isn't it?"

Grale bent over to look more closely at their faces. They were both young, late twenties, with long hair, tie-dyed shirts, and worn jeans.

"No, it's not a free country, not here," he replied. "How did you get to this place?"

"We just started looking for a wall to work on," Chad replied. "And we got lost."

"You are not welcome here," Grale warned them.

"Where is here?" Adrian asked.

"The third circle of hell," Grale said. "And if you return, you will never leave again. Am I clear?"

Both men's eyes widened with fear and they nodded. "We won't," they promised.

Grale turned to his younger guard. "Brother Louis, please escort these two back to where they can find their way out," he said. "And if they give you any trouble . . . shoot them."

"With pleasure," Louis said. "Okay, you two, up and out of here. Let me see your wrists so I can untie you."

When the guardian and his prisoners were gone, Harvey turned to Grale. "That's the farthest any of these so-called artists have made it," he said. "I don't like it. Maybe we need to crack down a little harder."

"I don't like it either, brother, but what would you have us do? Do we start killing kids because they want to spray-paint on a subway tunnel?" Grale asked. "But you're right, we need to do something or find a new home." He cocked his head to the side as if some new thought troubled him, then shrugged. "We'll talk later, but I've got to go."

Pulling the hood of his robe over his head, Grale hurried away. "Artists," he growled.

Bruce Knight looked up at the teenage vendor behind the counter at the Nathan's Famous hot dog stand at Coney Island.

"Okay, buddy, what will it be?" asked the vendor.

"Um, I'll have a regular dog and an order of cheese fries," Knight replied.

A few minutes later, he walked away from Nathan's and headed for the boardwalk that ran along Brighton Beach. He noticed two large, tough-looking men lounging against a wall, wearing identical black leather coats. Aware that they'd fallen in behind him, he kept walking as he'd been told when he had called the number his former employer had sent him to arrange a meeting with Nadya Malovo's faux cousin, Boris Kazanov. "He'll tell you where and when. Just listen to what he has to say and let Nadya know," he was told.

For the millionth time, Knight second-guessed himself for telling Grale about Malovo. He'd orginally thought that he would inform Grale that she was in town, working for the feds, and had mentioned Kane, and then remove himself as her attorney.

But Grale had other ideas. "I cannot force you to stay on as her attorney or report on what she says," he said, "but you've seen the evidence against her; you know she has committed great evil and it is in her to do more. I can't do anything about her at the moment, but ridding the world of Kazanov would be a blow for righteousness."

Grale had not told him what he had planned for Kazanov, but he was sure it wouldn't be pleasant. *It has to be better than what he's done to Kane,* he thought, shuddering at the image of the insane former mayoral candidate. However, now he wasn't sure who would win a confrontation between Kazanov, his henchmen, and Grale, especially after seeing the size and demeanor of the men who were following him. He suspected that if Grale lost, Kazanov wouldn't think too kindly of the man who set him up.

Although he had been aware of Grale's vigilante activities when he lived with the Mole People, Knight had never committed any illegal acts, much less murder. He knew that others went with Grale on some of his hunting forays, but he'd never been asked to participate. Until now.

"I understand that this form of justice isn't in you," Grale said. "But perhaps if I recount some of his past deeds, you'll feel better when he is gone." His friend had then gone on to describe several of the brutal, sadistic murders allegedly committed by the vicious Russian hit man until Knight was sick to his stomach and agreed to go ahead with the meeting. "But that's as far as I'll go and —" he began to say.

Grale had interrupted with a smile, his eyes bright with anticipation of the meeting. "I wouldn't ask you to do more, brother," he said. "This is between me and one of the Evil One's minions."

When Knight called the number he'd been given by Malovo, a man with a heavily accented Russian voice answered, *"Da?"*

Knight responded as he had been instructed. "Nadya Malovo wishes to send her greetings to her cousin Boris," he said.

There was a moment's hesitation on the

other end of the line and then another voice — this one deeper, rougher, and somehow more malevolent — spoke. "Who are you?" he asked gruffly.

"Um, I'm Nadya's attorney, am I speaking to Boris?" he'd replied.

Instead of answering, the man had given him an order. "In two nights, go to Nathan's in Coney Island," he'd said. "Buy a hot dog and fries and then walk down the boardwalk toward Coney Island Avenue. You will see two men, my men, but do not be alarmed. They will follow you . . . for your protection." Knight could have sworn that the man chuckled when he said those last few words, then added, "The bitch's 'cousin' will contact you when he is sure you haven't been followed."

"Okay, I —" Knight started to reply.

"No more talk," the man snarled. "And, Mr. Attorney . . ."

"Yes?"

"If this is a trick, your client's cousin will slit you open like a hog and eat your liver as you watch." Then the phone went dead.

The thought of being slit open and cannibalized was foremost in his mind as he approached a particularly dark area of the boardwalk where the lights on the path seemed to have been removed. Knight remembered how he had once read that the Brighton Beach area was also known as Little Odessa for its large number of Russian immigrants. The article had also noted that it was the New York home of the Russian Mafia, which it claimed was more violent than the worst street gang.

As he moved into the dark area of the boardwalk, Knight noticed that although it was a pleasant night for early spring, just a little cool with a slight ocean breeze, there were no strolling couples, or joggers, or anyone else coming toward him. Glancing behind, he could not see anyone following beyond the two hulking figures of Kazanov's men. He was alone.

Suddenly, a dark shadow separated itself from the stone wall on his left. A man larger than either of the two behind him stood in front, blocking his way. He could just make out the man's scarred and brutal face in the light of the half moon that had risen out to sea; his nose looked like a misshapen potato, bright feral eyes gleamed beneath heavy brows, and his breath stank when he opened his mouth to speak.

"Mr. Attorney," the man sneered. "What word do you bring me from my 'cousin' Nadya?"

"I . . . I . . . ," Knight stammered, suddenly weak in the knees. He'd never felt such a palpable presence of evil before and his only thought was to escape. *Where's Grale? Why am I alone?* His terror threatened to consume him.

" 'I . . . I . . . I . . . ,' " Kazanov mimicked. "Come, little mouse, before the cat swallows you or you piss in your pants, what did she say? Or do I have to cut the words out of your mouth?" As he spoke, the Russian pulled a long, wicked-looking straight razor from his coat.

Somehow, Knight managed to squeak out the words he'd been told to say. "The Halloween party this year will be in the Village. And your cousin hopes you will bring the family."

Kazanov furrowed his brow and then laughed loudly but without humor. "Tell my cousin that we will be happy to attend," he said. "However, we will need assurances that our traveling expenses will be covered. Do you understand?"

Knight nodded. "Yes, I'll tell her and —"

Out of the gloom behind Kazanov's men, a voice spoke. "Booger hong-ree," it said. " 'Pare some change, misters?"

Kazanov snarled. "Beat it, you piece of crap."

"By St. Peter, this *poproshika* smells like

231

rotting meat," one of the men gasped as he and his comrade turned to face the large shadow that had materialized behind them. "Get away, scum."

In spite of his fear, Knight smiled slightly and even welcomed the stench of the Walking Booger, though he wondered what one man — even one as large as this one — could do against three. He quickly learned when with surprising speed, Booger stepped toward one of Kazanov's men and with one hand around his throat, lifted him off the ground like he was a bag of cotton. He then dropped the man to the boardwalk, where he lay choking and clawing at air, his larynx having been crushed by the immense hand of Booger.

The second of Kazanov's men moved to attack Booger but suddenly an arrow appeared in his back, and then another and another. He too fell to the boardwalk; he shuddered once and died in a pool of blood.

"You set me up! You die," Kazanov growled, and began to move toward Knight with his razor. But Knight felt himself lifted off his feet and tossed to the sand beyond the boardwalk.

It was now Kazanov facing off with Booger, who was as large as the Russian and fifty pounds heavier. But Booger had no intention of engaging him. Instead, he left that fight for the man who jumped to the boardwalk from behind the wall.

"Kazanov, your evil is at an end!" David Grale shouted.

The Russian whirled to face the new threat. "So, I will have to kill three now," he spat.

"You won't be killing anyone," Grale replied. "And don't worry about my friends, I am all that is needed to send your soul to hell, from whence it came."

"I will slit your throat and pull your beating heart from it, ghoul!" Kazanov screamed, and lunged at Grale, slashing with his razor.

Lying in terror on the sand, at first Knight wondered why Booger merely watched his friend being attacked by the much larger man. But then he was reminded of his own feeble attempts to ward off Grale when they first met.

The Russian found himself cutting at air as his opponent moved easily beyond his reach. Ducking and weaving, Grale moved in quickly, slashing with his own crescent-shaped blade. He cut — an arm, a leg, across the big man's face — before Kazanov could react except to grunt in pain.

After several minutes of this, Kazanov

stood panting, weaving slightly, now holding his razor as if to ward off another attack. "I will pay you beyond your wildest dreams to go," he offered.

"My wildest dreams are to see you and your kind gone from the world," Grale said. "In case you are wondering, you are experiencing what the Chinese call death by a thousand cuts. Your evil blood is draining from your body, and the more you exert yourself, the faster the Reaper approaches and the time of your returning to your master arrives."

Kazanov stumbled a bit forward, then caught himself. He seemed spent, his arm with the razor dropping to his side. He stumbled a bit more toward Grale, as if on his last legs, but it was a trick. Fiercely, he slashed at the robed opponent in front of him. "Die, you bastard!" he screamed.

The move nearly caught Grale as the razor cut through a sleeve of his robe. But it was not fast enough. The attack threw Kazanov's balance off and he fell to his knees.

As quick as a panther, Grale jumped behind him and, with one swift movement, cut the killer's throat from ear to ear. Kazanov dropped his razor and his hands went to his neck as though he could stop the blood that spurted from his arteries and veins. There was a gurgling sound as blood poured down his windpipe, and then he collapsed, his body twitching.

Grale stood for a moment over his opponent before bending over and wiping his blade on Kazanov's coat. Standing back up, he announced, "Thus another evil leaves the world."

Looking over at Knight, who was slowly picking himself up, he smiled, his teeth gleaming in the moonlight. "Are you okay?" he inquired.

Knight shook his head and then leaned over and retched. When he finished, he looked again at Kazanov and then Grale. "This was revenge, not justice."

Grale looked back for a moment and then nodded. "You're right," he said. "But I'll leave the niceties of bringing evil men into courts, trying them, sending them to prison, and then letting them out again a few years later to brutalize and butcher more innocent people to the legal system." He then turned to Booger, who'd stood motionless the whole time. "Ready to go, my friend?" he asked.

The giant nodded. "Booger hong-ree."

Grale smiled. "So am I. What do you say we go get a hot dog at Nathan's?"

Booger smiled. "Yum, 'ot dog and fries."

"Sure, a hot dog and fries. You deserve it. Going to join us, Bruce?" Grale asked. "My treat."

Knight looked up at the stars and then shook his head. "No. I seem to have lost my appetite. I'm just going to go home."

"Sweet dreams," Grale replied. Then he and Booger walked off toward the bright lights of Coney Island.

16

"Taking Gilgamesh out for a walk, Babe," Marlene called out over her shoulder as her 150-pound presa canario guard dog bounded around her legs like a puppy. When Karp didn't answer, she turned around to where he was sitting on the couch in the living room of their loft, apparently lost in thought. "Butch?"

Karp looked up suddenly as if he'd been dreaming. "What?"

"Dog. Walk," Marlene replied, holding up a leash.

"Oh, uh, no, thanks," he said absently, then pointed at the papers on the coffee table in front of him. "I want to look these over again."

Marlene sighed inwardly. She knew he was referring to the detective investigative reports, known as DD-5s, from the murder of David Ellis, which included the shooting of ADA Kenny Katz and subsequent killing of the shooter, Kathryn Boole, by one of the Reverend C. G. Westlund's bodyguards, Frank Bernsen.

What a week it had been for the media. First there were the shootings in front of the courthouse, which had been followed by a whirlwind of stories and editorials, some of which had even blamed her husband's insistence that the Ellises be tried for fostering the environment that pushed Kathryn Boole over the edge. Of course, Westlund had picked up on the theme and run with it.

The shootings had been followed two days later by the bizarre killings of a notorious Russian hit man, Boris Kazanov, and two of his known associates on the boardwalk along Brighton Beach. According to the medical examiner's report, Kazanov had been cut dozens of times, none of them fatal, "but enough to cause the victim to lose a significant amount of blood while still living." The fatal wound had nearly severed his head.

If that hadn't been weird enough, one of the other victims — a man with a rap sheet as long as he was tall — had suffered a broken neck and crushed larynx. The coroner's report had noted bruising on the victim's neck, "consistent with finger and thumb marks left by a human hand . . . a very large human hand." And, perhaps the oddest death of the three, the last victim had been pierced by three arrows, "any one of which would have been fatal," according to the ME.

Curious, Marlene had called Butch's cousin Ivgeny Karchovski, a Russian gangster living in Brooklyn's Brighton Beach, to ask if he might know something about the murders that the newspapers weren't reporting. Although involved in illegal activites, especially smuggling Eastern Bloc and Russian immigrants into the country and bootleg caviar and furs, Karchovski did not deal in drugs, weapons, or prostitution, which made him okay in her book. He carried on his business quietly and without bloodshed unless threatened, at which point the former Russian Army colonel could be quite ruthless with his competitors.

"If it was a gang hit, no one is taking responsibility for it," Ivgeny told her. "It is good riddance though to a brutal monster, but it would take some — how do you Americans say . . . *gonads* to take on Kazanov and his men. To be honest, I think he must have pissed off a madman to have met such a fate."

Marlene had told her husband what his

cousin said, but his response had been, "It's the Brooklyn DAO's problem." It was an atypically short retort for him, but she understood that his mind was on the shooting — and Westlund.

Obviously the trial had been postponed. One of the defendants was dead; the other, Nonie Ellis, who remained out on bail, had been hospitalized for acute depression and was basically incommunicado. And the lead prosecutor had suffered a gunshot wound to the shoulder.

Katz had been fortunate that the bullet had passed through his shoulder, nicking bone but missing the major blood vessels and nerves. He'd been released from the hospital two days after the shooting, and although he'd been ordered home for several more days' bed rest, he'd appeared in the office that afternoon ready to discuss how to proceed. But that still had not been decided.

Marlene knew that Butch was torn over what to do. The legal justification behind the original reckless-manslaughter charge still applied to Nonie Ellis. But her husband was a compassionate man who believed in tempering justice with mercy, and it grieved him that the woman had not only lost her son but now her husband.

What to do about Nonie Ellis wasn't the only aspect of the shootings that troubled her husband. On the surface, Boole's actions appeared to confirm Gilbert Murrow's fears. A mentally unhinged follower of Westlund had snapped and acted upon his virulent rhetoric.

However, Butch thought there was more behind it. "I understand why she chose to shoot at Guma and Katz, and then me," he'd told her earlier that evening. "Westlund has pretty much painted us as devils incarnate to his followers. But her first target was Ellis, and that bothers me. Apparently, she must have heard that he planned to plead guilty, and I guess I can see that Boole would view that as a denunciation of her guru. But was that enough to scream 'Judas' and gun David down in front of a courthouse in broad daylight and then start blasting away at us? I wonder if Westlund and his henchmen were aware that David Ellis was going to give a Q & A statement." He'd tapped the yellow legal pad he always carried with him when dissecting the facts surrounding a case. "I'd give a year's salary to know what Ellis was going to say."

According to the police reports, Boole had not left any written or verbal statements to indicate her thinking in the hours and days before she acted. She lived in a small apartment near the Avenue A building and apparently didn't have a computer, so there were no e-mails, nor were there handwritten notes. "The apartment was clean," Fulton had told Karp, "almost too clean, but the homicide guys got there pretty damn quick and sealed it off. No one would have had time to sanitize it."

"At least not after the shooting," Karp added.

Karp had been particularly incensed that Westlund had profited from Boole's death. She apparently owned the building that housed the End of Days Reformation Church of Jesus Christ Resurrected, as well as the preacher's living quarters, and she'd left it all to him, in addition to the rest of her estate.

"Well, wasn't that convenient for him," Marlene said. "A win-win. The trial goes away, maybe. David Ellis is dead so whatever he was going to say went with him to the grave, and so does the opportunity to ask Boole, a middle-aged widow with no prior record, why she decided to commit murder. To top it all off, he gets her building, which has to be worth a ton, plus her money."

"And a life insurance policy made out to him," Karp added, clenching his jaw. "And where'd she get the gun? It was unregistered, with no fingerprints on it except for hers."

Westlund's bodyguard Frank Bernsen had been arrested at the scene. But as he'd claimed immediately after the shooting, he had a concealed-weapons license and had acted to prevent Boole from shooting Karp. The police reports bore out his version of events: that after shooting Ellis and Katz, Boole had turned her gun on Karp; when, after first lowering it, she'd raised it again as if to fire, Bernsen shot first.

Initial reports had not turned up much on Bernsen. He'd apparently served in the military and had a few misdemeanor assaults and a DUI, but no felonies — which would have prevented him from getting a concealed-weapons permit — and no prison time.

Marlene was glad that Bernsen had pulled the trigger, or she might have been a widow. But she knew that didn't make her husband feel any better about the woman's death.

There was even less on Westlund than Bernsen. All they knew was that he was originally from West Virginia and had worked as a coal miner until apparently deciding to become a minister. His "divinity degree" was of the mail-order variety, but there were no laws against that.

"You think he was behind it," Marlene said before Gilgamesh let her know that it was time to go out for his last walk of the night.

"Believing someone is factually guilty of a crime doesn't mean I have the evidence to do anything about it," he'd replied, citing the mantra of his office. "But someday, I'd like nothing better than to make that son of a bitch pay for this."

"We'll be back in a half hour," Marlene said, but her husband had already gone back to looking at the DD-5s, so she opened the door and took the elevator down to the street-level exit.

As she left the building with Gilgamesh and turned north to walk up Crosby, Marlene became aware that a shadowy figure on the other side of the street was walking in the same direction. She paused when the person began to cross.

"Marlene Ciampi?" a woman's voice inquired. She was dressed in a dark hooded sweatshirt that shadowed her face.

Marlene looked down at Gilgamesh, who was attentive and watching the stranger, but he wasn't growling or giving any other signal that he sensed danger. She decided to go with her dog's intuition.

"Yes," she replied. "And who are you?"

The woman stopped between two cars parked next to the curb near where Marlene stood. She looked up and down the block and then pulled back the hood of her sweatshirt. "My name is Nonie Ellis," she said. "I believe you know who I am."

Marlene's jaw dropped. "I thought you were in —"

"In the hospital." Ellis finished the sentence. "I was. They let me out this evening."

"Why —"

"Am I talking to you? Because I think there are some things your husband should know about C. G. Westlund."

Marlene pointed to her loft building. "Apparently you know where we live," she said. "Butch — my husband — is upstairs. Why don't you come talk to him yourself?"

Ellis shook her head. "I'm scared," she replied. "I think Westlund got Kathryn Boole to kill my husband. But I'm not going to testify against him. You can investigate what I tell you, and I hope you and your husband can do something with it. But when we're done talking, I'm leaving town."

"I'm pretty sure the terms of your bail require you to remain in the city," Marlene noted.

"It does, but I don't care," Ellis replied. "I'm going."

"My husband would see that you're placed in protective custody," Marlene argued. "You'd be safe."

"And if your investigation couldn't prove that Westlund was guilty of anything, or he got off? I think he'd kill me, too. At least this way, I'll get a head start."

"I could stop you," Marlene said. "My dog would hold you here until the cops arrive."

"But you won't," Ellis said. "I read an article about you . . . about how you've helped other women. And how you don't always follow the rules."

She's got me there, Marlene thought. "So what do you want to tell me?"

"Not here," Ellis said, again looking up and down the block. "I tried to be careful coming over, but I may have been followed. Is there somewhere we could go?"

Marlene pointed farther up the block. "The Housing Works Bookstore is open," she said. "They serve a mean cup of coffee and there are some private nooks where we'd know if someone else came in. After we're done, you can sneak out the back way."

An hour and a half later, Marlene walked

back in the front door of her family home. Her husband looked up as she took off her coat and hat.

"There you are," he said. "I was getting worried . . ." Suddenly he stopped. He knew the look on her face spelled trouble. "What's up?"

It took about forty-five minutes for Marlene to tell him what Nonie Ellis had said, and another twenty minutes for him to run out of questions as he took notes. At last he set his pencil down on the legal pad and sat back on the couch.

"It's a start," Karp said. "Of course, it all needs to be checked out and expanded before I can take it to a grand jury. I'll get Clay to —"

"I'm going to Memphis," Marlene interrupted. "That son of a bitch, as you so rightly labeled him, has done this to other people. I know it."

Karp shook his head. "I don't think that's a good idea," he said. "This is a police matter."

Marlene wasn't having it. "You send detectives down there and it's a fishing expedition," she said. "Westlund, or LaFontaine if that's his real name, will go to the press and raise hell about your trying to crucify him. I need to try to find some of these other people, and they'll talk to me more than they will a cop."

"You know I have to pick up Nonie Ellis," he said. "I need to get a statement from her and get her to testify against Westlund."

"Good luck," Marlene said. "No telling which way she went after we finished. And besides, this is my case; she asked me to look into it. I'm a private investigator and that's what I'm going to do."

They argued a little longer, then their eyes locked. Karp knew that there was no way to stop her, so he reached out to hug her and whispered in her ear, "Say hi to Elvis for me, and be careful."

17

Agent Michael Rolles tossed the *New York Post* on the kitchen table in front of Nadya Malovo, who'd been moved to a safe house in New Rochelle in Westchester County, just north of Manhattan and the Bronx. Or, as George M. Cohan had once said, "Just forty-five minutes from Broadway."

The agent was steamed. "Was this necessary? We sometimes had need of Boris Kazanov's . . . talents."

Malovo glanced at the headline: RUSSIAN MOBSTER BEHEADED. She shrugged. "I needed to know that the message had been delivered — both messages — as well as demonstrate to you what we're dealing with."

Rolles slammed his hand on the table. "I still don't get what this psychopath . . . What's his name, Grale? . . . What's he got to do with what you're doing for us?"

"Everything," Malovo replied.

"And how do you know what Knight told him? He might have mentioned the meet-up with Kazanov and that's it."

"That's what I'm about to find out," Malovo replied.

"How were you so sure that Knight would go to Grale? And how does a two-bit lawyer like Knight know this spook?"

"I know what men want, even queers," Malovo said, winking at Rolles, happy to be out of prison garb and into a snug pair of blue jeans and tight, curve-revealing sweater. "And Knight is my business."

Rolles glared but then smirked. "And what does Knight want?" he asked. "He doesn't seem interested in your vaunted sexual magnetism. Then again, maybe you're losing your touch. Getting too old for the seduction game, Nadya?"

Malovo laughed. "Touché! But there are many ways to seduce men; tits and ass are just one."

"And Knight?"

She pointed to the newspaper. "He has a debt to repay. I've never understood it but men with ethics consider repaying debts a matter of honor. Not something you would understand. Now, be a good boy and go find out what's taking my attorney so long this morning."

Rolles stood. "And when can I expect to know how all of this adds up?"

"When I'm ready. I demonstrated that I can deliver with the ferry attack. You looked like a hero, and if you play your cards right, you will again."

Rolles suddenly reached across the table and tapped Malovo on her forehead. "I'm counting on it, bitch. But remember, there's nothing I'd like better than to put a bullet right here."

Malovo didn't flinch. She just smiled, her green eyes glittering. "Maybe you'll have that opportunity someday," she said. "But until then we must work together."

A few minutes later there was a knock on the door. Malovo picked up the newspaper and appeared to be reading the front page when Knight entered. She had worked up a few tears and now exclaimed, "This is terrible! My cousin was murdered!"

"I know, it was a terrible shock when I heard," Knight replied. "It must have happened shortly after I saw him."

"You were able to meet him then?"

"Yes. On the boardwalk . . . where he was killed. Somebody must have followed him. Some other gangsters, I guess."

"That must have been it," Malovo said.

"He had many enemies."

"The newspapers said he was suspected in a number of murders," Knight said, pointing at the *Post*. "And in some gangland killings."

Malovo shrugged. "You know how the American press works; everything is exaggerated and it doesn't matter what the truth is. Still, I know he was not a good man . . . as I was not a good woman. Yet, when you have no family, losing the last member besides yourself is hard. He was not such a bad person when he was a child, and those are the memories I have of him."

A look of pain crossed Knight's face. *A man with a conscience,* Malovo thought. *Such weakness is useful.*

"Well, whatever his faults, I'm sorry for your loss," Knight said. "No one deserves to be murdered."

"Thank you, you're very kind," Malovo replied, then added somewhat shyly, "I'm just glad that you weren't hurt, too." *Never hurts to see if he can't also be seduced,* she thought before changing the subject. "Were you able to speak to Boris?"

"Yes. I don't understand what that was all about. A party in the Village on Halloween? The Village always has its annual parade, but I take it you were passing some sort of message, and I have to say I don't like being used in that fashion."

"I apologize," Malovo said. "You don't have to believe me, but I was actually trying to prevent a crime."

"Why not tell your federal handlers? Isn't that what you're supposed to be doing?" Knight asked.

"This had to do with family business, not national security," Malovo answered. "They're only interested in terrorism, not something as mundane as . . . well, I won't trouble you with the specifics." She changed direction. "What did Boris say?"

"He said he and his family would attend but wanted assurances that his traveling expenses would be covered," Knight said.

"Ah, always the businessman," Malovo said, shaking her head. "By 'traveling expenses' he meant that he wanted to be paid to call off the event." She hesitated, as if she couldn't decide whether to say anything more, but then couldn't help herself. "I take it that as a defense attorney you are acquainted with the district attorney Karp?" she asked, letting her very real hatred of the man put an edge in her voice.

"By reputation," Knight said. "I never faced him in court, but I don't think he loses much, if at all. If we had to go up against him, I'd be worried. But it seems to me that the feds have you pretty well insulated against the New York charges, so long as you fulfill your commitments . . ."

"I will do my part," Malovo said. "You may have seen the news about how the authorities stopped an attack on the Liberty Island ferry. That was thanks to me. But don't be too sure about Karp not being able to get to me," Malovo retorted, her voice growing angrier. "Karp is devious, and he hates me. A colleague of mine, Imam Jabbar, thought he had a deal with the feds, too. They were going to let him leave the country, but Karp waited until he was traveling to the airport in New Jersey and had passed out of the Manhattan federal jurisdiction. Then he had the local cops pull over a U.S. Marshals motorcade and arrest him. I don't think it's any coincidence that the marshal in charge of that motorcade who allowed Jabbar to be taken from her custody is the same marshal who watches my every move, Jennifer Capers. I wouldn't put it past Karp to be working on some deal with her to do the same thing when the feds are through with me."

"Well, we're aware that it happened once, so we know what to watch for," Knight said. He paused. "You seem to have quite a bit of animosity for Karp, above what even his actions to bring you to court would warrant."

"I hate him," Malovo spat. "I have broken laws, but there are others — powerful men, of course — who have broken more than I have . . . who use people like me for their dirty work, and he does nothing. I believe that he does their bidding."

Knight frowned. "That doesn't sound like him. He has a pretty squeaky-clean reputation. Who are these men?"

"Perhaps he makes such a noise about being so clean to cover his real activities," Malovo said. "These men, they call themselves the Sons of Man. They're a very old sort of criminal fraternity and have infiltrated nearly all of American society — politics, the military, business, law, even entertainment. I know these men, I have worked for them, and because of that they wish me dead."

"I'd have a hard time believing that Karp would be involved with them," Knight said.

"Perhaps," Malovo said. "But have you ever wondered why he and his family are repeatedly 'attacked' by criminals and terrorists and yet remain unscathed? Maybe these attacks are not real or are designed to fail in order to generate sympathy and to make him appear the hero. I do not know, but I suspect they are grooming him for higher office."

Knight shook his head. "This is all just too fantastic," he said.

"Is it? Think about some of the so-called terrorist attacks, including those in which I've been used like a pawn on a chessboard," Malovo retorted. "Why is it that the district attorney of New York County, and his family, are so involved in these matters that have nothing to do with his position? Why does this family always seem to be in the right place at the right time? Wouldn't it be more fantastic to say that this is all coincidence?"

Knight suddenly thought of Grale's take on coincidence. "How about divine intervention?"

Malovo smirked. "God does not exist. And coincidence can be stretched to the breaking point." She waved her hand. "Believe me or not, it doesn't matter. But I have something I want you to do."

"What?"

"I want you to set up a meeting with Karp."

Knight's jaw dropped. "Why?"

Malovo arched her eyebrow. "Because I want to give him a statement. Perhaps my conscience is bothering me, and I want to relieve myself of this burden of guilt I carry."

"As your attorney, I'd strongly advise against this," Knight said. "What do you hope to accomplish? He has a reputation for not accepting lesser pleas and he already has a slam-dunk case against you. I'm just trying to make sure you stay in federal custody, because if he gets his hands on you —"

"Just make the appointment," Malovo suddenly hissed.

Knight stopped and, seeing the look in her eyes, shrugged and nodded. "When?"

"Don't you Americans have a saying, 'There is no time like the present'? How about tomorrow morning? His office."

"His office?" Knight asked. "They probably will want to do it here."

"Then no statement," Malovo replied. "You tell Karp that I want to make a full confession, and he will get his little friends to get me there."

"I'll tell him."

"Good. You may go now and make your phone call. I will see you again tomorrow in the office of the district attorney."

When Knight was gone, Rolles reentered the room. "I think it's a dangerous game to be bringing Karp into this. The man is sharp, and like you were saying to Knight, he seems to have more than his share of —"

"Luck?" Malovo scoffed. "Call it what you will but there's one thing about luck. Whether it's good or bad, sooner or later it changes. My luck has been bad ever since I came to know of Butch Karp and his family; his has been extraordinarily good. It is time for a change, but I will not count on luck. In the past, I have not taken him into account, which was a mistake on my part; this time, however, I plan to use him."

"Use him how?"

"As bait," Malovo answered with a wolfish grin. "As bait."

18

As she waited in the Memphis Office of Dr. Charles Aronberg, Marlene browsed about, looking at the items hanging on the wood-paneled walls. There were the usual impressive college and medical school diplomas, including one for pediatric oncology, as well as a dozen photographs of a fit-looking man she assumed was the doctor climbing mountains, skiing, scuba-diving, and otherwise enjoying life.

However, there was one wall that particularly grabbed her attention. It was covered with dozens of snapshots of children and childish art drawn in crayons, colored pencils, and felt-tipped markers with small, heartfelt messages of thanks. One framed photo of a girl who appeared to be about twelve years old reminded her of Lucy at the same age. It was signed "The Drummond Family," thanking Aronberg "for the gift of time."

"She was a beautiful child," a man's voice behind her said. "I still grieve that I couldn't save her, and that was ten years ago."

Marlene turned to see the man whom she recognized from the photographs on the wall. He was fiftyish, tall and tan, with silver hair and gray-green eyes that were shiny with tears even now. "That must be incredibly difficult for a physician," she said.

Chuck Aronberg studied her for a moment and then nodded. "It is," he admitted. "It's one of those things they don't teach you in medical school, particularly in oncology, and that's how to cope with knowing that a large percentage of your patients are going to die no matter what you do. And when you choose pediatric oncology, they die far too young."

"How do you let it go?" Marlene asked.

The doctor shrugged. "You don't," he replied. "In fact, early on I got to the point where I nearly got out of this particular field and thought about going into family medicine, where I could treat colds, mend broken arms, and warn my patients about the dangers of cholesterol. To be honest, I was seriously depressed." He walked over and stood next to her, looking at the wall, then reached out to touch the photograph of the Drummond girl. "It was about the same time I lost the fight for Abby," he said. "I was sitting at my desk, numb, when her parents came by to thank me for giving them the time to say their good-byes. I remember her mother, Sherri, in particular saying that even a few months had been a tremendous gift and they hadn't wasted an hour or a day. It gave me a whole new way of looking at my work, so here I still am, ten years later."

As he spoke, the doctor's voice grew husky and Marlene could feel the depth of his grief. He turned and walked over to a couch, pointing to a chair next to it. "Please, have a seat," he said, and when she was settled, went on. "So my secretary says that you wanted to talk to me about Micah Ellis. I've wondered what became of him."

"I'm sorry to have to tell you this, but he died last November," Marlene said as gently as she could.

Aronberg hung his head. After a moment, he nodded. "I was afraid of that," he said. "Can you tell me where he died? Where was he being treated?"

Marlene explained the circumstances around Micah's death without going into what had happened since; she wanted to hear what the doctor would say first.

Aronberg's eyes flashed with anger. "Since

when are prayers and medicine mutually exclusive?"

"They're not in my book," Marlene said. "Can you tell me about his treatment and prognosis?"

Aronberg shook his head. "I would love to, but I'm afraid there's not much I can say," he said apologetically. "I'm sorry, Ms. Ciampi, but I'm sure you'll understand that I cannot discuss a patient's medical history, not without a subpoena."

"I'm an attorney, so I do understand privileged information," Marlene replied. "I was just hoping that because he died, you'd be able to tell me."

"Again, I'm sorry, I truly am, because there's plenty I'd like to say."

"Well, can I ask you a few general questions about astrocytomas, which were the cause of death for Micah Ellis according to the New York Medical Examiner's Office?" Marlene asked.

"By all means," Aronberg said, and gave her a brief explanation of the disease and the general course of treatment.

When she was finished asking medical questions, Marlene said, "Does the name C. G. Westlund mean anything to you?"

Aronberg shook his head. "Not that I can recall."

"How about the Reverend John LaFontaine?"

The doctor's eyebrows shot up. "Now, that name I recognize. A year ago, maybe a year and a half, a Memphis police detective came by the office. He said he was investigating the death of one of my former patients' fathers. He didn't tell me much, but he asked if I'd heard of LaFontaine. I'm afraid I wasn't much help; I didn't know the name. However, the interesting thing about your bringing it up now is that patient also stopped coming in for treatment and is deceased." The doctor stopped talking and frowned. "You think there's something up with this LaFontaine character?"

"He was apparently the minister who talked Micah's family into forgoing medical treatment for faith healing," Marlene replied.

Aronberg furrowed his brow. "I don't like it, and it's so reckless when dealing with a child's life," he said. "But it's not against the law to preach, I guess."

"Maybe not," Marlene said. "But if you don't mind, I'd rather not discuss Westlund's, or LaFontaine's, criminality, or lack thereof, until I know for certain what I'm talking about. Do you recall the detective's name who asked you about LaFontaine?"

Aronberg opened a drawer in his desk and after a brief search took out a business card and handed it to Marlene. "I have no idea why I kept this," he said. "Dumb luck I guess."

Marlene smiled as she read the card. "Or divine intervention. Detective Willie 'Wink' Winkler? Wink? He goes by his nickname?"

The doctor smiled. "Y'all are in the South, and we sometimes are a little different when it comes to naming our babies."

Marlene laughed and got up to leave. "Thank you for your time. It's been a genuine pleasure to meet you."

"The pleasure was mine," Aronberg said, also rising and extending his hand. "I wish there was more I could do. If you have any questions I can answer within the bounds of my oath, please call."

"Thank you, doctor, I will."

As Marlene turned to head for the door, Aronberg added, "Ms. Ciampi, get that subpoena and I'll be more than happy to speak about Micah."

19

"Bruce, there's someone here to see you."

Knight glanced at the intercom and then looked at his watch. It was almost five, and he was exhausted. *Meeting with a Russian assassin in the morning and then calling the district attorney and asking for a meeting will do that to you,* he thought. "I'm sorry, but I'm busy," he said. "Would you please ask whoever it is to make an appointment and come back tomorrow?"

"He says to tell you that David wants to see you," Danielle replied.

A chill went up Knight's spine. The images of one man choking to death, another twitching with arrows protruding from his body, and a third spurting blood from his slashed neck had not left his mind for very long, waking or asleep. Now Grale had sent Warren, or one of his other followers, to summon him to his lair. He sighed and got up from his desk.

To his surprise when he opened the door to his reception area he didn't find Warren but Grale himself. He was dressed like any other casual New Yorker in blue jeans, a green T-shirt, a light jacket, and running shoes. His long brown hair was tied back in a ponytail, his beard and mustache were neatly trimmed, and in spite of his too-pale skin and sunken eyes, he was still a good-looking man. He was happily chatting up Knight's secretary, who giggled at something he said.

Grale looked up and smiled. "Hey, Bruce," he said, "I know you're busy, but would you have a minute?"

"Sure," Knight replied. "Danielle, you can go. I'll lock up."

Danielle looked disappointed for a moment and she glanced at Grale, which caused Knight to experience a twinge of jealousy. "Well, if you're sure," she said. "I do have to take my mom grocery shopping and she lives in Brooklyn."

"You have to like a girl who's good to her mother," Grale said. "But be careful, Brooklyn can be a dangerous place for a young woman."

So says the serial killer, Knight thought.

Danielle beamed. "I was raised in Brooklyn, and I'm pretty tough."

"I'm sure you are." Grale smiled.

"Uh, good night, Danielle," Knight said. "David, please come in."

"Nice girl," Grale said when Knight closed the door behind them.

"Yes, she is," Knight replied as he took a seat behind his desk. Then, without knowing why he said it, he added, "And I want to keep her out of all of this. These are dangerous people we're dealing with —"

"And by that, you are including me," Grale finished, sitting down across from his friend.

"No, I meant, well, I uh . . ."

Grale laughed, a lighter version than the last time Knight had seen him, with Kazanov's blood dripping from his knife. "It's okay, Bruce," he said. "I am a dangerous person, some times more than others, especially when the darkness is on me. But today the sun is shining, on me and in my soul."

"That's good," Knight replied. Not knowing what else to say, he sat silently.

Grale looked at him for a moment before sighing and nodding his head. "I'm sorry I put you through that the other night. It was unfair, and frightening, I'm sure. All I can say is that Kazanov and his henchmen were evil men whom the law has been unable, or unwilling, to deal with. And while it would hardly seem possible given Kazanov's atrocities, Nadya Malovo is even worse, or at least her deeds are done on a grander scale."

"It was still murder," Knight replied. "And now I'm an accessory to murder. But even more than that, I believe in the justice system. I believe that every man, or woman, no matter how heinous we believe them to be, deserves a fair trial and to be found guilty beyond a reasonable doubt before a sentence is passed, and that the sentence should be handed down by a judge, not an executioner."

Grale's eyes narrowed. "What about the victims of these killers? The law had plenty of opportunities to do something about Kazanov. The same thing with Malovo. But what's your vaunted justice system going to do to her? . . . Give her a whole new life, that's what."

"I'm not arguing that the law never fails," Knight said. "And it fails miserably in cases like Kazanov and Malovo. But where does it stop? Who decides? You?"

"Yes," Grale said. "Sometimes I decide. And someday I may have to pay for that when your beloved system, which allows people like those two to commit their crimes and get away with it, catches me and puts me on death row."

As he spoke, Grale's voice hardened and his dark eyebrows knitted. But then his face softened and he leaned forward to look Knight in the eyes. "Look, old friend, I do understand where you're coming from, and I don't expect you to countenance what I do. But I'm asking you, pleading with you, to help me keep track of what Malovo's saying and doing. I don't think, and I can't believe that anyone who is aware of her past thinks, that she has turned over a new leaf, even just to get out of prison. She's planning something, and that means innocent people are going to die. I won't involve you again in any of my exploits, and I will never ask you to compromise your ethics again when this is through. But I need your help now."

Knight thought about it and at last nodded his head. "I'm already in, David, and I do owe you my life." He then told Grale what Malovo had said about Kazanov. "Apparently there was something planned for the Halloween festivities in the Village. She says she was trying to stop it."

"If she was, it wasn't out of concern for anyone but herself," Grale said. "But go on."

"Well, I don't know what to make of it," Knight said. "But she also seems to think that the district attorney, Butch Karp, is tied up with some nefarious group called the Sons of Man."

"Ridiculous," Grale interjected.

"That's essentially what I said," Knight agreed. "But she brought up what on the surface sounded like good points . . . that he and his family appear to have been targeted, or at least involved in any number of events that would seem on their face to have little to do with his being the district attorney of New York. And at the same time, nothing happens to them."

"God does favor that family," Grale agreed. "Which is part of the reason I've taken a particular interest in watching out for them."

"Well, I found it far-fetched, but that's what she was saying."

Grale nodded and then appeared lost in thought as he pursed his lips and stroked his beard with one hand. "Was there anything else?"

"Yes, she asked me to set up a meeting tomorrow morning with Karp," Knight said. "She says she's going to confess to the charges against her, including multiple counts of murder."

"What?!"

"That was my response," Knight said. "I

270

mean, if she cooperates with the feds she's not going to have to worry about the local charges. But still, why hand Karp her head on a silver platter?"

Grale frowned. "This is what I mean," he said. "She's up to something. Something to do with this Halloween parade and Karp."

"What about her comment that Karp is in bed with this other group?"

"I don't —" Grale started to deny the accusation but then stopped and suddenly looked worried. "I have a hard time believing it, but on the other hand . . ." He stopped talking for a moment and then added, "I need to think about some of this."

A few minutes later, when Grale and Knight exited the office, they found Danielle still sitting in her seat. "I thought you were going home," Knight said.

"I had a little more filing to do," she replied, glancing at Grale.

"Good help is hard to find," Grale commented, making the young woman blush.

"Apparently, I'm very lucky," Knight said with a laugh, which caused her to blush further.

"Well, I need to run," Grale said. "Don't be a stranger."

"I won't," Knight answered.

"Nice guy," Danielle said when they were

271

alone. "He married?"

Knight fought the urge to respond jealously. "You have no idea how nice," he said with a sigh. "But he's one of those guys who's sort of married to his job."

20

It was late afternoon when Marlene left Dr.
Aronberg's office. A thunderstorm had
blown up since she'd entered the building,
darkening the sky, and she barely made it to
her rented SUV before marble-sized hail
began pelting the parking lot and everything
in it.

As she waited for the storm to pass, she
pulled Detective Winkler's business card
from her purse and called, but only got his
voice mail. "Hello, this is Marlene Ciampi,"
she said. "I'm a private investigator from
New York City, and I'm in Memphis looking into the activities of a Reverend C. G.
Westlund, who you may know as the Reverend John LaFontaine. Dr. Aronberg gave
me your card. I'd like to talk." She gave her
cell number and hung up.

Lightning flashed overhead and was immediately followed by a crash of thunder
that made her jump. *Settle down, Marlene,*

she told herself as she typed an address Nonie Ellis had given her into the car's GPS system. *This weather's got you jumping around like a cat at a dog show and you need to concentrate.*

A map popped up and she put the car in gear. Moments later she was driving through a pouring rainstorm to East Memphis and into a neighborhood of ill-kept yards bearing clapboard houses in desperate need of paint, hammers, and nails. She pulled up in front of one particularly dilapidated house whose roof had sagged toward the middle so badly that a waterfall of rain poured down in front of the steps leading up to the door. As she waited for a break in the rain before getting out of her car, she thought about meeting Nonie Ellis the night before.

Sitting in a nook at the Housing Works Bookstore in Manhattan, Nonie described how Westlund, known to her at the time as the Reverend John LaFontaine, had gained her trust and wormed his way into her heart. "I was blind with fear for my son," she recalled. "The chemo and radiation treatments were horrible, bad enough that Micah begged to die."

"Wait a minute," Marlene had interrupted. "Micah was treated. You knew he was sick enough to need chemotherapy and radiation?"

Nonie had hung her head and told her about Dr. Aronberg and the astrocytoma diagnosis and treatments before continuing. "Then when everything seemed darkest and Micah was hanging on by a thread, Westlund showed up at the door. He seemed to know so much without our telling him — that we had a sick boy in the house; that he had brain cancer; that he'd been treated with chemo, which he called 'Satan's poisons'; even that David and I weren't real regular at going to church. He seemed sent from God, and when he offered to pray for Micah . . . well, I would have believed in anything if it saved my son, and even David, who was skeptical, came around. And it seemed to work. I mean, Micah's health improved to the point where he seemed like a normal, healthy little boy again by the time we moved to New York. By that point, I would have done just about anything for Westlund."

Nonie Ellis had broken down and started to cry, and it had taken her several minutes to pull herself together. "My husband was a good man," she said, sniffling and dabbing at her tears. "He knew that Micah needed more than prayers, but he went along with it because of me. I don't know if you've been told, but David was going to plead guilty. He left me a voice mail message that I didn't get until it was too late. He didn't come home that night, said he'd been walking around thinking. . . . He thought I was having an affair with Westlund."

"Were you?" Marlene had asked.

Nonie shook her head. "No," she said. "Looking back, I know now that some of his suggestive remarks and the hugging — even offering me a place to stay at his loft after David was shot — were attempts to seduce me," she said. "I am pretty sure though that he was having sex with Kathryn Boole."

Nonie stopped talking again for a moment and sighed heavily. "I know that Kathryn killed my husband and even tried to kill yours. But I just feel sorry for her, especially because it was my fault she met Westlund in the first place. She was just a lonely depressed woman who'd lost her husband and wanted to feel loved and needed again. Westlund knows how to feed on that."

Her last statement made Nonie laugh bitterly. "I know the feeling," she said. "No, I wasn't having sex with Westlund, but maybe what I let him have was worse. He couldn't have my heart — I lost that when Micah died and was too devastated to remember I owed David my love, too. But I gave Westlund my soul; I made a deal with the devil because I thought he could save my son. David and your husband are right: we were guilty of killing Micah. Me more than my husband."

Nonie had handed Marlene a letter from a life insurance company. "David found this," she said. "I think it was the final straw."

As Marlene quickly read the letter, Nonie explained how shortly after the family moved to New York, Westlund had appeared at their apartment door with his "church accountant," Frank Bernsen. "He had Frank talk to us about taking out a two-hundred-and-fifty-thousand-dollar whole-life policy on Micah," she said. "Frank said that someday it would pay for Micah's college and that he might find it difficult to get life insurance when he was an adult if his disease returned. It actually made sense. Then he asked that we consider not just taking out the policy but signing over the death benefits to Westlund and the church just in case 'God calls Micah home as a child before the policy matures.' Westlund called it an act of faith and said that if Micah had to die because it was God's will, then at least some good would come of it. That's when David balked. He didn't say anything to Westlund, or to me really. He was probably afraid I'd defend Westlund; I was pretty hard on him about things like that. But I could tell he was disturbed by it, and he wouldn't agree to take out a policy."

Nonie bit her lip. "That's when Westlund was at his best. He didn't get mad or stop coming over to pray for Micah. I could tell he was hurt, or I should say putting on a good act of being hurt, but he dropped the subject. Instead he talked a lot about how his ministry was suffering because there wasn't any money and how he might have to go back to Tennessee. I was desperate to keep him here, so I asked him how I could get David to sign a policy. He said he didn't think it was possible because David lacked faith. Then he suggested that I take out the policy and that Frank would forge David's signature."

"You didn't have a problem with that?" Marlene had asked.

Nonie shook her head. "He said that God would understand that I did it to further His Word," she said.

"What about the insurance company checking on Micah's medical records?" Marlene asked. "They wouldn't have issued a policy if they'd known he was being treated for astrocytomas."

"I asked about that, too," Nonie replied. "But he said that the Lord would blind the insurance investigator because it was for God's work. He even convinced me that it wasn't really lying to say that Micah didn't have any medical problems because we did not believe in doctors or their diagnoses. And it never came up. They didn't find Micah's records in Memphis. They gave me the policy and Frank pretended he was David and signed it."

"That's fraud," Marlene pointed out.

"I know, but . . ." Nonie hesitated and then looked up into Marlene's eyes. "I'm sure you think I'm nuts . . . that I went off the deep end . . . and I guess I did. I just don't know how to explain how a guy like Westlund can get inside of you. You want to believe so bad that everything he says is gospel. He said that even David would someday thank me when we could use the money for Micah's education. So I went along with his plan."

Marlene held up the letter from the insurance company. "But then they sent this, saying they weren't going to pay until after the outcome of the trial," she said. "So Westlund needs you both to be found not guilty in order for the check to be cut."

"I know he was surprised that the district attorney charged us," Nonie said. She leaned forward and grabbed Marlene's hands. "I think he's done this before and nothing happened to the parents."

"He needs to be stopped," Marlene had replied. "You need to talk to my husband and tell him all of this."

Nonie withdrew her hands. "I can't," she said. "I'm not going to put myself through a trial. I'm afraid, Ms. Ciampi. I think he got Kathryn Boole to kill David and had Bernsen there to make sure Kathryn didn't live to talk about it. I think he wanted me to stay with him to seduce me but also to keep an eye on me. I think he's capable of having me killed, too."

No amount of persuasion could change Nonie Ellis's mind. But before she'd escaped out the back door of the bookstore, she'd given Marlene the names and addresses of two women in Memphis. "Maybe they'll talk to you," she said.

One woman she knew only as "Sister Sarah," who was apparently one of Westlund/LaFontaine's most ardent supporters. "We met her shortly after meeting Westlund," Nonie had said. "She had a son named Kevin who the doctors said was going to die, but he lived."

The other woman, Monique LaRhonda Hale, had not been as fortunate. "Her daughter died," Nonie confided. "Westlund later told me it was because the Hales had lost faith and had secretly gone back to the doctors."

Nonie had paused, then added, "When I think about it, Monique and I have a lot in common. We both lost our children, and our husbands were killed."

The alarm bells went off in Marlene's head. "What do you mean both husbands were killed?"

"It was terrible," Nonie said. "After their daughter died, Monique's husband was mugged. They lived in a bad neighborhood in East Memphis and somebody beat him to death with a metal bar."

Nonie knew where Monique lived because she'd gone with Westlund on one of his home visits and helped pray over her daughter. It was the home that Marlene now found herself sitting in front of as a thunderstorm crashed and banged all around her.

Looking at the property, Marlene wondered if anybody was living there now. It was early evening and the cloud cover had brought darkness, but there were no lights on in the house. An old, rusted-out Ford station wagon sat in the driveway. A child's bicycle leaned against the sagging porch with knee-high weeds growing up through the spokes; judging by the rusted chain and flat tires, it had been a long time since it had last been used.

When the rain let up, Marlene dashed across the muddy front lawn and up onto the porch, where she knocked on the unpainted door. In her peripheral vision, she saw someone peep from behind the curtain drawn across the living room window. But no one answered the door.

Marlene knocked again. "Hello, Mrs. Hale? Could I please speak to you?"

"Go away," a woman's voice answered from behind the door.

"Please, it's important," Marlene pleaded.

"I don't care."

Marlene leaned her head toward the door. She could feel the woman's presence on the other side of the door. "Please, Monique," she said quietly. "This is about your daughter, and your husband."

"I said I don't want to talk to you," Monique Hale said angrily. "Y'all can carry yourself out of here or I'll call the police."

"Call then," Marlene said. "But first I want you to know that another child has died. He might have been saved but a con man named C. G. Westlund — you may know him as John LaFontaine — talked his parents into not seeking medical help."

"Which child?"

"Micah Ellis."

"I was 'fraid of that," the woman said. "Nonie must be taking it hard. She was tight with LaFontaine."

"Nonie's missing," Marlene said. "And David's dead . . . murdered by one of LaFontaine's followers."

The woman was silent for a full minute before speaking. "I'd like to help," she said. "But I just can't. My child is dead and my husband is dead. Ain't nothing goin' to change that."

"He needs to be stopped, Mrs. Hale," Marlene said.

"I'm scared. I know he killed my Charlie. Him and his thugs."

"I'll see that you're protected, Mrs. Hale," Marlene said. "My husband is the district attorney of New York, and I know he will do everything he can to help you . . . . Mrs. Hale, somebody needs to speak up for Charlie, Micah, Nonie, David, and your daughter . . ."

"Natalie. My daughter's name was Natalie, after her grandmother."

"Someone needs to speak for Natalie, too," Marlene said.

At last Marlene heard the security chain sliding and the dead bolt clicking open. A small pale woman with stringy brown hair and a high forehead peered out. "Come on in," she said, "and I'll make us some tea."

Almost two hours later, Marlene left the Hale residence and called her husband to fill him in on the conversations with Aronberg and Hale.

"Marlene, you never cease to amaze," he said. "I think I better send Clay and Guma down to get statements. And maybe it's time you let them finish this with that Memphis detective."

"You know better than that, Butch," she replied.

"Yeah, I do, but I thought I'd try," he said. "Don't suppose it would matter much to say I miss you and want you to come home. My world just isn't the same without you in it."

"Now, that's what I love to hear, even though I haven't even been gone for a night yet," she laughed. "And you know I have to see this debacle through to the end."

"So what's next?" Butch asked.

"I'm off to find Sister Sarah," Marlene said.

"Marlene, LaFontaine and his crew are thugs. They'll use violence; be careful."

"I will," Marlene said. Suddenly she missed her husband. The darkness she was stepping into was so seedy, and he had always been so resolute against such evil. "So what's happening with you?"

"You'll never guess who wants to give me a statement, a full confession, tomorrow morning," Karp replied.

"The Mad Terrorist, Sheik Khalid Mohammed."

Karp laughed. "I can only wish."

"Who then?"

"Nadya Malovo. Here in my office, first thing in the morning."

Marlene sat in silence. Alarm bells were going off again. "I don't think I need to tell you that it's you who needs to be careful, more than me," she said. "That woman is the most dangerous person I've ever known."

"She's just one crazy lady and security will be tight," her husband replied.

A chill ran up Marlene's spine. "She is a very evil woman, and if she asked for this, you know she's up to something."

Hanging up, Marlene entered the address Nonie had given her for Sister Sarah into the GPS. Nonie had said she'd only been there once, when Westlund apparently needed something from his devotee. "He told me to wait in the car," she recalled. "He was in there at least a half hour. So I sat there looking at the number on her townhome, 2214, all that time, waiting for him, and the street address was easy. Park Place."

This time the GPS took her to a much nicer neighborhood and a row of modest townhomes. The rain had stopped, and Marlene had gotten out of the car and started to walk toward 2214 when a young man came out of the home next door.

"You looking for Sarah?" he asked.

"Yes," Marlene replied, "do you know if she's in?"

The man brushed his long hair back with his fingers and eyed her suspiciously. "You a cop?"

"No, just an old friend," Marlene lied. "I was just passing through town and hoped to say hi."

"She's probably at work."

"She's working nights?" Marlene asked.

"She wouldn't make any money doing her thing by working days."

"I thought she was a schoolteacher," Marlene said.

The man laughed. "The only thing she teaches is how to take your clothes off. She's a stripper."

Marlene smiled. "She went back to the old job? What about her son, Kevin, who's watching him?"

The man looked confused. "What son? I ain't never seen no kid, and she's never said nothin' about a boy."

"It's been a few years since I saw her last, but a mutual friend said she had a boy and he was real sick," Marlene said.

The man shook his head. "If Sarah has a kid, it's the best-kept secret in this neighborhood."

The young man gave Marlene the once-over. "You a stripper, too? You got a nice little body. You was probably something back in the day."

Marlene fixed him with her one good eye. "Exactly what do you mean 'back in the day'?"

The young man smiled and held up his hands. "No offense, ma'am. I just meant that if you're this hot now, you must have been on fire in your twenties."

"That's better," Marlene said with a smile. "Nice save. So where's she doing the bump and grind?"

"Gentleman's Club on Lamar Avenue."

When Marlene got back in her car, she noticed she had a call from a Memphis-area-code phone. "This is Detective Wink Winkler returning your call. I'd like to talk to you, too. I'm out of town until tomorrow but will be in the office on Poplar Avenue by midafternoon. Stop by."

A half hour later, Marlene pulled into the parking lot of the Gentleman's Club strip joint. It was early yet and the parking lot wasn't very full, so it wasn't tough to spot the new BMW with the vanity license plate that read SARAH.

Marlene entered the establishment and when her eyes adjusted to the low light, she was soon aware that she was the only unaccompanied woman in the place except for those gyrating on the dozen stages scattered around the spacious room. A pretty, young black woman with bare breasts walked up to her. "Welcome to the Gentleman's Club," she said with a smile.

"Uh, thank you," Marlene replied, trying not to be overly conscious of the fact that she was talking to a woman dressed in nothing more than short shorts. "I'm looking for Sarah."

The woman gave Marlene a knowing smile. "I know she swings both ways," she said. "And I like sensual women, too. Maybe we can all get together after work?"

"Sorry, but I'm kind of a one-woman gal," she said.

"Too bad," the black woman replied with a pout. "But Sarah's about ready to go on. She's over there on stage four." She nodded to a stage where a strobe light had begun to flash.

Marlene thanked her and headed for a seat near the stage. A half-dozen men were scattered in the rows closest to the stage, but undeterred, she found a seat next to the stage. To the sound of Madonna's "Like a Virgin," a dark-haired white woman dressed like a schoolgirl pranced out on the stage, licking a large lollipop that she tossed to the closest of her admirers.

A man sitting to Marlene's left got up from his table and sat down next to her. "Maybe when she's off work we can all get together, have a little fun?"

"Beat it, creep," Marlene snarled. "What's with you people and your threesomes?"

"Just trying to be friendly," the man said, standing up and leaving in a huff.

Marlene shook her head. *Maybe I should have just waited for her to come home,* she thought.

Near the end of her dance and wearing nothing but a G-string, the dancer spotted Marlene and smiled before turning her attention back to the men also seated in the front row holding up dollar bills.

Not exactly the image I had of Sister Sarah, Marlene thought, smiling back.

After the music stopped and she picked up the dollar bills tossed at her, the stripper strolled over to where Marlene sat. "Hi, honey," she said.

"Hi, I liked your dance," Marlene replied, noting that on closer inspection Sister Sarah appeared to be in mortal combat with the aging process.

"Thank you," Sarah replied. "I get off at one. Stick around and maybe I'll give you a private show."

"Would you have a few minutes to talk now?" Marlene asked.

Sarah's demeanor changed. "You a cop?"

"How come everybody keeps asking me that? You have a guilty conscience?" Marlene said, but she wasn't smiling either. "No, I'm just a friend of Nonie Ellis and I'd like to ask you a few questions about the Reverend LaFontaine."

"I don't know no Nonie and no LaFontaine," Sarah replied, and started to turn away.

"Nonie says you do," Marlene replied. "She even knew where you lived, 'cause LaFontaine took her there when he was visiting you. I went by there a little earlier, met your neighbor."

"So?"

"So where's your son, Kevin?"

"He's with his father," Sarah said. "They live out of state."

"Yeah? What state?"

"California. I gotta go."

"That must be tough on you," Marlene said. "Your boy survives this terrible disease and then goes off to live with his dad on the other side of the country."

"Yeah, it's rough. I've got to —"

"Go. Yeah, I know. You need to go shake your ass for a bunch of leering strangers. Not quite the saint that Nonie described."

Sarah looked at the stage and shrugged. "Everybody's got to make a living," she said.

"Can I talk to you after work?"

"I don't get off until three and I'll be too tired."

"How about tomorrow morning then?" Marlene asked. "After you get up."

"I don't get up before noon."

"I'll bring breakfast," Marlene replied, handing the dancer one of her business cards. "In the meantime, if you want to talk before that, call me."

" 'Marlene Ciampi, private investigator,' " Sarah read. "You're not Nonie's friend."

"On the contrary, I may be her only friend," Marlene replied. "And I take that seriously. I'll see you tomorrow. And don't make me come looking for you."

21

"So this is where the famous Butch Karp presides over the machinations of American justice," Nadya Malovo said as she sauntered into his office through the private entrance. "As I expected, old-fashioned, like the man himself . . . lots of wood and leather upholstery. All business." She sniffed. "And I detect cigar smoke, though it is old and only lingers like a memory of days gone past."

She turned to look directly at Karp with a smirk on her face. "I take it you do not smoke cigars."

"Have a seat, Ms. Malovo," Karp said, standing beside the conference table.

"But of course not, that would be a vice for a man of such integrity. May I?" Malovo asked, nodding toward a wall of his office that was completely filled by books.

"Be my guest."

Karp continued standing as the assassin

walked over to the bookshelves, followed by U.S. Marshal Jen Capers and two men, a tall, steely-eyed, square-jawed type he assumed was a federal agent, and a plump shorter man. *Her attorney Bruce Knight, I presume.* He wondered briefly what Knight thought of Malovo. *Surely he's seen the file on her. Everyone deserves representation, but it can't be easy defending evil incarnate.*

"The usual legal books," Malovo noted. "But I'm impressed with the others. Melville. Faulkner. Descartes. Jefferson. Plato. . . . The complete set of Federalist Papers. Have you actually read all of these books?"

"Most of them belonged to Francis Garrahy, one of my predecessors," Karp replied evenly. "But yes, I've read them all. Now, I understand you're here to confess to certain criminal acts, not comment on the décor of my office or the content of my library."

Malovo laughed. "Yes, this is not a social call," she agreed, but then seemed to notice Clay Fulton, who was sitting in a corner chair. He had not gotten up when she came in. "Ah, Mr. Fulton. It's been a long time. No hard feelings I hope."

Fulton didn't reply except to glare at her. Several years earlier, he'd been part of a police convoy escorting Andrew Kane to a psychiatric evaluation facility in upstate New York when it was attacked by terrorists led by Malovo. The purpose had been to free Kane. But they'd used a school bus loaded with children to draw the police escort in, murdering the children as well as the officers who went to their aid. Malovo had shot Fulton in the leg but left him alive to carry his tale to Karp.

Malovo smiled. "I guess not," she said, "but looks like we're on the same team now."

Fulton ignored her comment as Karp turned to the others. "Good morning, Marshal Capers. You want to introduce your party?"

"Morning, Mr. Karp," Capers said. "This is federal agent Michael Rolles and defense attorney Bruce Knight, who is representing Ms. Malovo."

Karp pointed to the conference table set up to the side of his desk. "If Ms. Malovo and Mr. Knight would have a seat at the table, and the rest of you make yourselves comfortable anywhere else, I'll call the stenographer in." He pressed a button on his intercom. "Would you please tell Dennis that we're ready for him?"

Dennis Sheen entered the room and took a seat at the end of the table as Karp sat on one side and Malovo and her attorney sat on the other. Capers and Rolles pulled up chairs behind her.

When the stenographer nodded to indicate that he was ready, Karp proceeded. "Here today in my office is Nadya Malovo and her attorney Bruce Knight. Ms. Malovo I am informed that you have been apprised of your Miranda rights and have conferred this morning with your lawyer Mr. Knight regarding your rights and your request to make an incriminating statement regarding criminal acts you committed in New York. Correct?"

"Yes," Malovo said.

"Are you now willing to waive your rights and make your statement in the presence of your lawyer?"

"Yes."

"Have you been coerced or promised anything by me, or anyone else, to make these statements?"

"Not at all."

"Ms. Malovo, it is a fact that you initiated this meeting with me to make this statement. This was of your own doing?"

"Yes, absolutely."

Karp nodded. "Then let's get going."

Three hours later, Karp pushed back from the table. Over the course of the interrogation, Malovo had admitted to complicity in dozens of murders and violent crimes, from the killing of the schoolchildren when Fulton was shot to deadly bombings of restaurants, knifings, shootings, stranglings, and even an attempt to blow up the Brooklyn Bridge and incinerate the lower end of Manhattan with a ship filled with natural gas. Everyone in the room seemed stunned, even those who were aware of her crimes.

"I think that's about it for my questions," Karp said. "Is there anything you'd like to add?"

Smiling, Malovo shook her head. "That wasn't enough? But no, not at this time, though perhaps someday we will have the opportunity to speak again."

"Only if you want to take the witness stand at your trial," Karp replied.

"What trial?" Malovo sneered, her eyes glittering, whether with anger or glee he wasn't sure. "You will have to live with the knowledge that I am enjoying my new life, tucked away in some quiet little American town. Perhaps I will have a husband and get a dog."

"We both know that will never happen," Karp replied without emotion.

Malovo's eyes glimmered even brighter, and there was no mistaking the hatred in them. But she smiled again. "There is one thing," she said. "A small gesture to you. And that is to warn you that you and your family are in danger."

"Is that a threat?" Karp asked evenly.

"Not from me," she replied. "I do not know the details yet. However, I am aware of a plot that has something to do with your plan to be the grand marshal at the Halloween parade in the Village."

"Hold on a minute," Rolles said, getting to his feet. "You haven't said anything about this to me. The agreement is that you talk to me first."

"That is all I know at this time," Malovo said to the agent. "When I learn more details, I will, of course, tell you first. However, since I probably will not be speaking to Mr. Karp again, I wanted to pass this on personally. . . . After all, our relationship precedes yours and mine."

Five minutes later, when Malovo and the others were gone, Karp sat quietly at the table tapping on a yellow legal pad. He looked over at Fulton, who'd remained quiet throughout the interrogation. "So what do you think?"

"I think we had her dead to rights before this confession," Fulton replied. "But that just put her on death row."

"Except that her deal with the feds will keep her out of our hands," Karp noted. He thought about it a little more, then shook his head. "She wasn't confessing; she was bragging."

"I agree," Fulton said. "Throwing it in our faces, knowing we can't do anything about it."

"But why?"

The detective shrugged his big shoulders. "Because she's a soulless sociopath?"

"She is that," Karp said. "But she's a very calculating and manipulating soulless sociopath. I don't think Nadya Malovo does anything without some ulterior motive, and I'm not sure taunting us is all she's up to."

"Well, when you figure it out, let me know," Fulton said. "And hopefully it will be something that will give me the chance to repay her for the hole she put in my leg."

Karp nodded. "Hopefully you'll aim a bit higher."

The discussion was ended by Mrs. Milquetost on the intercom. "Agent Jaxon is here to see you."

"Send him in, Darla," he said.

When Jaxon entered a moment later, Karp asked, "So you hear it all?"

"Yeah. Thanks for setting that up," Jaxon replied. "Would have liked her to talk more about the Sons of Man; she didn't give up anybody we aren't already aware of."

"Maybe she wasn't privy to who was pulling all the strings."

"Yeah, maybe. I appreciate your letting me listen in."

"I'll shoot you a copy of the transcript as soon as I get it back. Maybe there's something in it. In the meantime, were you able to get anything on those two names I gave you?" Karp asked.

Jaxon reached into his coat pocket and pulled out a folded sheet of paper. "You're not supposed to have this," he said, laying it on the table in front of Karp.

"I understand," Karp replied as he read it. Then he swore. "The reason nothing came up on the records search for Bernsen and Westlund, whose real name apparently is LaFontaine, is because they're informants for the ATF?"

"Looks that way," Jaxon replied. "Apparently they got into some big trouble in Mississippi and were agreeable to working with the boys with Alcohol and Tobacco to infiltrate the Brothers of the South motorcycle club in Tuscaloosa. The ATF didn't want them showing up if, heaven forbid, they got pulled over for a speeding ticket or some freelance larceny. So their records, and fingerprints, are kept in a 'need-to-know only' federal database. I had to pull some strings to get it, but at least I knew where to look."

"The felony convictions mean Bernsen isn't allowed to carry a firearm, much less apply for a concealed-weapons permit," Fulton said, scowling. "I'll pick the son of a bitch up now."

"Can't do it," Jaxon replied, and pointed at the paper in Karp's hand. "At least not using that. They don't have an official record, and my ass would be grass for giving it to you."

"Might be better this way," Karp said after thinking for a moment. "I've already filled Clay in on what's going on, but Marlene's in Memphis looking into LaFontaine's activities. Might not want to tip him off now."

Karp then filled Jaxon in on what Marlene had learned. "What time are you and Guma flying down?" he asked Fulton.

"First flight we could get was four o'clock," the detective replied. He stood up. "In fact, I need to go wrap up a few details, then find Guma and get out to LaGuardia."

"Good luck," Karp said.

"Don't think I'll need it," Fulton replied.

"We're just mopping up after Hurricane
Marlene."

22

The Memphis police detective's droopy hound-dog face remained unresponsive as he sat back in a chair listening to Marlene. Tall and thin as a rail, Wink Winkler didn't say a word for several moments after she finished and he had closed his notebook. She wondered if he was just going to dismiss her as some crackpot private investigator.

Then he smiled. "I sure do appreciate you, ma'am," he said with a southern drawl that reminded her of Johnny Cash. "I knew there was something wrong about that son of a bitch LaFontaine, pardon my French. I just couldn't piece it together fast enough, and then he skipped town so I couldn't keep tabs on him neither."

They were sitting in the detective squad room of the Memphis Police Department, and he now pushed a manila folder across the table to her. "I shouldn't be talking to you about an open case," he continued.

"But after you left your message, I did a little calling around myself. Got some friends with the NYPD, and while they might be damn Yankees, I can trust 'em, and they said you and your husband — who you failed to mention is the DA up there — are good folks and that if you said something was important, then I needed to listen to you real careful. And glad I did."

Winkler explained that when Charlie Hale was beaten and later died, the case had been handed to him to investigate along with a dozen others. "We're not New York City when it comes to homicides," he said. "But we average more than a hundred and fifty a year, which for a city the size of Memphis is more per capita than New York by quite a bit. In fact, there have been times, unfortunately, when we earned the 'Murder Capital of the United States' moniker. Most of these murders are drug-related, or domestic violence, and we either catch the killer right out of the box or they go unsolved. Looking at the Hale case, I didn't initially hold out much hope. Charlie wasn't unknown to us. He had a half-dozen convictions on his record, mostly simple assaults and minor drug-possession-type charges; done a little time in the county jail, that's about it. As you know, he and his missus lived in a pretty tough neighborhood, one of the highest crime areas in Shelby County. I figured he either crossed one of his dealer friends or just wasn't careful enough when he went out that night."

"So what changed your mind, Wink?" Marlene asked.

"I don't know, a hunch maybe," Winkler answered. "I didn't have any leads, no weapon, no witnesses . . . the perps took his wallet and watch, so it looked like a robbery. But the first time I talked to his wife, there was another woman there who insisted on staying for 'moral support' and I couldn't get the two apart. Something just bothered me . . ."

"This other woman a pretty brunette, late thirties?"

"Yeah . . . wouldn't give her name but when I heard your story right away I made the connection to this 'Sister Sarah' you told me about. Anyway, Monique didn't say much. She said she had no idea who might want to hurt her husband. But she seemed scared and it just kept bugging me, so I waited a few days and then sat down the block from her house until I was pretty sure no one else was there, and then went back to talk to her."

Winkler shook his head. "She was not

happy to see me," he said. "About as nervous as a possum in the middle of a pack of hounds. But she lightened up some when I saw the photo of her daughter and we started talkin' about the poor kid. She said they'd been getting treatment at the children's hospital with Dr. Aronberg, but stopped going to the doctor when this LaFontaine character showed up at their door with his spiel about faith healing and all. She got up and peeped out the window, and then said that her husband was unhappy with the preacher after their daughter died, something 'bout an insurance policy. Sounds like the same thing you've run into with the Ellis family. But right about then, this other woman shows up again, like she'd been watching the house, too. And that was it; Monique shut down and I never could get another word out of her."

"Were you able to find out anything about LaFontaine?" Marlene asked.

"Not much," Winkler admitted. "He'd registered his 'church,' and I'm using the term loosely, for tax purposes with himself and this Frank Bernsen character as the church officers. But otherwise, he was clean as a whistle. I smelled ex-con all over him when we talked, but he was cool as a cucumber — shook his head over 'poor Charlie

Hale' but didn't know anything. Guess it all makes sense in light of what your husband told you about the ATF wiping their records — nothing but a bunch of rogue cowboys in that agency."

"Just remember that information was on the QT, Wink," Marlene reminded him. "Our best revenge will be to take their little pals down."

"Gotcha," Winkler replied. "I won't say a thing. But I will keep it in mind the next time those ol' boys come askin' for favors."

"You talked to Dr. Aronberg, too," Marlene noted.

"Yes, ma'am," Winkler replied. "Good man but didn't have much to contribute. Was treating Natalie; then the family stopped coming in and didn't respond to telephone calls. Glad I had the sense to leave my business card with him."

"I am, too," Marlene said. "So if you're thinking like I'm thinking, this LaFontaine is a con man and he works these families with sick kids. Gets some of them to donate 'to the church' and others to take out these insurance policies under fraudulent terms and sign the benefits over to him."

"Looks that way," Winkler said. "But how'd he know who to target?"

Marlene thought about it for a minute. "I

think it would have to be somebody on the inside who knew these families and their kids," she said.

The detective frowned. "You think Aronberg —"

Marlene was shaking her head before he could finish his sentence. "No, I don't," she said. "Of course it's a possibility, but I'd bet my bank account that his love for those kids and his anger at LaFontaine were all genuine. But he's a good place to start to figure out who was feeding LaFontaine the information. I think I'll drop by after I leave here."

Winkler nodded. "Let me know what you find out," he said. "In the meantime, I'm worried about Monique Hale. She was frightened, and apparently with good cause. I'm going to go pick her up and get her to a safe location until the bad guys are off the street. I don't know that I'm going to be able to put a case together against LaFontaine for the murder of her husband, but if I can't, I still want to make sure she's okay in case you need her in New York."

Marlene looked at her watch. "That reminds me. I have to pick up the two guys I was telling you about, Assistant DA Ray Guma and Detective Clay Fulton, at the airport at six. They're going to want to get statements from Aronberg and Monique, too. Maybe the three of you can do that together. In the meantime, I'm going to see if Sister Sarah is willing to cooperate."

"Maybe I should pick her up, too," Winkler said.

"Let me have a shot at her first," Marlene said. "If she's a pro at the con game, she may be a pretty tough cookie to crack. But if I can convince her that cooperating is her best chance to avoid taking an acting-in-concert murder rap, she may roll over on LaFontaine and his henchman, Frank Bernsen. One thing about good con artists is that they know when the jig is up. And besides, I think she may be susceptible to a woman's touch."

Winkler laughed. "Have to admit, Marlene, it's worked on me a time or two. But let me know how it goes. If she doesn't talk to you nice, I'll haul her butt in here and do it the old-fashioned way."

"Deal, Wink," Marlene said with a grin.

An hour later, Marlene again found herself in Dr. Aronberg's office. She'd called his office and learned that he was treating a patient but would meet her as soon as he was done. She was still looking at the photographs on his wall when he entered.

"Ms. Ciampi, this is both a pleasant surprise and a bit of serendipity," he said.

"Why is that?"

"Well, I was going to call you when I finished my rounds this morning," he said. "I've been giving a lot of thought to what you told me yesterday, particularly regarding the life insurance scam. I just couldn't see how a company would have issued a policy for Natalie Hale or Micah Ellis, not once they'd looked into their medical records."

"And?"

"And I decided to play Sherlock Holmes," Aronberg said lightly, though his smile then faded into a frown. "When I was at the hospital, I tried to pull up their records and they weren't there."

"What do you mean they weren't there?"

"They don't exist. They've been expunged," Aronberg said, his voice growing angrier.

"You're sure they existed?" Marlene asked. "Or that they wouldn't have been moved to some storage facility because the children weren't being treated, or had died?"

"I'm absolutely positive they were there," Aronberg said. "One of my assistants and I made numerous entries from diagnosis through treatment. In fact, I have copies of those records in my own computer. As for some special storage area for the files of children who stop treatment or are deceased, there's no such thing to my knowledge. And besides, I did a search of all hospital records; those names don't exist in the hospital's database."

"Who would have access to those computer files?"

Aronberg shrugged. "There are a number of people. Doctors, such as myself, but generally only to their own patients' files. The tech guys, of course, and some of the administrative staff."

Marlene's brow furrowed and she quickly filled the physician in on her conversation with Detective Winkler. "So who would know which children and families to target?"

"If what you're telling me about how this LaFontaine works is right," Aronberg said, "he not only would have to know which children have been diagnosed with potentially fatal diseases, he would need at least a basic understanding of the disease and how it progresses. Apparently, part of how the parents get sucked into his scheme relies on his knowing that the child will appear to be getting better, which often occurs once the effects of chemo and radiation wear off and the body begins to heal itself."

Aronberg pondered for a moment. "I'd say we're looking at a medical professional, probably a physician."

Marlene suddenly recalled something Nonie had told her about how LaFontaine seemed to know so much about the family. "This person might also have access to some family history, such as their religious affiliations and employment records. I guess that's the sort of thing a professional con man would be able to pull out of his hat; one of the characteristics of a grifter is having good intuition. But it also might be a clue."

Aronberg nodded. "When they come in, the parents fill in a pretty extensive form that covers family history, including questions about religious affiliations — we do try to meet their spiritual as well as physical needs through the hospital's ministerial staff. And many of our patients' families can't afford the treatments and have to apply for financial aid, so there's a lot of that information as well."

"All right, let's narrow it down," Marlene said. "Who would have the medical knowledge, and access to the computers and this personal information?"

Aronberg thought about it and then a lightbulb seemed to go off in his mind. His face fell and tears came to his eyes. "I can think of one person for sure," he said. "But I have a hard time believing it. He's a friend and a colleague, a good doctor, though he's an administrator now." He paused and shook his head. "I can't fathom why he would do such a thing."

"I'm sorry," Marlene said. "But people do things out of character for all sorts of reasons."

Aronberg's face had grown gray and grim. "I'm sorry, too. But I can't think of anything more evil than preying on a sick child and that child's parents. If he participated in this, then he's not the man I thought I knew, and he needs to pay for it."

"His name?" Marlene asked.

"Dr. Maury Holstein. He's my brother-in-law."

As soon as Marlene got out of Aronberg's office and into her car, she called the Memphis detective. "Hey, Wink, you able to get Monique Hale?" she asked.

"I went by and nobody was home," the detective answered. "I got an unmarked car sitting down the block, so when she shows we'll get her. What about you? What did Doc Aronberg have to say?"

Marlene told him about her conversation

with the doctor.

Winkler whistled. "That's a hell of a thing. You think Aronberg will warn him?"

Marlene thought about it. She had a plan in mind and it would fail if Aronberg decided to warn his brother-in-law. *Not this guy,* she told herself, *not the guy who still cries over a child he couldn't save ten years ago.* "No," she said. "I think we're safe there. I asked him if he'd be available to give a statement when Guma and Fulton arrive and he said yes. In the meantime, I have a plan to get this Dr. Holstein to lead us back to LaFontaine."

"What are you thinkin'?"

"Well, I'd like to know how he reacts if a certain Memphis police detective comes nosing around, asking questions," she said.

"And maybe he'll panic and start making calls to a certain flimflam man in New York?" Winkler said with a chuckle. "I'll want to get a subpoena for that phone record, and any others he may have made back when LaFontaine was still in town. But I know a friendly judge and between what you've got, your boys coming in from New York, and a little arm-twisting, I think that won't be a problem. In fact, I think I'll go chat with Dr. Holstein right now and set this in motion."

Before Marlene could answer, her cell phone buzzed and indicated she had a text message from a Memphis area code. "Hold on a second," she said. "Maybe this is Monique."

Instead the text read: "Will talk. Meet me at the club at 6. Sarah."

Marlene told the detective about the text. "I'll never make it," she said. "I have to pick up my guys."

"Maybe I should meet Sarah," Winkler suggested. "We could all get together after that at headquarters."

Marlene thought about it. "No. She's expecting me," she decided. "A cop shows up instead and she may lawyer up. She's not the big fish here; LaFontaine, or Westlund, or whatever his real name is, he's the big one we don't want to get away. Guma and Fulton will just have to cool their heels."

"Tell you what," Winkler said. "I'll go roust Holstein and then pick up your guys myself. We can get a statement from Aronberg and hopefully Monique Hale will show up by then. Maybe you can get Sister Sarah to give up the whole shebang."

"Yeah, maybe," Marlene replied. "I'll stay in contact."

23

Ned Blanchett pulled Lucy closer as they walked with arms around each other's waists. "I still don't think this is a good idea," he said, looking around at the dark shadows beneath the trees of Central Park.

"Don't worry, baby, we're being watched," Lucy replied. She, too, had been studying the shadows that took over the areas between the lampposts and had seen the figures flitting from tree to rock to tree.

"That's what I'm afraid of," Blanchett groused.

"What? I thought my knight in shining armor wasn't afraid of anything," Lucy said, stopping to rise up on her tiptoes to kiss her fiancé.

"Um, meeting at night in a park with a serial killer who commands an army of street people and lives underground will pretty much do it," Blanchett argued. "Especially when I got my girl to watch out for, too."

"Your girl is probably the safest person in this park tonight," Lucy said.

"So you don't have a problem with the fact that your friend has murdered more people than Ted Bundy?"

Lucy stopped and frowned. "I don't mean to make light of David's actions," she said. "But it's complicated. The people he's killed —"

"Yeah, I know, all bad men who deserved it," Blanchett said.

"What about the fact that we — meaning our agency — sometimes kill people without the benefit of a trial?" Lucy retorted. "Does it make it okay just because we get a pass from the government?"

"They're enemy combatants," Blanchett said.

"Some have been U.S. citizens," Lucy replied before sighing. "I don't want to get into this argument and it's not really relevant to how I see David Grale. He also saved me when I was being tortured and sexually assaulted by a man who had murdered and raped women and children for pleasure."

"And for that I will be forever grateful," Blanchett said. "But I can't condone one man being judge, jury, and executioner."

"I understand, sweetheart," Lucy said softly, patting him on the cheek before turning to continue their stroll. "But he asked to speak to me, and so I'm going to listen."

They walked on without talking for several more minutes until they'd passed the Loeb Boathouse in the heart of the park. Lucy pointed ahead. "There's our man. Hmmm, I didn't know David had a dog."

Blanchett squinted at the dark figures who had materialized out of the surrounding shadows and waited beneath a lamppost: a tall man with a dog on a leash and two more large men behind them. But as they drew closer, he suddenly whispered, "I don't think that's a dog."

The young couple came to a halt when they were ten feet away from the others. "Oh God, David, now what?" Lucy asked, her hand covering her mouth.

David Grale smiled. "Good evening, Lucy. I believe you've met my pet," he said, yanking on a leash he had attached to the collar of the man at his feet. "Come here, dog, show your face."

A man crouching next to him on all fours snarled and looked up at Lucy. Even in the dim light she thought she saw a moment of recognition on the creature's face, but then it was gone, replaced by a look of insane rage. He snarled at her like a junkyard mongrel and then cringed as if he expected to be beat.

"Kane!" Lucy cried out as she looked down at the ravaged face of the man. She hated him, and yet felt pity and tried to move toward him. When Blanchett stepped forward to follow her, the two men with Grale jumped forward to intercept the pair.

"That's far enough, Lucy," Grale warned her.

"This is wrong," she replied.

"Wrong? It is merely the beginning of the eternal torment he will be suffering for his crimes," Grale said, his dark eyes seeming to be on the edge of insanity as well.

"He's a human being," Lucy argued.

"He's a demon in a human body," Grale responded. Then, as if they'd been discussing the weather, he turned to Blanchett and held out his hand. "And this must be your fiancé. You're a lucky man."

Blanchett ignored the proffered hand. "I'm aware of that," he said. "But Lucy's right. No man — and he is a man — deserves to be treated so cruelly. In fact, no dog deserves such a fate either."

"David, please, Kane could be very useful to our agency," Lucy pleaded. "He could be the key to destroying the Sons of Man once and for all. Turn him over to us."

Grale dropped his hand and looked down at Kane, who sat on his haunches staring at the ground and gibbering to himself. "That might have been an option if he was capable of anything but what you see now," he replied. "But he is quite insane. We all know he was a liar and deceiver even when he was capable of rational thought; now his mind is gone and nothing of use comes from him."

"He could be treated and then questioned," Lucy said. "Let us lock him up and find out."

"Lock him up?" Grale said scathingly. "Your father, who I trust more than almost any other man, had him in custody and yet he escaped. And remember what Kane's agents were willing to do in order to accomplish that . . . or have you forgotten the children and police officers who were murdered in cold blood? They will stop at nothing to free him again, and the Sons of Man have infiltrated everywhere, including the federal prison system."

"David, you are better than this . . . ," Lucy said.

"Enough! I didn't ask to meet with you to argue the fate of Andrew Kane. He is my dog and will remain so until his soul is sent back to his dark master."

Lucy's face fell. "Then what is it you sent Warren for?" she asked angrily.

Grale's own face softened. "Well, I'd like to think you may have come just to see an old friend. It's been a long time."

"I would have preferred to do it under different circumstances," Lucy replied.

"Undoubtedly," Grale said, "but the circumstances are what they are."

"Then what?"

"I wanted to let you know, so that you can pass it on to whoever needs it, that Nadya Malovo is in some way mixed up in a plot planned for Halloween in the Village involving your dad and family," Grale said.

When Lucy didn't reply, he nodded and smiled slightly. "I see that this information is not entirely new to you."

"Is that it?"

"No," Grale said. "Maybe you don't know that whatever the plot involves, Malovo arranged it with Boris Kazanov. She claims that she was trying to call it off, though I doubt it was for any noble reason."

"Maybe she thought it would mess up her deal," Blanchett suggested.

"So that was you on the boardwalk in Brighton Beach," Lucy interjected. "I should have known. The papers were saying it was a gangland killing, but the arrows and knife work . . . who else but David Grale and company."

Grale started to speak but was interrupted by one of his bodyguards' sudden coughing fit. His face changed from grim satisfaction to one of compassion as he reached out and patted his man on the back. "Are you all right, Brother Harvey?" he inquired.

Harvey continued to gasp for breath before nodding. "I'll be okay," he said.

"That doesn't sound good," Lucy commented.

"He and I both share a common affliction with *Mycobacterium tuberculosis*," Grale answered. "We seem to be in a race to see who will meet our Maker first."

"You need to go to a hospital," Lucy said. "Both of you."

Grale shook his head. "It appears to be a particularly virulent strain and resistant to all antibiotics," he said. "It's all right. Harvey actually looks forward to shuffling off this mortal coil. Rather than feeling pity for my dog here though, you might save it for this good man instead. His wife and child were raped and murdered eight years ago by an evil man who'd just been let out of prison after serving only four years for a similar crime, the result of your justice system's plea bargaining. Unable to cope, he turned to alcohol and lived on the streets, which is where we met. He hasn't had a drop in four years, and you want to know what cured him? I'll give you a hint: it wasn't Alcoholics Anonymous or rehab. It was justice, true justice."

"True justice?" Lucy asked.

"Yes," Harvey answered. "Father David helped me hunt down the bastard who butchered my family when the parole board let him go after eight years. You want to know what he was doing? He was shacking up with a thirteen-year-old girl he had so drugged up that she couldn't stand up to leave after I slit his throat."

"But is that justice or revenge?" Lucy questioned.

"Both," Grale said. "Justice and a large dose of revenge. But at the end of the day, one more sexual predator who will never harm a woman or child again. But we digress. I've let you know what I've learned about Malovo."

"I'll pass on the information about the Kazanov connection," Lucy said. "Thank you for that."

For a moment, a sad look crossed Grale's face. "Whatever our differences in how we deal with evil men, we are all on the side of good," he said. He smiled, though the look remained. "So, I hear the two of you are getting married."

"Next spring," Lucy said, looking up at Blanchett.

"I'm happy for you," Grale said. "I still remember the gangly teenager who helped me feed the homeless at the shelter."

For a moment, Lucy forgot about the dangers and the leashed human being at Grale's feet and laughed. "I had such a crush on you," she said. "Before you . . . before . . ."

"Before it became apparent that I was a serial killer," Grale said, bemused. "I suppose that would put a damper on a young girl's ardor. But it's time for us to return to our home sweet home."

"David, let us take Kane," Lucy pleaded again. "Escort us to the police station. He won't be going anywhere."

"Sorry, Lucy, the answer is still no," Grale replied, tugging slightly on the leash. "This dog belongs with his master, and he's of no use to you." He pulled on the leash a little harder. "Come dog, heel."

Kane whimpered and looked one last time at Lucy before his lip curled and he obediently turned to follow his master back into the shadows, leaving Lucy and Ned alone.

"So, you had a crush on David Grale?"

Blanchett said.

"Yes, when I was a girl," Lucy said, then laughed. "Apparently I have questionable taste in men."

"Until me, you mean," Blanchett said, giving her a hug and a kiss. "I saved you from yourself."

"Lucky me," Lucy replied and kissed him back.

As the young couple walked back the way they had come, another dark figure pressed himself back into the shadows of the Loeb Boathouse where he'd been watching the meeting from afar. He licked his thin lips and smiled at the thought of the riches that would be coming his way and the sweetness of revenge.

24

Marlene approached the turn for the Gentleman's Club but then spotted the BMW with SARAH imprinted on the license plate beneath a streetlight up ahead. She continued past the parking lot and drove up alongside the car, rolling her window down. She was surprised to see not only Sarah but Monique Hale, in the passenger seat, her eyes wide with fright.

"Can't talk here," Sarah said. "Follow me."

Before Marlene could respond, Sarah sped off. So she pulled out behind her car and called Winkler.

"I don't like it," Winkler said. "Let her go and we'll pick her up. I can get a patrol car there in five minutes or less."

"Let me see what's going on first," Marlene responded. "I don't know why Monique is with her but if she's in trouble, it's my fault and I need to stay with her."

A familiar voice broke into the conversation. "Marlene, it's Clay," Fulton said. "I agree with Detective Winkler. I know you won't stop, but you stay back, you hear me?"

"I hear you, Clay," Marlene replied. "Welcome to Memphis. I assume Mr. Guma is with you and Wink has filled you two in on what's been happening."

"Yes on both counts," Fulton replied. "What's going on now?"

"We're turning off the highway and onto a two-lane road," Marlene said. "And she's speeding up."

For the next twenty minutes, as the sky grew darker, Marlene followed the BMW as it made a series of turns onto roads, many of them unmarked, that appeared to be leading farther out into the country. The clouds overhead, which had been threatening to rain all day, suddenly began to let loose.

About the same time, the BMW slowed, while behind Marlene headlights appeared, which she soon identified as belonging to a truck. "Looks like they've got me penned in," she told the men listening. "Wait a second, I'm getting a call. It's a Memphis area code but I don't recognize the number. I'll get back to you in a second." She pushed the button to switch to the new caller.

"Throw your phone on the road where I can see it," a man's voice demanded.

"What?"

"Throw your phone out the window on the road *now* or we shoot the Hale bitch!" the man snarled into the phone.

"How do I know you won't shoot her, and then me, anyway?" she asked.

"You don't," the man said. "But I'd prefer not to. We're just going to tie you up and leave you out here for a spell so we can get away."

"Who's 'we'? Sarah, you, and LaFontaine?"

"Never you mind; do as you're told or I'll be forced to shoot you both. Now chuck the phone where I can see it and then follow Sarah!"

Marlene thought quickly. She grabbed the GPS unit from the dash. Hoping that in the semidark and from a car it would look enough like a cell phone, she tossed it out the window. Apparently it was good enough, as the BMW started to move again and the truck pulled up directly behind her and honked. She put the car into Drive and followed, placing her cell phone on the seat next to her. She pressed the Speakerphone button and then called Winkler. When the detective answered, she explained what was happening.

"And, Clay, I have to say that your insistence on the family having cell phones with the locater application built in may just pay off," she said, giving him the telephone number to call and password so he could ask the phone company to pinpoint her location.

"Marlene, it's still going to take us too long to get to you. Step on it and leave this guy behind," Fulton said.

"Can't, Clay," Marlene said. "I should have known that as soon as I talked to Sarah they'd go after Monique."

"Have you seen any road signs or other landmarks?" The voice was Winkler's.

"Nothing," Marlene replied. "Wait . . . we're going past what looks like an old service station. Definitely closed down and boarded up. The sign says AJ's . . . and I can't read the rest."

"AJ's Gas and Oil," Winkler said. "I know it. You're near the Mississippi. We're on the way. Ten minutes."

"Step on it, boys," Marlene said. She reached down and felt inside her purse for the .380. Locating the little pistol, she tucked it into her pants and covered it with the blouse she was wearing.

As they continued to drive, she described

the surrounding area as best she could with the twilight giving way to the night. "We seem to be following the river now," she said. "But it's quite a ways below."

"You're on a bluff above the river," Winkler said. "I know where you're at. We'll be there in five."

"Can you make it sooner? We're stopping."

Marlene was suddenly aware of the figure of a large man outside her window. He was pointing a large-caliber revolver at her. "Put your hands on the wheel!" he shouted.

With no other choice, Marlene did as she was told, wondering how fast he could react if she went for the gun in her pants. *Not fast enough,* she thought.

The man reached forward and opened her car door. "Get out," he barked, keeping the gun pointed at her head. She did as she was told and he saw the cell phone on the seat. "What the fuck," he snarled, and struck her on the side of her head with his gun, knocking her to the ground.

Sarah walked up with Monique Hale, whose hands were tied in front of her. "You going to do her here?"

"No, over at the cliff," the man said. "She and the other one are going in the river. The water's high with all this rain; the cops won't find their bodies until New Orleans, if then."

Woozy, Marlene tried to think of something to save herself and Monique Hale. She pointed at the cell phone. "The cops are listening to everything," she said. "And they'll be here in a few minutes. Give yourself up before you take this too far."

Keeping his gun trained on her, the man reached inside and grabbed the phone. He looked at it. "There's nobody on the line," he said with a smile. "There ain't nobody coming for you."

Marlene looked hard at the man in the glow of her car's headlights. "And to think I wanted to thank you for saving my husband," she said.

"What in the hell are you talking about?"

"You're Frank Bernsen; you shot Kathryn Boole before she could shoot my husband, Butch Karp. You got away with that one, but I really don't think you want the heat that will come with shooting the wife of the district attorney."

Bernsen hesitated, then nodded toward a path beyond the parked BMW. "I got friends in high places, we'll just have to disappear for a bit," he said. "Now get up and walk."

The rain was letting up and a full moon was rising in the east when the two prisoners and their captors reached the edge of a steep embankment. Marlene could just make out the dark waters of the Mississippi far below.

"That's far enough," Bernsen shouted. "On your knees."

"No," Marlene said as Monique fell to her knees and started to sob next to her. She was still feeling woozy from the blow to her head and could feel her blood mixing with the rain running down her face. "If you're going to shoot me, I'll be standing up when you do."

Sarah shook her head. "I'm going back to the car, Frank," she said. "I don't have the stomach for this." She started to turn but stopped when he pointed his gun at her.

"Over with the others," he said.

Sarah's eyes widened in fear. "You can't shoot me, Frank," she pleaded. "Me and John go way back."

"Sorry, Sarah," Bernsen said, though there was nothing apologetic in his voice. "But he told me you had to go, too. You know how he feels about loose ends."

Sarah tried to run, but Bernsen aimed at the back of her head and pulled the trigger. The gun roared and the woman's body was flung forward into the mud.

It was all over quickly, but it was enough

time for Marlene to pull her gun and squeeze off a shot at Bernsen. The big man grunted in pain and doubled over as the bullet struck his stomach, but as she tried to shoot again, her gun jammed.

With a groan Bernsen straightened up, his face angry and frightened, but when he realized she couldn't shoot again, he smiled and leveled his gun at Monique. "Nice try, bitch. Tell the devil hello for me, but first you're going to have to watch your friend die and know that it was your fault."

Marlene did the only thing she could think of; she turned and dove at Monique Hale. She heard Bernsen's gun go off and felt the bullet tear into her shoulder, but her momentum carried her and the other woman over the edge of the bluff and down into the swirling waters of the river.

The plunge took her and Monique beneath the surface. With one arm wounded and the opposite hand holding on to the woman, she kicked as hard as she could. It seemed like forever before they broke through the surface, gasping for air.

"I can't swim!" Monique cried out as she thrashed around and nearly broke Marlene's grip.

"Kick your legs as hard as you can!" Marlene shouted.

There was the sound of another gunshot and a bullet zipped into the water close to Marlene's head. She looked up and back at the dark figure of Bernsen, now some twenty-five yards upstream from where they'd been swept away. He was taking aim, but suddenly he whirled in the other direction and pointed his gun. Several flashes of light followed, accompanied by the sound of more shots. Moments later his body tumbled backward over the edge of the embankment and down into the river.

Almost immediately, the dark figures of three more men appeared at the edge of the bluff. "Help!" Marlene screamed as the current dragged her and her struggling witness downstream. One of the men jumped and landed in the water with a splash, but she lost sight of him as her head went under again.

Fighting one more time to the surface, Marlene sucked in air. But she knew she was losing the fight to stay up and growing weaker from the loss of blood while trying to keep her grip on Monique.

I'm going to die, she thought as the waters closed over her head again. She used her last bit of strength to try to lift Monique's head above the surface. *Sorry, Butch. Sorry, kids. I love you all.*

As consciousness started to ebb, Marlene felt the burden of Monique's body being taken from her. At the same time, she felt herself being pulled up toward a soft light. *Jesus,* she thought, *thank you.*

"Missus, can you hear me?" a deep, strong voice said to her. "Hold on, now. I got you and your friend. Help is on the way."

Marlene opened her eyes and found herself looking into the broad worried face of an older black man she didn't know. Behind him the moon rose above the bluff. There was the sound of someone splashing behind her and her savior looked up. "Glad to see you, mister," he said. "I got them both by the hand, but I can't quite get 'em in the boat."

"Start with this one," a voice she recognized as Fulton's said behind her. She felt his strong hands around her waist and with a mighty shove, he launched her upward and, with the other man's assistance, into the boat. She lay there in the bottom of the wooden rowboat, not quite comprehending what was happening; a moment later, the unconscious body of Monique Hale landed next to her. Then Fulton hauled himself in over the side.

"I'm Detective Clay Fulton," she heard her friend tell the boat's owner. "I can't thank you enough."

"My pleasure, Mr. Fulton, the name's Lonnie Lynn," the man replied. "Lucky I was after some catfish tonight, or these ladies might have been fish food. Mind tellin' me what all the shootin' was about?"

"Tell you what," Fulton replied. "Get me to the nearest telephone, and I'll fill you in. In the meantime, my friend's been shot, and I need to apply pressure to the wound."

"You go right ahead," Lynn said. "I need to get these oars going or we'll be in Louisiana before you can shake a stick. We can talk later."

Fulton's face swam into Marlene's vision. "Hang in there, kid," he said as he pressed down hard on her wound, causing her to cry out in pain. "Jesus, Marlene, don't you think you're getting a little old for this?"

Marlene smiled. "I wouldn't want to miss all the fun," she croaked, and then lost consciousness.

25

Karp waited patiently as the tough-looking police sergeant placed his hand on the Bible and was sworn in as the People's next witness. They were in the second day of the trial of John LaFontaine, a.k.a. the Reverend C. G. Westlund, in front of New York State Supreme Court judge Henry Gresham Temple III and just getting to the heart of the matter.

Outside, Indian summer had given way to fall, with the deciduous trees in Manhattan putting on a display of color that amazed even longtime locals. However, it reminded Karp that Halloween, and his appearance as the grand marshal of the annual parade in the Village, was only a few days away. He wondered briefly how that night would go, but at the moment his focus had to be on the trial, and more narrowly on his witness Sergeant Trent Sadler: "Did there come a time when one of the men with the defendant attempted to prevent you from doing your duty?"

Karp turned toward the spectator section and smiled slightly at his wife, who was sitting a few rows back behind the prosecution table. When he'd received the call from Fulton that Marlene had been shot and was in the hospital, it was all he could do not to hop on the next plane and fly to Memphis. But she was the one who stopped him.

"I'm okay," she'd said, taking the phone from the detective. "Katz and I will have matching scars, but I'm more worried that when Westlund, or LaFontaine, doesn't hear from Bernsen, he'll skip town. Talk to Fulton and Detective Winkler, but there's plenty to arrest him on now. You can baby me later."

Karp had talked to the two detectives and then acted quickly. When two of Fulton's detectives arrived at the Avenue A loft, LaFontaine was already packing several suitcases, one of which contained more than $200,000 cash. He'd been arrested, however, without incident and taken to the DAO, where Karp had been waiting for him in an interview room.

As expected, the itinerant preacher had refused to give Karp a statement and demanded a lawyer, which had ended their

338

conversation. However, not before they'd engaged in a little back-and-forth.

"You'll never make it stick, Karp," LaFontaine said scathingly.

"You're going to swing on this one, LaFontaine," Karp replied evenly. "No plea bargain. No rationalizing. Just the trial, conviction, and prison." It wasn't the sort of give-and-take he would normally have engaged in with a defendant, but in this case, he had a reason.

Shortly thereafter, Karp went before a grand jury, which indicted LaFontaine for depraved-indifference murder.

LaFontaine had invoked his right not to talk to Karp. But that didn't prevent him from issuing statements to the media — mostly through his lawyer and the public relations firm they hired — from his cell in the Tombs. The gloves, as thin as they had been before, were all the way off now. The Jewish district attorney of New York County was anti-God and anti-Christianity, especially fundamentalist Christianity, as represented by the Reverend John LaFontaine and faith healing. And much to his consternation, all Gilbert Murrow could counter with was that the DAO would not try the case in the media but would let the facts speak for themselves at trial.

Unfortunately — *Or fortunately, depending on how you see two fewer dirtbags in the world,* Karp thought — Frank Bernsen had not survived being shot by Marlene and then Fulton, though the official cause of death was drowning in the Mississippi River. Nor had Sister Sarah, whose full name had been Sarah Westerberg, the owner of a lengthy criminal record that included larceny, criminal impersonation, and prostitution, made it to the hospital alive with a gaping head wound.

Their deaths had benefitted LaFontaine in two ways. They could not roll over on their boss. His defense attorney, J. R. Rottingham, a rotund, bug-eyed, blustering self-anointed sage who fancied himself a constitutional scholar, had been quoted early and often saying that any "alleged" criminal activity would have been conducted by Frank Bernsen and Sarah Westerberg without the knowledge of his client, "who would be shocked if the allegations are true."

This was a case without a smoking gun, or even a single dramatic witness who could pull it all together from the witness stand, especially as Nonie Ellis was still missing. It was a case that would be built of small pieces, from the ground up.

There had been some discussion in the

office, particularly between him and Guma, who was sitting second chair, about whether to dismiss "without prejudice" the indictment against LaFontaine until Ellis could be located; a warrant had been issued for her, but she'd disappeared. But both men had agreed that LaFontaine would run, possibly with the help of the ATF, which had so far refused to cooperate.

So, feeling somewhat like a fighter going for the heavyweight title with a hand tied behind his back, Karp had nevertheless entered the ring. As he'd stated in his opening remarks earlier that week, the People would prove that John LaFontaine, a.k.a. C. G. Westlund, had systematically preyed on the vulnerable families of seriously ill children, including the Ellises. That he'd identified his targets in Memphis with the aid of hospital administrator Dr. Maury Holstein, and that he'd used his position as the families' spiritual adviser to dissuade them from seeking medical attention for their kids, "knowing full well that these innocent children would die painful, lingering, and preventable deaths while their parents, who had given their trust to this man and feared his condemnation, stood by praying and watching helplessly."

As he spoke, Karp had walked over to face

the defense table, staring implacably down at LaFontaine, whose long hair was swept back behind his ears, and his beard had been neatly trimmed. The false preacher had done his best to smile up at him, though it had come off as strained. "And he did it not out of religious conviction," Karp said, accusing him to his face, "but for the most venal, despicable motive of all: he did it for money. And that, ladies and gentlemen, is what we will prove, so that you will have no choice but to find this . . . this charlatan, this flimflam man . . . guilty of depraved-indifference murder."

The defense had countered as expected: that LaFontaine was being persecuted for his religious beliefs, "which are at the very heart and soul of our rights as Americans." He was only a spiritual adviser to whom frightened families had turned in times of great crisis.

"Did he express to them his own dearly held belief that only God heals, and only God decides who lives and who dies? Of course," Rottingham said as he stood in front of the jurors and looked from face to face. "But isn't the expression of one's religious beliefs one of our most dearly held rights? It didn't mean he forced anyone to adhere to his beliefs. The only people responsible for not seeking medical attention for Micah Ellis are his parents."

Knowing that he would have to deal with the insurance policy issue, Rottingham had then blamed it on Frank Bernsen and Sarah Westerberg, though without admitting that there had been any wrongdoing. "And if it is shown — and that, ladies and gentlemen, is a *big* if — that anyone would profit from the death of Micah Ellis, it was not my client, but two other persons. One of them connected with the ministry, yes, but operating without the Reverend LaFontaine's knowledge. Two people who unfortunately — or might I suggest conveniently for the persecution, I mean prosecution, of my client — died in Memphis during a shootout with the police, and so they are not with us to answer our questions."

Following the opening statements, Karp had moved quickly through his witnesses. He called Assistant Medical Examiner Dr. Gail Manning to testify that Micah Ellis had died from general organ failure caused by brain tumors. She said there was evidence of seizures and that the boy was probably blind, unable to control his muscles, "and in extreme pain that was not alleviated by any commonly used painkillers" when he

343

slipped into a coma and died.

Dr. Manning had been followed by the paramedics, Justin Raskov and Donald Bailey, who'd been called to the scene where Micah Ellis lay dying in his parents' apartment. They relayed how LaFontaine and two of his men had blocked their way into the building.

"That guy there," Bailey said, pointing at LaFontaine, "stood in front of the door with his men and quoted Scripture, saying that we couldn't pass and if we tried, he'd come out with a sword against us."

"Surely you understood that my client was speaking in biblical hyperbole?" Rotterdam asked on cross-examination.

"I took it as a direct threat," Bailey countered. "It wouldn't have been the first time some nut with a sword came at me in New York City. It was pretty clear he and his boys weren't going to let us in, not until the cops showed up, and even then one of them tried to attack the cops."

"Was the man who tried to attack the police officers named Frank?" Karp then asked on redirect.

"Yes, I believe it was. That guy there," Bailey said, again pointing at LaFontaine, "called him Brother Frank. The cops hauled his butt off to jail."

Now, on the second day of the trial, Karp called Sadler to the stand to recount his version of the facts. "Sergeant, explain to the jury the facts and circumstances as you observed them when you arrived at the scene." he said.

"The defendant and two other men attempted to prevent me and the paramedics from going into the apartment to aid the sick child."

"And did he refuse to comply with a direct, lawful order from you to move out of the way?"

"He did."

"At some point, sergeant, one of the men with the defendant attempted to prevent you from doing your duty?"

Sadler looked straight at Karp. "Yes, one, Frank Bernsen, attempted to assault me and my officers. He was subsequently subdued, arrested, and charged with assault on a police officer and attempting to interfere with emergency personnel in the performance of their duties."

"During this obstruction and assault by Bernsen what, if anything, was the defendant doing?"

"The defendant was in charge and gave Bernsen one of these," the sergeant said, demonstrating LaFontaine's gesture.

"Let the record reflect that the witness indicated the defendant used his head in such a manner as to direct Frank Bernsen to physically confront the police sergeant and his men," Karp said.

A few questions later, after discussing what the sergeant encountered inside the apartment, Karp asked, "What, if anything, occurred as Micah Ellis was being loaded into the ambulance?"

"A large crowd of what I guess you'd call the defendant's followers had gathered on the sidewalk and were trying to prevent the paramedics from transporting the boy."

"How was the defendant involved in this?" Karp asked.

"He was egging them on," the sergeant said. "He invoked some religious injunction and said in substance that we were affronting the will of God. And that's when some of the crowd began to demand that we stop and moved forward in a confrontational manner."

"And how did you respond?" Karp asked.

"I called for backup," Sadler replied. "It was getting pretty dicey but then the kid's father asked everybody to settle down and that seemed to calm the crowd."

"I have no further questions, Your Honor," Karp said, turning toward Judge Temple.

"Your witness, Mr. Rottingham," the judge, a heavyset, round-faced man known for being a straightforward, matter-of-fact, and short-tempered jurist, said.

"Did the defendant actually say anything to encourage Frank Bernsen to move toward you in a manner you assumed to be an attack?" Rottingham said as he rose from his seat.

"I didn't assume anything," Sadler shot back. "If I hadn't sidestepped him and stuck him with a Taser, he would have been on me."

"So you say."

"So I know."

"But you haven't answered my question," Rottingham said. "Did my client say anything to Frank Bernsen to instigate this alleged assault?"

"No. Like I indicated, just the head motion," Sadler retorted. "But it was clear as day what he wanted."

"To you maybe."

"Yes, to me, and to my men, and to others as well."

"And when the boy was taken — against his parents' will —"

"The mother's will maybe; the father was okay with it," Sadler said, correcting him.

"Okay, against the mother's will from the

apartment," Rottingham continued, "did the Reverend LaFontaine attempt to physically block the paramedics?"

"No."

"So all he did was voice his displeasure?"

"He was agitating the crowd, trying to get them to stop us."

"Did he say that?"

"No, he implied it."

"I see, so you're a mind reader," Rottingham said scathingly. "Did anyone in this crowd attempt to physically stop the paramedics from transporting Micah Ellis to the hospital?"

"No. Like I said, the father interceded and things calmed down."

"So essentially, the Reverend LaFontaine and his congregation were exercising their free speech rights?"

"No, that would not be the case," Sadler shot back. "Inciting to violence and obstructing police action is not a First Amendment right, most respectfully."

After the midmorning break, Karp called Dr. Aronberg to the stand and began by asking him to lay out the chronology of Micah's diagnosis and treatment. "It was hard on the boy," the doctor said, "but I was encouraged by the results. But then he failed to return for post-treatment checkups, and his parents did not respond to our attempts to contact them."

"What is the likelihood he would have survived if this treatment plan had continued?" Karp asked.

"With his type of tumor, which was slow-growing, the survival rate is about seventy percent if we get to it in time and treat it aggressively," Aronberg said.

"And if untreated?"

"The child would die."

"Doctor, you are aware of what happened to Micah Ellis and Natalie Hale, is that correct?"

Aronberg dropped his head for a moment and then nodded, looking up. "Yes, they are deceased."

"And did you recently look for their medical records at the hospital where they were treated by you?"

"I did."

"What did you find?"

"Nothing. Their records had been expunged."

"Is that unusual?"

"Yes. It's simply not done . . . at least it's not supposed to be done."

"Can you think of any legitimate reason why they would have been expunged?"

"No. There is no legitimate reason to expunge patient records."

"Is this something that could have happened by accident, or say a power failure, or any other reason aside from an intentional effort to get rid of these records?"

"No. It was intentional. Even the backup files had been erased."

"Objection!" Rottingham bellowed. "The witness is not competent to come to that conclusion. I ask that his answer be stricken from the record!"

Judge Temple held up his hand to have Rottingham hold his thought. He then leaned toward the witness and asked, "Doctor, how do you conclude that this was intentional?"

"Your Honor, when I was questioned about this matter, I conducted my own inquiry with the hospital computer technicians," he said. "They demonstrated how the system works, including its fail-safes that would prevent anything except an intentional purging of the records. Which in their experience, and mine, had never occurred before."

"Very well, thank you, doctor," Temple said, and turned back to Rottingham. "Do you wish to probe further, now that you've opened the door?"

Red-faced, Rottingham stood silently, reached into his vest pocket, and withdrew a handkerchief that he used to mop his brow. He then sat down, ignoring the angry glare of his client.

Karp let Dr. Aronberg's explanation sink in for a moment and then changed direction slightly. "Doctor, when a new patient is admitted to the hospital for treatment, do they — or in the case of a minor, do their parents — fill out any forms regarding family history, religious preferences, and economic status?"

"Yes, a fairly large document actually, particularly if they are applying for financial assistance."

"So this form might indicate which religious denomination the parents might adhere to?"

"Yes."

"And whether one or both parents were unemployed?"

"Yes."

"So someone with access to this form, as well as the medical records, would know quite a bit about the patient and his family, including their home address?"

"Absolutely."

"And who would have access to the medical records and this personal information?"

"Someone in the hospital administration."

"Thank you, doctor, those are all of my questions for now," Karp said.

Rottingham rose and walked over to the jury box, turning to Aronberg as he asked his question. "Do patients with Micah's diagnosis always die if untreated?"

The doctor looked at him for a long moment before answering. "As with any disease, there are extremely rare instances of an astrocytoma tumor going into spontaneous remission."

"And what causes a spontaneous remission?" Rottingham asked, looking now at the jury.

"We don't always understand the mechanism," Aronberg admitted. "We do know that the human mind and body sometimes surprise us with their ability to combat disease without medical assistance."

"Or what some people might call a miracle, or divine intervention?"

"Perhaps," Aronberg said. "And I have no problem with the idea of divine intervention, though I believe that God works through the intellect of human beings and that, God-inspired or not, there is a scientific reason behind spontaneous remission that is beyond our current understanding."

"That's a nice speech, doctor," Rottingham said, "but what it boils down to is that sometimes spontaneous remissions, or what some people would call miracles, occur and you don't have a scientific, or medical, explanation for it. Isn't that true?"

"That's correct," Aronberg said.

"But until, or perhaps I should say *if,* that day comes, when you can explain these occurrences, your thoughts on the matter are no more valid than those of someone who believes that a spontaneous remission is an act of God."

"I suppose so," the doctor replied.

Rottingham strolled over to the defense table and stood next to his client. "Doctor, have you ever had any contact with the Reverend LaFontaine?"

"No."

"Have you ever seen him before arriving in this courtroom?"

"No."

"Did the parents of Micah Ellis or Natalie Hale ever tell you that they were no longer going to allow their children to be treated by you because the Reverend LaFontaine told them not to?"

"No."

"And, doctor, in your research into the expunged records, did you turn up anything that indicated that the Reverend LaFontaine had anything to do with it?" Rottingham asked, placing a hand on his client's shoulder.

Aronberg looked down at his hands. "No, I saw nothing to indicate he was involved."

Rottingham smiled. "Thank you, no more questions."

As Aronberg stepped down and passed between the defense and prosecution tables, Karp glanced at LaFontaine, who was looking at him with a slight smirk on his face. *Pride before the fall,* Karp thought, and turned away.

26

Karp was still thinking about Lafontaine's smirk, and ego, when he hurried into the reception area of his office, where Darla Milquetost told him, "Your visitors are already here." She pointed to the larger room where Nadya Malovo and company waited before adding, "That woman gives me the creeps."

Karp laughed. "She has that effect on a lot of people."

"Oh, by the way, I'm not exactly sure where this came from, it was on my desk after I let them into the meeting room and got them coffee," Milquetost said, handing him an envelope, "but it's addressed to you."

Walking into the room, Karp quickly took in the scene. Seated at the conference table were Nadya Malovo, her attorney Bruce Knight, Espey Jaxon, and Mike Rolles. Marshal Jen Capers was standing behind her prisoner, talking quietly to Clay Fulton.

Malovo spoke first. "It is my good friend Butch Karp," she said. "Apparently we will have yet another conversation that does not involve a witness stand."

Karp, tight-lipped, ignored her as he made his way around the table and took a seat. He looked at Jaxon. "So I got your message; what's up?"

Jaxon pointed. "Hello, Butch. I'll defer here to Agent Rolles, who called me just before I called you this morning and asked for this meeting."

Karp raised an eyebrow and looked at the other agent, who said, "As you know, Nadya has been hearing from her sources for months now about a possible terrorist attack aimed at the parade in the Village on Halloween night. She's been in contact with these people in the past week and the threat has gained credibility."

"It has gone from the planning to implementation stage," Malovo said.

"We've been worried for some time about the possibility of this particular attack," Rolles added. "Think about it. The parade draws two million spectators and fifty thousand participants, almost all of them wearing costumes, and all crammed into a one-mile stretch of Sixth Avenue. Although the NYPD tries to control entrance to the parade itself from the side streets, it's nearly impossible, not to mention there are several subway stops in that immediate area."

"It's a security nightmare," Jaxon said. "With everyone in costume, the police can't check beneath each robe and look in every backpack or behind every mask."

"Osama bin Laden could have come as himself," Malovo interjected, "and everybody would have congratulated him on his costume."

"So where do we go from here? Call off the parade?" Fulton asked.

The room went quiet until Rolles cleared his throat and spoke. "National security policy has been to keep these threats quiet," he said. "While we believe that this particular threat is very credible, if we stopped events every time there was a credible threat — meaning we are aware that some lone wolf or group is planning something — there would be no football games or World Series or concerts."

"There is something else," Malovo interjected. "Along with a desire to strike a major blow against America, those behind this operation have one very specific target."

"And that is?" Karp asked.

"You," she replied with a smile. "Apparently, they have tired of your . . . *interfer-*

ence with their plans and want to repay you for the downfall of my former colleagues Amir al-Sistani and the imam Jabbar. These are people who believe in revenge."

"That does it; whatever happens with the parade, you're out," Fulton snarled, glaring at Malovo. "We'll make up some excuse . . . work or illness or —"

Karp held up his hand. "Hold on, Clay," he said. "I don't see how I can live with saving myself while agreeing to allow this parade to go forward."

"It might actually work against us," Malovo said. "If they don't see you, they will assume that their plan has been discovered. But they have a separate Plan B."

"And what is that?" Fulton scowled.

Malovo shrugged. "I haven't been able to find out yet. But if they stay with the original plan, we have a better chance of stopping them. I think they may even be growing suspicious of me . . . after the ferry attack was thwarted, they have been more circumspect, though they have still needed Ajmaani — me of course — to supply them with their materials and financing. They are expecting me to be at the parade, too."

"You're not going to any parade," Capers argued.

Malovo looked at Rolles, who shook his

head. "I'm afraid that she has to," he said. "Not only would her absence warn them that something isn't right, she can identify at least some of the participants."

"If you know who these people are, why not just intercept them now?" Fulton said.

"It may have to do with their distrust of me," Malovo explained, "or they've learned not to put all of their eggs in one basket — that is the saying, no? — but I have only been able to meet with the two main leaders. There has been no contact with their teams."

"Then take down the leaders and the plan falls apart," Fulton said.

"It is my understanding that if the two are captured or killed, the others will carry out Plan B," she replied. "It may not be as dramatic as attacking the parade and trying to kill our friend Butch, but I am convinced it will be deadly and I have no idea how to stop it."

"Nadya meets with these guys the night before Halloween. We'll be tracking these two and we'll try to intercept them before the parade if we can get them all together," Rolles said. "But I think we need to be thinking in terms of making these guys think that their plan is working."

Malovo turned from Rolles to Karp. "So,

I guess you will be the bait to catch these fish. So what will your costume be, Butch? I am going as Little Red Riding Hood; perhaps you should be Big Bad Wolf, no?"

Karp mused. "The world is truly upside down."

Laughing, Malovo left with Rolles and Capers. When they were gone, Fulton sat down at the table. "You know she's egging you on to be at the parade," he said. "And it's not so she can help catch terrorists."

"I know, Clay," Karp replied. "But I don't see any other choice." He looked at his legal pad and saw the envelope that Milquetost had handed him stuffed in the pages. He opened it and read a note inside, then looked at his watch. "I have to be back to court in fifteen minutes. But I want to go get a newspaper."

Fulton frowned. "I'll go get it," he said. "You got enough on your plate."

Karp smiled. "Nah, I can use a breath of fresh air, too. Something about that woman; she's truly the queen of darkness."

Fulton laughed. "I know just what you mean."

27

As Karp turned to watch, a side door in the courtroom opened and a frightened-looking man timidly entered. He stood for a moment as if debating whether to try to turn and run despite the imposing presence behind him of the large black detective who escorted him from the witness waiting room.

"Please approach the stand to be sworn in," Judge Temple directed the man, who swallowed hard, adjusted his tie, nodded, and walked toward the low swinging gate between the spectator section and the well of the court. He glanced once at the defendant, who sat looking at him with an eerie smile plastered to his face, and then at Karp before fixing his eyes ahead on the court clerk who waited.

The phrase "stuck between a rock and a hard place" comes to mind, Karp thought as the man swore to tell the truth and took a seat in the witness box alongside the jury rail. He wondered if the red flush on the man's cheeks was due to fear, shame, or embarrassment — or likely all three. It was certainly not the nip in the October air outside. Dr. Maury Holstein had not spent much time outside at all since his arrest that past April for his participation in the grand larceny/fraud case still pending against him and LaFontaine in Tennessee.

At Marlene's suggestion, Detective Winkler had called Holstein following the shooting and asked if he could come in to talk to him about "the Reverend John LaFontaine and some irregularities in hospital patient records." As expected, the doctor panicked and called LaFontaine in New York City to ask what he should do.

LaFontaine was smart enough not to say much. "I don't know what you're talking about," the crafty con man responded. "And don't call here again." But scared, and now alone, Holstein had persisted with several more calls.

That was enough to link Holstein to LaFontaine and to get the Memphis judge, who had sufficient probable cause, to issue a wiretap order and authorize a subpoena for hospital telephone and computer records. The hospital records revealed numerous calls from Holstein's office to cell phones registered to the Holy Covenant Church of Jesus Christ Reformed when LaFontaine was still in Memphis. And while the computer records had been wiped clean of references to Micah Ellis and Natalie Hale, a forensic computer expert had been able to determine that the records had existed and had been deleted from a computer in Holstein's office.

Given the nature of the fraudulent schemes, Holstein was arrested. He'd immediately cracked under questioning from Winkler and Fulton and then gave a comprehensive, incriminating recorded statement to Guma.

When Guma asked what could have possibly driven him to become part of such an evil plot, the doctor began to cry. He had a gambling problem and was in the hole for fifty thousand dollars to LaFontaine's thugs, who had approached him with a deal: "I could wind up in the Mississippi with a bullet in my head, or I could go along with the program. My debt would be forgiven, and I'd get paid."

However, the threat wasn't the only thing that sealed the deal. He'd been having an affair with a stripper named Sarah at the Gentleman's Club. "They got some photos of me with her at a motel and said that if I ever told, they'd give them to my wife and put them on Facebook."

Holstein had turned over the photographs, one of which Karp showed him on the witness stand after establishing that the doctor had been blackmailed into getting involved in a plan to identify seriously ill children being treated at the hospital. "Is this the woman you knew as Sarah?" he asked.

The doctor looked up and then quickly back down. He nodded his head.

"You're going to have to answer yes or no loud enough for the court reporter and the jurors to hear you," Karp said.

"Yes, that's her . . . and me," Holstein said.

Karp entered the photograph into evidence and then showed it to the jury before continuing his questioning. "Do you see the man who approached you about this plan sitting in the courtroom?"

"Yes, that's him," Holstein said, pointing.

"Let the record reflect that the witness identified the defendant," Karp said. "And what did he ask you to do?"

"He wanted me to identify children who were being treated for illnesses that if untreated would result in their deaths," Holstein said.

"Did he say why?"

Holstein shook his head. "Only that he

had a plan to make money."

"What else did he ask you to do?"

"He said I had to erase their patient records."

"He say why?"

"No, only that I had to do it or my wife would get those photographs and I'd be killed."

"Did he ask you to do anything else?"

"Yes, he wanted the personal-information packet that the families fill out when the patient is admitted to the hospital."

"Did he want to know anything else?"

"Yes. He asked me about the diseases the kids were being treated for . . . how they would respond to treatment . . . how long they would live without medical intervention."

Karp walked over to the jury box and looked at the jurors' shocked faces before turning back to the witness. "Doctor, why didn't you go to the police with this?"

Holstein looked down at his hands and appeared to be crying, but he finally lifted his head and said, "I was afraid. And embarrassed."

"So you were willing to let children go untreated, children that you knew would die without medical help, because you were afraid and embarrassed?" Karp said, not bothering to hide the disgust that he felt in his heart.

Covering his face with his hands, Holstein let out a sob. "Yes. I was that bedeviled."

Karp gave Holstein a few moments to recover and then resumed his questioning. "Doctor, how often did you meet with the defendant?"

Holstein shrugged. "Only a few times. Sometimes he'd call, or I was supposed to call him."

Karp nodded and turned to the judge. "Your Honor, at this time I'd like to show the witness this file marked People's Exhibit Twenty-five for identification."

"Go ahead," Temple said.

Handing Holstein several sheets of paper, Karp asked, "Doctor, do you recognize the information contained on these papers, People's Exhibit Twenty-five for identification?"

"Yes, they are telephone records of calls I made to LaFontaine or from him to me."

"But those are just numbers," Karp noted. "How do you know they're to the defendant?"

Holstein shrugged. "That's who I called. Or sometimes his man Frank."

Karp took the telephone records back from Holstein and offered them into evidence. "You mentioned someone named Frank. Did you know Frank's last name?"

"No."

"Did you ever see Frank and can you describe him?"

"Yes. Big guy, about as big as LaFontaine. He had a beard, kind of rough-looking . . . dark hair, brown eyes . . . he had a scar below one eye."

"You mentioned that in addition to your gambling debt being forgiven, you were paid. How were you paid?"

"In cash."

"Who gave you the cash?" Karp asked.

"Frank," Holstein said. "He'd bring it in an envelope. And once Sarah brought it to my home and handed it to me in front of my wife."

"How did you explain that?"

"I said it was a payment from a patient," he said. "I don't think my wife believed me."

"Doctor, are you still married?" Karp asked.

"My wife has filed for divorce."

"And are you a free man?"

Holstein shook his head. "No," he said. "I'm an inmate in a Tennessee prison. I pleaded guilty to larceny and have to serve at least two years. I've also lost my medical license."

"Have you been offered any sort of deal by my office, or a district attorney in Tennessee, in exchange for your truthful testimony here today?"

"No. You wouldn't agree to anything. And to be honest, I don't deserve it."

"On that, doctor, we agree," Karp said, and turned to the judge. "I have no further questions."

Rottingham rose and approached the witness stand, where he stood looking at Holstein for a minute as if studying some loathsome creature. He shook his head. "So *Mr.* Holstein, as I gather you are no longer a doctor," he said, "do you have any proof that you ever met my client?"

"What do you mean?"

Rottingham shrugged. "Oh, I don't know . . . a photograph of the two of you together? Is there someone who saw him with you in your office?"

"No. We met at the Gentleman's Club."

"A strip joint," Rottingham said. "Surely someone would have seen you there."

"Maybe. I don't know of anyone."

"You don't know of anyone because maybe you never actually met with Reverend LaFontaine."

"Is that a question?" Holstein replied.

"Because if it is, I did meet with him, several times."

"So you say, but there's no proof of this."

Holstein sat silently, just staring at LaFontaine.

"And you say that those phone calls from your telephone were to LaFontaine. But are you aware that the cell phone was registered only in the name of the Holy Covenant Church of Jesus Christ Reformed?"

"That's his church," Holstein said, pointing at LaFontaine.

"It was," Rottingham said. "But was anybody else associated with the church?"

"Well, yes, Frank," Holstein replied, now looking directly at his interrogator. "And maybe Sarah, I don't know."

"That's right, you don't," Rottingham said. "And we don't know who it was you actually called, do we?"

"I called LaFontaine, but sometimes I talked to Frank."

"Mr. Holstein, do you have any proof that the cash you received came from LaFontaine?"

"It was part of the deal I made with him."

Rottingham walked over to the evidence table, where he picked up the photograph of Holstein with Sarah Westerberg. He held it up and showed it to Holstein, who looked down, and then to the jurors. "I only see two people in this rather explicit photograph," he said. "One is you, and the other is a woman you've identified as Sarah, a stripper you were fooling around with behind your wife's back. Is that correct?"

"Yes."

"The Reverend LaFontaine is not in this photograph, is he?"

"No."

Rottingham sneered. "I have no further use for this witness, Your Honor."

Asked if he wanted to question Holstein further, Karp rose and requested that the recording between the doctor and LaFontaine after Detective Winkler's initial call be played.

"John, I got a call from a detective, he wants to know about you and the kids' records. What do I do?"

"I don't know what you're talking about. And don't call here again."

Karp looked up at Holstein. "Doctor, when did you place that call?"

"In April, after the detective called and said he wanted to talk to me."

"And who did you call?"

"LaFontaine."

"John LaFontaine. Is that right?"

"Yes."

"Not Frank."

"No."

"Not Sarah."

"No."

Karp turned and pointed at the defendant, who for a moment lost his composure and scowled. "That man sitting at the defense table, the defendant, John LaFontaine. Is that right?"

"Yes."

Recovering, LaFontaine yelled, "I forgive you!"

"I'll leave that to God," Holstein replied as the judge banged his gavel. "I can't even forgive myself."

The judge pointed at LaFontaine. "There will be no more outbursts," he said, and turned to Karp. "Do you have any more questions for this witness, Mr. Karp?"

"Just one, Your Honor," Karp replied. "Dr. Holstein, did the defendant at any time express any sort of remorse for what the two of you conspired to do to these children and their families?"

Holstein shook his head. "No, the only thing he ever said was, 'The brats are probably going to die anyway, somebody might as well make a buck.' "

28

Marlene glanced quickly at the note her husband had given her as they sat on the couch that evening in their loft, before handing it back. " 'Talk to Warren.' Any idea who left it?"

"Darla swears it wasn't on her desk before everyone arrived for the meeting at lunch," Karp replied. "She says that everyone was sort of milling around in the reception area before going into the conference room, so it could have been one of them. Or maybe someone slipped in and out of the office while she was getting coffee."

"But whoever it was wants you to talk to Dirty Warren. And then he tells you that David Grale wants to meet with you?"

"That's about the size of it," Karp replied. "He says it has to do with Malovo and the Halloween parade, and that I have to come alone."

A car honked outside the building. "I

believe my chariot awaits," Karp said. He stood and walked over to the coatrack at the front door and pulled on a brimmed hat he rarely wore and a heavy trenchcoat. "I'm off," he announced.

Marlene hopped up from the couch and walked over to give him a kiss. "What's with the Humphrey Bogart look?"

"Just trying to look the part, schweetheart," he replied in his best Bogie.

"Ah, of all the gin joints in all the towns in all the world, you had to walk into mine," Marlene said with a smile. "Sure you don't want me to go with you, Rick?"

"Nah, the boys and Lucy will be back from the synagogue in a half hour and want dinner," he said. "This won't take long. And besides, we'll always have Paris."

Marlene laughed and patted him on the chest. "Well, just remember that David has his own agenda," she said. "If he thought it would further God's work, he'd sacrifice you."

"I'll listen with the proverbial grain of salt," Karp replied, and walked out of the apartment.

Reaching the street-level foyer, Karp stepped outside and up to the yellow cab that waited at the curb. One of the uniformed police officers assigned to the two patrol cars outside his residence was already talking to the driver.

"Evening, Mr. Karp," the officer said. "This guy says you called for a cab?"

"That's right, Eddie," Karp replied. "I'm meeting someone. It's for a case."

"I'd be happy to drive you," Officer Eddie said.

"That's okay," Karp replied. "I'm trying to do this low-key."

"That's why the Sam Spade look," Officer Eddie said. "But Chief Fulton will have my butt in a sling if I let you go somewhere without an escort."

"I'll clear it with Clay," Karp said, turning to the cab driver. "I'm sure Mr. . . ."

"Farouk," the cab driver said helpfully.

"Mr. Farouk will deliver me to my meeting and return me safe and sound," Karp said.

The officer looked doubtfully at the cab driver and then shrugged. "Well, as long as you clear it with the chief . . ."

"I promise," Karp replied.

"And you take the cab back and forth . . . no walking around," Officer Eddie insisted. He pointed a finger at the cab driver. "I have your name and cab number, no funny business."

"Business is not funny," Farouk replied with a frown.

"Now that that's settled, I need to get going," Karp said, and got into the back of the cab.

"Where to, sir?" the cabbie asked, looking in the rearview mirror.

"You know where the Bowery Mission is?" Karp asked.

"Yes, sir," Farouk answered, then realized what Karp was asking. "But oh no, sir, you don't want to go there. It's a rough place."

"And yet to the Bowery Mission I must go, my friend," Karp replied. "Step on it."

Fifteen minutes later, the cab pulled up to the front of a large dour brick building with a red neon sign that announced it as the home of the Bowery Mission. Looking out the window, Karp was not surprised to see the sidewalk in front of the mission crowded with small knots of unkempt, and in some cases dangerous-looking, homeless men and even a few women.

"Are you sure, sir?" Farouk asked. "If something was to happen to you, the police officer will make it very bad for me."

"Nothing's going to happen," Karp replied. "You've done a great job so far, and I'll make sure your superiors hear about it. Now if you can wait twenty minutes or so,

I'll make it worth your while."

Farouk handed him a business card. "Thank you, kind sir. Call me when you are ready and I will be here in a jiffy," he said. "I do not like the look of these men and I would prefer to drive around the block until you call."

Karp glanced out the window and noticed that some of the rougher looking men were eyeing the cab and moseying over for a closer look. Then he saw Dirty Warren Bennett and the Walking Booger emerge from the shadows of the alley next to the building and walk swiftly toward the cab.

"Aha," Karp said with a grin, "my friends are here to meet me." He opened the cab door and stepped out onto the sidewalk.

Seeing a well-dressed man exit the cab, some of the sidewalk denizens picked up the pace toward him, but then Booger swerved to intercept them. The huge man bellowed something incoherent, but in a loud and aggressive tone, and the others shied away and went back to their places in front of the building.

"Hello, Mr. Karp . . . son of a bitch crap whoop whoop . . . thanks for coming," Dirty Warren Bennett said. "He's waiting inside."

Bennett then led the way back to the alley and a side entrance to the building. He knocked and another big man opened the door. "This is . . . oh boy oh boy nuts tits . . . him, Harvey."

The man nodded and started to say something that sounded like a greeting, but a coughing fit took him. So he just stepped aside and pointed down a hallway.

Karp was led through a small maze of hallways and through a couple of storage rooms whose shelves were stacked with canned goods, bags of rice, and blankets. His guide led him to a door and there knocked again. A muffled reply came from within, at which Bennett opened the door. "Go ahead . . . whoop bastard . . . he wants to talk to you alone," the little man said.

Walking into what appeared to be a reading room with shelves full of books and several overstuffed chairs with lamps next to them, Karp stopped short as David Grale rose from his seat. It had been some time since they'd last seen each other and Karp was shocked by how gaunt and ill the man looked; the pale skin that covered his face and hands — the only parts visible — looked stretched and fragile, and dark circles hung beneath his eyes like purple half moons.

"Hello, Mr. Karp," Grale said, extending a hand, "thank you for coming."

"Hi, David," Karp replied, wondering why it was that once again he found himself in the presence of a sociopathic killer and yet felt completely safe. "Warren said you had something important you wanted to talk to me about regarding Nadya Malovo and the Halloween parade."

A look of sadness passed across Grale's face. "Yes, there's no time for pleasantries, even if I wasn't who and what I am," he said after a moment. "I have some information I'd like to share and, if you'll listen to what I have to say, a plan that I think may benefit us both."

"I'm willing to listen," Karp replied. "But if you're going to admit to any crimes, David, I think you should seek counsel first."

Grale looked surprised and then laughed. "You are the last of an honorable breed, Mr. Karp," he said. "A serial killer asks to meet with you to discuss stopping another killer, and you offer to protect his rights." The look of sorrow again crossed his face. "I truly appreciate who and what you are, Mr. Karp. Maybe someday you will have occasion to read me those rights; however, there is no need at this moment."

Karp smiled. "Good. I'd rather not attempt to make a citizen's arrest, not on your turf anyway."

Grale laughed. "You never know, perhaps I'd go along docilely as a lamb," he said. "Then again" — he gave Karp a funny look — "a little bird told me that Nadya Malovo is spreading a rumor that you are actually in league with the Sons of Man."

Karp's eyebrows shot up. "That's a new one," he said. "This wouldn't be the same little bird that left a note in my office telling me to speak to Warren at lunch today?"

"I wouldn't know about that," Grale said. "But apparently that evil woman would like to sow dissension among friends — or is she correct and you've gone over to the dark side?"

"But what about what I've done to thwart the Sons of Man and prosecute its members when they break the law?" Karp asked.

"All part of a smoke screen to keep you above reproach," Grale replied. "At least according to Malovo. But don't worry; if I truly believed that, you would be dead already. I do think it provides us with an opportunity. She believes that she can divide us, which means while she knows there is a certain 'connectivity,' she is unaware of our long and varied history . . . as well as my great affection for you and your family."

Karp nodded. "So what does this have to do with the Halloween parade?" he asked.

"I will tell you that Lucy filled me in on your meeting and discussion in Central Park, and while I'm on that subject, I'm asking you to turn Andrew Kane over to us for prosecution."

At the suggestion, Grale frowned, and for a moment Karp was taken aback by the sudden flash of insane anger he saw in the man's eyes. "I'm not here to discuss Andrew Kane," he snarled before controlling himself with great effort. "Excuse me, I didn't mean to lose my cool, but that subject isn't up for discussion. However, Malovo and her Halloween plotting is. . . . My little bird told me that after this she will have completed what the feds are asking of her and will then be placed in the witness protection program."

It was Karp's turn to frown. "You're sure of this?" he asked.

"My information is top-notch," Grale replied. "Obviously, that would not please you, or your friend Espey Jaxon, who I take it hopes to get more information about the Sons of Man from her before any such reward."

"Go on," Karp said.

"Well, I don't believe that Nadya Malovo sees herself fitting into the witness protection program," Grale said. "I'm not sure how she plans to pull it off, but I think her plot is much grander than that. And I think I have a way of foiling her, and at the same time giving you and me what we want."

"I'm all ears," Karp replied.

An hour later, Karp arrived outside of his loft. He tipped Farouk handsomely and got out of the taxi. He looked over the top of the cab at the officers in their patrol cars and waved.

Just as he turned, a dark shadow emerged from the alley next to the building and moved swiftly toward Karp. Something in the figure's hand flashed.

"Look out!" Farouk shouted. "He's got a knife!"

Karp turned and warded off the downward slash of the knife with his forearm. The blade tore through the arm of his trenchcoat. With his other hand, he punched his assailant in the face, knocking him back.

"Stop, police!" an officer shouted from across the street.

The hooded attacker looked over at the police cars and then ran back into the alley as two officers came to the rescue. One of them pursued the attacker into the dark while the other stopped to check on Karp.

"You okay?" the officer asked.

"Yeah, I'm fine," Karp replied, then held up the sleeve of his coat. "That was pretty close."

The sound of a gunshot came from the alley. Karp and the other officer ran to the entrance and peered into the dark.

A moment later, Officer Eddie emerged from the shadows. "He got away," he said. "The guy ran like he can see in the dark. I got a shot off but I don't know if I hit him."

The other officer spoke into the radio transmitter on his shoulder. "All nearby units respond to Crosby and Grand. Be on the lookout for a white male, dark hooded sweatshirt. Suspect is armed."

"Did you get a good look at him?" Officer Eddie asked.

Karp nodded. "Yeah. I know him."

"Great! What's his name? We'll have a dozen cars surrounding this place in two minutes."

"His name is Grale. David Grale. There's a few warrants out for him; he's wanted for a half-dozen murders."

The other officer pointed to Karp's sliced coat. "And now attempted murder of the district attorney. Guy's moving up in the world."

29

Fulton arrived the next morning to drive him to the courthouse. "After your little incident with David Grale last night, the press is going to have the place surrounded like Fort Apache," the detective said. "I talked to Murrow and his phone has been ringing off the hook."

The detective held up a copy of the *New York Post*. **HOLY GRALE SLASHES DA,** the detective read. "Butch, the *Post* devoted four pages to Grale, his background, the Mole People, and all the killings he's responsible for. They even quoted your cab driver."

Karp smiled. "You mean the press cares if a mad killer tries to assassinate the district attorney?"

"So when you going to tell me what this is all about?"

"You drive, and I'll fill you in."

Five minutes later, Fulton knew the story

but it didn't make him happy. "It's risky as hell," he said. "You're relying on a half-mad sociopath who has his own agenda."

"Half-mad?" Karp replied with a smile as he got out of the car at the Hogan Place exit, ignoring the shouted questions of the media who were camped outside the security barrier. "I think you're giving him some credit that may or may not be due. But I think in this case, his agenda meshes with ours. And it may be our best bet to avert a disaster."

"I still don't have to like it," Fulton said.

"Neither do I, my friend, neither do I. But get a call in to Jaxon and see if he'll meet at lunch."

Karp was still thinking about Grale and his conversation with Fulton an hour later when Judge Temple asked him to call his next witness.

"Thank you, Your Honor," he said, rising. "The People call Monique LaRhonda Hale."

A minute later, Fulton escorted the woman into the courtroom. She saw LaFontaine and his lawyer staring at her and immediately burst into tears.

Karp's heart went out to her as she approached her seat in the witness box like a condemned prisoner going to her execution.

But he needed her; he had fought tooth and nail to have her testimony admitted under the "prior bad acts" doctrine to show that what had happened to Micah Ellis and his parents was part of a pattern of criminal behavior engaged in by the defendant — a sinister scheme to defraud vulnerable moms and dads in search of a "miracle" to save their ailing child.

Now he had to take the frightened, weeping woman, who'd lost her child and her husband, through the painful memories that began when her daughter, Natalie, got sick and went to the Children's Hospital to be treated. And that led to the day LaFontaine had shown up at her doorstep shortly after Natalie's final chemotherapy session had ended.

"He seemed to know everything about us," Hale testified. "He even knew that my husband had some run-ins with the law, but he said he knew that Charlie had turned his life around and that if we had total faith in the Lord, Natalie could be cured. But we had to stop taking her to the hospital."

"Why not just continue the medical treatments?" Karp asked.

"She was just so sick, and the doctor said he couldn't guarantee that she would get well," Hale replied. "But John — Reverend

LaFontaine — was so sure of himself. He said that God would work through him to cure her if we proved we believed in Him."

"Did Natalie seem to get better?"

"Yes, we prayed a lot and it seemed to work."

"Did the defendant ever bring anyone else over to your house to help with these prayers?"

"Yes. Sometimes Nonie Ellis was with him, and sometimes Sister Sarah. They both had little boys who were also being healed through prayer."

"Did Sister Sarah have a last name?"

"I'm sure she did, but I didn't know it."

Karp showed her a mug shot of Sarah Westerberg and asked, "Do you recognize the individual depicted in this photo, People's Exhibit Thirty for identification?"

"Yes, that's her, that's Sister Sarah."

He then showed her a photograph of Nonie Ellis.

"That's Nonie."

"Did you ever meet their little boys?"

"I met Micah," Hale responded. "She brought him over a couple of times to play with Natalie. He was such a nice little boy, and Nonie was a dear."

"How about Sarah's child? Did you meet him?"

Hale shook her head. "I think his name was Kevin. But no, she never brought him over."

"Mrs. Hale, at some point did your relationship with the defendant become more than just that of a spiritual adviser and one of his followers?"

Hale, who had been doing better since the questioning started, bit her lip and started to cry again. "Yes, one day when my husband, Charlie, was out, he came over and said that he had fallen in love with me. That Jesus had appeared to him in a dream and said that God blessed our love. He said that our union in Christ would prove how committed I was and that it would help Natalie."

"So you became lovers?"

"Yes."

"And at some point did your lover, the defendant, come to you with a proposal regarding life insurance for Natalie?"

"Yes. He asked if Brother Frank, one of the men in his church, could talk to me about life insurance."

"Were Brother Frank and LaFontaine close?"

"Oh yes, Brother Frank came with him to the house several times. They seemed like good friends."

"And did Brother Frank talk to you about life insurance?"

"Yes. He said that someday a policy would be worth a lot of money and we could use it for Natalie's college education or her —" At that point Hale broke down again and needed a few moments to recover before going on. "Or for her wedding."

"But it was a life insurance policy that would pay in the event of Natalie's death?"

Hale shook her head. "Yes. He said that as long as we kept the faith we didn't have to worry about that. But he said that if something did happen to her — he made it seem like Charlie couldn't be trusted — at least some good could come of it by helping LaFontaine's ministry."

"So the death benefits were assigned to LaFontaine and his church?"

"Yes."

"Did your husband go along with the plan?"

"No. He was suspicious of LaFontaine . . . I think he knew that there was something going on between us. But anyway, he wouldn't sign it."

"So how did you get the policy?"

"John talked me into letting Frank pretend to be Charlie and Frank signed it."

"Did an insurance salesman ever come to

your house and ask for the family's medical history?"

"Yes. But John said that I shouldn't tell him about Natalie. He said that it would be the same as saying that the doctors had cured Natalie, and that would be an affront to God."

"To your knowledge did the insurance agent learn about Natalie's condition?"

"I guess not," she replied. "Because they gave me the policy."

Karp had walked over to the witness stand and poured her a cup of water from the pitcher next to the witness box. He handed it to her.

Then, standing in close proximity to the jury rail, the judge's dais, and the witness box, Karp said, "Mrs. Hale, I know this has to be very hard on you; your daughter, Natalie, passed away."

"Yes. My little girl died."

"And the life insurance company paid the death benefits?"

"Yes."

"Which were signed over to the defendant, John LaFontaine, and his church?"

"Yes."

As the woman cried quietly, Karp gently asked, "Mrs. Hale, did there come a time when your intimate relationship with the defendant ended?"

Hale nodded and dabbed at her eyes. "I felt so guilty," she said. "I told him it was over, which didn't seem to bother him. Then I told Charlie about the affair and the life insurance policy."

"What was Charlie's response?"

"He was angry, so angry. He went to confront LaFontaine."

"Were you there when the confrontation took place?"

"No."

"Do you know firsthand what was said?"

"No."

Karp left it at that. There were some things he could not bring up. He couldn't talk about what had happened to Charlie Hale. Nor, after vigorous pretrial arguments from Rottingham, was he allowed to enter the underlying facts into evidence, because of its collateral nature, including questioning Monique Hale about the night of the shootings. The judge had agreed with Rottingham that there was not enough evidence connecting the event with LaFontaine and that it would be highly prejudicial and outweigh any probative value.

With Hale on the stand, Rottingham now did his best to portray her as an adulteress who had been spurned by her lover and had wanted the insurance money for herself and her husband.

"Mrs. Hale," he said, emphasizing the "Mrs." "You were married at the time you began having sex with the Reverend LaFontaine?"

"Yes."

"Did he force himself upon you?"

"No, he said he was in love and that Jesus told him it was a beautiful thing in the eyes of God and it would help Natalie."

"That's your take," the defense lawyer said scathingly. "But you don't have any letters or e-mails to that effect, do you?"

"No. That's just what he —"

"And did the Reverend LaFontaine somehow force you to stop taking Natalie to the hospital for treatment?" Rottingham interrupted.

"No. But he said that if we did, it would show we didn't have faith in God and that he wouldn't pray with us anymore."

Rottingham questioned Hale as to whether it was possible that she was confusing Sister Sarah with Nonie Ellis — the two women did resemble each other — and that the former had never visited her home with LaFontaine. But Hale was adamant that Sarah Westerberg had been with the defendant.

"Was my client with Frank Bernsen when he came over to talk about the life insurance policy?" Rottingham asked.

"No, he just asked if Frank could talk to me about it and said that he would consider it a personal favor."

"And was my client present when Frank Bernsen pretended to be your husband and signed the agreement with the representative of the life insurance company?"

"No."

"And are you aware that as the financial officer of the Holy Covenant Church of Jesus Christ Reformed, Frank Bernsen had complete access to the church bank account?"

"No. I was never told any of that . . . I wouldn't have cared."

"Yes, all you cared about was your sexual liaisons outside of your marriage with my client, isn't that true?"

"No, I —"

"No further questions, Your Honor," Rottingham said, cutting her off.

Karp rose quickly and said, "I believe before your answer was clipped by Mr. Rottingham, you were going to answer his question regarding what you cared about. Would you please answer that question now?"

"Yes, I cared about my little girl," Hale

said, and burst into tears.

"Did the defendant convince you that the only way to save your daughter was to stop seeking medical attention and place your faith in him?" Karp said, letting the anger rise in his voice.

"Yes. And I believed him."

30

"So everyone is clear about their responsibilities for tomorrow's event?"

Nadya Malovo asked her question in Chechen and then looked at each of the three men sitting across the table from her in the dimly lit basement of a run-down house occupying the middle of a trashed neighborhood in Brooklyn's Bedford-Stuyvesant.

"All are ready for the glorious attack," one man replied, also in Chechen, while a second typed a reply into the laptop computer in front of him and then pressed a button to send his message.

Malovo looked down at the laptop in front of her as the second man's message appeared. "We will move into place at the sound of the explosions," the message read, "and wait for you there." She smiled and nodded.

Although the four had been speaking for

fifteen minutes, the real conversation was being carried out on the laptops. Sometimes Malovo would ask a question out loud and the first man would give a carefully scripted answer, while the other typed out what she really wanted to know. Sometimes she would ask a question aloud for the first man as well as type another on her laptop to send to the second man.

She found it humorous that she and the second man were "chatting" on Facebook. The reason for the subterfuge waited in a utility company van parked down the street from the house. Inside the van, federal agents listened in on the spoken conversation with directional microphones that she'd been assured would capture every word — a device she'd anticipated and used to her benefit.

Two of the men across from her were longtime associates, ex–Russian military special forces and now paid assassins. Both spoke Chechen and English flawlessly, the former helpful when trying to pass as Islamic terrorists from the breakaway Muslim country of Chechnya. With a big payoff looming, she knew they could be trusted and she respected their skills.

The third man, the traitor, she felt nothing but scorn for, but she needed him and so turned on the charm. "Are you okay, my friend?" she typed, and then smiled in a way that had melted harder hearts than the one this little man possessed.

The man licked his thin lips nervously but smiled and nodded. "I'll be ready," he typed.

"So what will you be wearing for Halloween?" Malovo said aloud.

The first man laughed. "Why, we will be dressed as terrorists," he said, reading from the script. "We hope the infidels will appreciate the irony."

The second man didn't bother to type. She already knew the real answer.

"How many mujahideen?" she asked aloud.

As instructed, the first man hesitated before answering her, as though suspicious of the question. "Enough," he said. "We have spread out so in case one group is discovered, there will be more to carry out the glorious mission. They will wait for your signal and then begin the attack. You will be on the northwest corner of Sixth Avenue and Eighth Street."

"Yes," Malovo replied. "Dressed as Little Red Riding Hood."

"Little Red Riding Hood?" the first man asked in English, as if he didn't understand the description.

"Yes, a fairy tale," Malovo replied. "A hooded red cape, carrying a basket. I will be standing with a man dressed as a wolf. Never mind . . . it is part of the fairy tale."

"Who is this 'wolf'?" the first man asked suspiciously.

"One of our benefactors," Malovo replied. "He wishes to observe the event firsthand. I vouch for him, and remember we are all working for Allah's glory."

"Praise be to Allah," the man replied.

Finished with the conversation, Malovo got up and climbed the stairs from the basement into the kitchen, where a half-dozen young black men pieced together suicide vests. "*Allahu akbar,* Ajmaani," said one of the men nearby, who was stuffing ball bearings into the pockets and lining of one of the vests.

"*Allahu akbar,*" Malovo replied. "It appears that you are almost ready for martyrdom!"

"Yes," the man answered. He pointed to boxes stacked next to the kitchen door. "We will be wolves among the sheep."

"Um, yes, a wonderful blow for Allah," Malovo said. "Remember, at my signal, rush the float with the enemy Karp on board."

"How will we know him? Will he be wearing a costume?"

"He is the grand marshal and will be on

the last float. A tall man, but I do not know how he will be dressed. Now make your peace with Allah, and someday soon, we will all meet again in paradise."

31

Sitting next to Guma at the prosecution table, Karp made notes on his yellow legal pad and pretended not to be interested in what was occurring across the aisle. But it was hard not to smile as Rottingham leaned in close to LaFontaine, arguing quietly yet vigorously. Twice the defense attorney looked back over his shoulder at him before turning back to his client. But whatever he was saying, it was having no effect, as the defendant continued to shake his head and argue back.

Karp heard the door at the rear of the courtroom open and turned in his seat to look back as a woman in sunglasses entered wearing a scarf over her blond hair. Dressed in slacks, a blouse, and a faded beige jacket, she looked like the sort of courtroom spectator who frequented trials where there had been a lot of publicity. The woman looked around for a moment before walking up and taking a seat next to Marlene, who'd called shortly before Karp left for the courtroom to say that she was going to attend the trial that morning. Marlene scooted over a little bit to make room but didn't say anything to the woman as she gave Karp a slight smile.

Smiling back, Karp then turned his attention to the defense table. At last Rottingham's shoulders sagged and he nodded. Rising from his seat and addressing Judge Temple, he announced, "The defense calls John LaFontaine."

Karp managed to keep a straight face, but his heart skipped a triumphant beat. They were now into the second day of the defense's case, and his plan to bait LaFontaine into taking the stand had worked.

After Monique Hale's testimony, Karp had wrapped up the People's case by calling investigators from the insurance companies that had written policies for Natalie Hale and Micah Ellis. The investigators testified that efforts had been made to search national databases for medical records pertaining to the children, but other than typical childhood issues that had shown up in the records of family doctors, there was nothing. On cross-examination, Rottingham had done little more than get the investigators to agree that it was not unusual for death benefits to be assigned to churches and other charitable organizations.

Karp's last witness had been a handwriting expert. He testified that whoever had signed the insurance applications as Charles Hale and David Ellis "was the same person, neither of whom were the real Mr. Hale or Mr. Ellis."

After Kenny Katz was shot trying to protect Ray Guma from Kathryn Boole's rampage, there had been no question that Karp would prosecute the case. The question had been how best to go about it, as it was no slam-dunk. The strategy he settled on had risks, but they were calculated risks he decided to take in part by studying his opponent's behavior and concluding that the man's ego could be used against him.

One of the earliest clues had been how LaFontaine, still going by the name Reverend C. G. Westlund, sought out the media spotlight after the Ellises had been charged. Of course, Karp knew that the defendant had been worried that if they were successfully prosecuted, the insurance company wouldn't pay, but there was more to it than that. LaFontaine had taken the chance that someone with whom he'd had previous dealings — such as Monique Hale — might see him on the national news and expose him. But he clearly enjoyed being a First Amendment poster boy and the support, as well as the funding, of those who'd rallied to his cause.

Some of it came down to understanding that LaFontaine was a man who practiced an extremely evil con game based on his ability to persuade parents not to seek medical attention for their sick children; it took a master manipulator to compromise such a strong bond. He was sure that LaFontaine believed he could sell ice cream to Eskimos and every success had convinced him that he was unstoppable.

Karp was sure that LaFontaine had even used his powers of persuasion on Kathryn Boole, preying on her loneliness, to seduce his way into her bed and her will. Then he convinced the woman, who'd never committed a crime in her life, to murder David Ellis. When she'd done his bidding, he ruthlessly, cold-bloodedly set her up to be killed by his own man, or any police officers present, to "protect" Karp.

After the arrest, Karp had known that LaFontaine wasn't going to confess or even say much before invoking his right to silence. But Karp had counted on the man wanting to engage in a war of words and knew he could get under LaFontaine's skin by challenging him and his ego. Then, during the trial, whether it was in his opening statement or with witnesses on the stand, Karp used every opportunity to belittle LaFontaine and paint him as a venal, evil bully who could only take on the weak. He'd made sure the defendant saw his looks of disgust and contempt and had been pleased to note how hard it had been for the egomaniac to control his rage at the insults.

After Karp had presented the People's case in chief, Judge Temple had adjourned for lunch, saying that the defense would begin its case immediately afterward. True to formal procedure, Rottingham made the pro forma motion to dismiss at the conclusion of the People's case by arguing that the prosecution had failed to present sufficient evidence to convict his client, and as was routinely done, Judge Temple had denied the motion.

So after lunch, Rottingham had started by calling an "expert" in faith healing to the stand. The man cited half a dozen anecdotal instances in which patients had been told that there was no hope, that their diseases were incurable and they were going to die.

"But through prayer and the intercession of men of faith, they are alive today," declared the witness, who had written a book on the subject.

That witness had been followed by a "faith psychologist," who claimed that "scientific" data she'd assembled demonstrated that the human body responded to prayer "so long as there is a strong correlation between the intercession and the victim's beliefs." And because a child picks up on the beliefs of parents, it was also necessary that "the care-givers be committed to the faith-healing process as well." As "proof," she showed the jurors "before-and-after photographic im-ages" of patients' magnetic fields — "Or auras, if you prefer the term," she said — that she claimed demonstrated significant improvement in their health.

Karp challenged both witnesses in the same manner, questioning whether their theories were "generally accepted within the scientific community," to which both, after complaining that the scientific community was not open to "matters of faith," admit-ted they were not. They also admitted that none of their studies involved the defendant.

Rottingham then called E. Webster Har-ding, a constitutional law professor from Harvard, to testify that LaFontaine's actions

404

were protected under the religious-freedom articles of the First Amendment. "We, as Americans, may not agree with any particular religious practice," Harding, an effete little man in a wool coat with leather elbow patches, sniffed, "but we believe in tolerance; the individual's right to worship as he or she sees fit is inviolate constitutionally."

On cross-examination, Karp queried, "Does one's exercise of his First Amendment rights immunize him from child abuse, Mr. Harding?"

"No, I would have to say not," Harding said.

"And, Mr. Harding, does one's exercise of his constitutional rights immunize him from murder?"

"No, of course not," Harding huffed.

As Harding left the stand, Karp sat down and leaned over to Guma. "Was Bill Buckley ever right when he wrote that he'd rather be governed by the first two hundred individuals whose names appear in the Boston phone book than by the entire faculty at Harvard, particularly its law school," he said, then winked. "Okay, so I added the last part."

When Temple prepared to adjourn for the day, Rottingham gave no indication what his plan for the morning would be. There was the possibility that he would rest the defense's case and try to make the point in his summation that the prosecution had failed to prove his client guilty beyond a reasonable doubt.

However, Karp bet that LaFontaine wouldn't pass up the opportunity to demonstrate how smart he was by putting one over on the DA, the jury, the court, and the entire justice system. Nevertheless, it had been a restless night, between wondering whether LaFontaine would take the stand and preparing for it, as well as the looming threat of the Halloween parade in two days.

Following the "assault" by David Grale, Fulton saw to it that extra police units were assigned outside the Crosby Street loft, keeping reporters, television crews, and the public, including LaFontaine's supporters, at bay. All press calls to the DAO regarding the matter were fielded by chief administrative aide Gilbert Murrow, who had "no further comment."

The NYPD handled inquiries their own way. "We take this matter extremely seriously," Police Commissioner Timothy Murphy said at a press conference. "We are searching for this individual and ask the public to report any sightings of him. However, do not approach or try to detain him; we consider him armed and extremely dangerous." A police media intern had then handed out a police-artist sketch of Grale, essentially a scruffy, white, bearded male with deep-set eyes in a hooded sweatshirt, a description that fit a good percentage of New York's population.

The next morning, Fulton again dropped Karp off at the Hogan Place entrance, where, other than a brief wave of the hand, he did not respond to shouted questions from the media. An hour later, Karp smiled inwardly as Rottingham called LaFontaine to the stand.

"All right, Mr. LaFontaine . . . ," Judge Temple began to say.

"Reverend LaFontaine, please, Your Honor," the defendant corrected him as he stood and brushed back his long hair with his fingers.

The judge studied him balefully for a moment before shrugging. "Okay, Reverend LaFontaine, would you please approach the witness stand to be sworn in."

LaFontaine rose and nodded to the jurors before striding to the witness stand. As he stood in the witness box he was asked by the court clerk if he would tell the truth and nothing but the truth. He raised his chin and replied, "Of course. I do not lie."

"The jury is here to determine that, Mr. LaFontaine. You may be seated," Temple growled, and turned to Rottingham. "You may begin your examination."

"Thank you, Your Honor," Rottingham replied, turning to his witness. "I'd like to begin by clearing something up for the jury. In his opening remarks, Mr. Karp noted that when you came to New York City, you used the name C. G. Westlund. Would you explain why to the jury?"

LaFontaine heaved a dramatic sigh and then looked at the jurors. "There is a simple answer: I feared for my safety. As I'm sure you good people know, men of faith are often persecuted for speaking the truth. As Jesus said, 'Know that if they hate you, they hated me first.' "

"I would also like you to explain how you came to be addressed as 'reverend'; did you attend a college or university to get a degree in religious studies?" Rottingham asked.

"I did not," LaFontaine answered. "I was called to do the Lord's work from the streets where I had been living a life of sin until I met a man who talked to me about Jesus. That's when the truth struck me like a bolt of lightning from heaven, and I was saved. This same man, a gifted street preacher himself, said I had a gift and that it was my calling to go out into an evil world and spread the Good Word."

"So then you are not a reverend?" Rottingham asked.

"Oh, but I am," LaFontaine answered. "I admit though that the appellation is something I applied for from an online school that offers such things. I would not have bothered except that — praise the Lord — my flock was growing to the point that I needed a church so that I could reach more sinners. My financial adviser, Frank Bernsen, suggested that I needed the title so that we could apply for nonprofit-organization status."

"So then you are a reverend in name only?"

"Well, I don't think the title makes the man. I have made myself a student of the Bible, harkening back to my days as a boy growing up in Memphis, Tennessee, on the knee of my grandmother, a God-fearing woman if ever there was one," LaFontaine said. "And if I might add . . ."

"Please," Rottingham said, encouraging him.

"I don't believe that Saint Paul or any of the apostles had divinity degrees either," LaFontaine finished with a chuckle.

"I believe you're correct there," Rottingham said with a smile. "But let's move on. Do you know Dr. Aronberg?"

"I do not," LaFontaine said.

"How about Dr. Holstein?"

"I saw him for the first time when he appeared on this witness stand."

"So how do you feel about the fact that Holstein testified that he met with you several times and that you asked him to identify sick children and give you private personal information regarding their families?"

A sad look crossed LaFontaine's rugged face. "I would swear to you that he was bearing false witness against me. I do not know the man. Nor have I ever spoken to him, until oddly, on the night of my arrest, I received a telephone call from a Memphis number I did not recognize. The caller made some sort of statement about an investigation, and I asked him not to call me again. I thought it was a wrong number, or perhaps someone calling for Mr. Bernsen on what he thought was a church telephone number, but I have since learned it was Dr. Holstein."

"Then why would he make such claims against you?"

LaFontaine thought about it, then shook

his head. "I have prayed greatly over this, but I cannot say that I know what is in the man's heart. Maybe he is trying to escape punishment for his own sins by cooperating with those who would like to see me fail in my work. As I said before, some men, particularly nonbelievers" — he stopped and looked pointedly at Karp — "seek to bring down men of God. They hate the truth. So-called physicians, in particular, are threatened by someone who preaches that all healing comes from God, who also is the only judge of who shall live and who shall die."

"What about the allegations that, with the help of Dr. Holstein, you targeted families with seriously ill children for personal gain?"

"It's a lie," LaFontaine declared, his blue eyes flashing with righteous indignation. "As I said, I do not know that man, nor have I specifically sought out families with ill children. I do believe that God gave me the gift of insight. Some might call it intuition, though I believe its origins are divine, but I sometimes 'know' when someone is suffering, to the point of even being able to decipher the physical cause. Or, for instance, when someone is down on their luck and needs a Christian hand out of the muck."

"Do you profit from this gift?" Rottingham asked.

LaFontaine again paused as if deep in thought. "I guess it would depend on what you mean by 'profit,' " he said. "I certainly profit spiritually by helping others find the Lord. I grow stronger with each sinner I turn toward the truth."

"I mean 'profit' more in the traditional sense," Rottingham said, "as in money or some other tangible assets."

"Again, it would depend on what you mean by 'profit,' " LaFontaine said. "I have been blessed that some believers donate to my ministry so that others may hear the Word and be saved. I try to live a simple life as I shepherd my flock."

"What about these insurance policies that the district attorney has alluded to?" Rottingham asked. "Were you aware of them?"

"I was," LaFontaine answered, "but only after the fact. My brother in Christ Frank Bernsen informed me after the unfortunate deaths of Micah Ellis and Natalie Hale that the families had taken out these policies and assigned the benefits to the church."

"You did not ask them to do this?" Rottingham asked.

"I did not," LaFontaine replied. "I was certainly grateful for their gifts. But it isn't the sort of thing I would have even thought of requesting."

"So how did these come about?"

LaFontaine's big head dropped to his chest. He appeared to be speaking, or praying, under his breath. When he looked up, there were tears in his eyes. "I had believed that the families made these gifts of their own volition. However — it tears at my heart to reach this conclusion, and I still don't believe it — if such a thing was proposed to these good families, then I guess it would have had to have been by my brother Frank Bernsen."

"How long have you known Mr. Bernsen?"

"Many years," LaFontaine said. "We were both sinners on the street when I was saved. Through my example, Frank was saved, too. . . . So I believed."

"How did you meet Monique and Charlie Hale?" Rottingham asked.

"I believe Frank told me that there was a family with a sick child in need of healing," LaFontaine said.

"So you didn't just appear out of the blue?"

"No. Frank gave me their address and said they asked me to stop by as they were disenchanted with the physicians attending their daughter."

"And what about the Ellis family?"

LaFontaine thought about it for a moment and then his face fell again as though he'd just reached another difficult conclusion. "I believe Frank told me about them as well. This was before I met the Hales. Yes, I'm sure Frank also informed me that they had a sick child and the father, David — a good, good man — was out of work and struggling."

Rottingham nodded and walked over to the evidence table, where he picked up a photograph. "The jury has heard about this woman, Sarah Westerberg, or as I believe Monique Hale referred to her, 'Sister Sarah.' Was she known to you?"

LaFontaine studied the photo but after several moments shook his head. "I'm sorry, I looked at that photograph when Mr. Karp showed it to the jury and I just can't place her," he said. "Of course, I meet many people in my ministry. Some come to the church once and never come back. Others I talk to on the street and may or may not see again. I don't just minister to families with sick children. I am called upon by our good Lord and Savior to seek out sinners wherever they may be. Perhaps I met her, but I don't recall."

"So if Monique Hale says that she would

come with you to prayer sessions at her house . . . ?"

"I'm sorry, but she's mistaken."

"What about Nonie Ellis," Rottingham said, "did she go with you to prayer sessions at the Hale residence?"

"Yes, of course," LaFontaine said. "I've found it very beneficial for these families to comfort one another and encourage each other to seek the true road of Jesus Christ."

"Would you say there is a resemblance between Nonie Ellis and the woman identified as Sarah Westerberg?"

LaFontaine frowned and looked up at the ceiling. "Well, I've never thought about it, but yes, there is. They are about the same age and build. Both have brown hair and brown eyes."

The defense attorney returned the photograph. "Reverend LaFontaine, you sat here patiently while Monique Hale described having had a sexual relationship with you."

"Yes."

"Would you care to respond to that accusation now?"

LaFontaine's eyes flashed with anger. "I have never had sex with that woman!"

Guma nudged Karp and whispered, "What's next? 'What's the meaning of "sex" '?"

"Is this the first time you've heard that accusation?"

"No," LaFontaine answered. "After the death of Natalie Hale, Monique's husband approached me and accused me of having sex with his wife and said he was going to expose me unless I returned the money paid by the insurance company."

"And what was your response?"

"I, of course, told him that it was untrue," LaFontaine said. "But I also said that I was not going to be blackmailed and that if he wanted the church to give him the money, he could request that in a civilized manner and I would see to it."

"What happened?"

LaFontaine shook his head. "I'm afraid that Mr. Hale was involved in some nefarious activities and my understanding is that he was murdered, possibly as a result."

"Did Monique Hale ask for the money back or attempt to blackmail you with this allegation of a sexual liaison?"

"No," LaFontaine said. "To be honest, I thought we remained friends and brother and sister in Christ. I have no idea why she has chosen to say these things about me. But greed can be a powerful motivator."

Rottingham was quiet for a moment, as though absorbing the wisdom of his client.

He walked thoughtfully over toward the jury box before turning back to face LaFontaine. "Reverend LaFontaine, did you ever tell the Hales or the Ellises to quit taking their children to see the physicians who were treating them?"

"I did not," LaFontaine replied.

"How do you talk to people who need spiritual help like the Hales and Ellises?"

LaFontaine looked from juror to juror before answering. "When someone invites me into their home to talk about the Good Word, I am careful to explain that I am just relaying my beliefs," he said. "I truly believe that all healing comes from God and that if we place our faith in God, He will reward us with His compassion and love. I do believe that you cannot say, 'I place my faith one hundred percent in God to heal my child,' and then turn around and hedge your bets. But that's just what I believe, and I don't demand that others believe as I do."

"What of those who place their faith in God, and yet their child still dies?"

LaFontaine looked sadly at his defense attorney and then up at the ceiling as he mouthed some words before looking down. "I do not claim to know why God sometimes calls these innocent angels back to Him even when we ask that they be saved. I am just a man and do not know His purposes; I can only help these families ask for His mercy."

"Thank you, Reverend LaFontaine," Rottingham said quietly before turning to the judge. "No further questions, Your Honor."

Judge Temple looked at the clock hanging over the entrance to the courtroom and then addressed counsel and the jurors. "We have reached the lunch hour," he said. "Mr. Karp, will you be cross-examining this witness?"

Karp rose from his seat to answer. "Without a doubt, Your Honor, without a doubt."

32

Karp looked at his watch as he entered his office. "Okay, gang," he announced. "I have forty-five minutes before I'm due back in court." He looked around the room at the people gathered there. Espey Jaxon. Jen Capers. Lucy. Ned Blanchett. Clay Fulton.

Jaxon shook his head. "Listen to the man," he said. "By tomorrow morning, the world may have gone to hell in a handbasket with him first in line, but he's working on his summation."

"We all do what we can to fight the good fight, Espey," Karp replied. "Right now I'm trying to deal with one evil man. I'll leave it to you spooks to handle the hordes from hell."

"We'll try," Jaxon said. "By the way, you okay?"

Karp frowned. "Yeah, sure, why?"

"The attack by David Grale," Jaxon replied. "I mean, it's not every day that a serial killer leaps out of the shadows and tries to knife the district attorney of New York County."

Feeling the eyes of the others boring into him, Karp shrugged. "He wrecked a favorite trench coat, that's about it. . . . So I take it the reason for this visit has to do with tonight's festivities?"

"Nice deflection," Jaxon replied. "And yes, this has to do with tonight."

"But Malovo and her handler aren't part of the conversation?" Karp asked.

"They must not have seen the memo," Jaxon replied.

"I see," Karp replied, gathering more from the statement than was said. "So what's the memo regarding?"

"This has to do with a meeting Malovo had last night in Bed-Stuy with at least some of the elements of this threat," Jaxon said. "We know that there were at least eight men in the house. At some point, she broke away from the others with one, maybe two, of the men, who appear to be leaders of this cell, or cells, and carried on a conversation for about twenty minutes."

"They reveal any details?" Karp said.

"Some," Jaxon said, "which we were able to pick up with directional microphones, but we don't have a complete picture, and for some of it we have to rely on Malovo's observations, which are always suspect."

"Undoubtedly," Karp said. "For instance?"

"For instance, she claims that the attack will be made with exploding vests — suicide vests — packed with C4 and ball bearings," Jaxon said.

Karp grimaced. "I've been wondering how long it was going to take someone to pull a Tel Aviv–shopping mall attack here," he said. "A lot of casualties, indeterminate casualties. These bastards don't care who they kill. What else?"

"Apparently, they'll be dressed as terrorists," Jaxon answered. "And the irony is that they'll probably walk right into the crowd on Halloween and nobody will think twice."

"So why don't we pick them up now?" Karp asked. "Disrupt their plans."

Jaxon shook his head. "I wish it was that simple," he said. "But some of what we heard indicated that there is more than one cell and that the Bed-Stuy group isn't alone. We're tracking them, of course. Anybody goes out of that house and we've got a tail on him. But as of a half hour ago, they were mostly lying low and there's been no other contact. If it's all we got, we'll grab these guys before they hit the street, but we're hoping there's a staging area where the cells will get together and we can round up the whole lot."

"One thing we picked up," Capers interjected, "is that they are all going to wait for a signal from Ajmaani, a.k.a. Malovo, who will be dressed as Little Red Riding Hood and standing on the northwest corner of Sixth Avenue and Eighth Street."

"What's supposed to happen then?" Karp asked.

The others all exchanged a look. "They're supposed to rush the float you're on, and when they get close enough, blow themselves up."

"There could be a few thousand people in the area around the float," Karp noted.

No one said anything until Jaxon spoke again. "I think we have time to play the recording of this conversation," he said. "Then Lucy would like to say a few words." He pulled a small digital recorder from his coat pocket and pressed the Play button.

Most of the recording had to do with Malovo asking if the preparations were complete and the attackers knew what to do.

"So what will you be wearing for Halloween?"

"Why, we will be dressed as terrorists. We

hope the infidels will appreciate the irony."

"How many mujahideen?"

"Enough. We have spread out so in case one group is discovered, there will be more to carry out the glorious mission. They will wait for your signal and then begin the attack. You will be on the northwest corner of Sixth Avenue and Eighth Street."

"Yes. Dressed as Little Red Riding Hood."

"Little Red Riding Hood?"

"Yes, a fairy tale. A hooded red cape, carrying a basket. I will be standing with a man dressed as a wolf. Never mind . . . it is part of the fairy tale."

"Who is this 'wolf'?"

"One of our benefactors. He wishes to observe the event firsthand. I vouch for him, and remember we are all working for Allah's glory."

"Praise be to Allah."

Jaxon stopped the recording for a moment. "At this point she leaves the man she has been talking to and goes upstairs, where, according to her anyway, the others are busy making bombs." He pressed the Play button again.

"Allahu akbar, *Ajmaani.*"

"Allahu akbar. *It appears that you are almost ready for martyrdom!*"

"Yes. We will be wolves among the sheep."

423

"Um, yes, a wonderful blow for Allah. Re-member, at my signal, rush the float with the enemy Karp on board."

"How will we know him? Will he be wearing a costume?"

"He is the grand marshal and will be on the last float. A tall man, but I do not know how he will be dressed. Now make your peace with Allah, and someday soon, we will all meet again in paradise."

The recording ended and Jaxon placed the machine on the table. "By the way, how will you be dressed?" Jaxon asked.

Karp smiled. "The Grim Reaper of course."

"I hope there's not much business for you tonight," Jaxon replied, then turned to Karp's daughter. "Lucy, you want to take it from here?"

Lucy nodded and turned toward her dad. "I've listened to that recording dozens of times," she said, "and every time confirms what I thought when I was first hearing it in that van. Something's not right. In the van, it was just a hunch. But now I'm sure. My first clue was that although Malovo and that first male we heard both speak excel-lent Chechen, neither of them is, in fact, Chechen. They are so good they could even fool someone from Chechnya who might think any small irregularities were regional differences, like the difference between a Bronx accent and someone from Texas. And these irregularities are so slight that at first I couldn't quite put my finger on what was troubling me."

"Help your old man out here," Karp said. "What are you getting at?"

"That Malovo and her pal are both native Russian speakers," Lucy said. "They're very well trained, and I'd bet the guy has lived in Chechnya so long that he's even picked up some of the nuances that are native to the southern part of the country. But every once in a while, he slips; a little bit of Russian creeps in. So the question becomes: Why is Malovo pretending that this guy is from Chechnya?"

"To fool you guys who are listening," Karp said.

"Certainly, if he's something more than he seems — such as a Russian-trained agent," Lucy said. "But I think it's also to fool those other men in the house."

Karp glanced at Jaxon, who acknowledged the look with a smile. "Your kid never ceases to amaze," the agent said.

Lucy blushed and then continued with her discoveries. "It was nothing really. Any polyglot fluent in Russian and Chechen could have picked up on it."

"Yes, but there's more," Jaxon said. "Please continue."

"Well, my next observation isn't so much about the telltale markers for native speakers," Lucy replied, "as it is about speech patterns. Anybody who spends their life listening to and absorbing languages will tell you that there is a huge difference between someone who is responding to questions off the cuff and someone who is reading something aloud. I think the guy responding to Malovo is reading his answers."

"But why?" Karp asked.

"Well, obviously Malovo knew we were listening in, so she could have been making sure we heard what she wanted us to hear," Lucy said. "But I heard more than she bargained for. When I was trying to pick up what was off about the guy's Chechen and speech patterns, I turned up the volume. That's when I heard it, and confirmed it by getting our audio techs to cut the voices out."

"Heard what?" Karp said, playing along.

"Espey, would you replay some of that recording, please, and play it loud?" Lucy said.

Jaxon picked up the recorder and turned

up the volume before playing it again. "There, did you hear that?" Lucy said after the man responded to one of Malovo's questions.

"Hear what?" Karp said.

"Play it again, Espey," Lucy said. "And, Dad, this time try to tune out the voices and listen to what's in the background."

Jaxon played the recording again. This time, Karp nodded. "I hear some sort of tapping."

Lucy laughed. "Espey, tell him how you figured out what the tapping is."

Jaxon grinned. "Well I guess this one shows my age, but when she was just starting out, Janis Joplin made a recording in which someone can be heard typing in the background. It's a classic."

"It's typing?" Karp said. "But who's typing?"

"A third person," Lucy said. "I think it was too much for the first speaker to carry on the faux conversation and type at the same time. What I think is going on is Malovo has one conversation for our ears, and in the meantime, she's looking at responses from a second guy on a computer — something she doesn't want us to know about, something she's cooking up with her fellow Russians. And I don't think it's martyrdom."

Jaxon gave Karp an appraising look. "I can see the wheels turning in that head," he said. "You want to let us in on what you're thinking?"

Karp sat for a moment looking at the others, then leaned forward. "I've been debating whether to talk to you about this — not because I don't trust you; you know better than that," he said. "But because I didn't want to compromise your positions." He looked at Capers and added, "Especially yours, Jen."

"Oooh, this sounds intriguing," Lucy said.

"Maybe so," Karp agreed. "Anyway, I think I had better tell you about a conversation I had with our favorite serial killer the other night."

"We were wondering when we were going to hear the real story," Jaxon said. "Go ahead, I believe you have our undivided attention."

33

LaFontaine settled himself in the witness chair and smiled across the well of the court at the jurors. He then swiveled toward Temple as the judge banged his gavel.

"I'll remind you, Reverend LaFontaine, that you are still under oath," Temple said.

"Yes, thank you, Your Honor. And God bless you," LaFontaine said before turning back to the jurors, adding, "And God bless you folks for taking time out of your busy lives."

Without changing his expression, Karp glanced at the jurors to see how they reacted to the defendant's words. He noted that two older women, one black and one white, smiled in return and nodded their heads slightly toward the defendant. He remembered from the jury-selection process that both were regular churchgoers, and it had been clear that the defense wanted them on the jury, which Guma had noted with trepidation.

However, Karp argued that the strategy could backfire on the defense. "No one likes to have their faith sullied by a charlatan," he had pointed out. "It's our job to prove that's what he is, and we'll be okay."

Now was the moment he would try to do that, and hope that he could help the jurors see through LaFontaine's veneer of deceit. As he stood waiting for the judge's okay to begin, he wondered if the defendant was as confident as he appeared on the stand. *Probably,* he thought. *His ego has him convinced that he's pulled the wool over everyone's eyes.*

Judge Temple looked at him. "Mr. Karp, are you ready to begin your cross-examination?"

"I am, Your Honor." *Time to remove the wool.* He walked over to stand next to the jury rail. "Mr. LaFontaine —"

"Reverend LaFontaine."

"*Mister* LaFontaine, you've testified that while you express your belief — if it truly is your belief — that faith healing requires complete devotion to the power of prayer while eschewing commonly accepted medical intervention, you do not require your followers to do the same?" Karp asked.

"That's correct," LaFontaine replied. "I explain what I believe and why, as it is

430

outlined in the Bible, and then leave it to others to choose their path."

"You do not threaten to withhold your spiritual guidance, or threaten to excommunicate followers from your church if they choose to seek commonly accepted medical intervention?"

"I do not."

"So if Monique Hale says that you do, she is lying?"

LaFontaine shrugged. "Perhaps she misunderstood."

"I see. And did the paramedics and police officers who testified earlier in the trial that you attempted to block their efforts to reach Micah Ellis, who would subsequently die from lack of medical attention, misunderstand you?"

"I disagree with the characterization that I blocked their way," LaFontaine said. "I was trying to impart that the wishes of the family were to rely on prayer as opposed to doctors to save their son. But they didn't care to listen."

"Did you threaten to come at them with a sword?"

"I was speaking biblically," LaFontaine said. "It isn't me who will come down with the sword of righteousness on the heads of sinners. It is the Lord."

"But you told the paramedics that their services weren't needed. And you refused to let them and the police officers pass, saying that you would come at them with a sword. And you intimated to your friend Frank Bernsen that he should attack the police officer."

"I did no such thing," LaFontaine said. "Frank may have been trying to protect the family and thus overreacted, but it was not at my request."

"Mr. LaFontaine, were you subsequently charged by my office with obstructing emergency personnel from the performance of their duties?"

"I was."

"And were you found guilty?"

"I was. Unfairly I might add."

"And was Mr. Bernsen also charged with obstruction, as well as attempted assault on a police officer?"

"He was."

"And was he found guilty?"

"Yes."

Karp walked over to the prosecution table and picked up a manila folder, but for the moment he just carried it with him back over to the jury rail. "Let's talk for a moment about Mr. Bernsen. Would you say the two of you were close?"

"We go way back," LaFontaine said.

"How far back?"

LaFontaine shrugged. "Twenty years, maybe more."

"And where did you meet Mr. Bernsen?"

Rottingham jumped to his feet. "Objection! What is the relevance of this line of questioning?"

Karp turned to the judge. "Your Honor, the defendant and counsel have made Frank Bernsen the fall guy for any wrongs that may have been committed in the name of Mr. LaFontaine and his church. And as we all know, Mr. Bernsen will not appear in this courtroom to defend himself or answer questions."

"I'll allow it," Temple said. "Overruled; the witness may answer the question."

"We met at the Shelby County Penal Farm," LaFontaine said.

"And what were you doing there?"

"Serving time."

"For what?"

"Me, for kiting checks," LaFontaine said. "Frank was in for assault."

"Kiting checks," Karp said. "A type of fraud, right? You pretended to be someone you were not and illegally obtained cash, goods, or services, correct?"

"Yes," LaFontaine admitted.

"How many other crimes have you and Frank Bernsen been convicted of?" Karp asked. "And let's just stick to the felonies."

"Objection!" Rottingham shouted again. "Now Mr. Karp is fishing."

"On the contrary, I am taking careful aim," Karp replied, holding up the manila folder. "This is fair game, particularly as any prior conviction, like fraud, may relate to moral depravity. The defendant's criminal record may most certainly be considered by the jurors with respect to the defendant's so-called credibility, as Mr. Rottingham well knows."

"Your Honor, may we approach the bench?" demanded Rottingham as he lurched to his feet.

"Come on then," the judge replied.

"Your Honor, I request that this sidebar be on the record," Karp said. "May we have the stenographer record it?"

"Yes, indeed," Temple agreed.

Out of the jurors' hearing and with the steno in place, Rottingham pleaded with the judge. "We have no idea where these alleged criminal histories come from, nor have we had a chance to look them over. In addition, I object to them on grounds of relevance. Reverend LaFontaine has already admitted that prior to his conversion he and

Frank Bernsen led a life of sin, and he even just admitted to having been incarcerated for a crime."

The judge looked at Karp. "Your take?"

"Your Honor, we obtained these certified records by serving the Bureau of Alcohol, Tobacco, Firearms and Explosives with a warrant," Karp replied. "They'd been kept out of the national crime database due to this pair working as confidential informants for the ATF. The ATF wasn't happy about it, but we won the day. As for LaFontaine already admitting to one crime and a life of sin, he still holds himself as a paragon of virtue while casting blame and culpability on his partner in crime. As such this history is relevant. The defendant exposed himself to this sort of character impeachment when he took the stand. It's not the People's fault that he thought his record would be kept secret. I am offering these files in evidence and handing a complete copy to Mr. Rottingham."

Judge Temple nodded. "I'm going to allow it. Mr. Karp is right; your client chose to take the stand."

"Not on my recommendation," Rottingham mumbled.

"Mr. Rottingham, you may return to your seat," Temple told him. "The objection is overruled; the certified files regarding the defendant and one Frank Bernsen, People's Exhibit Thirty-five inclusively, is admitted into evidence."

"Thank you, Your Honor," Karp said. He walked up to the witness stand and handed one set of papers to LaFontaine. "In case you need to refresh your memory," he said as the defendant glared down at him. "Now, you want to read off the list of felonies for which you've been convicted?"

"As I said, before I saw the light I lived a life of sin —" LaFontaine tried to explain, but Karp cut him off.

"That's not what I asked. I asked you to read off the list of felonies for which you've been convicted," Karp demanded, his voice booming in the courtroom.

LaFontaine looked down at the papers. "Burglary. Assault. Robbery. Drug possession and distribution. Receiving stolen goods." He put the papers down.

"I believe you left one off," Karp said. "It's the second to the last one, right before 'receiving stolen goods.' "

"Impersonating a police officer," LaFontaine said.

"Impersonating a police officer," Karp said. "Pretending to be someone you were not. I guess a leopard doesn't change his spots."

"Objection!" Rottingham roared.

"I'll withdraw the comment, Your Honor," Karp replied. "Now, would you do the same with Frank Bernsen's record?"

LaFontaine looked back down at the pages. "Assault. Assault with a deadly weapon."

"A few of those, aren't there?" Karp commented.

"Yes. Sexual assault. Burglary. Receiving stolen goods. Impersonating a police officer."

"That last one, impersonating a police officer, that was for the same occurrence that you were convicted for, right?"

"Yes."

"How many years ago were you arrested and convicted for impersonating a police officer?" Karp asked.

"A little more than two years ago."

"Shortly before you met Monique and Charlie Hale, correct?"

"Yes."

Karp walked up to the witness stand and held out his hand to get the records back. "With all those convictions, how come you're not in prison, Mr. LaFontaine?"

"The Bureau of Alcohol, Tobacco, Firearms and Explosives offered us a deal," LaFontaine admitted. "If we worked with them against an outlaw motorcycle club, our records were going to be expunged."

"You were working as informants, right?" LaFontaine stared at Karp for a moment, then nodded. "Yeah."

"And an informant, or snitch, is someone who tells on someone else in order to get out of trouble, right?"

"That's one way of putting it."

"Sort of like you snitching on Frank Bernsen about the life insurance policies, right?"

"Objection."

"Sustained," Temple said. "Mr. Karp, let's save it for summations."

Karp nodded. "So, Mr. LaFontaine, if I'm right about the timing here, your conversion into a man of God happened about the same time you were making a deal with the ATF and shortly before you met the Hales. Am I correct?"

"I saw the light about that time, yes," LaFontaine said. "I was hurting in my soul for all the sins I'd committed and after I met that other preacher, I knew I needed to change."

"I see, and Frank changed with you?"

"I thought he had."

"Well, he's named as the chief financial officer for both of your churches, here and in Memphis," Karp said. "You lived with him. Blocked the doorway of an extremely ill child with him to prevent paramedics and police officers from performing their jobs with him. And if Monique Hale is to be believed, and the jury will determine that, you were almost inseparable and he did what you told him to do."

"I deny that," LaFontaine replied. "Frank was his own man."

"But he was your brother in crime?"

"He was also my brother in Christ."

"Except that according to your testimony, he must not have been living a simple, sin-free life like you."

"I guess not."

Karp paced slowly in front of the jury box before asking his next question. "I'm noticing that according to you, everybody else is a liar or simply mistaken. Is that true?"

"What do you mean?" LaFontaine scowled.

"Well, Monique Hale says you forbade her and her husband from seeking medical attention for their daughter, Natalie, and that you threatened to leave her alone spiritually and emotionally. That you were her lover. But that's all a lie, right?"

"Yes."

"And she testified that Sarah Westerberg used to come to her house with you to talk to her about faith healing; that was also a lie?"

"Yes."

"And Dr. Holstein says that it was you who approached him about targeting the families of ill children and expunging their records from hospital files, and that he spoke to you several times after that. But that's a lie?"

"Yes."

"They're all liars because they all have it in for men of God. Is that correct?"

LaFontaine shook his head. "Perhaps they've just been led astray by godless men."

"And was it godless men who threatened you so that you changed your name and moved to New York City?"

"I would think so."

"Did you report any of these threats to the police?"

"No. I didn't think they'd take me seriously."

"That wouldn't be because between you and Frank Bernsen, you had a pretty good record for violent crimes, would it?"

"I don't know."

"Mr. LaFontaine, do you have any proof

that these threats were real? Or maybe you were just skipping town because it was getting too hot for you in Memphis."

"I object to counsel's portrayal of my client's reasons for leaving Memphis," Rottingham said.

"Sustained. Just ask your question, Mr. Karp."

"Mr. LaFontaine, I asked if you have any proof whatsoever that you were threatened because of your religious practices in Memphis."

"No. The threats were anonymous."

Karp was quiet as he studied LaFontaine on the witness stand. *Time to change course,* he thought.

"Mr. LaFontaine," Karp said, "would you say you've done rather well for yourself since coming to New York City?"

"How do you mean?" LaFontaine asked.

"I mean, you told the jury that you live a simple life," Karp replied, "but let's examine that." He walked over to the prosecution table and picked up several sheets of paper. "Your Honor, we offer the bank records for the End of Days Reformation Church of Jesus Christ Resurrected as People's Exhibit Thirty-six cumulatively."

"No objection," said Rottingham wearily. He'd tried to keep the records out of the trial at a hearing and lost.

Karp handed the papers to LaFontaine while keeping another set for himself. "Mr. LaFontaine, would you read the dollar amount contained on the line designated as 'total deposits to date'?"

LaFontaine looked at the papers. "Eight hundred and thirty-seven thousand."

"That's eight hundred and thirty-seven thousand dollars, correct?"

"Yes."

"And where did that money come from?"

"Donations."

"Donations," Karp repeated. "And I believe that there is one major 'donation' that makes up the bulk of the deposits . . . one for eight hundred and twenty-five thousand dollars. Do you recall where that money came from?"

"The estate of Kathryn Boole," LaFontaine said. "She left it to me when she passed away in April."

"And the remaining twelve thousand dollars?"

"Smaller donations from members of the congregation."

"Mr. LaFontaine, did Mrs. Boole leave you anything else from her estate?"

"Yes, her will included a building on Avenue A where she generously allowed our church to meet."

"The church, as well as living quarters for yourself and Frank Bernsen, is that correct?" Karp asked.

"Yes, that's true."

"Would you describe these quarters as part of living a simple life?"

"It is a nice three-bedroom loft, but nothing fancy," LaFontaine said.

"Nothing fancy," Karp said as he walked over to the prosecution table and picked up another sheet of paper. "Your Honor, may I have the real estate brochure for the property on Avenue A that Mr. LaFontaine has just described as nothing fancy marked as People's Exhibit Thirty-seven for identification."

"Objection," Rottingham said, rising from his seat. "I don't see the relevance of this brochure."

"The relevance is that the defendant has described this 'donation' as nothing fancy," Karp replied. "The jurors can look at the brochure and decide for themselves if that description is apt."

"I'll allow it," Temple said.

"Thank you, Your Honor," Karp said, walking back to the witness stand and handing the real estate brochure to the defendant. "Mr. LaFontaine, does this brochure fairly and accurately depict the property you inherited from Kathryn Boole?"

"Yes, it does."

"Your Honor, the People offer this Exhibit Thirty-seven in evidence," Karp said.

"So granted," Temple ruled.

"Mr. LaFontaine, would you please read the description of the building from the brochure."

"It says it's a 'three-story building in an up-and-coming neighborhood on the Lower East Side with a large open first floor excellent for commercial use, a second floor containing four large office spaces' —"

"Hold on just a moment," Karp interrupted. "I just want to be clear about these office spaces. Who occupies them?"

"The church uses one and the others are leased to business tenants," LaFontaine replied.

"I didn't see any deposits from these leases on the bank statements," Karp said. "Are they behind on their rent or does the money go somewhere else?"

"The money goes into a corporation," LaFontaine said.

"And whose names are listed as officers in that corporation?" Karp asked.

"Mine and Frank Bernsen's."

"I see. And how much approximately do

you bring in a month from those leases?" Karp asked.

"There are three offices other than the church office and together they pay about twenty-one thousand a month," LaFontaine said.

"Twenty-one thousand," Karp said. "And does that money go into church activities or charities?"

"It's for living expenses," LaFontaine said.

"I see," Karp repeated. "For that simple life you lead."

LaFontaine glared at Karp but remained silent.

"Objection," Rottingham said, this time remaining in his seat. "Counsel keeps making superfluous comments that are not part of a legitimate cross-examination."

"No, Your Honor, counsel misspeaks, that's a very legitimate question and I await an answer," Karp shot back.

"I have no intention of quibbling with you, Mr. Karp," LaFontaine stated.

"Well then continue reading the description of the building," Karp said, pressing on.

" 'The property includes a fully furnished twelve-thousand-square-foot loft with three bedrooms, three baths, a state-of-the-art kitchen, granite counters, and hardwood floors,' " LaFontaine read, then looked up.

"Continue, Mr. LaFontaine, there's more," Karp said.

" 'An entertainment room including a fifteen-foot projection screen and seating for twenty. Formal dining room. Built-in sound system.' " LaFontaine stopped reading. "That's it."

"That's it," Karp agreed. "And what was the listed price for the building?"

"Three point two million dollars," LaFontaine said.

"Three point two million dollars," Karp repeated. "So I ask you again, Mr. LaFontaine, haven't you done pretty well for yourself since coming to New York City?"

"I don't think it's unusual for a minister to reap the rewards of a dedicated congregation," LaFontaine argued. "You could ask Billy Graham how much he makes in a year."

"Billy Graham isn't on the witness stand, Mr. LaFontaine," Karp said. "Nor is he accused of using his influence and position of trust to prevent parents from seeking medical attention so that he can reap extravagant 'donations' and life insurance policies."

"Objection! Your Honor, counsel is doing his summations in cross-examination!" Rottingham yelled.

Temple simply cocked his head. "I believe that your client drew the analogy. Overruled, but let's get back to questions and answers, Mr. Karp."

"Yes, Your Honor," Karp replied. "If the witness would answer my question, please?"

LaFontaine glared at Karp but then forced a smile. "I guess I've done pretty well due to the generosity of my congregation."

"And you stood to do even better on the death of Micah Ellis, is that correct?" Karp asked.

LaFontaine looked at his defense lawyer, who remained quiet. "The Ellises had taken out a life insurance policy in which the benefits were assigned to the church."

"The church of which you and Frank Bernsen were the sole officers — the only ones who could make withdrawals," Karp said, pressing him.

"Yes."

"And this was a similar policy to the one Monique Hale testified about?"

"Yes."

"Except there was a problem getting paid this time, wasn't there?"

"The insurance company has not yet paid."

"Why not?"

"Because the Ellises were charged with

reckless manslaughter, and if they'd been found guilty, the company wouldn't have paid. The company was waiting to see what would happen."

"Were the Ellises found guilty?"

"No."

"And why not?"

"I'm not sure. David Ellis is dead. I don't know what happened to his wife, Nonie. I guess she's still charged with reckless manslaughter."

"Are you aware that there is a warrant out for Nonie Ellis for failure to appear both in her own case and as a witness in this one?"

"I've been told that."

"Did you benefit by the death of David Ellis?"

LaFontaine scowled. "Of course not, David Ellis was a friend and trusted member of my congregation. I loved David. We were brothers in Christ!"

"Do you know what happened to David Ellis?"

"He was killed."

"By whom?"

"By Kathryn Boole. She shot him."

"Where did you shoot him?"

"In front of this courthouse."

"And what happened to Mrs. Boole?"

"She was subsequently shot and killed."

"By whom?"

"By Frank Bernsen . . . because, I might add, she had pointed a gun at you," LaFontaine said.

"Indeed, she was pointing a gun at me," Karp said. "Why did she shoot David Ellis?"

"I don't know," LaFontaine said. "She didn't tell me her plans."

"Do you recall your actions when David Ellis arrived in front of the courthouse, shortly before Mrs. Boole shot him?"

"I was part of a group protesting the charges against the Ellises," LaFontaine said.

"But what did you do and say when you saw David Ellis arrive at the courthouse?"

"I don't recall exactly," LaFontaine replied.

"Well, perhaps this recording of the events will refresh your recollection." Karp turned toward the judge. "Your Honor, I'd like to play a DVD of a newscast that recorded certain relevant events pertaining to this issue."

Judge Temple turned toward the jurors. "There's an old law school saying that argues you can use virtually anything to refresh the recollection of a witness, even a shoe. Mr. Karp will now show you part of a newscast taken from the day in question to

449

ascertain whether it will refresh the defendant's recollection. That's all it's being displayed for. You may proceed, Mr. Karp."

The lights in the courtroom were dimmed as a court clerk set up a television screen so that the jurors, judge, LaFontaine, and the spectators could all see it. Karp pressed a button on the lectern and a female television reporter appeared on the screen standing on the sidewalk in front of the Criminal Courts Building.

"This is Tessa Laine, and we're at the Manhattan Criminal Courts Building, where this morning jury selection is set to begin in the reckless-manslaughter case against David and Nonie Ellis. The Ellises are accused of not seeking proper medical attention for their son, Micah, who later died. As you can hear behind me, emotions are running high, particularly among a group of protesters across the street who claim that this prosecution is a violation of the parents' religious rights."

As Laine spoke, the camera panned across the street to take in the protesters led by LaFontaine. *"Ah, we believe that David Ellis has arrived,"* Laine said. *"There's no sign of his wife yet. That's odd, but for some reason the protesters seem to be angry with Mr. Ellis, who up to this point they've been supporting."*

The camera panned across the street, zeroing in on LaFontaine as he pointed at Ellis and shouted. " 'The fool says in his heart, "There is no God." They are corrupt, their deeds are vile.' " At that point, the protesters surged into the traffic, where they stopped cars and were met by police. However, one woman continued through the stopped cars.

"That's Kathryn Boole," Karp, who was standing next to the screen, said, pointing.

As the camera recorded, Boole pulled a handgun from her purse and walked up to David Ellis. "Judas!" she screamed, and then shot him.

Karp stopped the tape and signaled for the lights to be turned up again. "Mr. LaFontaine, does the tape we've just seen refresh your recollection regarding what you did when David Ellis arrived at the Criminal Courts Building?"

LaFontaine sat silently staring at Karp. Finally, he nodded.

"Please speak up, Mr. LaFontaine," Karp demanded.

Again there was silence from the defendant, before he shook his head, then answered. "Yes, it does."

"Objection! Your Honor, please, my client is not on trial — nor should he be — for the murder of David Ellis. He is not responsible for the actions of any one member of his congregation any more than Mr. Karp would be responsible if one of his assistant district attorneys walked out of the Criminal Courts Building this afternoon and shot a hot dog vendor. This is just an attempt to make my client guilty by association with a deranged woman."

"A deranged woman who was apparently enough in control of her faculties to give Mr. LaFontaine a three-point-two-million-dollar building and eight hundred and twenty-five thousand dollars cash," Karp argued. "Apparently she was sane enough for that! We just saw the defendant point at David Ellis and a minute later one of his followers turns into a murderer. This whole trial is about LaFontaine's influence over susceptible people."

"Enough!" Temple ordered. "Mr. Rottingham, I'm going to overrule your objection to the question, but I caution you and Mr. Karp to keep the rhetoric to yourselves. Now, Mr. Karp, do you want to continue without the additional comments?"

"Yes," Karp said, and turned back to LaFontaine. "How powerful do you believe your influence to be over members of your congregation?"

452

"I've said before that all I do is explain what I believe," LaFontaine retorted. "What they choose to do with that is up to them. They are all thinking individuals."

"Do you know why Kathryn Boole murdered David Ellis?"

"I do not."

"You have no idea why she would yell, 'Judas,' and then pull the trigger?"

"No idea."

"Would it be because if David Ellis was dead and Nonie beat the reckless-manslaughter charge, you would collect on the insurance policy?"

"I don't know what you're talking about."

"Was it because David Ellis planned to plead guilty to the charge and expose you as a fraud because of the insurance policy?"

"I have no knowledge of that."

"No? David Ellis never told you those were his plans?"

"I said he did not," LaFontaine snarled.

Karp stood in front of the witness stand with his hands on his hips, glaring up at the witness. "Mr. LaFontaine, right now there are two people in this courtroom who know that you just lied again under oath. Me and you!"

Rottingham again jumped to his feet, but before he could object, another voice shouted in the courtroom.

"No, Mr. Karp, there are three!"

Everyone in the courtroom turned to see who'd spoken. Karp was surprised as the woman who'd been sitting next to Marlene now stood up. She shook visibly as she removed the scarf, followed by a blond wig and dark glasses. "I'm Nonie Ellis, and I have something to say."

Karp looked at his wife, who gave him a knowing smile. He shook his head and glanced over at Rottingham, who stood with his mouth agape, and then up at LaFontaine. For the first time since he'd met the man, he saw fear in his eyes.

"Your Honor," Karp said, "I'd suggest that this might be a good time to adjourn so that we can sort this out."

Judge Temple closed his mouth, which had fallen open when Nonie Ellis shouted. He now recovered and banged his gavel. "Mr. Karp, I couldn't agree with you more. Court is adjourned. Uh, and happy Halloween."

34

Nadya Malovo smiled at federal agent Michael Rolles as they waited on the northwest corner of Sixth Avenue and 8th Street and watched the revelers pass them by tooting horns, beating drums, dancing, shouting, and laughing. "You make a good wolf; nice fangs," she said.

For once Rolles smiled back at her. "The better to eat you with, my dear," he growled.

"Promise, promises," Malovo replied as she adjusted her red hood and switched her picnic basket from one hand to the other, the folds of her cape hiding the fact that her wrists were cuffed with plastic ties.

They were both feeling good about the evening. She because her plan — for all its complexity and potential pitfalls — was coming to fruition. He because she'd finally let him in on her plan the night before, after she'd met with the men in Bedford-Stuyvesant, and he realized that it was going to work. All that he wanted — power and money — would soon be his.

Only outwardly was Rolles an agent for the National Inter-Departmental Security Administration. In reality, he worked for the Sons of Man, another one of its legion of foot soldiers who had been assigned to infiltrate the political, military, law enforcement, and business establishments of the United States. Many years earlier, he'd begun his double-agent life working for the Central Intelligence Agency until the World Trade Center attacks of 9/11. In the rush to consolidate and expand national security under one umbrella, the hierarchy of the Sons of Man had seen an opportunity and ordered Rolles and many others like him to switch agencies.

That past spring he'd been given the assignment of a lifetime. Malovo, whom the Sons of Man had used in the past for a variety of their nefarious plans, had gotten word out of her federal cell that she could deliver a very valuable prize. Her asking price was her freedom and enough money to live like a queen for the rest of her life, and not in some crummy witness protection program.

At least that was what she'd told Rolles when he showed up at the maximum-security federal penitentiary, ostensibly to try his hand at questioning her. When they'd agreed on the deal, they played it cool. At first she pretended that she was no more interested in talking to him about sleeper cells than she had been with any of the other federal agents, like Espey Jaxon. But over time, she had started to "divulge information" that led to the destruction and apprehension of some of the cells, including the one she goaded into attacking the Liberty Island ferry, and then let it be known that she was only going to cooperate with Rolles.

Even Rolles admitted to her that afternoon as they prepared for the final phase that her plan was brilliant. It incorporated three objectives that all fit in with the goals of his organization.

The first would be the terrorist act. If all went right hundreds of people would die that night and thousands more would be maimed. All of which would be televised around the country and the world. Most importantly, the fear and paranoia generated by such easily accomplished suicide attacks would be overwhelming. The comfort zone Americans were finally settling back into in the post-9/11 world would be destroyed in a moment of death and destruction. What little faith they had in their current leaders would evaporate and create a vacuum into which powerful, confident, and determined men would step, even if it required martial law and the suspension of certain constitutional protections.

The second facet of Malovo's plan was the assassination of Roger Karp, the district attorney of New York County. For too long he and his cursed family and friends had foiled the well-laid plans of the Sons of Man. Sometimes it was beyond all understanding how they had stopped the organization from accomplishing its goals, but enough was enough; it was time for him to die. That this fit with Malovo's desire for revenge made it all the sweeter to her.

However, it was the third part of her plan that truly mattered. The prize she had dangled in front of the Sons of Man was Andrew Kane, formerly the group's most powerful member. As she told Rolles when he was sent to find out if she could deliver what she promised, Kane was alive and being held captive by the madman David Grale. One of her trusted men on the outside, one of the Russians she'd met with the night before, had been approached by a traitor who told him about Kane and said he could help locate him.

She could only imagine the ripple of both excitement and fear that the news of Kane's whereabouts had sent through the clandestine organization. When he was in power, Kane had seen to it that billions of dollars of the organization's finances were shifted into accounts that only he could access. The Sons of Man had lost billions more due to Karp and his friends, while the organization was not bankrupt, the financial blows had crippled its ability to push its agenda. Getting access to the money Kane had squirreled away would put them again in the driver's seat.

However, even billions of dollars wasn't the most important reason that Malovo's plan to find Kane was so vital to the Sons of Man. Kane knew the identities of those members of the group who had yet to be discovered by Jaxon and his agency, one of the few agencies the Sons of Man had been unable to make any inroads into, mostly because of its small size.

As such, there were two possible outcomes for Kane if Malovo's plan worked. Hopefully, he could be "rescued" from Grale and then forced to divulge the information regarding the secret bank accounts. After that, he would be disposed of. However, if Kane couldn't be removed from Grale's lair, it was up to Rolles and his two men, as well as Malovo, to kill Kane and silence him forever.

Malovo was quite certain that Rolles was also supposed to kill her, too. She was a loose end. She knew too much. Of course, she had not told him all of her plan. The image of her former mentor lying in the bloodred snow flashed in her mind and the thought made her happy.

Fortunately, Rolles was as weak as any other man. She couldn't seduce him with her sexuality, but she played to his ambition. She looked up at him again, seeing past the fake canine nose and fangs, through the gray fur headpiece and floppy ears. He was thinking about all the rungs he would be jumping past on the Sons of Man ladder. *Maybe right into the inner circle and a seat at its table.*

As she watched a marching band of barebreasted women covered in body paint dance past, Malovo smiled again. *Knowing your enemy's plan allows you to make the first move.* This advice from her mentor had saved her many times, even if it had not saved him.

Waiting for word that the next phase had been completed, Malovo took in the scene around her. For more than a mile the

460

sidewalks were packed with people, most of them in costume watching the parade. She knew that the marchers had begun lining up early that afternoon, an amazing collection of some of the most outlandish and outrageous costumes. Skeletons and vampires. Satyrs and clowns. Giants on stilts strode by as drag queens in their element proudly posed for photographs with tourists. And at the tail end of the parade was the grand marshal's float — a cemetery with gravestones and ghosts, all presided over by the Grim Reaper.

It had disappointed her to learn that Karp's family would not be on the float with him, though it had not surprised her due to her own warnings about the terrorist threat. But the warnings had been necessary. The most difficult part of her plan had been to lure Grale and his men out of their lair. The traitor had told her that there was no way she could simply storm his stronghold, even if she could find it. He and his people knew the subterranean world and were masters at fighting in the dark. "And if he knows you're coming with too great a force to fight," the traitor had said, "he'll just take Kane and melt away into the dark."

She needed to know how to find Grale's home and Kane, and she needed Grale to

461

be out of it, which is where her attorney Bruce Knight came in. The traitor had told her that Knight had once lived with Grale and still helped with legal issues for his motley collection of Mole People. That meant he could contact Grale and would be trusted. She gambled that Knight could also be trusted to reveal what she was saying and doing to his old friend. *So much for attorney-client privilege,* she thought with a laugh.

Of all the potential pitfalls in her plan, Grale worried her the most. He answered to no one but himself and by all accounts was insane, which meant he might not react in a predictable way. So she'd come up with several traps to get him out from beneath the streets. The first was to offer herself as bait. She knew from the traitor that Grale felt he was on some sort of mission from God to rid Manhattan of evil. "He believes that you are inhabited by a very important demon," the traitor had told her. "If he thought he could get to you and kill you, he'd take any chance."

So she let it be known to Knight that she would be at the Halloween parade with very little protection. He would also try to stop a terrorist attack, seeing himself as a force for good, and therefore she made sure that Knight knew enough about the evening's plans to warn Grale.

She wasn't as sure about Grale's feelings about Karp. On the surface, they were enemies — Grale was a mass murderer and Karp was a by-the-book prosecutor. The traitor had warned that there was some sort of personal connection between Grale and Karp's family, but whether that extended to the man himself, he wasn't so sure. So she also came up with the idea of planting the seed that Karp worked for the Sons of Man, not such a farfetched idea for a madman. It had paid off when Rolles brought her the newspaper with the front-page story about Grale's attack on Karp.

Malovo looked around, wondering if any of the costumed revelers around her were actually an insane killer and his minions. It would be so easy to sidle up to her, just as, according to her plan, it would be so easy for a group of terrorists to join the parade with no one the wiser until the bombs started going off.

Looking across Sixth Avenue, Malovo scanned the crowd to pick out Agent Jaxon and U.S. Marshal Capers. She'd suggested that they stand apart from her as they kept an eye on the marchers and told them it would be easier to spot the terrorists on the parade route than next to her on a crowded sidewalk. She expected Capers to resist the notion of being so far away, but other than insisting that Malovo be cuffed and within arm's reach of Rolles, she agreed.

During a break between groups on the parade route, Malovo spotted the pair. Capers was dressed as a clown in whiteface and wearing a short, bright yellow high school marching band dress and a cowboy hat. Jaxon was dressed as a cowboy, complete with a six-shooter that Malovo knew was not just a prop.

Suddenly, Jaxon's hand flew to his ear, while on his side of the street, Rolles did the same thing. A moment later Rolles turned toward her and grinned. "They caught Grale," he said. "Apparently he got within about twenty feet of Karp's float before Fulton spotted him. And get this, he was dressed like a monk and almost made it through the security line."

Malovo laughed. Then Rolles put a finger to his lips and listened to his earpiece again, and again started to smile. "Just like a row of dominoes," he said. "I'm afraid yet another terrorist cell has been taken down."

This time Malovo nodded. She knew the second report was from Jaxon's antiterrorism team. The next phase was complete. Two blocks away, two sleeper cells of terrorists who'd been helping each other into suicide vests were in the custody of federal agents.

"It's done," Rolles said, looking down at her. "They will relax their guard now."

"Time for the next phase," Malovo said.

Rolles nodded and pulled a cell phone from his pocket. He pressed a number and then spoke into the receiver. "Move."

Suddenly, from a side street just up the block, a new group of marchers broke through the throng and the police barricade to join the parade. The group consisted of a dozen young women dressed identically to Malovo as Little Red Riding Hoods and a half-dozen men dressed as wolves like Rolles. The crowd laughed and cheered as the wolves chased the red-caped women toward Malovo and Rolles.

Malovo glanced back across the street and saw Capers frown, then suddenly realize what was happening and start trying to push her way through the crowd. Jaxon followed, drawing his gun.

It was too late. The Red Riding Hoods, who were just young women hired to play the part, surrounded Malovo and Rolles. "Let's go," he said to her, and started to move with the crowd.

She smiled. This was the part of the plan

she had not told him about. One of the wolves stepped up to her, cut the plastic wrist cuffs, and handed the knife he'd used to Malovo. It all happened so fast that Rolles did not have time to react before the blade cut through his stomach muscles and pierced his liver. She twisted the knife for both effect and pleasure, and then stabbed him twice more before he could reach out to push her away.

"Bitch," he snarled as he started to crumple to the ground.

"The better to kill you, my dear," she laughed, and then bent over and took the cell phone from his hand. She stood and looked at the wolf who had handed her the knife. *"Allahu akbar!"* she shouted, giving him the cell phone.

"Allahu akbar!" he shouted back, and with the other wolves began to run toward the back of the parade route, where the grand marshal's float was just beginning its journey.

Even those around Malovo did not realize what had happened as she danced off in the middle of the group of other Red Riding Hoods. Not until a pool of blood began to spread around the twitching body of Michael Rolles did anyone scream.

And by the time Capers and Jaxon reached the spot, Malovo was long gone.

35

Standing on top of the float, Karp saw them coming from two blocks away. A half-dozen figures dressed in gray fur with black noses and floppy ears running with purpose against the flow of the parade. Even at a distance he could tell that they moved like men weighed down by a heavy burden.

It was seeing their costumes, though, that had reminded him of one of the offhand comments made by the terrorists in the house with Nadya Malovo: "We will be like wolves among the sheep." And that's when he knew the identity of the men who'd been sent to kill him and many others.

The comment might have passed him by, but his daughter's discussion about how people sounded different when speaking naturally as opposed to reading had heightened his consciousness about speech patterns. Without knowing why it mattered, he noticed how Malovo's voice had caught when the man spoke before she recovered and tried to hide the slipup.

Now he knew what had been in the boxes that Jaxon's men had discovered at the Bed-Stuy house that afternoon. They had found the boxes when they took the terrorists into custody, but they'd been empty, and it wasn't until the agents discovered an old tunnel below the apartment building that had once been used to transport heating coal beneath the streets that they realized that one group of the terrorists had escaped with their costumes. The others who stayed back were just unwitting decoys, though murderous in their own right.

"It's the wolves, Clay!" he shouted at the large ghost standing next to him.

"The wolves?" Fulton repeated, then nodded. "I see them." He cued his radio. "We've spotted the targets. Five — no, six men dressed as wolves, running toward the float. On my signal, jam them! Take-down team, be ready!"

As his would-be assassins approached, Karp prayed that none of them would panic and attempt to detonate his vest until they were close to him. Although it was believed that the vests were going to be detonated by remote control, they couldn't be sure that there wasn't a manual means as well.

A block away, the wolves picked up speed. One of them held up a cell phone.

"Now!" Fulton shouted.

Screaming, *"Allahu akbar!"* the wolves halted in a semicircle in front of the float as the leader with the cell raised it high above his head and pressed the Send button. For a moment it seemed to Karp that time stopped and the world stood still. But instead of a blast followed by a million tiny steel balls flying through the air, tearing bodies to pieces, nothing happened.

The terrorists looked at each other in confusion. Several shouted again as the leader punched at the phone. But that was his last act before all six wolves were tackled hard and taken to the ground by two dozen burly NYPD SWAT officers dressed as Roman gladiators. Before any of the assassins could reach for a manual detonation device, their arms were wrenched behind their backs and each was subdued and cuffed by two officers while a third held a gun to the head of a prisoner.

Throwing back his cowl and removing his Death mask, Karp looked over at a pretty female ghost standing on his other side. "Nice work," he said.

"What?" Lucy said, still looking at the squirming wolves on the ground.

"The cell phone detonator," Karp said.

"Oh," she said. "It was nothing."

"Yeah, nothing, but it saved a lot of people," Karp replied.

It was Lucy who'd figured out that Malovo would want the suicide vests to explode simultaneously for maximum effect and the best way to do it would be to use cell phones attached to the vests as detonators. Her clue, as she explained in his office at lunch, had been the attack on the ferry. She'd been listening on some of the world's most sensitive audio equipment when she announced that the remaining terrorists on the crippled boat wanted to surrender. "No one was threatening to blow up the boat," she said. "But right before it exploded, I heard a cell phone ring. We checked transmissions to and from the vessel, including those from Aman Ghilzai that morning. At the exact moment of the explosion, there was a call placed to a cell phone on the boat from one of the apartment buildings overlooking the harbor."

Karp looked at Fulton. "We better set off the fireworks," he said.

"Blow 'em!" Fulton shouted into his radio.

The command was followed by several large explosions from the rooftops of buildings on either side of the grand marshal's float. As the crowd around the float, some of whom were still trying to figure out if the scene with the handcuffed wolves was real or a joke, cheered, the big detective smiled. "Sounded like a successful suicide attack to me," he shouted.

Karp nodded, wondering how the night would end, but grateful that so far it was without the deaths of many innocent people.

Pulling that off had been no small feat and had taken the full focus of Jaxon's team, as well as Karp and Fulton. That alone had been tough for Karp, who'd had to switch gears from the trial and sudden appearance of Nonie Ellis.

Fortunately, the good guys had several things working for them. One was knowing that everything Malovo and her accomplice had said aloud was intended to deceive them. Whatever she was planning, it didn't depend on the six men in the house who thought they were going to martyr themselves.

Of course, Jaxon's team still had to follow the men and, when they met with the other sleeper cell, take them down as they prepared for mayhem and murder. The two Russians Malovo had been speaking to had also left the house, but these men, and a third unidentified man who'd gone with them, were left for Grale to deal with as part of his bargain with Karp.

It was Grale who'd figured out that while Malovo and Rolles, whom they now assumed to be a double agent with the Sons of Man, were serious when planning the terrorist attack on the Halloween parade, it wasn't just to sow fear and terror, or even just to kill Karp. Those were just side benefits. Their main objective was to kill or capture Andrew Kane.

Grale had realized early on that a traitor was working against him. A man who'd been exiled from the Mole People and had somehow contacted Malovo and informed her that Kane, whose information would be invaluable to both law enforcement and the Sons of Man, was being held captive. This traitor had led her to Bruce Knight, whom she'd tried to use to sow disinformation.

Grale had countered by having one of his loyal followers contact the traitor and, in conversations, let himself be convinced to work for Malovo, too. Then Grale tested his theory by having his man tell the traitor that he would be meeting with Lucy Karp in Central Park and that he would have Kane with him. He'd been well aware of the man in the shadows at the boathouse.

"Whatever her plans, she is working hard

to make sure that my focus, and your focus, is on the Halloween parade," Grale had said at their meeting. "She's even tried to divide us by suggesting to me that you work with the Sons of Man. All of it to lure me away from my stronghold and her prize."

It was then that Grale had proposed his deal with Karp, who now looked north up Sixth Avenue. *It's in your hands now, David,* he thought just as two police officers led a struggling man dressed in a brown monk's robe up to the float.

"Let go of me . . . piss crap balls whoop whoop oh boy . . . you pissants, I'm working with the DA!" the man shouted.

An amused smile crossed Karp's face. "David Grale, I presume," he said.

One of the police officers pulled back the hood from the robe, and Dirty Warren Bennett grinned up at Karp, his face twitching. "Hey, Butch, I got a . . . oh boy oh boy . . . good one for you," the news vendor said. "What are the two things the Gypsy woman says to Lon Chaney Jr. in *The Wolf Man*?"

Karp laughed. "Let's see, 'Even a man who is pure in heart and says his prayers by night may become a wolf when the wolfbane blooms and the autumn moon is bright.' "

"Yeah, yeah, that's the . . . tits ass whoop . . . one everybody knows," Bennett said with a grin. "What's the other one?"

"Boy, that's a tough one," Karp replied.

"Woo-hooo!" Bennett cackled. "Tonight I'm going to . . . son of a bitch oh boy . . . win for once!"

Karp grinned. "Sorry to disappoint you, my friend, but how's this? 'The way you walked was thorny, through no fault of your own, but as the rain enters the soil, the river enters the sea, so tears run to a predestined end.' "

"Aw, I knew you'd get it . . . oh boy whoop whoop," Bennett said. He pointed down at the sewer cover he was standing on. "It just seemed appropriate . . . crap nuts . . . it being Halloween and the predestined end and all. You know what I mean?"

"Yes, Warren, I know exactly what you mean."

36

The little man crept like the rat he was through the sewers and pathways beneath the city until he came to the dimly lit junction of tunnels where he knew he would be challenged. "I'm looking for the entrance to the kingdom of heaven," he called out.

"And how do you gain entrance?" a voice shouted back from the dark outside the circle of light.

"The love of Christ," the man answered, praying that the password had not changed.

A moment later, another man stepped out of the shadows with his rifle pointed. "James? What are you doing here? You know David exiled you on pain of death!"

"I have important news for him, Brother Harvey," James said.

"And what might that be?" Harvey replied before a fit of coughing took him.

"That his reign is over," James snarled. "And so is your life."

Harvey looked up just as a red beam intersected his chest. The bullet that followed knocked him to the ground, so that he ended up sitting in a puddle of dirty water with his back against the tunnel wall. "Judas," he whispered.

"How's it feel, Harvey?" James asked, squatting so that he could peer in the dying man's eyes with a penlight. "What does it feel like to die?"

"Like freedom," Harvey replied, and died with a smile on his lips.

The traitor James stood up, confused. He'd thought there would be more satisfaction; Harvey had been the one to escort him from Grale's kingdom and kick him out onto the streets. But there wasn't more time to think about it as two more men walked up behind him and stood looking down at the dead man.

"Now what?" James asked.

"We wait for Malovo and Rolles," one of the men said, and looked at his watch. "They should be here any minute."

James nodded. He'd been the third man at the meeting with Malovo in Bedford-Stuyvesant and felt important because of the role he'd been given. After being kicked out of the kingdom, he'd brooded over his exile, thinking of ways to get even. Then he remembered a conversation Grale had had with Harvey regarding Boris Kazanov and the Russian gangster's ties to Malovo. So he went to Little Odessa in Brooklyn and let the word get out that he wanted to speak to Kazanov about "something worth a lot of money to Nadya Malovo."

The gangster had found him shortly after and listened to his story about the man Grale kept captive in his lair, Andrew Kane. He convinced Kazanov that Malovo would be willing to pay millions for the information and assistance. The brutal Russian had taken it from there.

James found Malovo extremely attractive and fantasized about what sex would be like with the blond goddess. He was surprised and delighted when she started flirting with him, suggesting that one of his rewards would be an intimate one.

Waiting with the two NIDSA agents for word of the explosions from lower Manhattan, James imagined how grateful Malovo would be when he delivered her prize. When they heard the signals, he practically ran through the sewers and tunnels to reach the junction where they were to take out the guard and wait for the others.

The moment he was waiting for soon arrived when Malovo ran up. But there was no sign of Rolles.

"He's dead," Malovo answered truthfully when the agents asked why he was not with her. "That son of a bitch Jaxon shot him at the Fourteenth Street subway station. I barely escaped. But I heard the explosions; that part of the mission is complete."

The two agents exchanged puzzled looks. "I don't believe you," one said, and raised his silenced submachine gun. But he never had a chance to pull the trigger before a bullet caught him in the mouth, killing him before he even fell to the ground.

The second agent was also too slow to react. He turned in the direction the bullet had come from but in doing so left himself exposed to Malovo, who thrust her knife up through the base of his skull and into his brain. His body spasmed and jerked before he, too, crumpled to the ground.

James watched the deaths of the two agents in terror. He backed up against the tunnel wall next to Harvey as two more men appeared out of the dark wearing night-vision goggles. "Please don't kill me," he squealed as Malovo turned toward him, blood dripping from her knife. "I helped you."

"So you did," Malovo said, "and for that reason, I am going to grant your wish and leave you here alive."

Hope crept into James's eyes. "Thank you, thank you," he cried. "I'll go now. I don't need any other reward."

"That's very generous of you," Malovo said with a harsh laugh. "But you weren't listening. I said I would leave you *here* alive. I'm sure Grale will appreciate the gesture when he returns and finds his home and his people destroyed." She turned to the other two men. "Tie him to the man he betrayed and let's go."

"But why?" James wailed.

"Because no one likes a traitor, James," Malovo said, patting him on the cheek. "Not even the people he works for."

James was still crying and pleading when Malovo and her two men left him. She'd needed him as the conduit to the other traitor who still lived with Grale to make sure that Kane hadn't been moved. And he'd been handy for luring the guard from his secret spot; a man with a rifle in the dark could have held her team off indefinitely. She'd originally used two of her men posing as graffiti artists to probe the defenses of the underground community and had decided that she needed to use James to set the guard up. But she didn't need him anymore.

The reason she didn't was because she now knew the way to the inner sanctum of Grale's lair courtesy of the new super hi-tech GPS chip in the cell phone that Bruce Knight had been given by his old boss. One of her men now led the way, holding a dim screen in front of his face that mapped their path in from those coordinates.

They traveled fast with their night-vision goggles and didn't encounter anyone along the way. As they approached the cavern where Grale held court and where, according to James, the madman kept Kane chained to a bolt in the ground next to his throne, she and her men slowed down and then stopped at the entrance. All was dark inside; their goggles didn't pick up a single living thing or any movement.

Malovo listened but there were no sounds other than the dripping of water on stone and the far-off rumble of a subway train. Cautiously she crept in, with her men following. She turned to the right, where, she'd been told, Grale kept his prisoner. That's when she saw the tall robed figure rise from a chair, and the cowering creature next to him.

She raised the submachine gun she'd taken from Rolles's man. But just as she was about to shoot, a blinding painful blast of light seared into her brain, stunning her.

Instantly, she knew what had happened. Someone had turned on a very bright light, overwhelming the night-vision goggles. She and her men tore the devices from their heads, but it did no good. They were essentially blind.

All three started shooting wildly in the direction they believed Grale had been standing, and then randomly about the cavern. It was of little use.

Malovo felt a net drop over her that quickly tightened, pinning her arms at her sides, while strong, rough hands grabbed her. As her vision returned, she looked down at the ground and saw her two accomplices lying in pools of blood, their throats slit.

Stunned, she looked up at the platform and saw three men who made her blood run cold. The first was her attorney Bruce Knight, who said, "I'm afraid I have to resign as your counsel."

The second was Andrew Kane, who laughed insanely before blurting out, "Welcome to my nightmare!"

And the last was David Grale, who held up a collar and a leash. He pointed to the ground next to his overstuffed chair. "Make yourself at home; you're going to be here for a while."

Far above the cavern, Halloween trick-or-treaters and partygoers stopped in their tracks as a woman's scream rose from the sewers and echoed down the subway tunnels. Many years later on Halloween nights, they would still be telling the tale of how their blood had curdled at that cry of sheer terror.

37

The morning after Halloween there was no rest for the wicked or the just in Judge Temple's courtroom. The day began in the judge's chambers, where Rottingham objected to Karp's plan to call Nonie Ellis to the stand, accusing Karp of "sandbagging" him.

As Karp listened to his counterpart complain vociferously, he thought about the whole turn of events since court adjourned the day before. As soon as the jury was out of the courtroom, Ellis had been taken into custody; read her rights, which she waived; and then escorted to the District Attorney's Office.

Just to play it safe, Karp called defense attorney Belinda Morrow King, who had been retained to represent David Ellis on the morning of his murder, to come in and talk to Nonie before proceeding. In the meantime, he got the lowdown from Marlene on how the fugitive just happened to show up in court and take a seat next to his wife.

Marlene explained that after he left for court that morning, she'd received a text from an unknown number asking to meet her at the Housing Works Bookstore. "I had no idea who it was from," she said. "I've met lots of people there, including David Grale. But it was Nonie."

Ellis said she'd been staying at an East Village shelter under an alias and following the trial in the newspapers. When she saw that LaFontaine might testify, she told Marlene, she decided that she wanted to attend the trial. However, she wasn't sure she was ready to turn herself in, and so she was hesitating.

"I was pretty sure that if she came and listened to that liar, she would come around," Marlene told him. "So I suggested she wear a disguise and that if she was afraid, she could sit next to me. I was as surprised as anyone when she popped up and revealed her identity."

King had met with Nonie in one of the DAO interview rooms. When the defense attorney came out, she shook her head and said, "It's your lucky day, Karp. She wants to plead guilty to reckless manslaughter and is willing to testify against LaFontaine.

She'll give you a statement now."

Before leaving for the parade, Karp had called Judge Temple at his home and asked for the hearing in the morning, expecting resistance from Rottingham. King had agreed to come, too, and backed up Karp's story that her client had indeed been a fugitive and only in that eleventh hour agreed to turn herself in. The judge then ruled that Ellis could be called by the People as a rebuttal witness.

Her appearance on the stand had been devastating to LaFontaine's defense. She not only supported the testimony of Monique Hale, clearly demonstrating how the defendant operated to gain the trust of his victims and then control them with threats of losing the "miracles he promised," but also added to it. "He said that Micah's death was because my husband, David, had lost faith and wanted to go back to the doctors," she testified tearfully.

When she was finished, Karp asked, "Mrs. Ellis, will you walk out of this courtroom today a free woman?"

Nonie shook her head. "No. I pled guilty to reckless manslaughter. I'll be going to prison."

"Were you offered any sort of deal or other consideration in exchange for your testimony?"

"Only that you would tell the judge at my sentencing if I told the truth."

As Nonie, visibly shaking with tears streaming down her face, stepped down from the witness box, LaFontaine suddenly shouted, "It is a mortal sin to bear false witness!"

The comment brought Nonie up short. But instead of letting it tear her down more, she seemed to gain strength from it. "Lying is not the sin I will answer for," she replied so that the jurors heard her clearly. "Lying and murdering children are your sins, and I wouldn't want to be in your shoes when you are brought before God."

Nonie Ellis was the last witness, and they broke early for lunch. "When we return," Judge Temple instructed the jurors, "the attorneys, beginning with Mr. Rottingham and ending with Mr. Karp, will deliver their final summations, after which I will charge you on the law and you will then begin your deliberations."

During the lunch break, Karp retreated to his office, where he found Espey Jaxon and Jen Capers waiting. New Yorkers had woken up to the news that once again, they and their iconic city had been the target of terrorists. The newspapers and television stations fell over themselves to describe what they knew, and some of what they didn't, about the attack on the Halloween parade, which they reported had specifically been aimed at District Attorney Roger Karp.

Six men dressed in wolf costumes and wearing suicide vests had been apprehended; another six had been arrested in a nearby apartment building before they could join in. The thwarting of the attack had been lauded by government press secretaries as a prime example of co-operation between federal and local law enforcement agencies.

In another loosely related incident, the press reported that a man at first believed to be the wanted killer David Grale had been taken into custody near Karp's float but had been released shortly after when his true identity was learned. "I don't know where they got that . . . whoop whoop . . . Grale stuff, never met the man. I was just having fun, minding my own . . . [expletive deleted] . . . business when the cops grabbed me," the *Times* quoted Warren Bennett as saying.

The police were still trying to determine if the murder of a man, whose identity was not being released pending notification of kin, on the parade route at Sixth Avenue and 8th Street was related to the terrorist act, according to the *Post*. Some witnesses claimed that the man's assailant was a tall blond woman wearing a Little Red Riding Hood costume, who had last been seen running north.

The media had not found out about the bodies of four men found in the East River. They'd been a topic of conversation in Karp's office that morning before the hearing in the judge's chambers. Two of the bodies were the two agents with the National Inter-Departmental Security Administration who had worked with Rolles on the Liberty Ferry mission; the other two were Russians with long criminal histories.

"I would guess they're some of Grale's work," Jaxon said. He'd looked over at Jen Capers, who'd been quiet since arriving in the office. The pair had essentially agreed to look the other way and allow Malovo to escape, which rankled Capers maybe more than Jaxon, as the U.S. Marshals service prided itself on never losing prisoners. But they both knew that if not for the deal Karp told them he made with Grale, Malovo would have gone into the WITSEC program and there would have been no chance to keep her from walking away and continuing her murderous endeavors.

"Do you think Grale will live up to his part of the bargain?" Capers said at last.

Karp thought about it for a moment and then nodded. "David Grale is many things, including a serial killer," he said. "But he is also a man of his word. I think he will. When, I don't know."

The lunch hour passed too quickly and it was time to head back to court, where Rottingham first tried to convince the jurors that the prosecution had failed to prove its case. His client was being persecuted, he said, for his religious beliefs.

"He believes that God, not doctors, heals and is the ultimate arbiter of who lives and dies," the defense attorney argued. "He expressed that belief to other people, such as the Hales and the Ellises, and then gave of himself to pray alongside their sick children. And for this, the district attorney wants to put him in prison for murder."

Rottingham shook his head as if he could not believe this travesty of justice. "And because some of his congregation were so pleased with his efforts — and I'd point out that they included the Hales and Ellises — they rewarded him with gifts and donations. But the district attorney says that somehow that makes him a murderer."

Pacing slowly across the jury box, Rottingham suddenly stopped. "But did Reverend LaFontaine stop these people from going to doctors? Did he tie them up? Did he threaten them with a gun? Or was it their choice? Their decision. Who is guilty of not providing proper care for their children, the parents or a man who asked God to help them?"

Rottingham had gone on along the same tangent for a half hour before making his final argument that if anyone had committed a crime — "and I put it to you that the district attorney would be hard-pressed to prove this case, too" — it was Holstein and Bernsen.

As he spoke, LaFontaine kept a wounded expression on his face, occasionally wiping a hand across his eyes. Then as Rottingham finished his summation and began to walk back to his seat, LaFontaine wiped at his eyes. "God bless you, my brother," he called out.

Karp frowned and stood to deliver his summation, changing his opening on the spot in response to LaFontaine's remarks. "Words come easily to some people," he said as he turned toward the defense table and pointed at the accused, "especially to that man, who wields words like weapons. Not as sharp as a knife, nor as brutal as a bullet, but just as effective, and for Micah Ellis, just as deadly."

For a long moment, Karp let his words sink in as he stared down at LaFontaine, who couldn't hold his gaze and looked away. Karp then walked slowly out into the well of the court until he stood in front of the jurors, gathering his thoughts for the final push. He began, piece by piece, going over the evidence and testimony, until he ended with Nonie Ellis.

"Mr. LaFontaine was fond of calling all of these people liars," Karp said. "But let's examine who's the liar here. Would it be paramedic Don Bailey or Sergeant Trent Sadler? And what would Dr. Holstein gain by lying? He's admitted his culpability in the fraud and lost his wife, his freedom, and his medical license in the process. And why would Monique Hale lie? Revenge of a scorned woman? She was hiding in her house in Memphis when investigators found her and convinced her that LaFontaine needed to be stopped before more mothers lost their children. And what about Nonie Ellis? Why didn't she just keep moving? Why come back and plead guilty to reckless manslaughter and face years in prison? So that she could lie about this man she had given her soul to?"

Karp held up his arm and pointed to LaFontaine. "There is only one liar in this tragedy, and he's sitting at the defense table."

Dropping his arm, Karp shrugged. "Mr. Rottingham would have you believe that there's a question of whether a crime was even committed," he said. "But I assure you that there was and that its chief perpetrator, the defendant, knew what he was doing. Why else erase the medical records of children from the hospital computer files if not to prepare the way for insurance fraud? And what would it take to collect on that fraud?"

Karp walked over to the prosecution table and picked up a school photograph of Micah Ellis. "It took the long, slow, horrific, terrifying, painful death of this frightened child whose parents had been convinced by that man," he said, pointing at LaFontaine, "to not seek medical help and place their faith in him. That man counted on a child's death so that he could collect on an insurance policy."

Karp put the photo down. "But the defense also wants to hedge its bet. Mr. Rottingham would like you to believe that even if the crime of murder was committed, there's no proof that his client was responsible. But who knocked on the doors of vulnerable parents, armed with the knowledge of their child's disease and the family's history, and then callously used that information to convince them that only he, as God's emissary, could provide a 'miracle' that would save their child? And who stood in front of the paramedics and police officers rushing to save a sick child? The defense would point at Frank Bernsen. But Sergeant Sadler, who has no reason to lie, said it was the defendant who was in charge, and the defendant who motioned for his man to attack. That same man incited the crowd to confront the men trying to load the dying boy in an ambulance.

"And that same man incited the crowd across the street from this courthouse last April until a lonely widow named Kathryn Boole, who had never committed a crime in her entire life, pulled a gun from her purse and, yelling, 'Judas,' killed David Ellis. And what a windfall her subsequent death proved to be for Mr. LaFontaine and his simple lifestyle."

Karp returned to the prosecution table and picked up the manila folder containing LaFontaine's criminal record. "Until that moment, Kathryn Boole was a model citizen. But not John LaFontaine. He has a criminal history as long as my arm, a violent history, a history of robbery, larceny, and fraud, including impersonating a police officer — pretending to be something he is not. And I would put it to you today, ladies and gentlemen," Karp said as he walked over to stand in front of LaFontaine, "that this man is still pretending to be something he is not."

Karp turned back to the jurors. "I believe that if you piece together all that you've heard and all that you've seen, and all that you will see in the deliberation room, you cannot help but conclude that as surely as a knife or a bullet, John LaFontaine's words and actions ended the life of Micah Ellis."

Karp looked from one juror to the next, saw tears in their eyes and their mouths set grimly. "The People are asking you to return a verdict of murder because we now know beyond any and all doubt, from the evidence, that this defendant acted under circumstances evincing a depraved and wicked indifference to human life by recklessly and deliberately deceiving and lying to claim that he was a man of God, all the time plotting the death of a child. And how do we know he evinced this depraved indifference? Remember the testimony of AME Dr. Gail Manning and pediatric oncologist Dr. Charles Aronberg as they described the torment and fear Micah went through, without so much as an aspirin to relieve the pain, before he died. And why did he have to face such a horrible death at the hands of the defendant? For the most venal, despicable, and depraved reason of all . . . money."

One last time, Karp faced LaFontaine and then walked back to the jury rail. "Ultimately, each one of us will face final judgment, and how ironic it will be for this defendant who pretended to be a man of God. He mocked the very content of the Bible he was thumping. How will he answer when he is judged by Him and asked, *'For what shall it profit a man, if he shall gain the whole world, and lose his soul?'* "

EPILOGUE

Butch Karp sat alone on the bench set back from the subway platform, staring across two sets of tracks at the wall opposite. Colored tiles set into a white tile background proclaimed that this was the South Ferry station, the southernmost on the island of Manhattan.

A little farther down the platform, Fulton talked quietly with Capers and Jaxon; beyond them four plainclothes cops waited. Every once in a while the others glanced his way, but for the most part they left him alone with his thoughts.

Karp glanced at his watch — it was one A.M. — and sighed. It had been a long day, beginning with the sentencing of John LaFontaine.

It had taken only six hours of deliberation before the jury had returned a guilty verdict. Standing as the jury foreman read the decision, LaFontaine had suddenly started cursing the jurors, the judge, and particularly Karp with a stream of invective that surprised even those who had not believed him to be a man of God. But then the rant had suddenly stopped as LaFontaine clutched at his chest and crumpled to the ground, his face turning purple as he fought for air.

"A doctor," he begged. "Get a doctor."

LaFontaine had survived the heart attack and today, two months later, was brought before the court for its judgment. This time he sat sullenly in his seat, occasionally glaring hatefully at Karp, while Judge Temple listened to his lawyer plead for leniency. Calling LaFontaine a "despicable human being," the judge sent him away for the maximum allowable, life with a mandatory minimum of twenty-five years.

As for Nonie Ellis, Judge Temple had given her a three-year suspended sentence. Part of her probation was that she work at the East Village Women's Shelter.

One of the bigger surprises was that Karp learned that Bruce Knight had reported himself to the New York State Bar Association for violating attorney-client privilege with his erstwhile client Nadya Malovo. Karp had informed the bar hearing officer about the beneficial role that Knight had played in preventing the terrorist attack. The bar determined that Knight would keep his license and set up a program to teach newly admitted lawyers a course in ethics at state bar headquarters in Manhattan.

In order to keep his law firm afloat and pay the bills, Marlene retained his services as her investigator in chief in her private practice, focusing mainly on protecting abused women and working in conjunction with the women's shelter.

After the sentencing and the end of the workday, Karp had been looking forward to a quiet evening at home with Marlene and the twins. But Warren Bennett had been waiting for him when he exited the Hogan Place side of the building.

"Hi, Butch," the little man greeted him. "David says he's ready to . . . oh boy fuck me . . . keep his side of the deal. Be on the downtown side of the South Ferry platform tonight at one. Oh, and you may want to . . . whoop whoop oh boy . . . bring Fulton and maybe a couple other guys. She can be a handful, you know."

As he sat now waiting, Karp wondered what he'd given up for this deal. That night at the Bowery Mission, Grale had proposed that if Karp and his friends allowed Malovo to escape so that he could spring his trap, he would eventually return her to Karp's custody to be tried.

In exchange, Grale wanted to "entertain" the femme fatale assassin long enough to get her to tell him everything she knew about the terrorists and criminals preying on New York City so that he could ramp up his vigilante war against evil. "I think the threat of spending her golden years in my loving care will be enough to get her to talk," he laughed. "Of course my inclination is to slit her throat and send her back to hell. But I understand that there is a 'greater good' of seeing her exposed by you in a New York courtroom."

Grale had apparently been a convincing host, as evidenced by the dead bombers and gangsters and other nefarious types the police kept finding with their throats cut. One of his alleged victims, however, was harder to figure out. The nude body of a man named James Blankenship had been found hanging by the neck from a tree in Central Park. "JUDAS" had been carved in his chest, and his dead hand clutched a small leather pouch containing thirty bright shiny dimes.

Karp became aware of the rumble of an approaching train. He stood up as the others in his party walked toward the yellow caution line on the platform and peered down the track. A headlight appeared and then an apparently empty train slid into the station.

The train was not, however, completely empty, nor did Karp see what he expected when the door in front of him opened. As agreed, Nadya Malovo was there, a dog collar around her throat and fastened by a leash to a pole. Her eyes were wild and darting, and judging by the bruises and other marks on her filthy body, her stay with the King of the Mole People had not been a pleasant one.

But there was also another passenger, also collared and leashed. In a corner, the beast that used to be Andrew Kane snarled and cowered, one insane eye glaring out of his devastated face.

There was an envelope pinned to his threadbare coat. Fulton removed it and handed it to Karp who opened it and read the letter he found inside.

"An early wedding present for Lucy. With love, David Grale."

ABOUT THE AUTHOR

Robert K. Tanenbaum has been bureau chief of the New York Criminal Courts where 250 new cases arrive daily, and he ran the homicide bureau of the New York District Attorney's office and deputy chief counsel to the congressional committee investigations into the assasinations of President John F. Kennedy and Dr. Martin Luther King, Jr. His previous works include the novels *Outrage, Betrayed, Captive, Escape, Malice, Fury,* and *Hoax* and true-crime books *The Piano Teacher, The True Story of a Psychotic Killer* and *Badge of the Assassin.*